MORE THAN A FEELING

CATE WOODS

Quercus

First published in Great Britain in 2018 by

Quercus Editions Ltd
Carmelite House
50 Victoria Embankment
London EC4Y 0DZ

An Hachette UK company
2

A CIP catalogue record for this book is available
from the British Library

PAPERBACK ISBN 978 1 78648 528 1
EBOOK ISBN 978 1 78648 527 4

www.quercusbooks.co.uk

Typeset by Jouve (UK), Milton Keynes

Printed and bound in Great Britain by Clays Ltd, Elcograf S.p.A.

Cate Woods made the most of her degree in Anglo-Saxon Literature by embarking on a career making tea on programmes including *The Big Breakfast*, *Who Wants to be a Millionaire* and *French & Saunders*. After narrowly missing out on the chance to become a Channel 5 weather girl she moved into journalism, where she interviewed every famous John, from Prescott to Bon Jovi, ghostwrote a weekly column for a footballer's wife and enjoyed a brief stint as one half of *Closer* magazine's gossip-columnist duo, 'Mr & Mrs Showbiz'. Cate left the magazine world in 2009 to pursue a full-time career ghostwriting celebrity autobiographies and novels. She lives in London with her husband (not Mr Showbiz) and two small children.

Also by Cate Woods:

Just Haven't Met You Yet

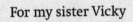

For my sister Vicky

PROLOGUE

Five Years Ago

'Girl, I am gagging over your look tonight. That headscarf – I *die!* Vintage Pucci?'

'Oxfam discount bin.' I grin, striking a pose. When a drag queen compliments your accessories, you can be pretty sure you're doing something right.

'Well, that was 20p fabulously spent, Miss Barb. Pussy is on fire!'

She bends down to give me a theatrical air-kiss on both cheeks: in wig and heels, self-styled 'door bitch' Madame Kiki Beaverhousen must be pushing seven foot. She lifts the rope and I slip under, sensing the mass scowl from the line of people waiting round the block who've just watched me shamelessly queue-jump.

'See you inside,' I say, waving to Madame Kiki, and disappear into the darkness beyond the doorway. All the signs are there: tonight is going to be fun.

As I make my way down the velvet-lined corridor, my step unconsciously falling in time with the music, excitement bubbles up inside me. I pass a large gilt mirror and pause to check my reflection. It took me two hours to get ready, which I guess is pretty standard for a Thursday night – after all, Thursday is the new Sunday, which was once the new Saturday, which used to be the new Friday . . . or something like that.

As well as the headscarf, I'm wearing a full-length pink kaftan with a jewelled neckline, armfuls of bangles and a pair of gold platform sandals (it's quite a casual club night, you understand, so I didn't want to overdo it), plus my signature make-up look: winged eyeliner, strong brows and pale, matte lips. Okay, I suppose it's not *my* signature make-up look – I stole it from Barbra, the divine Ms Streisand: my style icon, role model and all-year-round girl crush. My wardrobe of vintage and charity shop finds is entirely inspired by her own from the Sixties and Seventies. The woman is a goddess.

My Streisand obsession started over ten years ago when I was in my early teens. I have been blessed with a magnificent megalith of a nose, an impressive slab of nasal architecture that I'm now rightly proud of – although try telling a self-conscious fourteen-year-old who just wants to look like Britney Spears that big noses can be beautiful. I'd come home from school in tears one day, after yet another nose-based bullying, when my wonderful father sat me down and put on the film *The Way We Were*. I couldn't believe what I was seeing. There, on the screen, was MY nose, slap-bang in the middle of the face of the most beautiful woman I'd ever laid eyes on. My nose was getting to kiss Robert Redford! My nose was wearing the most fabulous pale-pink halter-neck jumpsuit! My nose was a *star*!

It was a life-changing moment, and it was then I decided that when I grew up I was going to *be* Barbra Streisand. And while I might not have her life – I'm yet to achieve the superstardom or multiple zeroes on my bank balance – I most certainly have her look, which in turn has led to me borrowing her name, too. To my work friends at least, I'm universally known as 'Barb'.

The corridor opens out into the bar and I spot a group of people I know. This club is currently a favourite with the fashion crowd: even if I turn up on my own, I know there'll be plenty of familiar faces here. I start working my way through the throng towards them.

'Barb! How are you, gorgeous?'

Tomo, a male model I've known for a few years – you probably know him, too, from countless ad campaigns – looms out of the crowd and wraps me in a bear hug.

'I'm just going to say hi to Riva, Delphine and the others,' I say, gesturing to the group by the bar when he pulls away.

'Okay, but first I've got a little proposition for you.' He reaches for my hand. 'Come with me . . .'

Models, male and female, tend to fall into two camps: they are either fetishised for their weirdness (these are the ones who look more alien than human – fashion simply *adores* a freak) or worshipped for their flawless beauty. With his achingly handsome face and gym-honed body, Tomo sits firmly in the latter category. He'd be an absolute nightmare to have as a boyfriend because he gets hit on constantly (by both men and women), but he's a great mate, plus we often end up in bed together anyway – and tonight, as he steers me towards a quiet corner of the bar, I'm guessing he has mischief on his mind.

'So I was thinking,' he says, snaking his arm around my waist, 'how about my favourite photographic assistant and I give this place a miss, and head straight back to mine?'

I look at him, eyebrows raised; I guess when you're this good-looking you can afford to be brazen. 'But I haven't even had a drink yet.'

'Well, I've got vodka in the freezer and champagne in the fridge, and if madame would like anything else, I will call my PA and get her to courier it over to the flat.' He pulls me closer and drops his voice to a husky murmur. 'How about it? I promise I'll make it worth your while . . .'

I chew my lip, thinking over this undeniably tempting offer. 'I really shouldn't, T, I've got an early start in the morning – Jay's shooting Nadia for *Harper's*. Besides,' I add, my armfuls of bracelets clanking in corroboration,

'I think I'm a bit overdressed for a private party at your place.'

Tomo leans towards me, until his perfectly symmetrical face is so close to mine I can feel the warmth of his breath, and whispers: 'But that's exactly what I was thinking . . .'

Looking into Tomo's dark eyes, and at his full-lipped mouth that I know from experience is highly proficient at kissing (and other oral pursuits), I'm *this* close to giving in – but it's already gone midnight, and I've got to be in the studio tomorrow for an eight o'clock start.

'Next time,' I manage with an apologetic smile.

Tomo fixes me with his trademark sex-look for a second longer, then shrugs. 'You're no fun anymore, Barb,' he says, but there's a grin in his voice and as we weave our way back towards the bar he loops his arm through mine. 'So how's work?'

'Oh, you know, brilliant and shit in equal measure.'

'I don't know how you hack working for Jay. I heard he was doing a shoot for *Vogue* the other day and he had a fit about the model being too fat. She was, like, sixteen or something, and he was screaming at the editor while this kid was sitting right in front of him!'

'Yep, I know, I was there.' I shake my head, despairing over my charmless boss. 'And people let him get away with it because he's an "artist"! He's just brought in this new rule that his female assistants have to wear nail varnish, because someone told him that's what Mario Testino does. I'm having to paint my nails every night because as soon as I start lugging the camera equipment and lighting around, they get chipped.'

'Well, look at it this way: once you've worked with Jay Patterson, your photography career will be sorted for life. That's got to be worth a daily manicure, right?'

Later that night I'm standing at the bar waiting to order a round of drinks. It's been a brilliant night – my face aches from laughing – but I can't be late for work; this job is far too important to me. I've told myself that I'm allowed one more vodka, a quick dance with Tomo (possibly also a kiss if I *promise* to behave) and then I really do have to go home. I've lost track of time and pull out my phone to check how late it is. When I look at the screen my hand flies to my mouth in shock.

Oh my God.

It's nearly 3 a.m., which means I need to be up again in four hours – but the *really* disturbing thing is the seventeen missed calls from my sister Tabitha. When I left our flat earlier this evening she was already on her way to bed. What the hell has happened?

'Another vodka tonic, Barb sweetheart?' asks the barman.

But I'm already turning away, fighting through the crowd so I can get outside to phone her back, panic flooding through me as I elbow my way towards the door. I try to think of a reason my little sister might need to get hold of me so urgently, but none of the possibilities I can come up with are reassuring.

After the heat of the club, the chill November air slams into me like a physical force. Gathering my kaftan tighter around me, I dial Tabitha's number and she answers immediately.

'Annie! Oh, thank God.'

Her voice is squeaky and breathless, as if she's on the edge of hysteria.

'Tabby? What's wrong? Where are you?'

'I'm at home. Annie, the ... the police are here. I ...'

She breaks off, collapsing into tears, sobbing uncontrollably.

'Tabitha, talk to me! Please! Tabby?'

But there's no reply, just the heartbreaking sound of her crying, and after a few moments an unfamiliar male voice comes on the line.

'Is this Ann Taylor?'

This use of my real name while I'm in full Barbra mode would usually grate, but right now I'm too panicked to care. 'Who is this?' I ask, voice trembling. My heart is racing, and I reach for the wall to keep myself upright. 'What's happened to my sister, is she hurt? Please, what's going on?'

'This is Sergeant Clive Ellis, Miss Taylor.' His tone is grave. 'And I'm afraid I'm going to need you to come home right away ...'

1

Present Day

I can't shake the feeling that I've forgotten something. It's been bugging me since I got on this bus, an unsettling niggle that I've left something important at home, and at each stop I've had to fight the urge to sprint back and check. To be honest it's taking the shine off this journey through the glorious sights of rainy south London – and the Stockwell one-way system is *so* lovely at this time of year.

Of course, the reason I'm feeling like this is because I know that I *have* left something important behind: my daughter Dorothea, aka Dot. She of the tiny shell-pink fists and bewitching smell. This is the first time I've been out of our flat without her since she was born, which was only twelve weeks ago, but time creeps by at three-toed sloth speed when you're measuring your days in naps and breast-feeds. When I left her in the capable arms of my best mate

Fiona a little while ago, closed the front door and took my first steps along our street unencumbered by buggy or changing bag, I kept checking behind me, furtive and twitchy, like I'd just been shoplifting in Boots. I managed to make it to the bus stop, but then the guilt kicked in. Oh good God, the *guilt*. From the outside I might have looked like your average badly dressed shoplifter, but inside my head the lunatics were taking over the asylum.

How can I have abandoned my baby? She's probably lying in her cot right now screaming for me while I swan off to go shopping – and not even shopping for her, shopping for myself! *I am a bad mother. Bad and selfish. I'm going to scar her for life. She'll grow into an emotionally stunted psychopath who won't be able to form healthy relationships or hold down a job and most likely will end up in prison, and it'll all be my fault because of that one time I went shopping and left her at home.*

I'm seriously regretting reading that book on attachment parenting.

Anyway, I felt so wretched about all this that I nearly turned around and went home, but then the bus drew up and I forced myself to get on board, mainly because I knew full well that Fiona, who is a tiny yet fearsome Northern Irish woman, would be 'ragin'' if I 'wimped out'.

There were no free seats so I resigned myself to standing, but then I realised that I could actually sit upstairs – no buggy! – and with more of a thrill than you'd think possible in the circumstances, I found myself a seat on the top deck. As the bus pulled away I turned my attention to the world outside, and as I gazed out of the window, my head propped against the smeary glass, it suddenly struck me how familiar the world looked: apart from some tired-looking Christmas decorations still looped around the streetlights, nothing much had changed since I last took this journey into town. I suppose there wasn't any reason why it *should* have changed – it had only been a few months, after all – but it's a shock to discover that while you've spent the past three months transforming beyond all recognition, the rest of the world has just been ... business as usual.

I found this strangely reassuring. Dot's birth catapulted me into the strange and scary universe of motherhood, a place where there were few certainties and even less sleep – and not even Alexa could provide the answers. But now here I was going shopping, sitting on the top deck of the 137, doing all those things I used to do before my world suddenly went mum-shaped. Annie Taylor is still here, folks! *She's alive!*

And now, as we trundle over Battersea Bridge towards the bright lights of Zone 1, my guilt over Dot is fading just a little, and I'm beginning to feel excited about the prospect of going shopping. For the first time in three months I am out in the big wide world on my own. Yup, it's just me and my long-neglected Visa card, hitting up the John Lewis ladies' wear department for some sexy lingerie.

Yes, I do know that John Lewis might not be the best place to look for sexy lingerie. My mate Jessica (who is in a dating frenzy post-divorce, so is an expert on such matters) insisted I go to Agent Provocateur, but apparently the assistants come into the changing room with you to fit the bras, and I'm really not up for that level of attention. There's a strong danger that if they get too 'hands-on', my boobs will go off like sprinklers, spraying milk over the racks of pom-pom mules and nipple clamps. Not to mention, I'm not supposed to be wearing underwired bras due to the breastfeeding, and even the thongs are underwired in that place. All in all, John Lewis feels like a far safer bet.

It's been a while since I thought about my body as anything other than a twenty-four-hour milk vending machine, but the reason I need something racier than my beige maternity bra is because this Saturday Luke and I are having our first post-baby date night. We're going for dinner at our favourite local restaurant, and then it will be full-speed ahead on the seduction highway, destination: Shag Town.

I can't say that sex is the first thing I want to do right now – sleep is actually at the top, middle and bottom of my list, dominating my every waking thought and even some of the sleeping ones too (I actually dreamt I was having a lie-in last week; it was wonderful – then Dot started crying and I woke up and discovered it was 2 a.m.). Also,

I'm a bit worried about the intercourse part of proceedings, primarily because I'm not that confident about the state of things *down there*.

How can I put this tastefully . . . ?

Imagine, if you will, a pretty cul-de-sac. It's a nice place to live; a 'desirable neighbourhood', in estate-agent speak. The accommodation is cosy and the front hedges neatly trimmed. But then one day an enormous wrecking ball smashes through it – KABOOOOOOM – transforming it into a hellish dual carriageway, big enough for those 'caution: wide load' lorries, flanked by a shamefully overgrown soft verge.

That's how I'm imagining my vagina, post-partum.

And if that wasn't enough of a passion-killer, my once-passable body now looks like a balloon that's been blown up and deflated multiple times until it's all sad and saggy. On the plus side, though, I am currently rocking quite the rack. I have boobs like the Titanic: gigantic, but leaky.

Is it terrible to admit that the idea of sex feels like a chore? It's not like Luke's been pressuring me (he's actually been really sweet about it, telling me to take my time and wait until I'm ready) but all of my multiple baby books agree on the fact that I should be 'intimate' with my partner by now. I'm also starting to worry that Dot is taking up so much of my attention Luke might be feeling neglected. I really don't want to become one of those couples who get so lost in parenthood that they start addressing each other as 'Mummy' and 'Daddy' and don't have anything to talk about apart from how many times their baby pooed that week. Luke would hate that.

The bus is now ploughing through the traffic around Hyde Park Corner, which isn't a million miles from Luke's office, and at the thought of being just a couple of streets away from him my face relaxes into a smile. *Luke*. I'm so lucky to have him. Handsome, successful, charming – at times I wonder if I'm punching above my weight. I knew he wouldn't be much of a nappy-changer, and he works such long hours I wouldn't expect him to be, but when I see him with Dot, cuddling her to sleep or tickling her until she dissolves into giggles, my heart melts with happiness. I glance out of the window again: I'm so close to his office, perhaps I should message him to see if he can pop out to meet me? It would be lovely to grab a few minutes together, just the two of us. I pull out my phone and write: 'Surprise! I'm near your office, can I buy my baby-daddy a coffee?' My finger hovers over 'send', but after a moment's consideration I hit the lock button instead. Wednesday is Luke's busy day at work, I probably shouldn't bother him.

The bus stops again, and moments later a twenty-something girl with enviable eyebrows and enormous headphones emerges onto the top deck. She takes a seat a couple of rows in front of me, the tinny bass still audible above the rumble of the bus. I feel a twitch of irritation:

possibly because of the too-loud music, but more likely because she reminds me of Barb, that distant version of myself who'd also had time to get her brows in shape and didn't give a shit what people thought of her. I miss that girl. Against my better judgement, I let my mind slide back to that horrible time five years ago when fun, fearless Barb suddenly vanished and was replaced by sensible, anxious Annie. If only I'd handled things better, and hadn't lost myself quite so dramatically, perhaps my life might have turned out differently? But then I wouldn't have met Luke, and we wouldn't have had Dot – and how could I ever regret that?

A little while later we grind to a halt at the traffic lights outside Selfridges. The January sales are in full swing and shoppers buttressed with Primark bags plough down the crowded pavements. There's a crowd gathered around the entrance to Bond Street station, and as I watch them milling around like goldfish, my eyes are drawn to a man waiting at the top of the steps leading down to the tube. Although I can only see him from the back, I would know those shoulders and that navy coat anywhere. It's Luke! I let out a little 'oh' of surprise. What on earth's he doing round here? Perhaps we can meet for that coffee after all!

I bang on the window, trying to get his attention, but he's so far away with so many people between us that I doubt he'd hear me even if I was standing on the street yelling his name. As I stare at him, trying to mentally will him to turn in my direction, a crowd of tourists ambles past, blocking him from view; now that he's out of sight, doubts start to edge in. *Was* that Luke? Perhaps I was mistaken: that navy coat isn't exactly unusual, and as far as I know he doesn't own a red beanie. He's not a red beanie kind of guy; he works in the legal department at a German investment bank. And why would Luke be loitering on Oxford Street on a Wednesday morning? He's usually stuck in some high-powered meeting around now. I must have been mistaken . . .

The bus inches forward and I fumble in my bag for my phone to call him, but then we creep to a standstill again and I get another glimpse of Luke – or his doppelgänger. Frustratingly I still can't see his face, or very much else of him. The little I can see, though, *feels* familiar. We've been together for three years; you should know, shouldn't you? My gut instinct is telling me I'm right. This man is about the same height as Luke and has a similar build and cool, slouchy way of standing. I'm *sure* it's him. Well, ninety-nine per cent sure. Eighty-five at the very least.

The bus starts to move and I realise I'm going to lose sight of him, so I make my way to the empty seats at the back in the hope of one last look, but the rain has just started again and with it umbrellas have begun mushrooming up around him. And then – hooray! – the crowds part, giving me a clear line of sight, and I feel sure that I'll be able to get a look at his face from this angle; except, as it turns out, I can't, because right where his face should be there's now another person – a woman – who is wrapping her arms around him, and his hands are hungrily pulling her towards him, and even from this far away I can see, without any room for doubt, that they are kissing.

2

There's a strangulated sort of choking noise, which I think must have come from me, and a rushing in my ears. Even though I'm sitting down I reach for the back of the seat in front to steady myself. *Jesus.* A surge of adrenaline pushes me to my feet and I lunge for the stop button, pounding at it frantically, and then race to the stairs and take them two at a time, stumbling on the last step and dropping my bag, the contents scattering as widely as if it had been detonated. The bus is packed and people tut and and huff as I scramble at their feet, muttering my apologies, trying to retrieve my phone, wallet and the surprising quantity of tampons that must have been lurking in the depths. A young man hands back my tube of nipple cream with a kind smile; in normal circumstances I'd be dying of embarrassment, but right now my brain is preoccupied trying to process what the fuck has just happened.

I shout to the driver to ask if he'll open the doors – we're stuck in traffic mere metres from the next bus stop – but when his eyes meet mine in the rear-view mirror he shakes his head.

'It's an emergency!' I shriek.

People look round, clearly thinking 'nutter'.

The driver glances at me again. 'I'm only permitted to stop at designated alighting points.'

An old woman sitting nearby asks: 'Are you ill?'

'No, I'm . . . I . . . just really need to get off.'

'Well, you'll have to wait like the rest of us,' she says, mouth puckered in disapproval.

I shoot one last beseeching look at the driver, but he is determinedly avoiding further eye contact so I hover by the doors, twitchy with impatience, my head exploding with visions of my boyfriend snogging another woman. I press my fists into my eyes, trying to block it all out. Come on, Annie, don't go assuming the worst. Luke wouldn't do that – we've just had a baby together, for Christ's sake! It must be a simple case of mistaken identity. I cling to this thought with the desperation of the drowning. There's absolutely no way that was Luke. I'm being ridiculous, and when he asks me to marry him over dinner this weekend – which actually isn't as far-fetched as it sounds, as he did ask me a question about ring sizes the other day – I'm going to think back to this moment and have a good laugh at how stupid I've been.

Unless . . . what if it *was* Luke? I'm hit by another wave of nausea. Is this because I haven't had sex with him since the baby? I catch sight of my reflection in the mirror over the doors and am far from reassured by what I see: the stringy, mouse-blonde hair with two inches of dark roots already escaping from its lopsided ponytail, a make-up-free face dominated by that wretched conk of a nose and the maternity clothes that I'm still wearing because I can't fit in my pre-pregnancy jeans. I certainly wouldn't want to have sex with this version of myself. Christ, have I driven Luke to have an affair by letting myself go? Is this all my fault?

After what feels like hours the doors finally open and I burst onto Oxford Street and race back towards Bond Street tube station. Moments later I'm standing on the spot where I saw him, frantically scanning the crowd for a flash of red hat, but he's nowhere to be seen. He's not in the station either, and there's no point me getting on a tube because if he has come this way, who knows in which direction he was headed. Dashing back up to street level, my heart hammering frantically in my chest, I pull out my phone and dial his number. *Come on, Luke, please be at your desk, let this all be a misunderstanding* ... It goes straight to voicemail. Perhaps he's in a meeting? Or maybe he's on the tube with *her*, heading to a hotel to have wild, adulterous sex. I bet *she* wears fucking Agent Provocateur underwear. Who the hell is she? All I saw was a camel-coloured coat and a light-coloured ponytail – or was it a hat? *Annie, focus* ... But the harder I try to visualise the scene, the quicker it slips away from me, until I'm left doubting that it even happened. Did I just imagine the whole thing? Is hallucinating something that can happen when you've recently given birth, along with the piles and stress incontinence? Does a weak pelvic floor lead to a weak mind? *Am I going mad?*

I try Luke's mobile again but it goes straight back to voicemail, as does his work number – so instead I call Fiona.

She answers the phone with a sigh. 'Dot is asleep and you're meant to be pretending you don't have a child for a few hours. Everything is grand. Now piss off.'

'No, please, Fi, don't go! I think I might have just seen Luke kissing another woman.'

There's a pause. 'You're joking.'

'Nope, deadly serious. I didn't get a proper look because I was on the bus, but I'm almost certain it was him.' Now the adrenaline is wearing off I can feel the tears coming. 'Please tell me I'm going mad and imagined the whole thing. Please.' I choke out the last word in a sob.

'Oh, I'm sure you have, love. I mean, Luke has his faults . . .' She lets that hang in the air and I feel a rush of irrational protectiveness towards my boyfriend.

'I hardly think forgetting our anniversary means he'll cheat on me,' I mutter.

'And your birthday . . .'

'That happened once! And he was really manic at work that month, I barely saw him.'

'Hmmm.' Fi clearly still hasn't forgiven him for that, but then as a friend she is staunchly loyal. 'Anyway, what I was going to say was that yer man may have his faults, but I don't think he'd be cheating on the mother of his child weeks after she gave birth. That would be a totally shitty thing to do. Luke's only a wee bit shitty.'

An idea suddenly hits me. 'Do you think I should go to his office, check if he's there?'

There's a pause as Fi thinks this over. 'You said you're almost certain it was Luke, but how good a look at him did you get?'

'Not brilliant. Just his back view really, and he was quite a long way off. And there were a lot of people in the way. And he was wearing a red hat that I've never seen before.'

'Okaaay ...'

'But it *felt* like him, honestly.' I feel a lump rising in my throat again. If Luke left me, how would I care for Dot? I don't have a job, Luke and I aren't married and he owns our flat. Best-case scenario, I'd be a homeless, unemployed single mum. As my future hurtles wildly out of control, with tragedy piling upon disaster on top of calamity, I ask, my voice quavering: 'Fi, what shall I do?'

'Darl, remember this is a crazy time for you right now,' she says gently. 'You're looking after Dot 24/7, you're short of sleep, your hormones are all over the place: your judgement is bound to be ... *impaired*. Perhaps this was just a totally understandable mix-up, like when you put your iPhone in the microwave last week.' (She's got a point – it's a miracle it still works after twenty seconds on defrost.) 'What I'm saying is, chances are you were mistaken and it wasn't Luke, so I think the best thing to do is just forget about this for now, enjoy your child-free time and then talk to him about it tonight.'

'You think I should just ask him outright?'

'Feck no, are you insane! Just get him chatting about what he got up to today and look out for signs of guilt, like avoidance of eye contact, defensiveness and stiff body movements.' (Fi once did work experience at *Cosmopolitan*, so she knows about this sort of thing.) 'Let me know what happens and we'll take it from there, but honestly, gorge, I'm sure there's nothing to worry about. Luke loves you and Dot and he wouldn't do anything to screw that up, I'm sure of it.'

She's absolutely right, of course. I'm hardly the most reliable of witnesses at the moment, and besides, Luke has never done anything to make me doubt his fidelity. He barely leaves the office: when would he have time for an affair?

'Thank you, love,' I say, feeling a glimmer of brightness. 'I'll see you in a few hours then. Um, before I go, though, how's Dottie? Has she done a poo yet?'

She sighs. 'Annie Amelia Taylor, you are not a mother today, you are a hot babe shopping for fuck-me knickers, remember?' But then, after a moment, she adds quietly: 'But if you *did* have a child, then she would be grand and very happy with her Auntie Fi. And I'm ignoring the poo question because *really*.'

I smile into the phone. 'I love you, Fi.'

'You too. Now get on with you and shop yourself stupid.'

And so that's exactly what I do. I squash my worries deep inside me, shove a lid on them and march straight to Agent Provocateur, where I buy a black lace bra and ribbon-tie knickers that cost nearly as much as Dot's pushchair. Then I go to Topshop and get a pair of spike-heeled ankle boots, a beaded clutch bag and two red lipsticks. I shop like a woman possessed, gorging on pretty things to distract me from the fears that are threatening to break free. It's only on the journey home that I realise I seem to have been shopping for the woman I glimpsed from the bus rather than for myself.

3

At just after 8 p.m., I hear Luke's key turning in our front
door, his feet stamping on the mat (one, two, three – the
same as every night) and then he appears at the kitchen
door, his six-foot-two figure filling the frame, a smile
crinkling the corners of his dark-lashed eyes. And despite
the emotions that are churning up my insides like socks
in a spin cycle, I feel, as usual, a thrill of excitement that
he's home – and that he's mine.

His navy coat is buttoned up over his suit and his hair
is slick with drizzle; he looks every inch the dashing,
Esquire-reading, half-Italian lawyer that he is. I try to visualise him wearing a red woolly beanie, but it's impossible;
the very idea of it is ridiculous.

It wasn't him, I tell myself, relief soothing my fears. *I've
got it all wrong.*

'You look nice,' he says, dropping a kiss on my forehead,
and I'm pleased he's noticed the make-up I hurriedly
slapped on after putting Dot to bed; it's the first time I've

worn lip gloss in months. 'Here, I got you a little something,' he adds, disappearing back into the hallway.

He returns holding out a bouquet classily wrapped in brown paper and raffia; these are no cut-price forecourt chrysanths, clearly. A thought immediately pops into my head – *cheaters buy flowers* – and I firmly shove it away.

'Your favourites.' Luke smiles. 'Peonies aren't easy to find in January, I can tell you.'

'Thank you, they're gorgeous. Um, what are they for?'

'Do I need a reason to buy you flowers?'

'No, of course not, but . . .'

He pulls me close and I rest my face on his chest, taking deep breaths of comfortingly familiar Luke smell.

'Well, for starters, they're because you're a fantastic mum. Because you have to get up and feed our daughter several times a night, and you never complain about it. Because you're beautiful, and I don't tell you that enough. Because I love you. I could go on . . .' He pulls away to look at my face. 'Okay?'

'Okay,' I say, returning his smile as he leans down to kiss me again, this time on the lips. His breath smells minty, as if he's recently brushed his teeth, perhaps to disguise the fact he's been kissing someone else . . .

Annie, stop it.

It is taking every milligram of my self-control not to blurt out: 'Were you snogging a strange woman on Oxford Street this morning and if so, then WHAT THE FUCK

WERE YOU DOING, YOU TOTAL FUCKING BASTARD?'
But that would be a dreadful idea. For starters, if it *was*
Luke I saw today then he'll deny it, obviously. I need to
take a subtler approach and then monitor him for signs
of deceit as Fi suggested. More importantly, however, now
that I'm here, snuggled up against him, I'm becoming
increasingly unsure that Luke would ever cheat on me.
Over the years we've been together, he's never given me
any reason to doubt him – and surely if he *was* having an
affair there would be some warning signs, such as a
change in his mood, or unexplained nights out? But quite
honestly, apart from the totally understandable post-baby
nookie drought, our relationship feels stronger than ever.
He actually said to me the other day, 'You and Dot have
made my life complete.' Those aren't the words of a cheating scumbag, are they?

Luke always likes to hear about what Dot and I have got
up to while he's been at work, so as I finish preparing dinner I tell him about our day, deliberately leaving out any
mention of my morning's outing while I decide whether
or not I should just forget the whole thing. Luckily, I have
big news: Dot rolled over for the first time this afternoon,
which according to all my baby books makes her something of a rolling prodigy.

'Well, she's obviously going to be sporty,' says Luke, his
eyes lighting up with pride. 'I should get a football for
her, get started on ball skills early . . . And how about we

take her skiing next year? I could look into it now, I bet we could get a really good deal if we book early . . . What do you think, Annie?'

I burst out laughing – not because the idea itself is laughable (although it actually is, because Dot won't even be two by then so may not even be walking, let alone skiing) – but because I'm overjoyed to hear Luke making plans for us as a family. I very much doubt a man who was thinking about running off with another woman would be so eager to fix up a holiday with his current girlfriend, especially this far in advance.

Yet for all the evidence suggesting that it wasn't Luke I saw this morning, the vision of the man in the red hat is seared into my mind. While Luke is upstairs changing out of his suit, I reluctantly come to the conclusion that I am going to have to ask him about it. Otherwise I'll forever have doubts, which will at some point in the future – no doubt in the middle of an argument about something totally unrelated – suddenly explode messily out of me.

By the time he comes back downstairs I have plated up the shepherd's pie, poured the wine and am sitting at the table waiting for him. I was pretty shambolic in the kitchen before Luke and I got together, but I've now got a solid repertoire of crowd-pleasing dishes under my belt. This is partly thanks to my friend Claris, who has her own catering company and has taught me her best easy-yet-impressive recipes, and partly because now I don't have a career I have no excuse *not* to be able to cook. Nowadays I even own an apron – *and* I wear it.

Luke slides into the seat opposite me. 'This looks delicious, *patatina*, thank you.' (Patatina is Luke's nickname for me. It means 'little potato' in Italian. It's endearing, apparently.)

'Great!' I say, a little too brightly. 'Buon appetito!'

As Luke tucks in, I take a large gulp of wine for courage. It's now or never . . .

'So,' I ask, my voice deliberately light, 'what did you get up to today?'

Luke shrugs, eyes on his plate. *Avoiding eye contact.* 'Not much, really. The usual crap.'

I try again. 'Did you get out of the office at all?'

'I nipped out at lunchtime to get some sushi, but that was it. You know what it's like on Wednesdays.' He waves his fork at his plate. 'This shepherd's pie is delicious, Annie.'

'I'm glad you like it,' I say, smiling through the jitters. 'So . . . you just had meetings all morning then?'

'Pretty much,' says Luke, still focused on his food. 'What have you done differently with this, Annie? Have you put lentils in it?'

Oh Christ, this is *torture*. Why doesn't he give me a straight answer? I've never really had a reason to analyse what he's saying quite so closely; perhaps Luke's always this vague, and I just haven't noticed? Clearly, I need to take a more direct approach.

I take a deep breath and just come out with it. 'Luke, do you have a red woolly hat? Like a beanie?'

Ah, *now* I've got his attention: he looks up and his eyes lock onto mine. I feel a stab of fear – what if he says yes? What am I going to do then? – but although his expression is quizzical, he doesn't look remotely guilty, and after a moment he shakes his head.

'Come on, I'm a Chelsea fan – remember? Wouldn't be seen dead in red. Why d'you ask?'

'Oh, there was one in the hallway this morning. I wondered if you'd dropped it.'

'It probably belongs to Damian,' shrugs Luke casually, mentioning our neighbour. 'He's a Gooner, poor bloke.'

And with that he returns to his food. Surely if it *was* him I saw today, my question would have indicated that he'd been caught red-handed – or rather, red-hatted – and there would be at least a flash of concern, or some inkling of guilt. I can't believe Luke is *that* good a liar.

I still feel the need to test him further though, to put my mind completely at rest.

'So, I had an interesting morning,' I say, after we eat in silence for a few moments.

'Oh yeah, what did you get up to?'

'Fi offered to babysit, so I went shopping.' And now for the killer blow: 'On Oxford Street.'

The moment I utter the words I hold my breath, on ten-terhooks for his reaction: I've as good as told him that I caught him cheating – if, indeed, the mystery cheater *was* him. But without even the slightest of pauses, Luke looks up and beams, his face radiating pleasure.

'That's fantastic! You were seriously overdue a bit of me-time. So how did it feel, being out in the real world again? Did you manage not to phone Fiona every five min-utes to check on Dottie?'

He looks so happy for me that I'm engulfed by a wave of shame. I've got this totally wrong, haven't I? I've thrown everything I had at Luke, but he gave me absolutely no cause to doubt him: there was no weird body language, no stiffness, no awkward silences. All I had to go on is a distant half-glimpse of someone who looks a bit like him (from the back) out of a grubby bus window – and this from a woman who recently microwaved her phone. If this was a court of law, the verdict would be unanimous: 'Not guilty, m'lud.'

I feel the tension drain from my body, and I realise just how much I've worked myself up over this non-event. Well, that was a waste of a day's brainpower on needless worrying.

After dinner we snuggle up on the sofa together and watch a film. Thanks to Luke's doting Italian mama Lucia, who regards feminism as the devil's work and raised her only son amongst four daughters as a prince, my boyfriend has some fairly old-fashioned views on gender roles (while he certainly wouldn't go as far as insisting that a woman's place is in the home, I know he's perfectly happy that he's the breadwinner and I'm in charge of the house and Dot). But tonight he is noticeably caring and attentive, fetching me a cup of tea and offering me a foot rub. He's certainly not acting like a man who's about to run off with another woman. If anything – and I don't think this is too much of a leap, in light of the ring-size query – he seems more like a man with marriage on his mind. I've never been that fussed about getting hitched, but since having Dot I'm definitely warming to the idea. It might be nice to have a party to make our little family official, and Dot would look seriously cute tottering down the aisle in a tutu and sparkly trainers. Perhaps Luke's feeling the same way too?

It's nearly 10 p.m. and I'm thinking about getting ready for bed when Luke's mobile starts to ring. I watch out of the corner of my eye as he picks it up, checks the caller ID, puts it back on the sofa without answering (screen down) and returns his attention to the TV. I feel an unpleasant stirring of something that I hope is indigestion.

'Aren't you going to get that?'

'Nope.'

'Anyone you know?'

Luke shrugs. 'Just work stuff. Whatever it is can certainly wait until morning.'

The ringing stops, and I have to firmly remind myself

that it's far from unusual for Luke to get work calls this late, and that I should be glad he's not interrupting our time together to deal with it.

I sit up and stretch. 'Well, I'm going to give Dot her dream feed and then call it a night.'

'Okay, patatina,' says Luke, leaning over for a kiss. 'I'll be up shortly.'

I'm halfway up the stairs when he calls to me. 'Oh, Annie, I nearly forgot; I'm afraid I'm going to have to work late on Friday.'

I stop in my tracks. Friday is the one day of the week he always comes home early so that he's here for Dot's bath and bedtime; I don't think he's ever missed it.

'Oh, that's a shame,' I say, trying to keep my voice level.

'Yeah, sorry, there are these important clients coming over from the States. But I'll make it up to you on Saturday night, I promise. Our big date, remember?'

Then he waggles his eyebrows suggestively, and despite myself I return his grin; he looks so excited. Plus am I really going to mistrust him forever just because I *imagined* seeing him cheat on me?

'Can't wait,' I say, blowing him a kiss.

Dot doesn't stir when I open her door and creep over to her cot. She is lying on her back and in the light from the hallway I can just make out her ridiculously long eyelashes, her tiny nose – Luke's, not mine, thank God – and that perfect pink rosebud mouth. I lean down until I'm close enough to hear her breathing and smell that gorgeous baby-scent and stay like that for a few moments in the warm darkness, just watching her sleep.

At times like this I'm almost frightened by the strength of my love for my daughter; in fact, I don't think the word 'love' really cuts it in this situation: this overwhelming, all-consuming, 24/7 obsession is something else entirely. Shortly after Dot was born, I remember watching a David Attenborough documentary in which a baby wildebeest wandered away from its herd while a hyena was circling, hungrily, and I was hit by such a fierce, desperate surge of protectiveness that it left me breathless. I realised then just how vulnerable I am now; I knew without a doubt that if anything bad ever happened to my child, it would destroy me.

Dot doesn't even open her eyes when I lift her from the cot and carry her over to the rocking chair in the corner where we have our late-night feeding sessions. She latches on instantly, her little mouth working away rhythmically; the breastfeeding comes so easily now I've almost forgotten the struggle we initially had to get the hang of it. While Dot's guzzling I pull out my phone to play Candy Crush (she can often be on there for a good half hour) and I discover a text from Fi.

How did it go? Anything to report? Hope all good. Call if you need to chat. Fx

After a moment's consideration, I start to type a very long text recounting the conversation I had with Luke this evening – his reaction, my conclusions, blah blah blah – but then, in the glow of the night light, my eyes fall on the silver-framed photo that hangs over Dot's cot. It was taken minutes after I'd given birth: Dot is just a tiny pink scrap lying on my chest, nuzzled into my neck, while I smile down at her, looking pretty good considering what I'd just been through. Luke has his arms around both of us and is gazing into the camera with an expression that hovers somewhere between astonishment and ecstasy. I love that picture; it's a perfect distillation of all the incredible emotions of that moment. And then I glance down at Dot, who is still chugging away at my boob, cheeks flushed, perfectly content with her little world. I drop a kiss on her head, then delete my original outpouring and write:

Thanks for checking up on me, Fi, but it was a false alarm. I'm going mad clearly! Nothing to worry about at all xxx

4

I have this theory that your name plays a significant role in deciding your destiny. Think about it: would Madonna have become the world's biggest star if she was named, say, Pam? Would Beyoncé be a bootylicious pop goddess if she'd been christened Janice? I don't think so. Which goes to show why I'm a little less than satisfied with my name: Ann. Three letters, none of which are even remotely interesting. Not for me a Tantalising T or a Brilliant B – I'm stuck with one Average and two Normals. My parents didn't even think to stick an Enigmatic at the end, which at least might have added a dash of French flair. So since I was a kid, I've tried to offset some of my name's blah-ness by going by Annie.

It doesn't help that my younger sister was given the far more dazzling name of Tabitha – and if Tabitha Taylor wasn't alliteratively alluring enough, she recently married a man named Jonathan Tempest, so is now Tabitha Taylor-Tempest, which sounds like the best character in a Jilly Cooper novel. As if to prove my brilliant name theory, Tabitha's life is like a character's in a Jilly Cooper novel, too: she works in an art gallery, her husband's family live in a Cotswolds manor house, she is kind and beautiful – with the cutest little button nose – *and* she makes jam in her spare time. I hope this doesn't sound like I'm jealous, because I'm not – I adore her. Tabby's three months pregnant and I can't wait to be an auntie – not least because none of my other close friends have had babies yet, so I'll finally have someone to talk to about blocked milk ducts and cradle cap.

Seeing as we're all in our thirties now, I guess it's quite surprising that I'm the only one of my group to have become a mum. Fiona is über-broody, but wants to wait until she and her fella Finn are married before starting a family; Claris, who I've known since primary school, is in a committed relationship with her new catering business; and my newly divorced friend Jessica has never wanted to be a mother, even when she was (briefly) married, because, and I quote, 'Having a child is so fucking predictable.' Also: 'I don't need the hassle.' And: 'A baby would get in the way of me having sex with lots of unsuitable men.' In the circumstances, I think it best for all concerned if she keeps her coil in.

I'd hoped I might make some mum friends at NCT antenatal classes, but Luke didn't want to go. His official excuse was that he was too busy at work, but I think it was more to do with the fact that he didn't fancy discussing vaginal mucus plugs or role-playing the different stages of labour with a roomful of strangers; he's just not that type of guy. Surprisingly, however, I did manage to get him to come to a hypnobirthing class – although that was only because it was on a Sunday when Chelsea weren't playing, and I told him he might get a massage.

That one class was all it took for Luke to realise that he would really prefer to be *outside* the hospital delivery suite while I was giving birth. He was extremely apologetic, but it was actually a relief: he's quite squeamish about bodily functions, and from what I understood there was a significant possibility of pooing during labour (me, not him) and I didn't want to have to worry about repulsing Luke on top of everything else that would be going on. Besides, while hypnobirthing might have scared off one birth partner, it supplied me with another, far better one: the class teacher, Sigrid.

If you could create the ideal person to help you through a twenty-eight-hour labour, including some intense forceps action, then it would be Sigrid. The woman should have 'human epidural' printed on her business card. She looks like a Scandinavian hippy goddess – all blonde plaits, freckles and open chakras – and just the sound of her voice is enough to send you into a blissed-out trance. Luke jokes that she's the living embodiment of joss sticks and mung beans, but then he's deeply suspicious of anything remotely 'alternative'.

As well as teaching hypnobirthing, Sigrid works as a doula, which is another word for someone you pay to allow you to scream at them during labour, and thank God she agreed to be mine for Dot's birth. Understandably, going through something akin to trench warfare creates a bond, and we've since become good friends; in fact, she's coming over to babysit Dot for our big date on Saturday night. Yet for all her earth motherliness, Sigrid doesn't have any children of her own, which means that I still have a vacancy for someone to moan/drink wine with in the afternoons. As a result, I've just started taking Dot to a mother and baby music group in the hope that I'll meet a like-minded soul who's not averse to mixing breastfeeding with booze.

Raggy Rhyme Time takes place every Thursday morning in our local church hall and is run by a middle-aged woman dressed up as a rag doll, with painted-on red cheeks, a ginger wool wig and the dead eyes of a long-term hostage. 'Raggy' plays the guitar and sings 'The Wheels on the Bus' while the mums sit in a circle shaking tambourines and the babies chew the mini-maracas and cry. As far as I can work out, the children get absolutely nothing out of this – as most of them are too young to sing, play the panpipes or even support the weight of their own heads – but at least the mums can feel that they are assisting the development of their offspring's cognitive and motor skills. Plus – more importantly – it provides an opportunity to complain about how little sleep you've had over custard creams at the end of the session.

Today is the second time I've been and I nod to a couple of women I recognise from last week. Dot slept through our first visit, but at least that gave me a chance to learn the actions to 'Wind the Bobbin Up', and today I try to get to grips with the twenty-seven new verses that have been added to 'Row, Row, Row Your Boat' since I was a child ('Row row row your boat, gently round a puddle . . .').

After the singing is finally finished and Raggy has disappeared off to neck some vodka, the mums congregate around the tea urn. All the excitement has sent Dot to sleep, so I put her in the pushchair and then, feeling like the new kid in class, approach one of the women I'm already on nodding terms with.

'Hello.' I smile brightly. 'How old's your little one?'

'Sienna's four months. Just got your first tooth, haven't you, poppet?'

We coo over her baby, who is dressed in what I'd call Princess Charlotte chic: smocked dress, cashmere cardigan and patent booties. In comparison, Dot's plain white Babygro makes her look like an asylum inmate – but at least it doesn't require dry-cleaning.

'I'm Annie,' I say. 'Mother of Dot.'

'Oh, you'll have to get used to introducing yourself like that,' chips in another woman, who is grappling her baby with the dexterity of a seasoned pro. 'My eldest is at nursery and I'm only ever addressed as "Theo's Mum". I don't think they even know my real name.'

Her real name, it turns out, is Margo, she is a mum of three, and once we get the initial parenting chat out of the way – 'Five hours' sleep? I had three and a half – *and* I've got mastitis in my left tit' – I discover that she is head of HR at a French aerospace company. Sienna's mum, it transpires, is director of a large publishing house, while another woman who joins us with her twins is the CFO of a Swiss bank. All this collective corporate brilliance, brainpower and ass-kicking-ness, now spent doing the 'Hokey Cokey'. It just seems . . . well, a bit of a waste.

'Do you work, Dot's Mum?' Margo asks me, refusing a Bourbon, which is probably why she's like a size six.

'Not anymore,' I say. The power-mums look disappointed, so I quickly add: 'But I used to be a fashion photographer – well, an assistant fashion photographer.'

'Really? That sounds fascinating!'

'It was. I loved it.'

'So why did you decide to stop working?'

'Well, I didn't really *decide* to stop, I . . .' I trail off, wondering how to explain what happened. I've just met these women; I'm nowhere near ready to air my dirty laundry yet. 'Life got in the way,' I say eventually. 'Who's for another custard cream?'

5

Dot is still asleep when we leave Raggy Rhyme Time, so I take the scenic walk home, which takes us through the poshest bit of Clapham and past the very exclusive estate agents where Fiona works. One of the unforeseen bonuses of having a baby is the amount of walking you end up doing while trying to get your child to sleep, or trying to keep them asleep, or just simply 'getting some fresh air'. I've never been that keen on exercise, but since having Dot I'm probably smashing 10,000 steps a day without even thinking about it.

Curtis Kinderbey Sales and Lettings is located on a pretty street that's predominantly made up of estate agents and trendy cafés where you can eat anything as long as it's avocado toast. I don't want to go into the office and risk waking Dot so I hover outside, covertly scanning the interior for Fiona while browsing the property details in the window. I gaze at the glossy photos of cinema rooms, marble staircases, indoor pools and cathedral-sized basements and try to stifle a twinge of envy. Jesus, there are some seriously lavish properties for sale here, all of them way, *way* beyond my means. For instance, five million for a small two-bedroom flat? Unless it's in Buckingham Palace and the price includes use of the Queen's best crown, that seems wildly overpriced.

Although I can't see Fi inside the office, I spot a few familiar faces – I know most of her colleagues from meeting her down the pub post-work, pre-Dot – but there's a bloke sitting at the desk nearest the window that I don't recognise. He's engrossed in something on his computer, which gives me the opportunity to check him out. He's young, probably mid-twenties, with a not-conventionally-handsome but interesting face, pale with wide-apart eyes. There's a definite touch of Benedict Cumberbatch about him. I'm still scrutinising him, trying to work out whether he's strangely attractive or just strange-looking when I realise he's no longer working at his computer but is instead staring back at me.

Cheeks flushing, I grin stupidly.

He mouths: 'Do you need some help?'

I give an apologetic head-shake in reply – do I *look* like I can afford a five-million-pound flat? – and am turning to walk away when I see Fiona bowling down the street towards me, a pocket dynamo in a pencil-skirt and stilettos.

'Annie!' She beams and holds out her arms. 'This *is* a

nice surprise. Come here, gorge, I need a hug. I've had a feckin' shite morning.'

'What's happened? Let's get a coffee and you can vent.'

We buy takeaway flat whites from the nearest avocado toast outlet, then amble along as Fi tells me about the sale of a huge and very expensive house on the common that she's spent months painstakingly negotiating, but which is now at risk because the buyer has 'sensed a presence from the spirit world' in the master en suite and will only go ahead with the sale if the vendor agrees to pay for an exorcism.

'Let me get this straight,' I say, trying not to laugh, 'this woman thinks the toilet is haunted?'

'Yup. She's feckin' mental.' She rolls her eyes and shakes her head dismissively. 'Finn's Uncle Derry is a priest, so I'm thinking I'll get him to come and say a few Hail Marys over the cistern and be done with it . . . Anyway, enough about work. Luke put your mind at rest last night, did he?'

'Absolutely,' I say. 'I think I must have imagined the whole thing. Sleep deprivation's a fucker!'

Fi turns to look at me. 'You absolutely sure, darlin'? Nothing you want to talk about?'

'Nope, everything's fine!'

After a slight pause, Fiona returns my smile. 'Grand,' she says. 'I'm so glad it all turned out okay.'

We walk on for a few moments in silence.

'I mean, there *was* this call to his mobile quite late in

the evening,' I say, 'and Luke told me he didn't want to answer it because it was work, but it's not unusual for him to get late work calls. And it's actually really sweet that he didn't want to interrupt our evening together, isn't it? And then he told me he had to work late tomorrow – but that happens, you know? Not on a Friday usually, it's true, but he can't choose when these important client things happen, can he? So really, I've got nothing to worry about at all – nothing *at all* – and it's definitely for the best if I just put the whole mix-up behind me, and move on. Don't you think?'

I stop and turn to Fiona, but her expression is not exactly reassuring.

'Fi? Do you think I need to worry?' My stomach lurches anxiously.

'No, no, not at all. But I sort of get the impression you might still be a *wee* bit concerned, so if you wanted to put your mind completely at rest then why don't you call his office and ask to check his diary?'

'What? No! That would be a terrible thing to do, like snooping through his phone or reading his emails. I'd be like some God-awful prying wife. No way.'

'Suit yourself, Saint Annie,' shrugs Fi. 'But at least you'd get some closure. All you need to do is call his PA and ask if there's anything in his schedule for tomorrow evening. Would that really be so bad?'

Once Fiona has gone back to the office, I loop back

across the common to prolong my walk home; I need time to think about what she has said. Although the sensible, rational part of me knows that I've got nothing to worry about, the emotional, irrational part of me – quite a large part, to be honest – is unconvinced. Try as I might, I can't get the image of the man in the red hat out of my mind. I hate the idea of checking up on Luke behind his back, but Fiona is right, at least this way I can put any lingering doubts to rest. Before I have second thoughts, I call the switchboard at Luke's office and ask to be put through to Vicky, his PA.

Efficient as ever, she picks up after just one ring.

'Luke Turner's office.'

'Oh Vicky, hi, it's Annie, Luke's, um, partner.' Girlfriend doesn't sound right now that we have a child together.

'Annie! How are you? And Dot?'

'Hard work.'

Vicky laughs knowingly. She is a mum of five; I am in awe of the woman.

'I'm afraid Luke's in a meeting. Do you need me to get a message to him?'

'No, no, I don't actually want to speak to him. The thing is, I'm trying to arrange a surprise dinner – a "thanks for being a great dad" sort of thing – and I wondered if you could check a date in his diary to see if he's free?'

'Aww, that's sweet of you, Annie, I'm sure Luke would love that. When are you thinking?'

'Tomorrow evening. Short notice, sorry.'

'Right, let me have a look ...' I hear brisk tapping at a keyboard. 'Okay, he's got a 4 p.m. meeting with Eckhart, and then ... you're in luck, it looks like he's free for the rest of the day!'

I feel my legs buckle under me and grab the pram for support. Luke lied to me – it *was* him in the red hat. Our daughter is only a few months old and he's having an affair. My hand flies to my mouth. *Luke is having an affair.*

'Oops, no, my mistake!' Vicky's tone is breezy, oblivious to my breakdown at the other end of the line. 'He's got a 7 p.m. meeting with the Americans. I'm so sorry, Annie, he's probably going to be stuck here until late.'

Giddy with relief, I can't stop myself from bursting into laughter.

'Annie? Is everything alright?'

'Yes, sorry, I ... Dot was just doing something funny. Thank you, Vicky, you've been *hugely* helpful.'

'My pleasure. Bring that gorgeous little girl into the office to see me sometime, okay?'

I flop down on a nearby bench, feeling as knackered as if I've just run a marathon. Thank God, at least now I can put the whole thing out of my mind. Unless ... What if Vicky's in on it, and Luke told her to lie to me about tomorrow night? Maybe *she's* the one he's been having the affair with?

No, that's ridiculous, Vicky's five-foot-nothing and

Kardashian-curvy; the woman I saw from the bus was built like a catwalk model. Come on, Annie, I know you're tired, but for pity's sake, get a grip. Whoever that was on Oxford Street, it definitely wasn't Luke.

6

After weeks of that most English of weather conditions – an opaque, white sky, oppressively low, that makes you feel like you're living in Tupperware – Saturday morning dawns clear and sunny with an Alpine nip to the air. And when I say 'dawns', this is not just a figure of speech: it's still dark when Dot wakes me and I watch the sun creep over the frosty rooftops while she has her milk.

The sight of sunshine acts like a triple-shot espresso, and despite the fact that most sane people are still asleep, I'm buzzing with positivity: it's the weekend, which means Luke is at home so I'll get a break from Dot-duties, and we've got our big date tonight! Best of all, I've finally seen off that maggoty worry that's been worming away inside me since Wednesday.

Dot finishes her breakfast, burps, then looks up at me with an expression that says, 'Oh, hey, didn't see you there', stretching up her hand to touch my face. I pretend to nibble her fingers, which makes her giggle like I'm the funniest person ever, so I do it again. I can't get enough of that baby chuckle – perhaps I should record it for my ringtone? At times like this I can almost forgive the early wake-up calls. Almost.

We occupy ourselves until half past eight when I notice Dot rubbing her ear. I deduce this to be one of those mythical 'sleepy cues' that all the baby books go on about, so I immediately dash back upstairs and put her down for a nap – dearly hoping I haven't missed the crucial 'nap window' – and then crawl back into bed with Luke, wondering whether mothers in Amazonian tribes worry about this shit. (Probably not, but while they may not be obsessing over 'The Top Ten Sleep Mistakes Parents Make', they *do* have to deal with the Brazilian wandering spider, so swings and roundabouts, really.)

Luke is asleep when I slide under the covers next to him, moulding myself against the length of his back. He stirs, and I enjoy the sensation of his muscles flexing and tightening beneath me.

'Hey, beautiful,' he murmurs, 'what time is it?'

'Eight thirty-ish. Dot's just gone down for a nap.'

He turns over to face me. 'You should have woken me up! I could have helped you with her.'

'You didn't get back until after midnight, I thought you'd need the lie-in.'

'Mmmm, I don't deserve you, patatina,' he murmurs, snaking his arms around me, and I try to ignore a stab of self-consciousness about the pockets of back fat that have stubbornly stayed put post-pregnancy.

We snooze until Dot wakes again, and then our day unfolds like most of our Saturdays now that we're parents – a stroll to the coffee shop, stopping at the pond to feed the ducks; tummy-time on the play mat; late showers and a fridge-foraged lunch of leftovers – except today there's the added frisson of knowing that we've got a proper, grown-up night together later. Every now and then I catch Luke's eye and I can tell from his smile that he's feeling the same spark of excitement I am.

Dinner is booked at 8 p.m. at a local restaurant that is close enough to be able to dash home if Dot needs a feed, yet treaty enough to make it worth getting dressed up for. Luke offers to take care of Dot's bath and bedtime routine, which gives me the luxury of a whole hour to transform myself from dowdy to slightly less dowdy.

I blow-dry my hair for the first time in ages, then realise that all the frizz was actually covering up inches of dark roots, so I tie it back into a ponytail, which looks marginally better. Wearing my new lingerie, lipstick and an old-but-reliable dress that skims over my flab and bigs up my boobs, I feel, if not a million bucks, then at least a few hundred thousand.

Luke is in the shower when Sigrid, our lovely doula, arrives for babysitting duties, looking like a really cool milkmaid in a white lacy dress with a leather biker jacket and this incredible pair of slouchy, studded boots. I'd ask her to borrow them, but my size sevens are probably twice the size of her exquisite fairy feet.

'Oh Annie, you look beautiful!' She gathers me into a hug, her white-blonde hair swishing around us both, smelling of summer meadows and sunshine. (And yes, I probably am slightly in love with her, but the woman helped me through some scarily intense shit, so I think I'm allowed a bit of a crush.)

'How are you, my darling?' Still holding me, Sigrid draws back and puts her head to one side. She has this way of looking at you like she's gazing into your soul; it would be impossible to lie to her, because she'd just *know*.

'I'm good. A little tired, but generally good. Except . . . Is it normal, after having a baby, to be, um, seeing things?'

'Seeing things?'

'Yeah, like thinking you've seen something, but you actually imagined it. Hallucinating, I suppose.'

Sigrid beams, showing cinematically-perfect teeth.

'Annie, you've just been through the most profound, intense and transformative experience of a woman's life. The energy pathways of your body are bound to be disrupted. I can certainly show you some yoga poses that will help rebalance your chi, but yes, in the circumstances I'd say a little hallucination is entirely within the realms of normal. Okay?'

'Okay.' I smile; I knew Sigrid would make me feel better. 'Luke's just getting ready, can I get you a drink?'

'I'd love a cup of tea, thank you, angel. Here, I've brought some Tung Ting Oolong with me.' She fishes in her bag and holds out a box of tea bags. 'It's quite a delicate leaf, so you'll need to leave the water for a few minutes after boiling ... Now, where's Dottie? Is she asleep already?'

'Yes, but go up and see her if you'd like.'

'Love to,' beams Sigrid, shrugging off her jacket. 'Back in a sec.'

As she pads upstairs, I head to the kitchen and put the kettle on, thinking once again how lucky I am to have Sigrid in my life. Thanks to her, I know I'll be able to relax tonight and focus on Luke, rather than worrying about how Dot is getting on. I should take her out for a nice lunch next week to thank her – or perhaps I could buy her a gift ... ?

The baby monitor is turned on in the nursery, and as I potter around in the kitchen, I hear Sigrid murmur, 'Hello, little one, how are you?'

I visualise her as she leans over the cot, perhaps stroking Dot's sleep-flushed cheek, and smile to myself; then after a few moments I hear a sort of rustling noise, and Sigrid says: 'She's grown so much since I last saw her.'

Now I hear Luke's voice. 'She rolled over the other day, did Annie tell you?'

Ah, those must have been his footsteps I heard a moment ago.

Sigrid says something in reply, but I'm loading glasses into the dishwasher and the clatter drowns out her response. I glance at the clock on the oven: quarter to eight. We should probably get going – the restaurant is only round the corner, but I can barely hobble in these heels.

Then, over the monitor I hear: 'Luke, no. Don't. Not here.'

I freeze, unease creeping over me like a chill. It's not Sigrid's words that unnerve me as much as her tone: urgent, guarded, breathless. I wait, straining to hear what comes next, but nothing more is said and as the seconds tick by I start to talk myself down from the ledge. *Get a grip, Annie, you're imagining things again. There's nothing to worry about.*

But then I hear a woman's gasp. It's the sort of gasp that happens involuntarily when someone touches you and you never want them to stop. And now Luke's voice, so soft that I can't make out what he's saying, although the end of it sounds very much like: '. . . can't stop thinking about you.'

I throw myself across the room to where the monitor is plugged in and frantically turn up the volume to its highest setting, every fibre of my being focused on listening, and, despite the horrible rushing sound in my ears, this time when Sigrid speaks I hear every word.

'I meant what I said to you on Wednesday, Luke. We can't keep doing this. I feel terrible about Annie.'

'I know, I know. Me too.' A sigh. 'Look, shall we still meet next week? Just to talk?'

A pause. 'You really think we're just going to talk?'

'Sigrid, I . . .'

And then there are no more words, just murmurs and gasps and moans, and it's clear as day what's going on: the father of my child is standing next to our sleeping daughter with the woman who dried my tears during labour and they are kissing, just like they were when I saw them the other day. And nearby, watching the pair of them, there is a photo of me holding my baby moments after I gave birth, taken just weeks ago, and they're too far gone to even care.

7

I can't do anything; I just stand there, paralysed, listening to the soft sounds coming over the monitor. Now that my worst fears have been proved right – actually no, not my worst fears, *worse* than my worst fears – I feel nothing. I'm literally numb. It's like my emotions have been packaged up in bubble wrap.

After a while – seconds? minutes? – Sigrid comes back into the kitchen, followed by Luke. They are bright-eyed and smiling, like they've had a few drinks. All I can do is stare at them, dazed. It feels like a pair of unicorns have just trotted into the kitchen.

'So,' beams Luke. 'Mystic Meg here reckons our daughter could grow up to be a professional footballer. I'm calling Chelsea FC first thing tomorrow.'

Sigrid gives him a jokey little shove. 'I didn't say that, I just said that she clearly has excellent muscle tone and is going to be an early walker.'

I just stare and stare, trying to force this terrible new

reality to sink in. This deadness I'm feeling is a bit discon-
certing; perhaps I'm in shock?

Luke is the first to notice that something is up, his
brow furrowing as he takes in my expression. 'Annie?
What is it?'

I still can't speak, but now Sigrid notices something
isn't quite right, too. Her smile fades and she glances
nervously at Luke. I can tell exactly what they're both
thinking: *what does she know?*

And then suddenly Dot's cry fills the room, amplified
by the monitor that is still turned up high, and I watch as
realisation spreads over Luke's face like a stain and the
implications sink in. His eyes go wide, his mouth hangs
slack, and he takes a step towards me and then stops, glancing over at Sigrid, whose expression is the mirror image of
his own. Dot mercifully goes silent again, returning to sleep.

God knows why, but I feel utterly calm, sort of like I'm
floating outside my body watching me watch them, but
it's the dangerous sort of calm that you know at some
point in the near future will shatter into jagged shards of
anger and pain.

I finally manage to speak. 'At what point did the two of
you start . . .' My voice cracks; I can't bring myself to finish the sentence.

Luke takes another step towards me, his arms outstretched. 'Annie, whatever you think you may have
heard, you've got it all wrong, honestly.'

'Don't touch me,' I snap, surprised by a sudden stab of emotion, a preview of the rage to come. But just as quickly as it hits, it fades, and that spooky calm returns. 'I asked you a question. Given the circumstances, I think it would be polite to answer.'

'Annie, what we've done is unforgivable,' says Sigrid, 'but it's not what you think, I promise you . . .'

'So I've been hallucinating again, have I? Or is fucking the new father all part of your post-birth service?'

She opens her mouth to speak, but I cut her off. 'Don't even try to talk your way out of this, because I saw the two of you at it last week. Not so averse to red hats after all, are you, Luke?'

'Annie, we haven't had sex, I swear to you.' Sigrid holds her hand to her chest, so bloody sincere, a paragon of perfect innocence and integrity.

Luke latches onto this, nodding furiously. 'We just kissed, that's all – nothing else!'

'Ah, so what just happened upstairs isn't such a big deal then?' This shuts them both up. 'To be honest, a one-off shag would have been almost easier to forgive, although no doubt you've been working yourselves up to that. Now, if you could please answer my original question, when did this start?'

The pair of them look shiftily at each other but say nothing. All I want is for them to tell me what happened so that I can get as far away from them as possible. The longer this silence drags on, the closer my composure is to exploding: I feel like a rubber band that is being slowly stretched, longer and tighter until it quivers, and I just know it's about to snap back.

Sigrid is the first to speak, destroying any remaining iota of respect I had for Luke. 'Do you remember that day when you were having trouble breastfeeding and you phoned asking me to come round and help? Well, after you'd gone to bed that evening, I stayed for a while and Luke and I chatted. Nothing happened that evening, but there was a . . . a spark.'

'Go on.'

'So we met up a few days later for a coffee,' says Sigrid.

'I phoned Sigrid to ask her to meet,' mumbles Luke. 'She didn't want to, but I pressured her into it.'

'But *why*?' My voice chokes with emotion, and I doggedly fight back the tears. 'I'd just given birth to your *child*! We were a family! Wasn't that enough for you? Am *I* not enough for you?'

'Of course you are, Annie, please, I love you . . .'

'Then why have you been chasing after *her*?'

'It's not like that at all! It's just – fuck, how can I explain . . .' He drags his hands through his hair, his eyes squeezed shut. 'It's like . . . after you had Dot, I was so in awe of you, of what you'd achieved. You *made* our daughter. You gave birth to her! It was mind-blowing, and I saw you in a whole new light. The sexual feelings I had towards you suddenly felt wildly inappropriate, because you were this incredible . . . creator of life. And I know it's absolutely no excuse, and what I've done is unforgivable, but I suppose because of that I sort of stopped seeing you as a . . . as a sexual being.'

'Jesus, spare me the Madonna and whore bullshit!' I erupt, my fury swelling by the second. 'I tell you, Luke, your mother has SO much to answer for . . .' I take a deep breath, trying to stay in control. 'So, because I had turned into the blessed Virgin Mary, you thought you'd try your luck with Ulrika-fucking-Jonsson over there.'

'It wasn't like that!' Luke looks helpless. 'Annie, you know what a huge shock it is, becoming a parent. You've found it tough too, haven't you?'

'*Everyone* finds it tough with a newborn baby, Luke, but most people manage not to have an affair as a coping mechanism.'

'Annie, I really wouldn't call this an affair . . .' murmurs Sigrid.

'Just shut up! Shut up!' I shriek, then take another breath to compose myself. 'Luke, do go on, I think you were just trying to talk your way out of this?'

He fixes me with a look of desperation, but ploughs on. 'What I was trying to explain was that I found fatherhood overwhelming. The idea that this new little person was entirely dependent on us for everything . . . I was shattered by the weight of the responsibility, Annie. And then Sigrid was just *there* and I . . . I liked the feeling of flirting, of being able to forget about all the responsibility for a bit and to be . . . free again, I suppose. And then one thing led to another and, well, here we are. I've got no excuse. I know I'm an arsehole.'

'No, you're far worse than that. You are a weak, pathetic little man, and you're a coward.' I turn to Sigrid. 'So what's your excuse? Chakras out of whack, were they?'

She just stares at her feet and says nothing, and I'm engulfed by such a surge of sadness that it virtually winds me. Sigrid's betrayal is almost worse than Luke's. This is the woman who handed me my baby after I had given birth, who held my hand while my poor, torn vagina was stitched back up again, who I trusted like a sister. The lump in my throat is making it hard to talk now and I know I can't keep it together for much longer, but I need to know every single sordid detail.

Digging my nails into my palms to stay in control, I turn back to Luke. 'So how many other times did you two "go for coffee"?'

'Two or three,' he mumbles. 'But we wouldn't have taken it any further.'

'Bullshit. I heard the two of you upstairs. You were planning on meeting up next week.'

'Annie, I love you, you've got to believe me!' Luke is begging me now, close to tears himself. 'I can't bear the thought of losing you and Dot. Nothing really happened,

I promise! This was just a stupid . . . moment of madness! Please, Annie, you need to get this in proportion!'

I can tell Luke regrets saying this as soon as the words are out of his mouth.

'*Get this in proportion?* Let me get this straight, just so we're all on the same page here. I've overheard my boyfriend, the father of my three-month-old baby, sticking his tongue down the throat of a woman I thought was my friend. What *exactly* do you suggest would be a proportionate reaction in this situation? Because personally, I feel I'm being pretty fucking reasonable, all things considered.'

Silence. Luke is standing with his hands shoved in his pockets, shoulders hunched, looking at me like a scolded Labrador, while Sigrid is snivelling in the corner. I turn to face her.

'Anything to say for yourself, Sigrid? Because really, I'm not sure this is a doula win. I can't say I'll be reviewing your services that favourably on Yell-dot-com after this.'

She is properly crying now, the tears sending rivers of mascara and bronzer running down her face. Not such a natural beauty after all, then.

'I'm so, so sorry, Annie,' she whispers. 'I never meant to hurt you.'

'Well, you have.' I close my eyes and the tears brim over. 'Just go. Get out.'

Thankfully she does, and quickly; moments later I hear

the door close behind her. The numbness is fading fast and anger and loathing are rushing in to take its place. I turn to face Luke and realise I'm shaking.

'How could you do this to me?' My breath is coming in gasps. 'We've just had a *baby*! My body is shot to pieces, I barely know who I am anymore, my hormones are all over the place and you decide *this* would be a good time to cheat on me! There might be a shittier time to do the dirty, but right now I can't think of it.'

'I'm so sorry,' says Luke, and I can't stand the sound of his whiny voice. 'It meant nothing, I promise you! Can we just sit down and talk about this, please, Annie?'

'No.'

'If you'd just give me a chance to explain . . .'

'I thought you explained already? Something about not fancying me anymore, wasn't it?'

'No, no, that's not it at all, I . . .'

'Fuck you, Luke.'

I slump to the floor, defeated, and finally the floodgates open, and it's almost a relief to allow the pain to pull me under. Luke comes over and tries to comfort me, but I can't bear for him to be anywhere near me; eventually he mutters something about 'giving me some space', and a little while later I hear the front door close.

I drag myself up to our bedroom and cry until the sheets are soaked and I'm blanketed by sodden tissues. Usually my friends – Fi, Jessica and Claris – and my sister,

Tabitha, would be the very first people I'd call in a crisis, but right now I can't face putting into words what's just happened. Because then I'd have to accept the fact that it actually has. Ridiculously, at some point during my sob-fest, I feel a tiny chink of hope when I think, 'I'll phone Sigrid in the morning, she'll know what I should do', and then I remember, and I squash my face into the pillow and howl. In fact, I quickly realise that it's better not to think at all, because when my brain does take charge, the likely consequences of tonight's bombshell leave me breathless with panic. Just a few hours ago my world felt calm, secure, but now the future is a terrifying blizzard of question-marks: where will Dot and I live? How will I support us? I feel like I'm barely coping with parenthood as it is – will I be up to raising her all on my own? And will I be able to trust anyone ever again?

Just after 1 a.m. Dot wakes wanting a feed, which is probably a good thing because it forces me to put my emotional breakdown on hold and drag myself downstairs to warm the milk that I pumped earlier this afternoon – and thank God I did, because I can't bear the thought of breastfeeding and passing any of these horrific, tortuous feelings onto Dot through my milk.

After a moment's protest over the bottle rather than the anticipated boob, Dot settles down and starts to drink. I watch her as she feeds – so tiny and perfect, bliss-fully unaware of the mess her parents have made of everything – and the tears flow constantly down my cheeks, as if a tap's been left on.

'I'm sorry, my darling,' I whisper, over and over. 'I'm so sorry.'

After her milk Dot falls back to sleep at once and I guess I must eventually too, because the next thing I know I'm being jolted awake by her cry again, and I open my eyes to see the grey dawn light filtering through a chink in the bedroom curtains. I've got a splitting headache and my whole body aches. The space next to me is empty – Luke hasn't come home. Perhaps he's with Sigrid. In my mind I see the two of them lying together, limbs entwined, reassuring each other that really, what they've done isn't *so* awful, and sympathising about poor, dumb Annie. The tears start again; it's almost a relief to let myself tumble back into that pit of despair, where I don't need to think about the future. But Dot's increasingly urgent cries pull me back out and I think: *no, I have to get a grip.* I need to be strong for Dot. I can wallow some other time, but right now I need to make a plan.

I feed Dot, get her dressed, and then while she's content on her play mat, I go in search of my phone. There are missed calls and messages from Luke, which I ignore; instead I dial my sister's number. It's still early, but Tabitha's never been one for lie-ins and I'm banking on the fact she'll already be up baking croissants or something. Sure enough, she picks up after a couple of rings.

'Hey, early bird,' she says. 'How are you?'

'Tabby, something's happened.' *Don't cry. Keep it together.*

'Annie? What is it?'

'It's Luke.' It's a struggle to get the words out. 'He's been . . . cheating on me. With Sigrid. The doula.'

There's a sharp intake of breath at the other end of the line. 'Jesus Christ.'

'I don't know what to do, Tabs. I just want to run away but I can't, because of Dot.' Despite my best efforts, I start to sob. 'Oh God, poor Dottie! What's going to happen to us?'

'Right, I'm coming to get you,' says Tabitha firmly. 'Pack a bag for you and one for Dot. Bring the essentials and don't worry if you forget something, Jon can always run out to the shops later. I'll be with you within the hour. You're going to stay in our spare room.'

'But that's your nursery . . .'

'Not yet, it isn't. We'll sort this out, alright?'

I feel wimperingly grateful to her for taking charge. 'Thank you, Tabby.'

'Where's Luke now?'

'I don't know. He left last night, I'm not sure where he's gone.'

'Well, if that bastard does appear, tell him he better not be there when I arrive, because if he is I won't be held liable for my actions.'

I manage a small smile; I've cried so much over the

past twelve hours it makes my face feel weird. 'Thank you, Tabby. I'm so sorry about all this.'

'Don't be, it's hardly your fault. I love you and I'll be there soon. We'll get through this, okay?'

'Okay.' I hesitate for a moment. 'Tabby?'

'Yes?'

I gulp down the lump in my throat. 'I wish Mum was here.'

8

Five years ago Tabby and I lost our parents. They were driving through France when a lorry lost control and ploughed into their car. They died instantly, the police assured us; they would have felt nothing, they wouldn't have suffered. For some reason I latched onto this obsessively in the days after the crash. I know it had been said to comfort us, but I questioned it endlessly: how do we really *know* they felt nothing? How can anyone know what happens in the moments before you die? Besides, *I* felt plenty. I had always been close to my parents – I would call my mum most days, and get home for Sunday lunch as often as my busy clubbing and lie-in schedule would allow – but their deaths hit me harder than I could ever have imagined. First it was an all-consuming grief, then bleak depression enlivened by occasional outbursts of fury: at the lorry driver, at the police, at the couple who my mum and dad had been holidaying with – even at my parents themselves. Suffice to say, I was not handling it at all well.

At the time of the crash I was living my best possible life, working as second assistant to a famous fashion photographer called Jay Patterson. For a girl who had wanted to be Annie Leibovitz since she was old enough to drool over the fashion shoots in *Vogue*, it was a dream job, and one that had taken me years of hard slog and shameless blagging to land. I had knocked on every door I could find – and if it stayed shut then I just booted it open.

As well as working alongside the industry's top names, the upsides to being Jay Patterson's bitch (well, deputy bitch) included worldwide travel, endless parties and designer freebies. The downsides were the total lack of job security and the fact that my boss was a cocaine-fuelled egomaniac who liked to pay prostitutes to wee on him. I had planned to stick it out with him for two more years because it would look good on my CV, but when I broke down in the wake of my parents' death and couldn't get out of bed, let alone to work, I was rapidly replaced by the next ruthlessly ambitious wannabe. It took me six months to get back on my feet, by which time the world of fashion had moved on; Barb was last season's boot-cut jean in a world of ripped skinnies. I managed to get the odd freelance photography job, but without any of my old drive or passion the bills started to mount up, and eventually I had to face facts: I could either be a homeless, aspiring photographer, or I could get a 'proper job' and pay the rent. I signed up with a secretarial temp agency and my first job was at a German investment bank, working for – you've guessed it – Luke.

By this time a year had passed since the crash and I was a very different girl to the ambitious extrovert of my photography days. I craved security; the unpredictability and chaos that I'd once found such a buzz now held zero appeal. My longest 'proper' relationship up until this point (I don't count the bed-hopping of my fashion years) had only lasted a year or so with a fellow photography student called Yoshi, who'd gone back to Tokyo once our course was finished – I still can't pass a Yo Sushi without getting a bit misty-eyed – but now I wanted nothing more than to settle down with a lovely, grown-up man who would look after poor little orphan Annie.

Luke was part of the corporate world, focused and hard-working, a traditional man's man. Not to mention he had a body like David Gandy. To this day, nobody can rock tailored pinstripe trousers quite like him. That first morning when I walked into his office to introduce myself, I think I might actually have said: 'Hi Luke, I'm Annie Taylor, the temp who'll be filling in for Vicky while she's on holiday, and, if I may say so, sir, *PHWOAR*.'

And if I didn't say it out loud, I certainly thought it.

The problem was, you could just tell that Luke was the

type who went for sweet, uncomplicated girls with swishy ponytails, not big-mouthed Barbra Streisand wannabes who liked dancing on tables with drag queens. I had already dialled down my look since my parents died – the Barbra outfits were inextricably linked with my darling dad, and it was too painful to be reminded of him every time I looked in the mirror, plus the clothes suggested an inner flamboyance and confidence that I no longer felt – so I just took it to the extreme. I guess most of us are guilty of tweaking ourselves to a degree to become the person we think the object of our affections will desire. I packed away the headscarves and kaftans, toned down my eyeliner and made myself into the girl I knew Luke would fancy. And actually, I felt ready to say goodbye to Barb. *This is just part of the growing-up process*, I thought; I'd fallen hard for Luke. Two months after we started dating, I came to stay at his flat in Clapham for the weekend and never left.

But while the new me – sweet, obliging Annie Taylor – might have ticked all his boxes, deep down I think I knew I wasn't being true to myself. This wasn't an issue to start with – when someone is falling in love with you, it's almost impossible not to love yourself too – but as time went on and I gradually began to piece myself back together again in the wake of my parents' death, this feeling became stronger. I started to miss Barb: her camera, headscarves, big gob and all – although by now she felt like a virtual stranger to me. And then I became a mum, which muddled up my identity still further, leaving me even more confused about who I am. I suppose you could say I was feeling a bit lost.

Well, now I really *am* lost.

Tabitha and her husband Jonathan move me and Dot into the spare room of their cottage in Fulham and instantly take charge. I spend the day in bed, wallowing in a swamp of teary self-pity, while Tabby force-feeds me toast and listens when I blather on about my life being over. Jonathan takes Dot for a walk and keeps her entertained. At some point that afternoon, waking me from a fitful doze, I hear the doorbell ring and moments later my sister's voice, angrier and shoutier than I've ever heard it, shortly followed by the door slamming. She later tells me that Luke turned up asking to see me.

'I don't think I've seen Tabs so furious,' Jonathan recalls; Tabby has forcibly ejected me from the bed and we're now sitting in the kitchen having supper.

'Well, I couldn't believe he had the cheek to turn up on the doorstep!' Tabby shakes her head. 'I told him to eff off, obviously.'

'Thank you,' I mutter, pushing my food around the plate. 'I'm just so sorry to get you both mixed up in this mess.'

'We're family, of course we want to help,' says Jonathan, reaching for my hand and giving it a squeeze. 'We're here for you and Dottie, always.'

I smile at him, tears prickling my eyes at his kindness; at least my sister landed a good 'un.

'Annie . . .' Tabby pauses, shifting in her seat, as if getting up the nerve to break bad news. 'I know Luke has behaved absolutely appallingly, but you do know . . . you're going to have to speak to him at some point, don't you?'

No fucking way, snaps a voice inside my head. 'Mmmm,' I say, vaguely.

'He told me he's desperate to make things right between you. He's clearly feeling terrible about what he's done. He doesn't look like he's slept at all.'

'Good. Fucking arsehole. Sorry, Jon.'

Jonathan comes from a very well-to-do family – I get the impression they own most of Gloucestershire – and is so well-mannered that I don't like swearing around him, but he just smiles.

'My dear, in the circumstances it is entirely warranted.'

We eat in silence for a bit – well, Tabby and Jonathan eat, I brood. Then Tabby says: 'I know it's early days, but have you had any thoughts about what you'll do?'

'Well, I'm not going back to our flat any time soon, that's for sure. Right now I don't want anything to do with Luke ever again . . .' I slump further into my chair. 'Oh, I don't know, it's way too soon to make any decisions.'

'I know, and that's exactly what I told him,' says Tabby stoutly. 'And he does realise he needs to give you some space. But ... Annie, he wanted me to make sure that you use your joint bank card – for anything that you and Dot need.'

Anger erupts inside me. 'I don't want that arsehole's money!'

Jonathan and Tabitha exchange glances. 'Sweetheart, this is not just about you,' says Tabby gently. 'You're going to need to support Dot, and Luke is her father. I know you want to punish him, but if you don't accept his help, the only people you'll hurt are you and Dot. This is really not something to be pig-headed about.'

She's right, of course. I've been carefully avoiding tackling the subject of where Dot and I will live – and, more importantly, what we'll live *on*. Tabitha and Jonathan insist that I can stay with them as long as I want, but they have a baby on the way, so they certainly don't need a self-pitying single mum squatting in their future nursery. That's got to be bad baby karma.

'Okay, I'll use his credit card,' I say eventually. 'But *only* until I get back on my feet. And then Luke Turner can stick his fucking Amex up his cheating arse.' I grimace. 'Sorry, Jon ...'

On Monday morning Tabitha and Jonathan go back to work (but only after making me promise to at least change out of my pyjamas) and for the next few days I stay in their spare room, marinating in self-pity. Time becomes a meaningless concept: I sleep during the day and lie awake at night, torturing myself with Luke and Sigrid's betrayal. Breastfeeds are the only way I have to mark the hours passing. I keep my phone switched off, primarily to avoid Luke, but also because I'm still not up to speaking to my friends just yet. In amongst the toxic stew of emotions I'm currently experiencing – anger, hatred, fear – I also feel deeply ashamed, as if I'm to blame for what happened because I somehow failed as a girlfriend. It's ridiculous, I know, but right now I'm too humiliated even to speak to Fi, Jessica and Claris. Tabitha has talked to them though, so at least they know Dot and I haven't been kidnapped, and she's assured me that they're there for me when I'm ready.

Thank God for Dot, who despite everything is her usual sunny, giggly self. Without her I'd most likely plunge back into depression. She's the only reason I have for getting out of bed; I can't allow myself to go full hermit when I've got her to care for. But in my bleakest times there are moments – and how I hate myself for this – when I find myself resenting my daughter. *If it wasn't for Dot*, whispers a voice inside me, *you could start a whole new life away from Luke. Because of her you're trapped forever* . . . These thoughts are mercifully fleeting, but my self-loathing peaks when they do creep out from under whatever dark stone they've been hiding.

When I'm not focusing on Dot, I brood endlessly over

what I should do next, and it takes me until Thursday to realise that I have two options. The easiest of these would be for me to move back in with Luke. Until he screwed it all up I was perfectly happy with him, and he *is* a good dad – do I really want to ruin Dot's future over a little snogging? And perhaps a lot of blokes have such moments of madness after becoming a father: not a midlife crisis so much as a *new*-life crisis. In France this is probably an accepted rite of passage – in fact, it could well be so commonplace that there's a name for it: '*une liaison amoureuse de bébé*' or something; I'll Google it. Yes, I should probably be more continental about Luke's indiscretion: put it behind me, sleep with one of Luke's mates to 'even things up', take up smoking and get back to what was admittedly a comfortable, happy life. But this option would obviously depend on me being able to forgive Luke; could I actually do that? Right now it feels as likely – and as welcome – as growing a third boob.

The other option sends me cowering under the covers. This would basically involve splitting up with Luke, moving out and getting a job. In other words: growing the fuck up. God, how I wish I still had just a fraction of my old self-belief! Barb would have never put up with this crap; she'd be out there getting shit done, fighting to make a fantastic new life for her and her daughter – not snivelling into her sister's spare duvet . . .

On Friday morning, Tabitha tells me that I'll be going out that evening.

I lift my head wearily from my porridge. 'No, I'm not.'

'Yes, you are. It's not good for you to be stuck inside.'

'I've been out! Dot and I went to the park yesterday. We fed the ducks.' I sigh. 'How I envy their simple, crust-fuelled existence . . .'

'I mean out *without* Dot. The girls have arranged a quiet dinner at a place nearby. You don't have to go for long, but you're going to go. Your friends are desperate to see you and it'll do you good.'

I try to come up with a reason to say no but I know Tabby's got me bang to rights on this one. 'Okay,' I say. 'You're right, as always.'

'I know I am,' Tabby smiles. 'Oh, and Annie? Maybe run a brush through your hair before you leave the house.'

9

I can think of very few instances where the maxim 'quality over quantity' doesn't hold true – in fact, nail varnish may be the only one I can come up with: better a dozen bottles of Rimmel than two Chanel, as regardless of price they all chip within twenty-four hours – but nowhere is it more apt than in the case of friends. So you have 1,837 Facebook friends? Good for you! You are truly #blessed. But how many of these people would drop everything and come over if you needed help unblocking your U-bend? How many of them even know where you live?

I am lucky enough to have three girlfriends of the very highest quality. Five-star, premium, A-grade mates, all of whom would be there like a shot for plumbing-related or indeed any other emergencies. Although I've collected them from different places over the years – I met Claris at school, Fiona through an ex-boyfriend while at college and Jessica on a sambuca-fuelled night out at a karaoke bar – we have melded together into a gang so seamlessly it's as if we were put together for a Netflix Originals series: 'So we've got the loud Irish one, the glamorous cougar, the serious yet sensitive entrepreneur and the tragic single mother – TV gold!'

So as much as I feel like hiding in Tabitha's spare room for the rest of my life, if anyone can make me feel brighter it'll be my friends – and I think I've *just* about got to the point where I can talk about what's happened without crying.

For some reason, Claris has booked dinner at the sort of place people go to for hen parties because no other establishment will have them. It's only 7 p.m., but there are already two bouncers at the door and the bar is rammed with people, an impressive number of whom are already drunk enough to be dancing. 'Gangnam Style' is playing on a loop and we spot our first set of comedy plastic boobs within seconds of arriving.

Claris, whose idea of a wild night out is a Beckett play at the National, a small glass of Merlot in the interval and then a taxi home, is mortified at her poor choice of venue.

'Oh God, I'm so sorry, I had no idea it would be like this!' She has to shout to make herself heard. 'I don't know this area at all, so I looked up local restaurants in *Time Out* and saw the name of this place and assumed it would be a nice old-fashioned pub, where we could sit by the fire and drink mulled cider. I thought it would have a cosy nook!'

Jessica snorts with laughter. 'Oh yeah, cos "Dick's Halfway Inn" certainly puts you in mind of cosy nooks.'

'I know! I didn't get the joke!' Claris looks close to tears. 'I was in a rush when I booked it, it wasn't too far from Tabitha's and it sounded . . . homely.' She looks over to me, desperately. 'I'm so sorry, Annie, this must be the last place you want to be right now. Do you want to go somewhere else?'

'Please don't worry, it's fine,' I bellow, as a woman in a bridal veil riding an inflatable penis staggers past. 'It's got, um, character.'

'Come on, let's sit down,' yells Fi, forging a path through the crowds. 'It looks a bit more civilised in the restaurant.'

It is not. We are seated next to a gang of blokes who are celebrating Geoff's divorce with a fancy dress bar crawl. Even in my self-absorbed fug, I register that their costume game is strong: Geoff has come as a giant prawn, one of his mates is a man-sized Heineken bottle and another is dressed in a sequinned gown, make-up and Miss World sash.

Geoff and pals are clearly in a 'chatty' mood; thankfully Fiona, who has a voice like an Ulster fishwife, booms, 'NOT INTERESTED, LADS', and that seems to do the trick.

Our waiter arrives bearing enormous laminated menus that are sticky with the fingerprints of stags and hens past.

'Hey there, ladies, and welcome to Dick's! How're you doing tonight?' He says it in a way that implies he's used to getting frenzied whooping in response. 'My name's Craig,' he goes on, unfazed by the tepid reception, 'and I'm here to get the fun started! Yeah!'

'I think we'll just order some drinks for now, thank you,' says Claris with a tight smile.

'Cocktails?' grins Craig, eyebrows raised, as if suggesting cunnilingus.

'Now you're talking,' purrs Jess, angling her cleavage in his direction. 'What would you suggest?'

'For you, I'd recommend the Leg Spreader,' smirks Craig. 'Or perhaps you'd prefer a Screaming Orgasm?'

She fixes him with a kittenish smile. 'Well, if you're offering, I'll take one followed by the other.'

They both laugh, while Fiona puts her head in her hands. 'Jess, are you *literally* trying to become Samantha from *Sex and the City*? Because that's what's happening.'

She shrugs. 'I can think of worse role models.'

'But we're here to support Annie,' whispers Claris. 'She's delicate right now.'

'Oh tsk, I'm just having a bit of fun.' Jess turns to face me. 'Annie, is my behaviour offending you?'

'Honestly guys, I'm fine.' I give them a reassuring smile. 'I'll be up for a glass of red if anyone else is?'

Fi scans the menu. 'Okay, let's get a bottle of the Shiraz and a couple of the sharing platters.'

'Meat or veggie?' asks Craig.

'One of each, I think.'

Craig jabs his finger at his tablet. 'Awesome, so that's one bottle of Giddy Creek vino, one "Fancy a Porking" meat platter, one "Lettuce Turnip the Beet" veggie platter and a Leg Spreader.' He pockets his tablet and collects up the menus. 'Back soon, ladies. Don't miss me too much!'

When he's left my friends turn to me, their faces uniformly concerned (apart from Jessica, who is still watching Craig's disappearing behind).

Claris reaches for my hand. 'So, how are you holding up?'

'Not very well.' I feel myself welling up and take a deep breath to stay in control. 'I'm so sorry I didn't call you after it happened, I just . . .'

'Don't you *dare* apologise,' says Fi. 'We've just been so worried about you. Do you feel up to telling us what happened?'

As it turns out, it's actually a relief to talk about it, to relive the events of that fateful Saturday for an audience, because the story's been stuck inside my head for so long that it feels a bit like the plot of a film rather than my actual life. I manage not to cry too much – just a bit of snivelling, no sobbing or gnashing of teeth – but then it's hard to have an emotional meltdown when there's a giant crustacean downing sambucas at the next table.

When I finish recounting what happened, Fiona reaches over and gathers me into a hug, her face steely.

'I'm gonna kill that fecker,' she says. 'And then I am going to telephone whoever the feck regulates doulas and report that witch for misconduct. And then I'll feckin' kill her too.'

Jessica exhales slowly, as if winded. 'I always feared Luke might have it in him to be a bit of a prick, but really, he's exceeded all expectations.' She shakes her head. 'What a total shit-bag.'

I nod grimly. 'He told Tabby he wants me to move back into the flat. Apparently he' – I make quote marks in the air – 'doesn't want to lose me and Dottie.'

Fiona and Jess snort with indignation, but Claris shushes them.

'And are you maybe ... *considering* that as an option, Annie?' she asks gently.

I sigh; it's difficult to give a straight answer because I change my own mind so often.

'After it first happened, I just assumed that I'd leave Luke. I couldn't ever imagine forgiving him, let alone trusting him again. I'd just be waiting for it to happen again. But as time has gone by, I'm wondering if my initial reaction might have been a bit, well, over the top.'

Jess' eyes go wide – and they were already saucer-like thanks to all the Botox. 'You are kidding, right? He cheated on you weeks after you had a baby! In the ranks of arsehole behaviour, that's just below shagging your mum and then blaming it on you for being fat.'

'But is kissing someone actually cheating?' I persist. 'Is it really worth splitting up over?'

'Arguably not if it's a one-off drunken snog, but what Luke did – a premeditated, calculated seduction – in my book is a clear-cut case of cheating,' says Jess. 'And, as you said yourself, the pair of them would have definitely ended up shagging at some point.'

I've been tormenting myself with the vision of Luke and Sigrid having sex, and the mention of it makes me feel sick.

'But Luke and I aren't the only people involved here, remember,' I say.

'I don't think Dottie would want you to be unhappy,' says Claris.

'But who's to say I *would* be unhappy? Luke says he's desperate to make things right. The bottom line is that he's Dot's dad. Don't I owe it to our daughter to at least give it another go?'

Just then Craig reappears with two huge platters of deep-fried things.

'Anything else I can get for you, ladies?' he asks, although this is clearly aimed at Jessica.

'No, we're fine, thank you,' replies Claris, in a tone that says, 'please stop encouraging our friend and leave us alone'.

'Well, okay then, enjoy!' grins Craig, in a tone that says, 'blimey, love, lighten up, I'm just having a bit of fun'. He winks at Jess and then, thankfully, disappears.

Once he's gone, Claris turns back to me. 'You were saying, Annie?'

I reach for a battered something and take a bite. It's possibly chicken. Or fish.

'Look, I know Luke's behaved terribly,' I sigh, 'but we're missing the bigger picture here, which is how I'd get by if I *did* leave him. I don't have a job. I have nowhere to live. I have nobody to help with Dottie ...' I tail off, over-whelmed by the hopelessness of the situation. 'I don't know, perhaps I should just suck it up and go home ...'

Geoff leans over from the neighbouring table, gestures to whatever the word is for a prawn's groin and bellows: 'You can suck *this* up, love!'

Miss World, the Heineken bottle and the others all fall about. Fiona jumps up with murder in her eyes, but Claris pulls her straight down again.

'Ignore it,' she mutters.

Jess tops up my wine. 'It's early days, Annie, things will become clearer over the next few weeks. You're still deal-ing with the shock – it's not the right time to make any long-term decisions. But whatever you *do* decide, I hope you know that you'll have all our support.' The others smile and nod their agreement. 'And in the meantime,' she goes on, 'we've been talking about how we can help you and Dot, and we've come up with a few ideas.'

'They're just suggestions,' adds Claris. 'But we thought it might help to have a few options when you're deciding what to do.'

I look around at my friends' eager faces. 'Okaaaay ...'

Jess wipes the grease off her fingers, and then puts both hands on the table as if meaning business.

'Right, so you know that since the divorce I've been knocking around in that big house all on my own . . .'

Fi shoots her a sceptical look. 'All on your own?'

'Okay, so occasionally the knocking *might* involve another party, but they're usually gone before breakfast . . . Anyway, the point is that I've been thinking about getting a lodger, and I was actually going to advertise, but the lodgers I'd like best in the world would be you and Dot.'

I feel a rush of love towards her. 'Oh Jess, that's so lovely of you, thank you. It's the most wonderful offer and I'd love to stay, but I couldn't possibly accept unless I was paying you rent. And apart from a little left over from Mum and Dad, I don't have the money.'

'I don't want a bloody penny from you,' she says smartly. 'But we thought you might say that, so Fi has got a suggestion.'

I turn to Fiona, who has a kid-at-Christmas grin on her face.

'I've lined you up a job interview at the estate agents,' she says. 'You're going to meet my boss on Wednesday next week!'

I stare at her open-mouthed, then glance at Claris and Jess who have the same excited expression.

'But I don't know the first thing about selling houses.'

Fiona waggles her finger at me. 'Ah, but you won't be

selling houses, you'll be *photographing* them. You know the photos you see on property details? Well, we've always used freelancers to take them, but they're unreliable and the standard is variable, to put it mildly. My boss, Karl, wants to get our own in-house photographer, and I can't think of a better choice than *you*, darlin' girl.'

My head is spinning; this is all moving so fast. 'Fi, I . . .'

'It's only part-time and the hours are flexible,' she continues. 'And I've already done such an excellent sales job on you with Karl that I reckon the job's yours if you want it.' She sits back, folds her arms and grins. 'What d'ya reckon, gorge? Ready to get the ol' camera out again?'

I don't know what to say. I'm overwhelmed at how thoughtful they've all been, and I really don't want to disappoint them, but how can I explain how . . . *useless* I feel right now?

Since getting together with Luke I've often thought about getting another job – Barb would be utterly scornful that I'm now a 'kept woman' – but the more time that has passed, the less confident I've become, and now the prospect of putting myself back out there again fills me with fear. I hate to admit it, but it's just been easier to stay at home and play Annie the housewife for Luke, especially because that's what he's wanted. And now, with Dot to think about and Luke having done the dirty, the idea of starting a new job feels like I'm standing at the foot of Everest ready to have a crack at the summit in trainers and a Pac-a-mac. Plus, if the thought of getting a job makes me feel sick with worry, the thought of leaving Dot with a stranger makes me even queasier.

'I'm not sure, Fi,' I say eventually. 'It is an amazing opportunity, but what would I do with Dot? She's still so tiny. And childcare is expensive . . .'

'Well, Luke will need to step up, obviously,' says Jess. 'She's his daughter, too, the very least that wanker can do is help pay for a childminder.'

'Or maybe you could take her with you on jobs,' suggests Fi with the blithe innocence of the child-free. 'Just strap her in one of those baby carrier thingummies and you'll be grand.'

My head is spinning and it feels like my heart is racing. I want to be strong for Dot, but it feels like my life is spiralling out of control. I'm only just coping at being a full-time mum, how on earth would I fit in a job as well?

'I don't know . . .' I say, chewing my lip.

Claris puts her arm around me and pulls me towards her. 'Annie, we know how tough it's been for you since your parents died, and now there's this horrible situation with Luke. You've had a really hard time of it. I know this won't be the easiest option, but I really think this job could be just the thing you need to get yourself back on track, to get some of that old Annie fight back. We all believe in you, but *you* need to start believing in yourself too.' The girls murmur their agreement. 'You can still go back to Luke if that's what you decide, but if you take this job you'll go back to him on your own terms, for the right reasons, rather than just because it made sense financially. In fact, it would probably be a *positive* thing for your relationship. And we'll be here to support you every step of the way.'

'And after photographing supermodels,' says Jess, 'taking pictures of kitchens will probably be a walk in the park.'

Fi nods enthusiastically. 'Seriously, it'll be a piece of piss for you, love.'

'Will you just meet with Fi's boss and see what he has to say?' asks Claris.

'He's a twat, but a harmless one,' adds Fiona.

I look around the table at my three dear friends who are all focused on me, eyes filled with expectation, waiting for my reply. It's obvious that they've spent a huge amount of time and effort thinking of ways to help me; in the circumstances, really, what else can I say?

'Alright.' I smile, hoping I'm hiding the panic that's bubbling up inside me. 'I'll go for the interview.'

But as they all hug me, and tell me how brave I'm being and how much they love me, a little voice in my head pipes up: *Don't worry, Annie, you don't have to do this. You can just make your excuses nearer the time.*

10

Jess lives in a huge Victorian villa on a tree-lined avenue just off Streatham High Road, a two-mile stretch of traffic and takeaways that's famous for being the longest high street in Europe. It doesn't quite have the charm of neighbouring Clapham, but fans of peri-peri hot wings will find much to delight here.

When Jess and her then-husband Leo bought the house three years ago, it was what estate agents would call 'a complete blank canvas': in other words, a rat-infested, damp-riddled, barely habitable dump. Jess and Leo started renovations immediately, but as the months went by, the state of the house became inversely proportional to the state of their marriage: as they lovingly restored the rooms, so their relationship crumbled. Shortly after the builders moved out, so Leo did too – although to be fair it wasn't really the house's fault that their marriage didn't work out. That had more to do with the fact that they'd got married during a drunken game of 'Truth or Dare' while on a long weekend in Las Vegas.

Anyway, Jess kept the house in the divorce and her and Leo are still good mates, so it's all ended sort of happily ever after. And despite its inauspicious beginnings, it *is* a lovely house: light, airy and with plenty of room to accommodate a lost soul and her baby daughter until she works out what the hell she's going to do with her life.

Jonathan and Tabitha drive us over to Streatham on Sunday morning. I've still only got the minimum of possessions that I grabbed when I left, but – thanks to the sheer amount of equipment babies seem to need these days – Jon's VW Polo is packed to the roof, and Dot and I are wedged in amongst our stuff on the backseat. It's a good job I left the nappy sanitiser bin and baby bath behind, otherwise we'd have needed a transit van.

'You will come and see us every weekend, won't you?' Tabby's face is etched with concern as she spins round to look at me. 'And if you need us we'll be here like a shot, okay?'

'Don't worry, Dottie and I will be absolutely fine.' I flash her an encouraging smile from behind the bottle steriliser and breast pump on my lap. 'It's going to be an adventure!'

But although I'm putting on a brave face – I've already caused my pregnant sister more than enough worry, after all – how I wish I could stay in Jon and Tabby's spare room for a while longer. As much as I love Jessica, the prospect of moving in with her feels like I'm being set adrift in the middle of an ocean with dark clouds gathering and no land in sight. At Tabby's I could hide away and let her deal with all the crap, but now I'm going to have to start taking responsibility and making some big and scary decisions – and the consequences of those decisions aren't just going to affect me, they're going to have a lifetime's impact on Dot.

As if reading my mind, Tabitha asks: 'Have you given any more thought to when you might meet up with Luke? He texted me again last night, Annie. He's desperate to see you both.'

At the mention of Luke's name, my insides clench in fury. He's been trying to contact me every day, leaving rambling, soul-baring voicemails and sending emails and messages; for somebody who doesn't usually 'do' emotions, he's being awfully chatty. I still can't bring myself to respond – the only thing I want to know from him is *why why why*, and so far his attempts at explaining just make me feel worse – but I do know that we need to talk. For Dot's sake, if nothing else.

'It's not going to get any easier the longer you leave it,' adds Tabby, her tone gentle.

'I do know that,' I say, 'but at the moment it's working out quite well for me pretending that Luke's been abducted by aliens and is undergoing painful and humiliating experimentation in their spacecraft.'

Tabby raises an eyebrow.

I sigh, defeated; she's right, of course. 'Okay, okay, I'll send him a text, see if he can meet up this week.'

'Atta girl.' Tabby smiles. 'If it's any consolation, I think Luke's torturing himself far worse than any alien with an anal-probe could do. And you never know, talking things through with him might even make you feel better . . .'

Yeah, and Sigrid and I might become best buddies, I think – but keep it to myself.

Jess answers the door dressed in a silky, lace-trimmed robe of the kind rarely seen outside Sharon Stone movies.

'Hello, lodgers!' She holds out her arms. 'Gimme that delicious baby.'

Dot is due a feed and is starting to grumble, but I pass her over. 'Thank you so much for this, Jess. I can't tell you how much I appreciate you having us to stay.'

She waves her hand dismissively. 'Honestly, Annie, I'm really looking forward to having you both here.' She looks over my shoulder, blowing kisses at the others who are unpacking our things from the car. 'Tabby, hi darling! And the gorgeous Jonathan, so lovely to see you . . .'

I peer past Jessica into the house. 'You're looking very . . . boudoir, Jess. Do you have, um, company?'

'Course not! But, you know – standards, angel. You never know who might turn up.'

Dot has now progressed to full-on crying, and Jess holds her out to me with an apologetic grimace. 'I think it's malfunctioning.'

'She's just hungry,' I say, raising my voice to be heard above the wailing. Meanwhile, the heap of baby paraphernalia in her stylish hallway is growing; I eye our clutter anxiously.

'Jess, are you quite sure that Dottie and I won't be in the way?'

She furrows her brow as best she can. 'In the way of what?'

'Of . . . well, you know . . . all the shagging.'

'Oh, don't worry about cramping my style, love, I'm going to put you in the attic, well out of the way of any random willies.' She beckons us through the hallway. 'Right, Tabby, Jonathan, everyone come through to the kitchen, I have coffee and croissants, and champagne for those of us who aren't lactating, pregnant or driving.' She gives a little tinkly laugh. 'Oops, just me then!'

After the others have gone, Jess helps me set up Dot's cot in her attic conversion and arrange the toys that we've brought with us. Once we've finished, the room looks wonderfully cheery: sunshine is pouring through the skylight and Jess has thoughtfully dotted jam-jars of daffodils around the place. We've got far more space here than we did at my sister's – plus an en-suite bathroom filled with lovely toiletries (Jess works in PR and gets tons of freebies) – but I still can't shake this feeling of unease. Am I doing the right thing bringing Dot here? Perhaps it would have been better to move back home, so I could sort things out with Luke. As much as I hate him right now, as the days pass by a tiny part of me is starting to miss him, too – and Tabby's right, I can't hide from him forever. Before I can change my mind, I dig out my phone and send him a text, telling him that Dot and I are now staying at Jessica's and asking if he wants to meet up one evening this week to talk. A reply appears almost immediately:

Annie, I'm so glad to hear from you! Could we possibly meet at home during the day so I can spend some time with Dottie too? I'll book it off work as holiday. Tuesday good for you? I'm missing you both so much xxx

Christ, Tuesday is the day after tomorrow. Well, better to get it over with, I suppose. I bash out a curt reply, telling him that Tuesday will be fine. What with this *and* the spectre of the job interview, it's shaping up to be quite a week . . .

Later that afternoon, while Dot naps in her cot and Jess goes to meet a friend for lunch, I lie down on my new bed. I'm exhausted: the emotional turmoil is taking its toll, and in addition, I've got a nagging toothache. Perhaps all my negativity is using my top right molar as a conduit? I pop some painkillers and am finally drifting off to sleep when a knock at the front door jolts me awake again. I lie there, hoping that whoever it is gives up and goes away, but moments later there's another knock, more insistent this time. *Damn.* I better not ignore it, as I'm sure that would be poor lodger etiquette, so I pull on a hoodie and trudge downstairs. I've been avoiding mirrors as much as possible, but Jess' house is full of them, and I catch glimpses of myself as I pass by. I look like the 'after' photo on those posters that warn of the damage caused by long-term crystal meth use. I just hope that it's not Luke at the door, hoping for an early reunion, because if he sees me like this he'll run straight back into Sigrid's lithe arms faster than you can say methamphetamine hydrochloride.

But it's not Luke. A woman with sleek brown hair is standing on the doorstep, two large cases at her feet, smiling like she's presenting the weather on breakfast telly. She's wearing so much make-up that I imagine she must get through at least two tubes of mascara a week – one for each tarantula-lashed eye – and her lips are plumped up like two glossy chipolatas.

'Are you Annie?'

'Yes,' I say, trying to figure out who she might be. 'Hello, er . . . ?'

The woman holds out her hand and I shake it, feeling a rush of shame at the state of my chewed, dirty nails next to her flawlessly manicured talons.

'I'm Mara,' she says, then tips her head to one side and

gives me a long look up and down. 'Hmmm, looks like we're gonna have a busy afternoon!'

I blink, confused. 'I'm really sorry, but I'm afraid Jess isn't here at the moment.'

'No probs, hon, we can get started without her.' Mara picks up her bags and walks past me into the hallway.

'Um, what exactly are we getting started on?'

'On *you*, silly!' Mara gives a little laugh. 'Did Jessica not mention I was coming? She booked me to cheer you up.'

For a horrible moment I wonder if Mara might be here to give me some sort of 'sexy lady-massage' – after all, one of Jess' favourite sayings is that we're all just a couple of vodkas away from being lesbians – but I'm pretty sure she wouldn't do that to me. At least, I *hope* she wouldn't.

'She warned me that I'd have my work cut out,' Mara goes on, 'and it looks like she wasn't lying!'

I just stand there like the sack of potatoes (and not cute little Italian ones) that I currently so closely resemble. 'I'm sorry, Mara, but what *is* your work exactly?'

'Waxing, nails, hair, tan, brows, lashes . . .' She reels off the list, checking them off on her fingers as she goes, then drops her voice and leans in towards me. 'I can do Botox and fillers too, although that's strictly hush-hush, what with me not being a doctor and that!' She giggles again. 'So, what shall we start with? Jessica booked me for the whole afternoon, so we'll probably have time to do the lot. Total makeover, yeah?'

By the time Jess arrives home an hour or so later, I've got glossy pale-pink nails (hands and feet) and I'm lying on Mara's fold-up treatment couch in the living room, mid-bikini wax, while Dot sits in her bouncy chair nearby. Jess hovers in the doorway, totally unfazed by the fact that my vagina is currently taking pride of place along-side her leather modular sofa.

'Howdy, kids, how are we getting on?'

I tip my head back to look at her. 'Jess, you should have told me Mara was coming!'

'I wanted it to be a surprise.'

'Well it was. And a very kind and lovely surprise too, thank you.'

Despite my initial horror at the thought of having to tackle my appearance, I'm actually enjoying this pampering session. It's been months since I spent any time on myself, but it turns out that improving your outside actually makes your insides feel better too. That is, until Mara rips off the first lot of wax.

'Holy shiiiiit!' Catching my breath, I raise my head to see what the hell is going on down there. 'Is there anything left?' I ask weakly.

'Oh yeah, don't worry, hon,' says Mara breezily. 'I'm giving you a natural Brazilian, which is a bit more bush than usual. I tend to find it more flattering on my mums.'

'Let's have a look,' says Jess, making her way into the room.

'Don't you dare!' I shriek. 'Things are far from pretty down there since it served as an escape hatch for a human being.'

Mara slaps on another lot of warm wax. 'It don't look *that* bad,' she muses. 'I've deffo seen worse, believe me.'

'Thank you, Mara, that's, um, nice to hear.'

'You're welcome.' I feel her start to tug at the edge of the wax. 'Right, another deep breath . . .'

There's a noise like Velcro ripping.

OW OW OW OW.

'Mara usually gives me a Hollywood,' says Jess. 'That's all of it taken off, the better to show off my perfect vagina.'

'How do you know it's perfect?' I mutter, my teeth gritted.

'Cos I get told. Apparently my vayjay looks like a beautiful origami flower.'

'Yeah, mine too, an origami flower that's been made by a toddler who accidentally rips off a petal and then screws it up into a ball.'

There's another tearing noise.

FUUUCCCCCKKK.

It's dark by the time Mara finally leaves, but my new best friend has worked miracles during her time here. I can see that I look better – my hair has been highlighted and trimmed, my brows tweezed and tinted. I drew the line at a spray tan, but the lash extensions are a bloody revelation; I reckon I look better than I have in ages. When I come into the kitchen to retrieve Dot from Jess, who's been playing with her while Mara blow-dried my hair, my daughter eyes me warily as if she isn't quite sure who I am.

'Awww, she doesn't recognise Mummy without her moustache,' pouts Jess. 'Seriously though, doll, you look amazing. Proper hot. Like the old Annie.'

The real surprise, however, is how much better I *feel*. It's as if much of my anxiety and self-doubt was ripped out with my pubes. I feel lighter, stronger – and a tiny bit sexy too.

It's just a shame that nobody will get to see the Brazilian (honestly, my vagina hasn't looked this spiffy in yonks) but even so, just knowing it's there has given me a much-needed confidence boost. If Luke really has stopped seeing me as a 'sexual being' as he claims, then hopefully my new look will prove him otherwise. I'm not trying to win him back with a flutter of my new lashes, you understand, but I want him to regret what he did to me with every fibre of his sorry being and beg me to take him back. It's petty, I know, but I want him to want me like he wanted Sigrid. Only then will I be able to decide whether or not I'm ever going to want *him* ever again.

11

Tuesday arrives far too quickly, and by 10 a.m. I'm walking down my street towards our flat with a dozing Dot strapped to me in her sling, feeling like I'm heading to an interview for a job that I'm not sure I even want.

The glow of confidence I had been left with after Mara worked her magic on Sunday has already begun to fade. Post-wax ingrowing hairs have already started appearing, giving my bikini line an alluring 'teenage acne' look. And it certainly doesn't help that I had a rough night with Dot, who woke up every hour and screamed for no apparent reason. By 4 a.m. I was so exhausted that I ventured onto baby website chatrooms, something I only do when I'm really desperate, as the people who post on there scare the living hell out of me. I was slightly reassured to discover that there is an actual thing called the 'Four-Month Sleep Regression', which could well be behind Dot's wakefulness; yet as ever when it comes to baby-care, the advice on how to deal with this was plentiful, authoritative and utterly contradictory. For example: you should be swaddling your baby to get her to sleep – or you should definitely *not* be swaddling her, and instead be rocking her in your arms ... WTF, have you lost your TINY MIND? Don't *ever* rock your baby to sleep, you moron! Do you want to still be rocking her to sleep when she's thirteen? No? Then put her back in her cot while she's awake and rub her back in a circular motion while making a soothing 'shhh-ing' noise (try imitating the sound of the sea on pebbles, or a gentle spring breeze rustling the trees) until she drifts contentedly back to sleep. This may take hours, but sleep will come ... Or sleep *won't* come, in which case pop a dummy in her mouth ... A dummy? Er, *hello*? What special kind of monster are you? NEVER EVER give your child a dummy, you will end up having to spend a fortune at the orthodontist, not to mention it's been proven that kids who have dummies grow up with lower IQs. It's not called a *dummy* for nothing, you know ...

And so on, ad infinitum.

By the time it was what normal people would consider to be morning, I had tried literally every piece of sleep-inducing advice on the internet – apart from the suggestion to 'add a tot of brandy to baby's milk', but only because I didn't have any to hand – however, the only thing that worked was plugging Dot back on my boob whenever she cried. 'Demand Feeding', I believe this is called, probably because it's so fucking demanding.

Anyway, thanks to Dot's night-time shenanigans, I'm currently feeling weary, tearful and vulnerable (plus the toothache's back again), which is a risky state to be in for meeting Luke. If he so much as offers to have Dot for one night, I'm liable to collapse weakly into his arms; I'd profess undying love in exchange for a few hours' undisturbed sleep.

As I make my way along our garden path, dragging out the last steps up to the house for as long as possible, I notice little green shoots have pushed up in the flowerbeds since I was last here. It's only been, what, nine days? Christ, it feels like months. I glance up at our kitchen window and all the emotions from the aftermath of that horrible Saturday night come flooding back – the shock, disbelief, betrayal and pain – and I get such a horrible queasy feeling in my stomach I wonder if I might actually be sick. Thankfully the moment passes, but I'm a little concerned about how I'm going to react when faced with Luke. Well, whatever happens, I'll do my best to remain calm and dignified. I most definitely have the moral high ground here and I intend to keep it that way.

Although I have my key with me, I ring the intercom on the communal front door. I assume Luke will just buzz me up, but moments later I hear feet on the stairs and then here he is at the front door, his dark hair flopping into his eyes, his smile a blend of hope and fear.

'Hello, Annie.'

He's wearing a white t-shirt and jeans; I'm not sure if this choice of outfit is deliberate, but I've often told him that this is what I like him in the best. And despite everything that's happened, I'm furious with myself to discover that I find him as attractive as ever. Damn his perfectly symmetrical face and muscular arms. But he looks troubled, and I note the dark shadows under his eyes with grim satisfaction.

'You look really great,' he says. 'Amazing, in fact.'

I just shrug in reply; I am not going to make this easy for him.

'How's Dottie?' He leans forward to try to see her face, which is pressed up against my chest.

'She's asleep,' I say, recoiling.

There's an awkward silence. Luke rubs the back of his neck; he looks extremely uncomfortable. *Excellent.*

'Thank you so much for coming over,' he says, after a few moments. 'I really appreciate it.'

I open my mouth to tell him that he can stuff his thanks, because I loathe him for what he's done to me – to our family – and that I'm only here for Dot's sake, but instead all that comes out is a muttered: 'S'okay.'

'Well then, let's go up,' he says, turning around and heading upstairs.

The flat looks just the same as when I left. My favourite denim jacket is still hanging by the front door (must remember to take that with me when I leave), my spotty wellies are lined up next to Luke's on the shoe rack, and there's a stack of unopened bank statements and mobile phone bills on the mantelpiece. So much has changed since I was last here, but, at the same time, nothing at all.

'Coffee?'

'Yes, thank you.'

I stand there awkwardly while Luke faffs around with the bean-grinder, stovetop espresso maker and milk whisk; being half-Italian, he reckons making coffee is his thing. It's certainly just about his only 'thing' in the kitchen.

'Looks like a lovely day out there,' he says, as he precisely measures out the coffee grounds.

'Mmm, feels almost spring-like,' I reply automatically.

'Yes, apparently we've seen the last of the frosty mornings for a while.'

God, this is weird. Anyone watching our exchange would think we'd never met before; it's like we're holding back the deluge of emotion with a wall of polite chit-chat. I'm just relieved that I've managed not to scream, cry or puke yet.

Luke puts the milk in the microwave to warm. 'Take a seat, I'll bring the coffee straight in,' he says, nodding towards the living room.

I walk through – and suddenly freeze. The living room smells ... different. Not unpleasant, but certainly not like it usually does. The smell is musky, floral – like a half-familiar fragrance ... Christ, that's not Sigrid's perfume, is it? Has she been here, rubbing her groin on the soft furnishings, like a cat marking its territory?

At this thought, my heart starts thumping in panic and perhaps that's what disturbs Dot, because at that moment she starts to stir and I look down to see her stretching and blinking up at me.

'Hey there, sleeping beauty,' I murmur, kissing her head. 'Let's get you out of there ...'

By the time Luke comes in with the coffee, I'm sitting on the sofa with Dot on my lap, looking through one of her favourite board-books.

His face lights up. 'Dottie!'

Dot looks uncertain for a moment, then she beams at Luke in delight. He scoops her up from my lap, swings her round and then hugs her to him.

'Oh, I've missed you so much, little girl ...' He stays like that for a while, eyes closed, just holding her to him and breathing in her scent, and my frozen heart thaws a little to see them together. When he opens his eyes again, they are bright with tears.

'How's she been?' he asks. 'Is she sleeping alright? Have you been coping on your own?'

'It's all fine. Dot's been amazing.'

He nods, takes a deep breath – and then the dam bursts.

'I'm so, so sorry for everything, Annie,' says Luke, his

voice cracking with emotion. 'I wish I could change what I did. It was a completely idiotic, fucked-up thing to do, but I'm desperate for us to be a family again. Please, tell me what I can do to make this better and I will do it.'

'Oh come on, Luke, really? You can't think it's that simple.'

'Why not? I screwed up – badly, I know – but I want to make it right again. Really, why *can't* it be that simple?'

'Because you betrayed me with one of my friends just after I'd had our baby. You destroyed our trust. You've made me feel like complete shit. You've taken what should have been one of the most special times in our lives and turned it into something hideous and painful.' I swallow down the large lump that's appeared in my throat again. 'Do you really think I can just *forget* about all that?'

'No, no, of course not, but I want to make this right.' He sits down next to me on the sofa, still clasping Dot, his eyes fixed on mine. 'Help me out here, Annie, please, how can I fix this?'

Honestly, you'd think he was talking about a broken dishwasher.

'There's nothing you can do to fix this. Well, apart from not cheating on me ever again. And I'm not at all sure that you can even manage that.'

'Annie, I swear that I will never do that to you again. You have to believe me.'

'But how can I believe *anything* you say now? You can't

just pick and choose when you trust someone, it's an all-or-nothing sort of thing, you know?' Then I remember the trace of mysterious perfume. 'Has Sigrid been here?'

Luke looks outraged. 'No!'

I narrow my eyes at him sceptically.

'Of course she hasn't! I haven't seen her since ... well, since that night.'

'Have you spoken to her?'

A look of guilt flashes across his face and I feel another surge of nausea. 'You bastard,' I mutter, shaking my head.

'We only spoke once, and that was only because she called me to ask if she should get in touch with you.'

I open my mouth to tell him *exactly* what I think of that suggestion, but Luke cuts in before I can speak. 'I told her that would be a terrible idea, okay? And I've had nothing more to do with her since.' He reaches out his hand for mine, but I pull it away. 'She means nothing to me, Annie, I promise you. I'm never going to see her again.'

I turn away from him; I don't want him to see the tears that are threatening to flow.

'I fucked up,' Luke goes on. '*Big time.* I've got no excuse for any of it. But I'm desperate to have you and Dot home so we can try and sort this out together. You two are my world. Please, I made a stupid mistake, but you *have* to give me a chance to make things right.'

'No, ordering fish when you wanted chicken is a stupid mistake. What you did is on another level altogether.'

He sighs. 'Won't you at least move back home so we can deal with this as a family?'

I turn to look at him. 'No, I'm going to stay at Jessica's for a while. I need space to try and process all this.'

He looks pained. 'How long's "a while"?'

'I don't know. As long as it takes for me to work out what's best for me and Dot in the future.'

'What do you mean?' Luke's voice suddenly has an edge. 'You're not seriously thinking about splitting up our family over this, are you?'

I gawp at him. 'What did you expect? You *cheated* on me. Surely it can't come as a surprise that I'm thinking about breaking up with you?'

'It was just a bloody kiss!' He runs his hand through his hair, exasperated. 'It meant nothing!'

I feel a surge of anger that leaves my chest tight and my heart pounding. I could so easily scream and rant at him, but I need to keep it together for Dot's sake.

'Luke, please tell me you know that kissing another woman – on several occasions, one of which happens to be next to your sleeping baby while your girlfriend is downstairs – is definitely not "nothing".'

That shuts him up. We sit next to each other without talking, brooding on our own thoughts and watching Dot, who is now lying on the floor with her toys. I knew this conversation wasn't going to be easy, but Luke seems to have assumed that he could just apologise and then our lives would go happily on as before. Does he really think this is something he can just brush under the carpet?

After a while I break the uneasy silence. 'You should probably know that I'm thinking about getting a job.'

I wasn't going to mention this, but after the way he's reacted I'm feeling bloody-minded.

Luke's head snaps up. I'm pleased to see he looks appalled. 'You're *what*?'

'Fiona has lined me up an interview to be the in-house photographer at her estate agents.'

'But what will happen to Dot?'

'Well, she could come with me to work. Or she could go to a childminder, or nursery.'

Luke stares at me, eyes widening in horror; you'd think I'd just suggested selling her for drugs.

'Annie, she's barely four months old!' He shakes his head. 'Absolutely no way.'

I manage to swallow my rage, although it's getting tougher to do so. 'Luke, are you *forbidding* me to get a job?'

'Of course not, but . . . I just don't think it's the best thing for our daughter right now.'

'Okay, do *you* want to stay home and look after her?'

'That's a ridiculous thing to suggest, you know I can't quit my job,' he snaps. 'I'm the one earning the money.'

Stay calm, Annie. 'Well, now I'm going to be earning some money too. And Dot will be perfectly fine.'

'She's far too young for this, Annie, she needs to be

with her mother.' He looks at me uncertainly, as if decid-ing just how far he should push this, before apparently settling on the nuclear option: 'Don't you think you should be putting Dot's needs first?'

Well, that does it: all the pent-up rage and resentment comes bursting out.

'How dare you suggest I wouldn't do my best for my daughter! Everything I do – *everything* – is done with Dot as my priority, and for you to suggest otherwise is . . . well . . . just about the worst thing you've ever done, apart from nearly *fucking the doula*!' My voice disappears in a squeak of fury. 'Oh, and while we're on the subject of put-ting others' needs first, shouldn't you perhaps have put mine and Dot's before those of your PENIS?'

So much for remaining calm and dignified. At the sound of my anger, Dot starts to cry. I scoop her up, clutch-ing her to me while I sob, wracked with guilt that I'm putting her through this trauma, but at the same time unable to stop myself from falling into a gulf of self-pity. *How could Luke do this to me?* I was just starting to work out my place in the world after being thrown off course by the loss of my parents – and, okay, so the photography thing hadn't worked out as I'd hoped, but being a good mother and loving partner, and creating a happy home, is just as valuable and fulfilling a role, right? Except now Luke has screwed that up for me as well, leaving me with no idea who I am or what I'm doing.

Wiping away a tear, I turn to glance at him: the look on his face suggests he's struggling to decide whether to hug me or get the hell out.

'Please, Annie, I'm not the enemy,' he says quietly. 'I love you, patatina, and I'm going to do whatever it takes to make us a family again.'

I turn away from him, swallowing down the bitter retort that's hovering on the tip of my tongue. Well, at least coming here today has helped me make one decision: whatever else happens, I am *definitely* going to that job interview tomorrow.

12

'Well, what do you think?' I strike a pose in the kitchen doorway. 'Would *you* hire me?'

Jess looks up from her toast and appraises my carefully selected job-interview outfit: a pair of black boot-cut trousers – maternity, though you really can't tell – a white shirt and an ancient black cardigan. It's a bit bobbly up close, but unless I'm going to be sitting on this bloke's lap for the interview, it'll be fine. (And if I *do* have to sit on his lap, then I won't be taking the job, thank you very much.)

Jess pulls a face. 'Wow, I didn't realise the interview was for the job of a silver-service waitress in 1993, but dressed like that, you'll ace it, babe.'

I look down at my outfit. 'It's not that bad, is it?'

'Yes.' She says it matter-of-factly. 'It makes you look like you've given up. Surely you must have something a little more inspiring in your wardrobe?'

'No – well, not anything suitable for a job interview.' I

brought back more clothes from the flat yesterday after seeing Luke, but it's been so long since I needed to wear anything remotely formal that my options were limited.

Jess takes another bite of toast. 'I miss the kaftans, Annie. Why not get those out again? Surely photographers are allowed to look a bit creative – even the ones who work for estate agents?'

I shake my head firmly. 'That was another lifetime.'

'But they suited you. They were who you were.'

'Not anymore,' I insist, pushing down the memories that bubble up inside; it pains me to remember how much more interesting Barb was. 'Anyway, have you seen what Fi and her colleagues wear? It's all sexy little suits and high heels, like a sluttier, modern-day *Mad Men*.'

'Well, you can't wear *that*. Seriously, I refuse to let you leave the house in it, someone might see you and think you're something to do with me.' Jessica hops off her stool and fastens her silky robe around her. 'Come on, kiddo, let's have a look in my room. I'm sure I've got something that won't make you look like someone's frumpy mum who never has sex.'

'But I *am* someone's frumpy mum who never has sex,' I mutter, following her upstairs.

Jess 'works from home' on Wednesdays (i.e. spends the day online shopping and swiping right) so is not only available for styling advice, but also, thankfully, Dot-sitting duties while I'm at the interview. I sit on her bed while she rifles through her extensive wardrobe, occasionally turning to scrutinise me, and she eventually pulls out a tomato-red trouser suit, holding it up with a triumphant 'tah-dah!'

I pull a face; it's a lovely colour, but way too look-at-me.

Jess glares back at me. 'Just try it on. It'll look fab on you.' She reaches inside the wardrobe again and holds out a spotty blouse. 'Here, put this underneath.'

And so I do as she says, partly because when Jess has made up her mind, resistance is futile, but mainly because she always looks great and I, quite frankly, don't.

As I get changed, Jess eyes my maternity bra nervously.

'Try not to leak on that blouse, love, it's dry-clean only ... Blimey, Annie, your tits are ginormous!'

'Yeah, well, Dot's overdue a feed so they're even bigger than usual.'

'Can I have a feel?' Before I can object, she jumps up and grabs my boobs. Honestly, the woman has zero respect for personal space; just because she enjoys being groped doesn't mean the rest of us do. 'Oh my God, that is crazy!' Her eyes go wide and she breaks into astonished giggles. 'They're all hard and lumpy, like they're filled with gravel!'

I pull away from her, buttoning up the blouse. 'Wow, thanks, you really know how to make a girl feel pretty,' I mutter. 'That's what happens when you're breastfeeding ... Right – what do you think? *Of the outfit?*'

'Perfect.' She grins with an approving nod. 'Smart, but sassy. The job's yours, hon.'

An hour later I'm sitting on a lime-green banquette in the reception area of Curtis Kinderbey Sales and Lettings anxiously awaiting the agency's manager, Karl. Fi has already popped over to say hello and made a joke about my suit clashing with the upholstery, which I'm sure was intended to help me relax, but has actually made me even more jittery. I knew I should have stuck with the waitress outfit; it may have been bland, but at least it was a more accurate reflection of my personality . . .

'Hey, you must be Annie. I'm Karl – great to meet you.'

I look up and come face to crotch with the tightest pair of pinstripe trousers I have ever seen. In fact, they aren't so much suit trousers as ankle-length Speedos. I know it's the trend these days, but honestly, you can see *everything*: penis, ball one, ball two – the whole shebang, all perfectly level with my eyes. I am desperate to unsee this, but at the same time I can't stop looking: it's hypnotic, like watching a really terrible act on *Britain's Got Talent*. Only with immense effort do I manage to drag my eyes away and up into the grinning face of a man who looks like he may well be fully aware, possibly even proud, of his car-crash crotch.

'Hello!' I jump up, flustered, and stick out my hand. 'Thank you so much for seeing me, Karl, it's a pleasure to meet you.' *And your entire reproductive system.*

'Let's go to my office so we can chat,' he says, turning around and treating me to the back view.

Like the rest of Curtis Kinderbey's premises, Karl's office is modern and minimalist. There is nothing on his desk apart from a bottled protein shake, and the only decorations are a large, numberless wall clock and a shelf of hideous glass and metal sculptures that on closer inspection appear to be awards.

'Ah, I see you've clocked the trophy cabinet,' grins Karl, gesturing for me to sit down. He points at each of the awards in turn. 'Best Lettings Negotiator 2009, Best Prestige Property Agency 2014 *and* 2015, Best Branch Manager 2016 – that last one was for yours truly.' Karl rocks back in his leather chair, chuckling to himself. 'Darren Wilson from Coxtons in Putney was convinced he had it in the bag – you should have seen his face when my name was read out!'

'Wow, that's really impressive,' I say, hoping flattery will make up for the earlier crotch embarrassment.

Karl takes a swig of his shake. 'But seriously, Annie, the reason Curtis Kinderbey Sales and Lettings is the award-winning market leader is because we're innovators, y'know? We're always thinking up ways to improve our client experience, because without our clients, what would we be?'

I assume this is a rhetorical question and politely wait

for him to continue, but it quickly becomes clear that Karl is expecting an answer.

'Oh! Ah, gosh, without your clients you'd be . . . well, I'm not entirely sure.' I laugh nervously. 'You'd be . . . out of business?'

'We'd be *nothing*, Annie.' He sits up and bangs his hand on the table. 'And *that's* the reason that you're here today.'

'Right. Great!'

Karl smiles, running a hand over his hair. He has the sort of hairstyle that looks like it's been moulded into place rather than brushed; it looks like glossy, brown Play-Doh.

'So, I'm not sure how much our little Fiona has told you' – he pronounces her name 'Faaay-ohh-narrr' in a broad, mock-Northern Irish accent – 'but I'm looking for a shit-hot professional photographer to help promote Curtis Kinderbey's selection of superior prestige properties.'

'It certainly sounds like a very interesting position.'

'Sure is, and an incredible opportunity for the right person. Have you brought your portfolio?'

'Ah. I'm afraid not, no.'

'No problemo, just give me the names of some property websites where I can see your work.'

God, this is awkward. 'I'm sorry, Karl, but I've never photographed houses before. Or flats. Or any sort of property, really.' I give an apologetic smile. 'I thought Fiona had told you that?'

Karl frowns. 'She told me you were an excellent photographer with years of experience.'

'Well yes, I have had quite a bit of experience . . .'

'Experience photographing *what*?'

'Models, mainly. I used to assist quite a well-known fashion photographer.'

'Give me some names.'

'I'm sorry . . . ?'

'Names. Of the models you photographed. Anyone I'd have heard of?' Karl leans forwards, hope etched across his features. 'That Kylie from the Kardashians?'

'Ah, no, it was a few years ago now, so Kylie was probably, um, still at school.'

'Cheryl Cole?'

'Sadly not, no, it was really more fashion models I worked with, rather than celebrities, like . . . Natalia Vodianova, for instance.'

Karl slumps back in his chair. 'Never heard of her,' he mutters, glancing over at the clock. I get the distinct impression that this job is rapidly slipping away from me, which means, of course, that I suddenly really, really want it.

Come on, Annie, think . . .

'Kate Moss!' I virtually yell. 'I did a *Vogue* shoot with her once.' (Probably better not to mention that I was there to make coffee and didn't even touch a camera.)

Karl's eyes light up. 'You worked for *Vogue*?'

I nod. 'Yup. And *GQ*, *Harper's*, *Esquire* . . .'

'Fantastic! Darren Wilson is going to *freak* when he hears about this. I bet you Coxtons don't have an *Esquire* photographer taking the marketing shots for *their* shitty properties . . .' He shakes his head, chuckling to himself, then glances up at me. 'You've got your own camera, right?'

'Yes, of course, a Canon digital SLR, and I've got a 10–20mm wide-angle lens that will be perfect for photographing property, as you can fit more of the room in the frame, which means—'

'Terrific, you've got the job.' He sticks his hand over the desk. 'Welcome to the team.'

As Karl walks me out through the office, I glance over at Fiona's desk and give her a surreptitious thumbs up; she grins and does a mini air-punch. I can't quite believe I've got a job, and so quickly, too! I was all primed to dazzle Karl with my technical property photography expertise – gleaned from a frenzied Googling session last night – but in the end it was Kate Moss who sealed the deal. (Thank you, Kate, I forgive you for bitching about the coffee at that *Vogue* shoot. Consider us quits.)

Out in reception Karl is telling me about his fitness regime and I'm trying my best to appear fascinated by the details of his Lacto-Paleo diet, when the door swings open and Benedict Cumberbatch walks in. Not *the* Benedict Cumberbatch, you understand, but the lookalike who I clocked in the office the other day. He greets Karl and then looks at me, his eyes lingering on mine a little longer than is entirely comfortable. I didn't quite appreciate how tall he is; he towers over Karl, and stands with a slight stoop as a result.

'Rudy, I'd like you to meet Annie Taylor,' says Karl. 'She's going to be our new property photographer. She used to work for *Maxim*, you know.'

Then Karl turns to me, his hand clamped chummily around Rudy's back.

'This is Rudy Sheen, he's a Curtis Kinderbey newbie too. He started as a negotiator just before Christmas but from his performance so far I'm expecting big things of him! Isn't that right, mate?'

Rudy's mouth forms a crooked line, which I think is meant to be a smile. Up close he looks even younger than I first thought, but there's something about him that gives an impression of maturity too: perhaps next to Karl's puppyish enthusiasm, his stillness and deliberate stare make him seem older than his years. In fact, with his skinny frame, messy dark hair and intense, wide-apart eyes, he looks more like a poet than an estate agent.

'You were here the other day, right?' he asks, his voice soft.

'Yes, I came to meet Fiona. She's a friend of mine.'

He nods, thinking this over. 'Well, I look forward to working with you, Annie.'

Again, the eye contact goes on for a few seconds more than you'd welcome in the circumstances, then he turns and walks into the office.

'Odd bloke,' murmurs Karl, watching him go. 'But honest to God, he could flog sand to the Saudis.'

I meet up with Jess and a sleeping Dot in a nearby café, where we have celebratory almond croissants. Jess keeps telling me how proud she is of me and how this is the start of an exciting new chapter in my life, and I'm trying to stay positive and enjoy the moment, but I can already feel worries creeping in to take the edge off my triumph. Is this really the best thing for Dot? How will I cope with a baby and a job? Am I up to this? And what the hell am I going to *wear*?

A little while later Jess and I are walking back to the bus stop when she nods at Dot's buggy and says thoughtfully: 'They're not like dogs, are they?'

'What aren't?'

'Babies. I pushed that pram around the common for an hour and not a single bloke gave me so much as a second look, whereas when I took my mum's pug to the park, I got chatted up by a golden retriever, a Border terrier *and* a working cocker, all in the time it took Madge to do her business.' Jess stares dreamily away into the distance. 'Man, that working cocker really knew how to work his cocker . . .'

I give her a playful shove. 'No, they're not known

for being great for pulling, babies. Quite the opposite, in fact.'

Jess nods. 'Unless, of course, you're a single bloke pushing a baby, which I understand is catnip for a certain type of female.'

'Mm-hmm,' I murmur vaguely. My mind is suddenly focused on the fact that if I *do* split up with Luke, then I'll be back in the third circle of hell that is the world of dating. It was bad enough the first time round, but with a child in tow and speeding towards my forties? That's going to be mission virtually impossible. Well, at least it's not something I'll have to think about for a long time yet – if at all, if Luke and I manage to sort out this mess . . .

'Annie, are you listening to me?'

I snap back to attention to find Jess looking at me.

'Sorry, love, what did you say?'

'I was just telling you about my brilliant idea to help you deal with all the crap going on in your life at the moment.'

'Great! What was it? Prozac? Carbohydrates? A holiday in Hawaii?'

'A one-night stand.'

I burst out laughing; proper loud guffaws. 'Yeah, because that's exactly what I need right now. To have a stranger judge my sad vagina and stretchmarks. That will be *super* helpful.'

'Just hear me out, will you?'

I shrug; there's no point trying to stop Jess when she's had one of her 'brilliant' ideas.

'Okay, so you're feeling pretty shitty about yourself right now, aren't you?'

'True.'

'And understandably so, after what that fucker did to you.' Jess puts an arm around my waist and gives me a squeeze. 'But if you came out with me for a night, you'd have men falling all over you, I guarantee it. We'll get dressed up, go to a bar, have a dance, get bought drinks and then . . . see where the evening takes us!'

'Home?' I deadpan.

Jess ignores me. 'You need to let yourself go for a night, forget about your responsibilities and remember what it's like to have *fun*. It'll be the best thing for you, Annie, I promise. Being seduced by a hot bloke will definitely help you get your groove back.' She glances at my cleavage. 'Besides, it's such a waste that nobody's getting to enjoy those magnificent tits. Apart from Dottie, of course.'

'Jess, I'm sorry to disappoint you, but I'm afraid I can't think of anything I'd like to do less.'

'But *why*?'

'Well, apart from the fact that I'm currently in a relationship' – Jess rolls her eyes at this – 'sex is absolutely the last thing on my mind right now.'

'But how can that even be possible? Sex is an essential

bodily function, like breathing, or having a poo. It's a *necessity*.'

I sigh. 'I know it's hard to understand, but it's like I'm too deep into motherhood to need it right now.'

Jess stares at me with an expression of total miscomprehension. This is going to be challenging.

'Okay,' I begin, 'you know on nature documentaries—'

'Like David Attenborough programmes?'

'Yes, that sort of thing.'

'I love David Attenborough,' muses Jess. 'He's such a fox. That voice . . .'

'*Jessica!*'

She grins apologetically.

'As I was saying, you know on nature documentaries when there's a lioness with cubs and a randy lion comes up and tries to get his end away, but the female is all like, "Leave it out, son, can't you see I'm busy with the kids?", and then swipes at him with her big furry paw? That's basically me right now.'

Jess is shaking her head. 'Nah, I guarantee if the right lion came along that lioness would be all like, "Mmm, how do you want me, babe?" You just need to meet a really hot lion.'

Gah, this is *impossible* . . .

'I'm not having a one-night stand, Jessica. That is literally not going to happen, so save your breath. I love you for trying to help me, but right now I need to focus on Dot and sorting things out with Luke.'

Jess puts on a sing-song voice, like she's trying to persuade a toddler. 'It would make you feel better . . .'

'No.'

Jess pouts. 'You used to do crazy impulsive shit like that all the time. You're no fun anymore.'

'I know, it's called motherhood.'

'Well, you weren't that much fun for a few years *before* motherhood, either,' mutters Jess.

13

I have another terrible night's sleep – although this time it's not Dot who's the cause of the frequent waking, but my toothache. Sometime around 4 a.m., when I'm speed-balling Neurofen and Paracetamol, past worrying about what it's doing to my milk supply, I come to the reluctant conclusion that I can't put it off any longer: I'm going to have to bite the bullet (*veeeery* gently, as biting is agony) and see the dentist.

I hate going to the dentist. It's not the actual dentistry part that bothers me; I'm not troubled by drilling or injections – I don't even mind when they scrape at your teeth like they're getting moss off an old brick wall. No, it's my dentist herself that's the problem. Her name is Dr Nowak and she is about twelve years old. With her blonde ponytail, pale-green scrubs and pink Crocs, she far more resembles a child beauty pageant contestant dressed up for the 'My Dream Job!!' round, rather than a qualified adult health professional. It's not her fault, I know, but she makes me feel old and an underachiever, also the last time I saw her she accused me of being a jaw-clencher, which is basically the same as calling me frigid. I guess I could just see a different dentist, but do you know how difficult it is to get on the list of an NHS practice? You pretty much have to wait until someone dies and then jump into their space – and I refuse to stake out the local undertakers just so I'm first in line for affordable dental care. So I stick with Dr Nowak and just see her as infrequently as possible. As a result, I am scrupulous with my dental hygiene – although clearly not scrupulous enough to prevent whatever has caused this toothache . . .

The magazines in the dental surgery waiting room are at least six months old, so I flick through a feature on how to get a 'banging beach bod', while trying to remain Zen at the thought of what awaits. Thankfully Dot is being looked after by Claris; she'd usually be busy with her new catering business, but luckily for me February is a fallow canapé month.

'Ann Taylor?'

I look up; the receptionist gives me the briefest of smiles. More of a grimace, really.

'Downstairs, please, room three.'

I gather my things together with a heavy heart and make my way down the staircase of dental doom. With each step, the knot in my stomach tightens and my jaw clenches – NO! Stop clenching, Annie! You are *not* a clencher, okay?

With immense reluctance I edge inside room three, but instead of finding Dr Nowak exuding patronising perkiness, there's an unfamiliar dark-haired woman waiting for me. She beckons me inside.

'Take a seat, please, Dr Ford will just be a minute.'

'Dr Ford? Is Dr Nowak on holiday?'

'No, I'm afraid she's moved practices. Dr Ford has taken over her list of patients.'

Yes! Well, today just got a whole lot better. I settle myself in the chair while the nurse – for I presume this is she – fastens a paper bib around my neck. Whoever this new dentist is, they've got to be an improvement on Dr Nowak. And then the door opens and in walks George Clooney's marginally sexier younger brother. Out of the corner of my eye, I see the nurse surreptitiously dab on some lip gloss.

The World's Hottest Dentist™ flashes a movie-star smile. 'Hello, I'm Dr Tom Ford.'

Even his voice is handsome: deep, growly and warm, like the voiceover on a whisky commercial.

'Tom Ford – like the fashion designer?'

'Exactly.' He grins. 'So, Miss Taylor, what can I do for you today?'

'Please, call me Annie.'

He arches one perfect, manly eyebrow. 'Like the orphan?'

I collapse into girlish giggles. Not only gorgeous, but funny too! Jess, I've just met that very hot lion you were talking about . . .

I tell Dr Ford about my toothache and he pays really close attention – I *knew* he'd be a good listener – and makes concerned noises that suggest he genuinely cares about my pain. The nurse hovers by his shoulder, hanging on his every word, fluttering her lashes in his direction; she clearly fancies the pants off him. Pathetic.

'Alright, Annie, let's take a look at what's going on, shall we?' That groin-tingling smile again.

'Yes,' I say. *Oh yes.*

He presses a button, there's a soft whirring sound and I feel the seat reclining until I'm almost horizontal. Like I'm lying in bed. Waiting . . . for Dr Ford. Waiting for him to come and . . . blimey, I'm actually getting a bit turned on here. Must be some sort of weird breastfeeding hormone surge.

Dr Ford scoots his stool towards me, then comes to a halt by my side, his feet planted masterfully apart. He's wearing Adidas Stan Smith trainers rather than those stupid Crocs. God, he's cool. I bet he has a motorbike. I look at his hands: so strong, so masterful and – *bollocks*, so married. But now he's putting on some latex gloves, so I can just pretend the ring's not there.

Dr Ford angles the light above me and then leans forward so his face is hovering just above mine, so close that

I can make out the flecks of gold in his green eyes and the white squint lines in his tanned skin that attest to winter sunshine; he's probably been heli-skiing or something similarly sexy and dangerous. He's wearing a surgical mask, but even that is a bit of a turn-on: like he's *forbidden* to speak, and can only use the power of touch to communicate his deepest desires. I lie there, staring into those bewitching eyes, waiting for him to touch me, my heart pounding, my lips gently parted . . .

'Open your mouth just a little wider, please, Annie.'

Open my what? Legs, was that, Doctor . . . ? I open my mouth as wide as I can. I intend to be the best patient Dr Ford has ever had. Once he's had me, no other patient will ever be good enough for him again. As I lie there, I catch the nurse's eye; Jesus, will you look at the face on her! Jealous, obviously.

For a moment nothing happens: it's like he's toying with me, teasing me, letting the anticipation build . . . And then – oh yes! – he places a finger in my mouth and presses my bottom jaw down, ever so gently, and I have to stop myself moaning with pleasure. I close my eyes and now my whole being is focused on the sensation of his fingers as they explore inside my mouth; gently probing, sliding between my lips . . .

'Right, I've done an oral cancer check and everything looks just fine.'

What? *No!* You're forbidden to speak, remember?

'Do you floss every day?'

'Yes,' I lie. Just get on with the probing!

'Excellent.' His green eyes crinkle into a smile, and all is forgiven. 'Now, open up again for me . . .'

Phew. I close my eyes, push my boobs out and breathlessly await Dr Ford and his magic, wedding-ring-less touch. I can sense him getting closer again and feel my cheeks flush and a pulsating warmth in my groin. And then . . .

Ouch! What the fuck? The expert fingers have been replaced by some sort of spiky metal instrument that's being poked with quite excessive vigour into my gums. Christ, that does *not* feel pleasant. In fact, it's totally killing my buzz. Perhaps I should try to imagine that this is some kind of kinky *50 Shades*-style sex game. *I've been a naughty girl, Master, prick me with your pricky metal thing, Master*. Problem is, I struggle to get excited about the idea of S&M. Pain is pain after all, even if it's 'sexy' pain – and whatever Dr Ford is doing really is quite painful.

After a while he loses the torture instrument, but the moment has passed. And then Dr Ford gets the nurse involved to take some x-rays – and I have zero interest in a threesome with that sour-faced cow.

Nevertheless, at the end of our time together I get the impression that Dr Ford might be a bit sad, like he's gutted I've got to leave.

'Okay, Annie, everything looks fine, but you're going to

need a filling in that top right molar, so I want to see you again soon.'

'Right, I see,' I say, quietly stoical, although inside I'm all: *hooray! Woo! More Dr Ford!*

'There's just one other thing,' he says, as I shrug on my coat as sexily as I'm able.

My phone number, Dr Ford? But what about your wife? I know there's this incredibly powerful attraction between us, but I'm just not the sort of woman who'd ever want to break up a marriage. Unless, of course, the two of you have been living apart for some time, due to your much-older wife's unreasonable behaviour, in which case . . .

'Do you clench your teeth?'

I give him a hard stare. Goodbye, Dr Ford. It was fun while it lasted.

Back upstairs, I'm waiting by the front desk while the receptionist struggles to find me an appointment sooner than six months' time and I realise that I'm smiling to myself: a proper, full-on beam. Well, that was an extremely interesting twenty minutes! After my chat with Jess, I was beginning to worry that my low sex drive was a cause for concern, so I'm overjoyed to discover that I do still have those feelings – and it feels really good to feel them again. There's hope for me yet. Screw you, Luke Turner, I *am* still a sexual being.

'Barb . . .?'

At the sound of the vaguely familiar female voice – and the shock of hearing someone address me as 'Barb' for the first time in years – I turn round to discover a short, curvy woman looking at me, brow creased in uncertainty. She is wearing an enormous pale-blue fur coat, possibly Muppet in origin, and her hair is an explosion of dark curls with a bright white streak at the front, like a bolt of lightning in a night sky or a very sexy skunk.

My mouth drops open in a delighted gawp: I'd know that 'fro anywhere.

'Oh my God, Riva!'

'It *is* you, Barb!' She throws her arms wide and rushes in for a hug. 'I haven't seen you since forever! Where the fuck you been, girl?'

Riva is one of London's most in-demand stylists, a fashion legend with a client list as sparkly as her be-ringed fingers, who I was lucky enough to work – and party – with back in my photography days.

'I almost didn't recognise you, babe,' she says, pulling back from our embrace to check me out. 'You look so . . .'

She gestures at my jeans and cardigan, grappling for the right word.

'Safe? Suburban? Housewifely?'

'Yeah, pretty much!' She laughs. 'What happened?'

'I turned into a safe, suburban housewife.' We grin at each other, fuelled by crazy, happy memories. 'But *you* haven't changed a bit, love! How have you been? Ooh, and how's Jethro?'

'He's got big. Can you believe he's now at school?'

'Noooo! I remember you being pregnant, it feels like last week.'

'I know, scary, right?' She smiles, and then wraps me in a hug again. 'God, it's really good to see you! What have you been up to? This is so weird, I was actually talking about you just the other day. I was with Delphine – remember her?' I nod, a snapshot of a willowy red-headed make-up artist flashing into my mind. 'She was asking if I knew what you were doing these days. We were reminiscing about your incredible outfits.'

I feel a twinge of self-consciousness about how much less incredible I must look to her now.

'Yeah, I sort of lost touch with a lot of the old crowd after I stopped working with Jay,' I say.

Riva looks away for a moment, clearly uncomfortable. 'I'm so sorry I didn't get in touch after . . . what happened. I didn't really know what to say, and then time passed and . . .' She tails off with an apologetic shrug.

'It's okay, I think a lot of people felt the same. I do understand, honestly. I went to ground for a while and then lost touch with too many friends.'

Riva gives my arm a sympathetic squeeze, and the awkwardness fades. 'Look, I've got an orthodontist appointment now – can you believe I'm getting fucking braces at the age of thirty-four? – but can we meet up for lunch sometime? I'd love to catch up, Barb.'

'That would be amazing,' I say. 'I don't really go by Barb anymore, though. It's just Annie these days.'

Riva gives a dismissive snort. 'Babe, you will *always* be Barb to me.'

As we swap numbers I notice her phone wallpaper is a photo of a gang of half-remembered faces on a night out. It's a strange feeling to discover that all this time my old life has been going on without me: the parties, laughs and adventures. Over the years I've been so careful not to dwell too much on my memories of that period because in my mind it had become so closely linked with losing my parents, but now that I'm here, faced with Riva, the living, breathing embodiment of my old life, all I remember is the fun we had together, and I feel a wave of nostalgia along with something that might possibly be regret.

'We used to have a lot of fun, didn't we?' I smile.

'Used to?' Riva gives a bark of laughter, then plants a smacker on my cheek. 'Darling, we still do!'

On the bus ride to Claris' house to collect Dot, my mind wanders back over my memories of Riva. Now that I'm a mum myself, it seems astonishing that the arrival of Riva's son, Jethro, seemed to have so little impact on her life; even with a baby in tow it was just business and pleasure as usual. There was one particular night at a club in Dalston: it must have been shortly after Jethro's birth, because I remember somebody saying we ought to wet the baby's head, and Riva replied that as she was the one who'd done all the work, it was *her* head that deserved wetting, and then a bottle of champagne magically appeared and she climbed on a table, shook it up and sprayed it all over herself like she was Beyoncé.

If I saw someone pull a stunt like that today, my thoughts would go as follows:

1) What a waste of champagne
2) That's going to be awfully sticky
3) I hope you've got a change of clothes with you
4) Someone might slip on that floor
5) Is it time to go home yet?

Back then, however, all I remember is the laughter.

At the time I didn't give Riva's post-natal partying a second thought, but now I can only marvel at how she managed it, especially because she was raising Jethro alone (she was a little hazy about Jethro's paternity after falling pregnant during a 'busy' work trip to the States). As someone who has developed a pathological fear of even the mildest of hangovers since becoming a mum, I have so many questions for her. For example: wasn't she tired the whole time? Like, so, *so* tired? Was she on some sort of miracle drug that kept her going – and, if so, where might one procure it? And where on earth was Jethro while she was dancing on tables?

Claris lives in her late grandmother's house, which is a mere ten-minute walk from Luke's place. Her granny Polly passed away last year on the very same day that she received a telegram from the Queen congratulating her on her 100th birthday. Apparently her last words were: 'Can you believe HRH's signature is printed? She didn't even bloody sign it herself!'

Granny Polly always was a stickler for good manners.

For Claris, the dark cloud cast by her beloved grandmother's death brought with it the silver lining of being left her beautiful home in one of the most desirable streets just off Clapham Common. Freed from the burden of London rental prices, Claris quit her job in cookery-book publishing and dedicated herself to her long-term ambition of setting up a catering company, called, in honour of her late granny, 'Polly Put the Kettle On'. As the name suggests, she specialises in afternoon tea, which means visitors to her flat are usually roped in to try whatever delicacy she's testing that week.

But as I walk up the front path, it's not the scent of freshly baked scones that wafts out to greet me, but Dot's urgent cries. I dash the last few steps and ring the doorbell, panicked about what might have happened, guilty about having abandoned my poor baby and worried about how my poor friend's been coping. Seriously, being a mother is non-stop *feels*.

Moments later a wild-eyed Claris opens the door with a wailing Dot in one hand and a bottle of milk in the other.

'Oh thank God, Annie!' She shoves me inside. 'I've been trying to give Dot her milk, but I think there might be something wrong with the bottle! She can't seem to get any out and she's been getting more and more upset and I DON'T KNOW WHAT TO DO!'

'Shhh, don't worry, I'm here now,' I say, trying to soothe them both. 'I'll just put her on the boob, that'll calm her down.'

We hustle into the living room, where the walls are still covered with Granny Polly's collection of antique oil paintings, which are so dark you can barely discern the subject matter (Racehorses? Boats? Ladies in large hats?) then I sit on the sofa and manoeuvre Dot into position, where she lunges at my nipple like a dog going after a treat.

'Ouch – easy, tiger,' I murmur, stroking her warm head as she gulps away.

Claris flops down next to me. 'Oh thank God,' she mutters again, this time in exhausted relief. 'She'd only been crying for a minute or so, but I have no idea what I'd have done if you hadn't turned up. I was seriously thinking about trying her with a piece of walnut sponge. What do you think the problem might have been?'

'Did you remove the travel cap from under the bottle's teat?'

'What?' Claris' eyes bulge in outrage. 'No! You didn't mention anything about a sodding travel cap!'

'I'm so sorry, I didn't even think about it. My fault, totally. That must have been really stressful.'

Claris raises her eyebrows as if to say, *you don't know the half of it* – but then relaxes into a smile. 'Well, no harm done. And she was a total delight before she got hungry. We had a walk on the common and read some books. She's clearly highly intelligent, Annie, she was very interested in the latest Hilary Mantel.' She gets up from the sofa, hands on hips. 'Now, what can I get you? Cup of tea? And I've been trying out a tahini and white chocolate cake that I'd love to get your thoughts on . . .'

After her feed, with Dot obligingly dozing in her pram, I tell Claris about my new hot dentist – leaving out some of the more eye-popping details, as I should probably save those for a more broad-minded audience (i.e. Jess). I thought Claris might disapprove of me lusting after another bloke while things with Luke are still so murky, as her moral compass has always been finely tuned, but instead she seems really pleased that I have – I quote – 'got a bit of your old spark back'.

I cut myself another slice of cake, which is possibly the best thing I've ever eaten.

'Talking about old sparks,' I say, 'when I was leaving

the dentist I bumped into a friend from my photography days. Riva – she's a stylist. I don't suppose you remember her?'

Claris thinks for a moment. 'No, but then I was always completely intimidated and flustered whenever I met your fashion friends. They were just so *cool*. Ooh, do you remember that model you had a bit of a thing with? What was his name ...?'

I grin; I know exactly who she's talking about. 'Tomo.'

'That was it!' Claris smiles, shaking her head. 'I couldn't even look him in the eye, he was just too beautiful ... So was it strange seeing this girl – Riva – again?'

I chew a mouthful of cake, thinking this over. 'Actually, not as strange as you might imagine. We're going to meet for lunch and I think we'll probably be able to just pick up where we left off years ago – although obviously our lives couldn't be more different.' I don't mean to, but I let out a sigh. 'Seeing her reminded me what fun we used to have. It made me miss my old job – my old life.'

'Well, I like the Annie of today far better,' says Claris stoutly. 'I hardly ever saw you back then, you were always jetting off somewhere glamorous or spending the entire weekend in a club.'

'Yes, but wasn't I more fun? I certainly think I was more interesting ...'

Claris shoots me a severe look. 'Annie Taylor, what could be more interesting and rewarding than raising a human being? I know how much you enjoyed the photography, but I guarantee that you wouldn't find all the partying and wild shenanigans half as appealing as you used to. People grow up and their lives change. Enjoy the memories, but don't ever regret the way things have turned out, not for a moment.' She tops up my tea from the pot. 'Besides, it would be impossible to have that sort of lifestyle with a child. The only time you used to be at home was when you were getting ready to go out!'

'But Riva . . .'

Claris looks at me quizzically. 'Riva what?'

I was going to say that Riva is a mum too and still manages to have a life with more to it than just naps and nappies, but think better of it.

'Doesn't matter,' I say. 'Right, enough about me, I want to hear what you've been up to . . .'

14

It's the start of my first working week, the day I rejoin the workforce and become a valued member of society once again. (And yes, I do know that being a mother is the most important job of all blah blah blah but you don't get paid for it, there are no lunch breaks and you can't even go to the loo without company. Plus, there's something fundamentally pleasing about having a job: doing an honest day's work in exchange for an honest day's pay. It's as satisfyingly straightforward as motherhood is bewilderingly complicated.)

Before Karl lets me loose with my camera on Curtis Kinderbey's portfolio of 'superior prestige properties', however, he has decided it would be a good idea for me to spend a day shadowing a member of his team to make sure I've got a feel for what he calls 'the C-K way' – or, as Fiona puts it, 'smiling and lying at the same time'.

On the way into the office I drop Dot off with her new childminder, a local woman called Helen who comes highly recommended. If you're entrusting your baby to a stranger, then you're going to want them to look like Helen: smiley, rosy-cheeked and in possession of a cosily ample bosom and a lovely house full of toys. Unfortunately, Dot didn't get the memo – or else she's just sick of being handed round to different babysitters (oh, hey there, Guilt, nice to see you again!) – and she howls as soon as we arrive.

Helen, bless her, does her best to put my mind at rest, reassuring me that Dot is sure to settle once I've gone; nevertheless, I arrive at Curtis Kinderbey already frazzled and wondering if this job is worth the heartache – and whether perhaps Luke was right after all about Dot needing to be with me. Weeing on your own is probably overrated anyway . . .

But then I think about the Raggy Rhyme Time power mums who seem to juggle multiple kids, executive jobs and *still* make time to get their nails done, and I think: *you've got this, Annie.*

'Ah, here she is, our little David Bailey!' Karl hustles over as quickly as his trousers allow, rubbing his hands together. 'So, are you ready to sell some houses, Annie?'

'Absolutely,' I say with a beaming, I've-got-this smile.

'Terrific, terrific . . . So, as I said to you on the phone, today will be an invaluable opportunity for you to observe how the business works first-hand and give you a helicopter view of the world of prestige property . . .'

As Karl rattles on, the management-speak flowing as freely as if he was reading straight out of a handbook, I sneak a look around the office for Fiona. There's no sign of her. Bugger. I'd hoped – we both had – that Karl would pair us up for today's outing, but it looks like I'm going to be palmed off on somebody else instead. Oh well, I know most of Fi's colleagues and they're a nice bunch; I'd be happy to tag along with any of them – any of them, that is, except for the inscrutable Rudy. I glance over to where he's sitting, his lanky frame hunched over his computer screen, long fingers drumming on the desk. I'm not exactly sure why, but he unsettles me. There's definitely something a bit off about him, like he's an alien who's trying to pass as human after careful observation of their behaviour . . .

'. . . so we'll touch base offline EOP. Sound good, Annie?'

I realise Karl has stopped talking and is now waiting for me to respond.

'Fantastic,' I say, brazing out my total ignorance of what he's just said with my best cheerleader smile. 'Let's do this!'

But Karl carries on looking at me, as if expecting me to do something. But what? I stopped listening after '. . . blue-sky thinking'. I look around, searching for a clue as to what's expected of me, and discover that Rudy is now standing by the door, coat on, and staring straight at me.

My heart sinking, I turn back to Karl, who makes a little shooing action with his hands like he's herding chickens. 'Chop chop, Annie, your carriage awaits.'

As I walk over to Rudy, he raises a hand in greeting. I can't say he looks pissed off to see me, but then he doesn't look particularly thrilled either. I feel a pang of shyness at the prospect of spending an entire day under that serious, unflinching gaze. He has the look of a man who would rather die than use an emoji. He probably hand-writes messages with a quill.

'Good morning,' he says as I approach.

I plaster on a grin. 'Hi Rudy! Thank you so much for letting me tag along today. I promise not to do anything stupid – well, I'll try not to, at least! Ha ha!'

My lame attempt at banter ignored, Rudy just nods then turns and heads out the door.

I'm actually quite intrigued to watch him at work, because I can't imagine how a man of so few words can possibly be any good at selling *anything*. Perhaps he persuades people to buy houses through the medium of mime, or interpretative dance.

I'm only comfortable with silence with someone I know well, so as we drive to the first appointment I can't stop myself from filling the chat-vacuum with mindless babble, spilling out all sorts of personal details as if I'm a lonely drunk sitting at a bar. I'm in the middle of telling Rudy all about Dot's meltdown at the childminder's, and how I'm worried that I'm actually a terrible mother, when it occurs to me this is really not an appropriate conversation to be having with a new work colleague. I immediately shut up and we drive on in silence. I'm staring out of the window, wondering if I should call Helen to check on Dot, when suddenly Rudy speaks.

'So you have a daughter?'

'Yes. Dot. She's four months old.'

He doesn't say anything else and I assume that's the end of our chat – really, he's *quite* the conversationalist – but after a few moments, he asks: 'How old are you?'

'Don't you know that it's rude to ask a lady her age?'

'Sorry,' he says, completely seriously.

'I'm joking! Thirty-one.' I turn to look at him. 'How old are *you*?'

'I'm twenty-two.'

'Well, you don't seem twenty-two.'

We're waiting at traffic lights and he glances at me with the beginning of a smile. 'How old do I seem, then?'

'Fifty,' I say. 'Possibly older.'

And now he breaks into a proper grin and I feel almost proud for making him smile like that: it was hard won, but at least I'm in no doubt that it's genuine. And it completely transforms his face; until now I hadn't even noticed that his eyes are different colours: one brown, one blue, like David Bowie, or a husky.

'Yeah, people often think I'm older than I am,' he says,

shifting into gear as the lights turn green. 'I guess I've just got one of those faces.'

A few minutes later we arrive at an imposing golden-bricked house and Rudy eases his car into the driveway behind two black Range Rovers and something sporty and super-expensive-looking, shaped like a wedge of Parmesan on wheels. The enormous front door is flagged by twin bay trees; Rudy presses the buzzer and we wait. I'm curious and more than a little intimidated: I've never been inside such a grand house before.

'We're being watched,' I mutter, nodding at the security cameras pointing menacingly at us from above the door.

Rudy just raises his eyebrows in response.

Moments later the door opens to reveal a petite woman, immaculately dressed in navy with gold jewellery and swept-back dark hair. The word 'elegant' immediately springs to mind, swiftly followed by 'loaded'.

'Good morning, I'm Rudy Sheen from Curtis Kinderbey and this is my associate, Annie Taylor.' His tone is considerably warmer and more upbeat than it was a moment ago. 'We have a valuation appointment at 9 a.m.'

The woman nods. 'Come through to the drawing room, I'll let Mrs Franklin know that you're here.' She shows us into a room that's straight out of 'Posh Interiors for Very Rich People' magazine. 'Can I get you a coffee or tea?' she asks.

'You're very kind, but nothing for me, thank you,' says Rudy with a gracious smile.

'No, thank you,' I mutter, stunned by all the luxury.

After she's gone I look around the enormous room, marvelling at how anyone can keep pale blue silk sofas so spotless – especially in light of the fact that there seem to be at least three children living here, judging by the silver-framed family photos that litter every surface.

'That woman isn't the owner then?' I whisper.

Rudy shakes his head. 'Housekeeper.'

Just then I hear the sound of approaching heels on marble and a woman appears in the doorway, pausing for just a moment as if posing for a photograph.

She is over six foot tall with the hair (and waist measurement) of a Barbie doll. God knows how old she is – anything between twenty and fifty seems possible – but I'm guessing she was once a model as I'm sure you can't be that beautiful and not try to make some money out of it. The most striking thing, however, is the sheer glossiness of her: glowing skin, glistening blonde mane, diamonds glinting all over her – she looks like she's powered by solar panels.

This is what rich looks like, I think. *And it's very, very shiny.*

'You're from Curtis Kinderbey?' she asks, already bored.

'We are, Mrs Franklin. I'm Rudy Sheen – we spoke on the phone last week? – and this is our property photographer, Annie Taylor.' He smiles in a way that suggests he's thrilled to be here. 'Thank you so much for taking the time to see us, we won't keep you long. Your house is exquisite.'

She glances around the room and sighs. 'Mmmm, we've outgrown the space,' she says, with an airy wave of a diamond-clad hand. 'I suppose you'll want to see the rest of it. This way . . .'

We trail Mrs Franklin around the house, my mind increasingly blown, as she points out the cinema room, the housekeeper's quarters and a 'mindfulness suite' with the careless complacency of someone who has absolutely no idea quite how incredible their home is, and how bloody lucky they are. You know that expression 'how the other half lives'? Well, this is how the other 0.000000001 per cent live.

We get only the briefest glimpse of each room before Mrs Franklin sweeps on. I would absolutely love to have a proper poke around – to check out her walk-in closet and have a nose through the beauty products in the master bathroom – and then I remember that I get to come back and photograph this place. It suddenly feels like an enormous treat.

The real revelation, though, is Rudy. Gone is the monosyllabic Mr Spock, and I finally understand why he's so good at selling houses. He is charming and engaging, flattering Mrs Franklin without being obsequious, and complimenting the antique furniture and art with what seems, to my ignorant ears at least, to be expert knowledge. Whether it's all bullshit, however, doesn't really matter, as Mrs Franklin laps it up; by the time we have finished the tour, she's putty in his hands, giggling coquettishly and touching his arm at every opportunity.

'I'll be in touch later today with the valuation,' says Rudy as she shows us out. 'You have a truly exceptional home, Mrs Franklin, and I'm confident that we can exceed your expectations in handling its sale.'

'Thank you, Rudy.' She smiles, her dental work outshining the diamonds. 'Obviously I'll have to discuss this with my husband, but if we're happy with the valuation, then I think we'll be able to work with you and Curtis Kinderbey as the sole agent.'

Bingo.

Back in the car, Rudy reverts to his inscrutable self, jotting down a few notes in a file, setting Google Maps for our next appointment and then reversing out of the driveway, all without saying a word.

When it becomes apparent that he doesn't intend on making any sort of comment on what, I assume, was a very successful appointment, I realise I'll have to get the ball rolling.

'That seemed to go well?'

Rudy's expression doesn't change. 'We'll see.'

I try again. 'I hope you don't mind me saying this, Rudy, but I wasn't expecting you to be quite so good at this. That really was quite a performance.'

'Performance,' he repeats, seeming amused. 'Yes, good choice of word. Because it's all an act, isn't it? I'm acting the part of an estate agent.'

'Well then, you're a really good actor.'

'I should hope so, I studied for three years at RADA.'

I turn to look at him, unsure whether he's joking. 'What, the world-famous and prestigious drama school RADA?'

'Yeah.'

'Are you serious?'

'Of course.'

I gawp at him, astonished. 'Then why the hell are you working as an estate agent?'

'Benedict Cumberbatch is stealing my roles,' he says.

I laugh, and Rudy smiles too. I realise how much more relaxed I feel around him than I did just an hour ago. He may not be particularly forthcoming, but he's refreshingly forthright – which means I don't feel shy about digging a little further.

'Seriously, what happened?' I ask. 'Why are you doing this if you trained as an actor?'

'I came to work at Curtis Kinderbey because I couldn't get an acting job. I still haven't got an acting job, so I'm still here. It's as simple as that.'

I nod slowly, pondering the correct response. 'I'm sorry,' I manage eventually.

'Don't be. It's actually proving useful experience for the acting – first-hand observation of human nature and all that. Besides, it was a choice between being an estate agent or a waiter, and this pays far more – and I get to hang out with interesting people.'

Was that last comment directed at me? I glance at him again, but his attention is focused on the road.

'Anyway,' Rudy goes on, 'from what I understand, this is a bit of a career departure for you too.'

'Well, I used to be an assistant to a fashion photographer, which I loved, and I was hoping to set up on my own, but then . . .' I shrug, deciding it's probably advisable to leave it at that. 'I've not worked for years actually, so this is all quite nerve-wracking.'

'Why did you give up the photography?'

I look out of the window, struggling to find a short answer. 'I screwed up, I suppose.' Then, not wanting to sound self-pitying, I add: 'It's complicated.'

Rudy pulls up outside a parade of shops and nods towards a café. 'We've got half an hour before our next appointment, so I can either follow Karl's instructions and tell you why you're so lucky to be working for Curtis Kinderbey or you can fill me in on your complicated life.' He unclicks his seatbelt. 'Up to you, but either way I want a coffee.'

The correct choice, of course, would be to shut up and

listen to the Curtis Kinderbey pep talk. Rudy certainly doesn't need to hear about my parents dying and my subsequent breakdown and how I met Luke and how we had Dot and how he cheated on me so I moved out to live with my cougar friend Jessica. This is most definitely *not* need-to-know information for a new work colleague. And yet over the next twenty minutes or so I tell him all this and much, much more, the words tumbling out #nofilter.

I don't expect or particularly want Rudy to comment or pass opinion on my ramblings, I just find myself wanting to talk; in a funny sort of way it's a relief to tell someone totally impartial about everything that's happened. I guess that's why people go to see priests. Rudy nods in places, makes the occasional remark, but is otherwise silent, and I presume as we get back in the car that there'll be no further mention of my confession.

'Thank you for listening,' I say, as he puts the key in the ignition.

'You're welcome.' Rudy checks his mirrors and then pulls away. 'And for what it's worth, I think you did the right thing.'

Well, that's a surprise. But does he mean having a baby? Leaving Luke? Moving in with Jessica? When it's clear he doesn't intend on elaborating, I ask: 'In what way?'

'Getting a job. I think it'll help.'

'Thank you,' I say. 'That's nice to hear.'

And it is. Coming from Rudy – the real Rudy, not the RADA-trained performing Rudy – it means a lot, and I almost believe it more than when my friends told me the exact same thing.

15

As it turns out, Fi was absolutely right: after working with models, photographing houses *is* a piece of piss. Houses don't turn up late for work, complain about the coffee or lock themselves in the toilet in tears because their boyfriend ran off with a Victoria's Secret Angel. I'm really enjoying taking photos again, Dot has stopped crying when I drop her off with Helen the childminder and Karl seems to be happy with what I've produced so far: all-in-all, this working-mum lark is going pretty well – touch wood. I'm sure Mr *Antiques Roadshow* Rudy would be able to tell exactly *what* sort of wood this is that I'm touching – 'ah, a superb rosewood bureau, early eighteenth century, with exquisite walnut herringbone cross-banding' – but to me it just looks old and expensive, like everything else in this house I'm photographing this morning. It's magnificent, decked out like a baronial Scottish castle, and the only people living here are an elderly couple and their Jack Russell. Who knew there were so many gazillionaires living in my neighbour-hood? I've never given much thought to what might be behind the high fences and security gates that you pass in some of the nicer streets round here, but these last two weeks working for Curtis Kinderbey have been quite the eye-opener.

My friends – and Rudy – were absolutely right about me feeling better about myself now that I'm taking pro-active steps to sort my life out rather than just sitting and waiting for it to happen to me. I'm currently working three days a week and plan to increase my hours over the next few months. Luke is insisting on paying for the childminder – even though I know he still strongly dis-agrees with me getting a job – which I'm grateful for, because without his help my wages would barely cover Helen's fees.

And despite my worries that I'd be out of my depth, the job itself is proving remarkably straightforward. I turn up at the property, the owner gives me a quick tour – or, even better, I pick up the keys from the Curtis Kinderbey office and give myself the tour – then I measure up the floor plan using a laser gadget and photograph each room.

Although the brief for these marketing photographs is pretty simple – 1. Make the space look as big/light as pos-sible; 2. That's it – there is some scope for creativity in how I stage the room. As I find my feet, I'm becoming more confident about moving furniture around to get the perfect shot. Depending on the size of the property, I can be in and out within an hour, although I imagine this morning's mansion will take a little longer. Quite why anyone needs six toilets I have no idea – especially when you're only a two-bum household – though I'm discovering that when you're loaded, such matters have little to do with need. Rich people have six bathrooms simply because they *can*.

Another interesting thing I've learnt from doing this job is just how nosy I am. It's actually quite addictive, the thrill you get from peeking inside wardrobes, opening drawers and looking through the private clutter of a stranger's life. And these people have such amazing stuff! Wood-fired pizza ovens built into the kitchen. Hand-embroidered silk wallpaper. Full-sized trees growing out of onyx-tiled atriums. Sauna and steam complexes in the garden. Ooh, and the shoes! I now get where the expression 'well-heeled' comes from: walk-in wardrobes with floor-to-ceiling shelves of colour-coordinated footwear appear to be *de rigueur* for the truly posh.

I probably shouldn't admit this, but I've started to take photos of some of the more beautiful things that I've come across during my work. It happened first in the second house that I was sent to photograph: I was measuring the floor plan in the kitchen when the sun suddenly came out, pouring through the skylight and lighting up an arrangement of dark red roses that sat on the Italian marble counter, next to a quilted Chanel handbag that had been casually abandoned. The composition was flawless, the lighting perfect: the artist in me could *see* what a stunning photo it would make; so before the light changed I got out my iPhone and took a quick snap.

For the rest of the day I kept sneaking a look at the picture. At first I felt guilty, as if I'd stolen something, but there was also a rush of excitement and pride at having captured something beautiful. This may sound wanky, but for the first time in years it felt like I had created art.

I honestly had no intention of taking any other photos of clients' possessions, but in the very next house I went to, there was a shelf of antique crystal perfume bottles in the master bathroom that looked like something out of a Victorian apothecary. Before I could talk myself out of it, I quickly took a shot – and, if I do say so myself, it was another beauty.

For a few days afterwards I half-expected to get an irate phone call from Karl about my flagrant snooping, but once again I got away with it, and since then I've sneaked one or two photos at each property I've visited. I've got pictures of sculptures, designer furs, a bed piled with a rainbow of silk pillows and even the inside of one of those mega-fridges which contained only champagne and caviar. My iPhone photo feed looks like it belongs to the wife of a Russian oligarch; whenever I look through the photos, I get a vicarious thrill of living a life of luxury and beauty – and they also satisfy my growing creative urges.

With my floor plan and marketing photos of the baronial Scottish castle complete (with a bonus arty snap of a full-sized stuffed stag for my private collection) I have a couple of hours to kill before my next appointment, so I decide to head into town to get some new clothes for Dot, who is straining at the poppers of all her Babygros. I'm waiting at the bus stop, sheltering from the drizzle, when my mobile starts vibrating in my pocket. As always, my first thought is automatically to wonder whether it's Luke. I can't help it; old habits die hard. I do miss him – at times so deeply that I wonder why I don't just put this whole mess behind me and move home – and Luke seems so desperate to make things right. He's stopped messaging me quite as much now, but he still phones or emails most days for Dot updates, and he always finishes by telling me how much he loves me. I guess you could say that my feelings towards him are, well, *mellowing*. For now, though, we've arranged that Luke will have Dot every other Friday night and Saturday, with tonight being our inaugural Daddy Day Care session. I'll miss Dot, of course, but ... Oh, who am I kidding, I am *massively* looking forward to a night off. I quite fancy spending it having a bath, a takeaway and then a blissful, undisturbed night of sleep, but the girls and Tabby are taking me out for dinner instead – which will of course be equally lovely. Plus I'll still be able to have a lie-in tomorrow.

When I check my phone, however, the caller is not Luke. I don't recognise the number; it's probably a client, or someone from Curtis Kinderbey.

'Hi, this is Annie Taylor speaking.'

'Annie, please don't hang up.' The soft voice is instantly and nauseatingly familiar. 'It's Sigrid.'

I freeze with the phone clamped to my head, opening and closing my mouth like a just-hooked trout, an alarm pounding inside my brain. Actually, it's not an alarm: it's my heart, thumping away as if I've just done a HIIT workout.

'Annie, are you still there? I know I have no right to ask you for anything, but I'd really like to talk to you.'

I take a moment to compose myself before answering, resolving to deal with the situation calmly and with dignity.

'What the fuck do you want?' Well, a bit of dignity.

'Annie, there are some things I need to say to you and I'm hoping your heart will allow you to hear me out. I think it might help start the healing process – for both us.'

'Sigrid, I don't give a shit about your healing process, and there's nothing you can say that will make me feel any better about what you've done.'

'But I think there might be. I've been meditating on my

actions and I really want to share some of the lessons I've learnt. I've already spoken to Luke about this and he . . .'

'Wait, you've been talking to Luke?'

There's silence at the other end of the line.

'Sigrid? When did you speak to him?'

A long pause. 'I didn't call to upset you.'

'I'm not upset, I just want to know what's going on between you and Luke.' *Deep breath, Annie. Calm and dignified.*

Sigrid gives a little huff of frustration; the conversation clearly isn't going the way she intended. 'Well, when I saw Luke a few days ago, we—'

'You *met* with him?' I choke the words out, my stomach twisting.

'Annie, I can hear how much pain you're still in and I'm truly sorry, but even if I spent the rest of my life apologising, it wouldn't change what happened. Talking about it just might, though. It's vital we keep lines of communication open so that all parties can grow and . . .'

I'm tense with the effort that it's taking me not to cry, but there's no way I'm going to give Sigrid the satisfaction of hearing poor, unenlightened Annie lose her rag. Swallowing my tears, I wrench the phone from my ear and jab at the screen to end the call. I realise that I'm shaking. Luke can't have done this to me, surely? Not after promising he'd never see her again. But Sigrid has no reason to lie, and it's not as if Luke hasn't betrayed me before. That *bastard.* There I was starting to think I should just forgive and forget, and all this time he's been meeting up with Sigrid and . . . and what? Having sex? It's certainly not out of the question. He lied to me about seeing her, so God only knows what else he has been lying about.

Before I have a chance to calm down, I phone Luke.

'Hey you!' He sounds delighted to hear from me. 'I was just going to call you to discuss plans for this weekend. I can't wait to see our little girl later.'

'Luke, have you been meeting up with Sigrid?'

The silence at the other end of the phone tells me everything I need to know.

'God, you really are pathetic. Just couldn't keep away, could you?'

'Annie, you need to calm down and listen to me.' Luke's voice has a hard edge. 'You've got this all wrong, I promise you.'

'What, so you haven't been meeting up with her then?'

'Sigrid turned up at my office last week and asked to see me. I got Vicky to tell her I would be in meetings all day, but she insisted on waiting. She wouldn't leave, Annie! In the end I said I would give her five minutes. She started telling me some bullshit about meditation, I said I wasn't interested and then she left. That was it, I swear.'

'And why the hell should I believe anything you tell me?'

'Because if I wanted to be with Sigrid, do you really think I'd be trying so hard to win you back?' He sighs, exasperated. 'Annie, I love you, all I want is for you and Dot to come home. Surely you can see that?'

I hesitate, trying to get my thoughts in some sort of order. I'm such a jumble of emotions that I find Luke's calm, rational manner infuriating. 'You could have refused to see her,' I mutter.

'You're right, and perhaps I should have, but she was there for hours, and it was starting to get embarrassing. I just wanted to get rid of her. But apart from that one time, I've had nothing to do with her.'

Despite my turmoil, I have to admit that he does sound like he's telling the truth – and I can certainly believe Sigrid is capable of such stalker-ish behaviour.

'Would you have told me any of this if I hadn't found out from Sigrid?' I ask.

'Of course I would!'

'Bullshit.'

A pause. 'Fine, I probably wouldn't.'

'Luke!'

'But only because I knew how much it would upset you, and because I *didn't do anything wrong*!' Another sigh; he clearly thinks I'm making a fuss over nothing. 'Annie, please stop trying to look for more reasons to hate me. All I want to do is to make things right with you. You need to start trusting me again.'

'Easier said than done.' And I end the call.

16

I stand at the bus stop, staring at my phone, jittery with adrenaline.

'Arsehole,' I mutter at the now dark screen, swiping away a tear.

The drizzle has now turned into a downpour, the skies so gloomy that passing cars are switching on their headlights. I need to find somewhere to calm down, get a hot drink and clean up the mascara that's probably smeared across my cheeks. *Like war-paint*, I think grimly – although I'm not exactly acting like a warrior right now. How I hate the person I become whenever I have anything to do with Luke. Despite my fears, I'm actually coping pretty well as a single mum: the job is working out okay, Dot's happy and although I'm tired *all the bloody time* I do feel quite proud that I'm making the best of a shitty situation. But one wrong word from Luke and I instantly turn into a needy, snivelling wreck.

I peer through the rain for a glimpse of the comforting

glow of a Starbucks or Costa, but I'm in a residential area and the sole option within umbrella-less dashing distance is a pub at the far end of the street. Although it's only late morning, it looks like the lights are on, and so, tucking my camera bag under my jacket for protection from the deluge, I pull up my collar and make a run for it.

The Admiral Nelson must be one of the few remaining pubs in the area that hasn't been converted into luxury apartments or had a Millennial makeover. Give it a couple of years and it will have an onsite micro-brewery and vegan brunch options; for now, however, it is the epitome of an old man's boozer: dark wood panelling, flickering fruit machines, Stella on tap and a carpet so gratuitously patterned it could hide an industrial waste spillage. The ghosts of cigarettes past still linger in the air, years after the smoking ban. I'm guessing a soya flat white will be out of the question.

There are only three other customers – all male, all seated at separate tables – who have the look of men who still rue the day that women got the vote. Suddenly, the idea of getting soaked to my knickers doesn't seem quite so unappealing: I think I'll use the toilets and then take my chances in the rain.

There's a bloke behind the bar restocking the fridge with tiny bottles of Britvic orange juice.

'Excuse me, which way to the Ladies?'

'Facilities are for customers only,' he says, without turning round.

Great. Well, I suppose I might as well be miserable here as anywhere else.

'Fine, I'll have a lime and soda, please.'

The barman gets up, clearly miffed at the inconvenience, and pours my drink. 'Anything else?'

I hesitate. The way he's looking at me I can tell he's thinking: *you don't belong in here, love.* God, I am so sick of being patronised by bloody men! I glance at the clock behind the bar: just after 11 a.m.

Fuck it.

'And a double vodka.'

'In the lime and soda?'

'Yes.' I boldly return his stare. 'Please.'

He turns to the row of optics with a shrug; he obviously thinks I have a drinking problem. Perhaps I should order some food as well . . .

'Could I please see the menu?'

'Kitchen doesn't open until midday.'

'Okay then, I'll have . . .' I look around for a suitable snack and spot a jar at the other end of the bar. 'What's in there?'

'Pickled eggs.'

'I'll take two. Early lunch.'

He looks dubious, but it's probably a nourishing choice. They sell hard-boiled eggs in snack pots in Pret, after all, and isn't pickling the latest health trend? Something to do with microbes . . .

I choose a table as far away from the other customers as possible and sit staring at the vodka and two pickled eggs on the little round table in front of me; what seemed like a sensible choice a moment ago now seems utterly bizarre. Why didn't I just leave here when I had the chance? There's probably a friendly café just around the corner: I could be smothering my sorrows right this minute with a hot chocolate and a buttered bun. Instead, I've stumbled into 1956 and a potential alcohol problem.

I take a tiny sip of my drink, feeling a not-unpleasant warmth from the vodka, trying not to cry again. Bloody, bloody Luke, this is all his fault . . .

Or is it? Perhaps it's *my* fault for letting him get to me . . .

No, Annie, you're being ridiculous. Luke is the father of your baby and he cheated on you: of course that's going to 'get' to you. You're not a robot.

I take another sip; this is going down surprisingly easily . . .

But now he's desperate to make things right, to be a family again – so that's a good thing, isn't it?

I take another large gulp of booze. *Yum.*

Trouble is, I'm really not sure I can ever trust him again.

My head is already feeling a bit swimmy; breastfeeding has turned me into a total lightweight. I take a nibble of egg – and spit it straight out into a napkin. Jesus, that's not food, it's a Bushtucker Trial! I have more vodka to get rid of the Domestos aftertaste and then some more, and discover my glass is now empty. Well, that barely touched the sides – but then pub measures are notoriously small, aren't they?

First things first: I need to get rid of those eggs – the reek of blocked drains is making me queasy – so I wrap them in a napkin and make a beeline for the Ladies, where I stuff them into a tampon bin, trying not to gag at the sulphurous stink. Then I brave the mirror and tackle my face, wiping away the smudges of mascara and re-applying my make-up, majoring on blusher and bronzer for the healthy glow of one who absolutely *does not* have a drink problem.

On leaving the Ladies, I march up to the bar, my confidence boosted by the make-up and infinitesimal amount of vodka coursing through my veins.

'I'll have a Bloody Mary, please. Double.'

I watch the barman pour in two teeny measures of vodka. Honestly, it's barely a teaspoonful.

'Could you put in an extra shot, please?'

He does so without comment. 'How were the pickled eggs?'

'Delicious, thank you.'

'My nan's recipe,' he says. 'She used to run this place. That's her over there.'

He puts my drink on the bar and nods at a framed photo of a woman who clearly eats a dozen pickled eggs for breakfast.

'She looks like quite a woman,' I say, perching on one of the stools. 'How much do I owe you for this?'

'On the house.' He grins. 'Nan would have insisted.'

I smile gratefully while thinking: *God, I really hope he's not responsible for emptying the tampon bins.*

By the time I leave the Admiral Nelson an hour or so later, the sun has come out, I have gained two Facebook friends – Clive the barman and Bob, one of the regulars (the others, Tony and Del, don't yet do social media, although they've promised me they'll take a look) – I have been treated to several of Clive's 'special' rum cocktails, and I am absolutely, undeniably shit-faced. It's a lovely, floaty drunkenness, though, not an angry, slurry one, and as I stroll back to the bus stop with the sunshine warming my face, I can't imagine why on earth I was getting so stressed out about Luke. Seriously, what's the big deal? I don't need that emotionally constipated loser! I am a strong, confident woman who can take on the world. Just like Clive's old nan, Gawd bless her.

As I fumble in my bag for some chewing gum, I stumble on an uneven paving slab – oopsy daisy! – but recover with a giggle. Honestly, pre-lunch drinking is *massively* underrated.

I eventually arrive at the next property, the penthouse

apartment of a flashy Thames-side development, half an hour behind schedule, but apparently the owner, an American investment banker, lives in New York so – no problemo. Judging by the number of security guards loitering in the marble-lined lobby, the residents here are strictly mega-bucks only. I have to put a code into the lift to get it to go to the penthouse, and when it reaches the top floor, the doors open straight out into the apartment.

'Woah, this place is uh-mazing!' I announce to the vast room, which has floor to ceiling windows facing the Houses of Parliament across the river. *Wow*. The view alone must be worth millions.

I spin around with outstretched arms and then belly-flop onto the sofa and lie there watching the boats gliding up and down the Thames, feeling pleasurably woozy. I actually start to drift off, but then my stomach rumbles with the force of an accelerating 747, reminding me that I haven't really eaten since breakfast. I am instantly overwhelmed by an urge for something fatty, salty or sugary – or, even better, all three – so I drag myself off the sofa and have a poke around the kitchen, singing Barbra Streisand hits at top volume. I might not have her look anymore, but boy, can I still belt out her back catalogue! Sadly, the kitchen cabinets are largely empty, apart from some jumbo tubs of whey protein and a half-finished bottle of Grey Goose, so I wander through to the bedroom, which is dominated by a bed on a raised plinth that would comfortably sleep at least a dozen supermodels (although only if they were lying on their sides, like a tin of sexy size-zero herrings). I slide open the expanse of fitted wardrobes to reveal a row of designer men's suits and a squash racquet. Honestly, this place couldn't be more of a millionaire bachelor cliché if it had a *50 Shades*-style sex dungeon in the airing cupboard. (It doesn't – I checked.) There is, however, some obviously big-ticket artwork about the place, including a huge Chinese vase that I earmark for an iPhone snap later. It's only then that I remember I'm supposed to be here to do some actual work. Doh!

The marketing photos are dead easy, because the rooms are so huge that there's no staging or trickery required, and I discover that photographing while pissed stops me obsessing over every tiny aspect of each shot like I usually do. I'm literally done in ten minutes. Result! Right, now for that vase . . .

I crouch down in front of it to get the best angle while effortlessly hitting the high notes in 'Woman in Love'. I hadn't actually realised before, but I'm a *really* good singer. I check the photo on the screen: yes, this is going to look bloody brilliant. Perhaps I should move it over by the window so I can get the Houses of Parliament in the background? It looks quite heavy, but if I get my shoulder under it, I'm sure I'll be able to shuffle it across the carpet ...

'Nice vase, isn't it?'

And then I spin round in shock to discover a man standing in front of the lift doors, which are closing behind him as silently as they apparently opened.

17

Despite my drunken state, I immediately notice two things about the new arrival. Firstly, he pronounces vase as 'vayse' rather than 'vaarse'. This clearly makes him American, which means he must be the owner, and therefore not in New York after all. And secondly, he is fit. As in, *well fit*. He is about my height, with a sandy-coloured beard, broad shoulders and the sort of chest that would make a perfect place to nestle your head. His nose, while not XXXL like mine, is impressively prominent and noble. The overall impression is of a sexy, suit-and-tie-clad lumberjack. Probably not everyone's cup of coffee, but, right now, most definitely mine.

'I'm so sorry, I was just taking a closer look,' I say, gesturing at the vase. 'I'm a big fan of, um, Ming Dynasty porcelain.' (If I've learnt anything from Rudy, it's that if you say something with enough confidence, people will believe you.)

'Right,' he says, narrowing his eyes. 'And you are?'

'Annie Taylor. From Kindis Curtebey – I mean Curtis Kinderbey. Curtis Kinderbey! Ha! The excellent estate agents. I've just been taking marketing photos. Not just vase photos, honest! Hahaha!'

He nods thoughtfully. 'Well, Annie Taylor from Curtis Kinderbey, you've got quite a loud singing voice. I could hear you from inside the lift – and I believe it's lead-lined and bomb-proof. Barbra would be proud of you.'

Before I realise it, I snigger. I know I'm being massively unprofessional, but I can't help it; nothing seems that important right now. Plus, he's smiling, so hopefully that means he's not going to report me for misconduct. *And* he knows his Barbra songs! Gosh, he really is *very* attractive ... Bloody hormones – or bloody alcohol. Could be either to blame right now, TBH ...

'Well, I better get my things together,' I say, making a particular effort not to slur my words. 'I will be out of your way in just one little tiny minute.'

'It's no problem, take your time.' He strolls into the room and slings his rucksack onto the sofa in such an assertively manly fashion that I immediately find myself imagining that I'm the rucksack and the sofa is his gigantic bed (minus the fishy supermodels).

'Can I get you a drink before you go?'

'Grey Goose and tonic, please.' Shit! It slipped out before I could stop myself. 'Just joking! Water would be super, thank you.'

A moment later he hands me a glass and then sits on the arm of the sofa fiddling with his phone as I pack up my camera. I keep taking surreptitious glances at him, just to reassure myself of his attractiveness, and get a shock one time when I discover he's looking straight back at me. Our eyes meet and he smiles; my cheeks flare red in response.

'This is such an amazing view,' I enthuse, trying to detract from how flustered I suddenly feel.

'I know, right?' he says, jumping up and crossing to the window with endearing enthusiasm. 'What this room really needs is a telescope – then you could look right inside the Houses of Parliament.'

'Ooh, that's an excellent idea! There's probably some juicy sex scandal going on right this moment.'

He turns to me, eyebrows raised. 'You reckon?'

Shit, I shouldn't have mentioned sex. That was inappropriate and makes me sound like a perv.

'Or just a . . . normal type of scandal,' I say quickly. 'Like bribery or something. And if you caught them in the act, you could sell the pictures to the newspapers and make loads of money.'

He gives a half-smile. 'And this would be the act of . . . ?'

I stare at him, mock-outraged. 'Bribery, of course!'

He laughs. He really is being very friendly, almost – and I'm sure I'm not imagining this – flirtatious. All the eye contact, the frequent smiles: yes, the signs are most definitely there. Ha, I've still got it!

'So, do you live nearby?' he asks.

'Not far,' I reply, putting on my coat while wondering: *is he asking that as polite chit-chat, or because he wants to get in my pants?* I swing my bag over my shoulder and turn to face him, a flame of anticipation flickering inside me. It's not just that I fancy him – although I blatantly do – but even in my drunkenness, I feel like here is someone who is *right* for me; we're definitely each other's sort of person. We might have only just met, but I know that for a fact.

'I better get going then,' I say, hoping he'll ask me not to.

He gets up off the sofa, another of those sexy smiles playing about his lips. I hadn't noticed before, but he's got the most amazing teeth: white (but not fake, Simon Cowell white), perfectly straight, totally American. A thought suddenly pops into my head: *if I made a move right now, he would respond.* I'm not sure where it came from, but now that it's in my head, it's firmly stuck there.

'Well, thank you for coming,' he says. 'It was great to meet you.'

'You too. The agency will be in touch with the photos and floor plan within the next few days.'

I turn and head towards the lift and although most of my focus is devoted to making sure I walk in a straight line, I can sense that he's following me. Sure enough, when I reach the doors I turn and discover he's right there next to me. He's still smiling – although his smile has now changed. This smile has a question in it.

There's a lightness in my head and my breathing is shallow. This is completely different from when I was lusting over Dr Tom 'Hot Dentist' Ford the other day, because this time I am 99.9 per cent sure the feelings are mutual – and I'm too pissed to care about the remaining 0.1 per cent. Our eyes are now locked; it's like he's daring me to make the first move.

So this actually happens in real life and not just in the movies, does it? You meet someone and there's an instant, compelling attraction? I feel a pleasurable stirring in the vicinity of my knickers as my hand hovers over the lift button, playing for time.

Go on, do it, urges my inner MILF. *I dare you.*

But what about Luke? He's Dot's dad, and we haven't officially broken up, after all.

Luke is screwing Sigrid. He's betrayed you again and again. He doesn't care about you.

I really should leave. I'm drunk and I don't know the first thing about this bloke.

Jess said you needed to have a one-night stand, didn't she? I'm sure a one-day stand would do the trick, too . . .

I take a step towards the American, trying to keep the drunken wobbling to a minimum, and fix him with my best seductive stare. We're standing so close that I get a whiff of his alluring, citrussy fragrance; I just hope the chewing gum has taken care of my own alluring vodka-y fragrance. A look appears in his eyes – it could be excitement, or it could also be confusion – but he makes no attempt to move. I do think that given the opportunity, most blokes wouldn't turn you down, so I take another step towards him, until we're standing close enough for me to reach out and touch his chest. And so I do.

His eyes flick down to my hand and then back to me with a quizzical look, but again, he doesn't move. Mission Control, we are *go*!

Is this completely unprofessional? Oh yes. Am I going to get fired? Probably! But right this moment I couldn't give a stuff. The flicker of anticipation has turned into a blaze of excitement. I am a strong, sexual woman. I used to do crazy stuff like this all the time; God knows I deserve a bit of fun.

Before I can change my mind, I lean in towards him for a kiss. I catch a glimpse of his expression, which is admittedly rather wide-eyed, but he doesn't pull away, and a moment later our mouths touch. His lips are soft and yielding and his beard just the right side of scratchy, and as I close my eyes, any worries are washed away in a flood of feel-good hormones and I surf the wild rush of oxytocin, letting myself be sucked down into a whirlpool of lust ... but now my head is starting to spin and actually

I'm feeling a bit queasy and I – *oh fuck fuck fuck what the fuck am I doing?*

I don't know which one of us pulls away first, but suddenly we're most definitely *not* kissing, and I've sobered up as quickly as if someone has just chucked a bucket of cold water over me.

My hand flies to my mouth in horror. I have literally just forced myself on someone. And not just a randy stranger in a bar, on a client in his own fucking home.

'I'm *so* sorry . . .' I am stammering, too mortified to string a sentence together. 'I can't . . . I don't know . . .'

Oh God, just look at his expression! He has the face of a man who's discovered he's just been given herpes. By me. Right now I can't begin to fathom why I ever thought he might want me to lunge at him. For all I know he might be married. Christ, he could be gay!

He wipes his mouth of my pickled-egg slobber and then runs a hand through his hair, clearly trying to work out how to deal with this sex-crazed lunatic.

'It's okay,' he says, his voice deliberately calm, as if negotiating with a terrorist. 'It's fine. Really, I . . .'

'No no no, I behaved appallingly, it's all my fault!' I hammer at the lift button. 'I feel absolutely terrible, I . . . I've had a hard week, personal issues, no excuse, but . . .' Thankfully the lift arrives and I dive in, lunging at the button to make the doors close, not daring to look back at him. *What have I done?*

Then I hear him say: 'Just wait a minute, I . . .'

But thankfully the lead-lined lift doors now glide silently closed, drowning out the rest of his sentence, sparing me further mortification. It's only then it occurs to me that I didn't even find out the poor bloke's name.

18

There's a tipping point between gloriously drunk and grimly hungover, which for me is heralded by a spinning head and a creeping awareness that I've just made a complete tit of myself – although said tittery is generally drunken dancing and/or karaoke, mere japes compared to forcing myself on a client. I'm usually nearing bed when I reach this state, but today I've plunged straight into the opening credits of The Hangover From Hell while sitting on the early afternoon bus back to Streatham surrounded by old ladies, mums with babies and a couple of nuns. I now realise that the reason we generally get pissed in the evening is because fewer people notice if you do embarrassing things in the dark. Also, self-loathing and existential angst are far worse during daylight hours. (Not to mention, there are fewer, if any, nuns around at night.)

I've done some dumb things in my life, but today I have literally scaled the Everest of idiocy. Best case scenario,

I'm going to be fired; worst, I'll be arrested for sexual assault. I get a sudden flashback to the American's appalled expression and am body-slammed by another wave of shame. Of course he didn't pull away when I threw myself at him: the poor bloke was in shock! I shakily cram down another mouthful of the kebab that I bought before getting on the bus and force it down along with my rising nausea. If today's taught me anything – apart from the questionable wisdom of pre-lunch boozing – it's that if a man's smile seems to have a question in it, that question isn't necessarily 'Fancy a snog?' It's actually more likely to be: 'Could you please get out of my home?' Or: 'Why are you looking at me in that weird way? Seriously, you're scaring me.'

I shrink into my seat, attempting to make myself invisible, and am hit by a visceral need to see Dot, to hold her close and remind myself that there *is* something good in my life, that I'm not a total fuck-up. But Luke's collecting her from the childminder today and keeping her with him tonight; besides, I definitely shouldn't be parenting in this state. I'm not even capable of looking after myself.

I have two more work appointments this afternoon, but there is no way I can struggle through those feeling the way I do now. I need my bed and the oblivion of sleep. I'm going to have to call Karl to let him know; I just hope to God that the American hasn't already phoned the office to report me for aggravated snoggery.

I dial Karl's direct line and it goes straight to voicemail; thank God, my first bit of good luck today . . .

'Um Karl, hi, it's Annie Taylor here. I've just finished up at the riverside penthouse apartment but I'm afraid I'm feeling really ill, sort of shivery and achy – in fact, I think I might be coming down with the flu – *cough cough* – so I'm going to have to go home to bed. I'm so sorry, I'll make sure the other photographs are done early next week. Sorry again. *Cough*. Bye.'

I catch one of the nuns' eyes; she knows I'm lying. She gives me a piously pursed-lip look that says: *you, my child, are going straight to hell.*

A few minutes later my phone vibrates with a Whats-App from Fi; Karl has obviously already been moaning about my unreliability.

Karl's said you're ill – what's going on, you okay? You better not wimp out of tonight x

Shit – dinner with the girls! I completely forgot about our monthly catch-up tonight. Well, there's no way I'm going to be up to that; I'll have to cancel. But what on earth to say? My response needs to be composed with care – the date's been in the diary for ages, it's the first chance we've all had to get together since I started the job – but I've pickled so many brain cells with booze that I don't have the ability to come up with a decent lie. In the end I take the easiest option: honesty, but just a hint of it.

I found out that Luke and Sigrid are still shagging this morning and didn't cope with it well. Can we talk later? Feeling terrible and need to sleep. So sorry xxx

I press send and then turn off my phone. My relief at the prospect of being left in peace outweighs the guilt at blowing out my mates. Thankfully Jess is not at home when I get there, so I go straight to bed and pull the duvet over me, still burning with shame, and let sleep consume me.

'Annie? Annie, are you okay?'

Safe inside my duvet cocoon, I become vaguely aware of voices nearby. Why are there people in my bedroom? What time is it? Oww, my head hurts ... Then the memory of what I've done smashes into me like an avalanche.

'Maybe she's ill.' That sounds like Claris; perhaps if I feign sleep, they'll all go away. I breathe extra slowly and loudly, to indicate a state of deep slumber.

'She's faking it, clearly.' Then I feel someone – probably Jess, because that was her voice – give me a shove. 'Come on, Annie, we know you're awake.'

'Leave her alone! We should let her rest.' I say a silent *thank you* to Claris.

'What *is* that ...?' Now I hear Tabby, and a rustling noise somewhere on the bed. 'It looks like ... ugh, a kebab – or what's left of it.'

'Gross!'

'Right, bollocks to this.' There's a sudden blinding light – that even with my eyes shut makes me flinch – and a rush of cold air as the duvet is ripped off me. 'Annie Taylor, what the feck is going on?'

With a moan, I curl into a ball and squeeze my eyes open a crack. Standing around my bed are Jess, Tabby, Claris and Fi, who is holding my duvet.

'Leave me alone,' I mutter – and then, hoping that being nice might help them take pity on me, I add: 'Please.'

Jess sits next to me on the bed. 'What's the story, babe? Fi told us about your cryptic phone message. What happened with Luke?'

I struggle up into a seated position, my stomach lurching like I'm on a waltzer. I put my head in my hands to try to stop the spinning.

'Why are you all here?' I ask weakly.

'We had a date, remember?' says Fi.

'And your phone was turned off,' says Tabby. She is cradling her growing bump and looking at me accusingly. Despite my feeble state, I make a mental note to have a proper chat with her about how she's getting on with the pregnancy; every time we've spoken lately it's been all about *my* dramas.

'And we were worried about you,' adds Claris, holding out a glass of water.

'So because Mohammed wouldn't come to the mountain, the mountain has come to Mohammed,' says Tabby. 'We've also ordered a takeaway, although it looks like you've beaten us to it.'

Everyone glances over at the remains of the doner spilling out onto the duvet, and my stomach churns again with nausea and shame, then I get a sudden, sickening flash of terror – *where the hell is my baby?* – and when my booze-addled brain remembers that Dot's with Luke, relief hits me with such force I almost get whiplash.

Jess leans towards me and sniffs, examining me with suspicion. 'Mmm, I thought as much. You've been drinking, haven't you?'

Claris looks worried. 'Annie, what's going on?'

I sip the water, trying to get my thoughts in order. There is absolutely no way I'm going to be able to fib my way out of this.

'I promise I'll tell you everything,' I say eventually. 'But could I please have a shower first?'

Fi nods. 'Right you are. We'll see you downstairs in fifteen minutes sharp.'

When I have finished recounting the day's events, leaving absolutely nothing out, there is silence around the kitchen table. The pizzas are sitting in front of us, still in their boxes, untouched.

Fi is the first to speak. 'What, so you just ... kissed him? Just like that?'

I nod miserably. Out of the corner of my eye, I see Claris and Tabby exchanging looks.

'With tongues?' asks Jess.

I close my eyes. 'I think so.'

'And there hadn't been any flirty banter beforehand?' Fi presses on. 'Nothing that might have given you the impression he was interested in taking things further?'

'Well, he *was* really friendly, but ...' I slump into my seat. 'Nope, nothing at all. He was polite and nice and because I was drunk, I took it as a come-on.' I drop my head into my hands with a groan. 'Oh God, what have I done ...'

Again, silence. That is not a good sign. This is a group that is never knowingly lost for words.

'Well, for me it's the pickled egg thing that's the worst bit of the whole tale,' says Jess breezily. 'Why didn't you just have a bag of crisps? Or some nuts? That would have been the sensible thing to order in a pub. But *pickled eggs*, Annie ...' She pulls a face. 'As for the rest of it, though – forget about it! The guy is probably boasting to his mates as we speak. You said so yourself, it's not like he pulled away or tried to stop you, did he? I bet he was enjoying it. Lucky bugger, I say. Honestly, you're making a huge deal out of nothing.'

'Jess, he's a *client*.' I look at Fi imploringly. 'Be honest, how bad do you think this is? Am I going to get fired?'

Jess hoots with laughter. 'Oh come on, there's absolutely no way he'll phone the office to complain. Can you imagine? "I'm afraid to say your lady photographer just forcibly kissed me, leaving me in a state of considerable distress." He'd be laughed off the phone!'

'Well, he'd be quite within his right to complain,' says my sister.

'Tabby, please, I feel bad enough as it is . . .'

'But just imagine if it was the other way round and *he* forced himself on *you*?' she goes on. 'Wouldn't you make a complaint? Because I know I bloody well would.'

There's nothing I can say to that, because she's absolutely right.

'Look, if he *does* phone the office to complain,' says Claris, 'which I'm quite sure he won't, you can just explain the situation with Luke, and how you were in shock over it. They'll understand.'

'But that's the other thing,' says Tabby. 'From what you've told us, Annie, it doesn't sound like Luke *is* sleeping with Sigrid again.'

I turn furiously to my sister. 'How can you defend him after everything that arsehole has done!'

She reaches for my hand. 'I'm not defending him. He's been a complete bastard and, believe me, I won't ever forgive him for what he did to you.' She gives my hand a sisterly squeeze. 'But what he said to you today made sense. He's certainly proved that he's desperate to win you back – why would he be bothering if he wanted to be with Sigrid? I really think he's telling you the truth this time. It certainly didn't warrant you going out and getting shit-faced.'

Jess grabs the bottle of wine and tops up all our glasses. 'This goes right back to what I've been saying all along, that you should dump Luke and move on. You're coping brilliantly without him and you clearly don't trust him – just get rid of the loser, he's dead weight!' Then she pulls the nearest pizza box towards her and takes a slice. 'So, was he hot? The American, I mean.'

'Jess!' Claris shoots her a *now-is-not-the-time* glare.

'Come on, we've got all the woe-is-me crap out of the way.' She leans towards me with a wicked grin. 'Now for the good bit.'

I can't help but smile. 'Yes, he was,' I admit eventually. 'Very hot. *And* he knew his Streisand songs.'

There is a mass eyebrow-raise around the table. The girls know just how much this would appeal to me.

'No excuse though, is it,' I add miserably.

Before I go to bed that night, I turn on my phone. As well as all the concerned messages from my friends earlier in the day, there's one that Luke sent this evening. It's a photo of Dot, smiling gummily and clutching a new teddy he must have bought her. This is my first night without her and I suddenly miss her with a fierceness that knocks the breath out of me. *My baby.* Just staring at the picture makes my heart ache, literally. After a while I manage to drag my attention away from the photo – although not without kissing the screen first – and read the message Luke has sent with it.

Goodnight, Mummy! Dot went to sleep very happily and now I'm here lying missing you, as usual. Please let me know what I can do to make things right between us, patatina, so we can be a family again. It's all I want. Sleep well, beautiful xxx

19

Today is Dot's first swimming lesson at Little Splashy Quackers. The local leisure centre offers baby swimming classes for far less than here, but I was won over by the Splashy Quackers' website with its cute underwater photos of babies happily wriggling about in their 'purpose-built pool heated to a balmy thirty-four degrees' and their claim to be 'south-west London's premier baby swimming experts'. For the money they're charging, I'm expecting Dot to be able to swim a length's butterfly (without arm-bands) by the end of the first lesson.

As with any new activity that involves transporting a ticking time bomb from A to B, I have given myself an extra hour to get to the pool to allow for poo-explosions, unscheduled feeds and the origami-like intricacies of the baby buggy. As it happens, however, this morning is one of those rare occasions when Dot doesn't throw any curve-balls, and we arrive at the pool with time to spare and smiles on both our faces. I can't work out why I'm feeling a bit strange – sort of floppy and heavy – until I realise that it must be because I'm actually quite relaxed.

While Dot lies on the changing mat, cooing happily and playing with her toes, I wriggle into my swimming costume, attempting to expose as little porridge-textured flesh as possible. Glancing around the communal changing room, I'm relieved to see that I'm not the only one who's had the idea of wearing a t-shirt over their costume as an extra layer of modesty, although one freak is actually wearing a bikini – and not one of those sporty ones with the sturdy straps, but the kind that's four teeny triangles tied together with dental floss, of the sort you might see on *Love Island*.

All the mums and one brave dad gather by the poolside as the previous class finishes, and we're all doing that thing where you covertly check out everyone else to decide who you might be friends with (not Bikini Woman, obvs). The bold ones are already striking up conversation, but I hang back, glad to have Dot to focus on. I really have no idea when I got so shy; once upon a time I would have already been up front organising the post-swim cocktails ...

'Hi there, everyone! I'm Meredith and I'll be your instructor on this beginners' baby swimming course.'

We all turn to look at the beaming Meredith, who has a broad South African accent – 'Welcome to Luttle Spleshy Queckers!' – and the muscular back and shoulders of a professional swimmer. Both of these things serve to re-assure me that Dot and I are in super-safe hands.

'Right, let's get those babies into the water,' she goes on. 'One at a time now, careful up the steps . . .'

The pool is like a giant bath that you have to climb a ladder to get into. Bikini Woman pushes to the front, keen to be first up the ladder to show off her flawless arse to the rest of us flaccid-rumped mortals. There is not a dimple, crease or blemish in sight; it's like she's made entirely out of plastic. The other mums are giving her envious looks, while the sole dad is openly gawping at the side-boob, under-boob and over-boob on display. My body didn't look anything like that even *before* it made a baby. Perhaps she had hers by surrogate? Yes, that must be it . . .

The water is so blissfully warm it's like taking a dip in the Maldives. Dot is delighted with her new surround-ings, bashing her fists against the water, giggling at the splashes and shrieking with delight. Meanwhile, Bikini Woman's baby is howling so loudly that Meredith has had to temporarily abandon a singalong because none of us can hear what we should do if we're happy and we know it. Bikini Woman looks embarrassed and flustered; I feel an unsisterly pang of Schadenfreude.

The class itself turns out to be more like playtime than an actual lesson, and Dot takes to it immediately. The singing, the splashing, the little rubber ducks they get to push around – she is in her element, and I'm thrilled to have found something that we can enjoy doing together. I'm just wondering if perhaps she's got real talent, and imagining myself as the Judy Murray of the swimming world, getting up at 4 a.m. every morning to drive Dot to training, when Meredith decides to take things up a notch.

'Right, the babies are doing so well I think we'll try our first dip underwater.' A frisson of anxious excitement passes through the group; this is the moment we've been waiting for. 'I'll come round to you individually, one at a time, to show your babies what to do,' adds Meredith.

I am *really* looking forward to this. Honestly, you should see how happy the babies look in the underwater photos on the website – it's like they're in their natural habitat, like little mer-babies! Perhaps I should get Dot a cuter swimsuit for her photos, maybe something with frills . . .

'Right, what's Baby's name?'

It takes me a moment to realise that Meredith is talking to me. *Oh.* I'm really not sure I'm that keen on going first. I mean, I love the idea of Dot swimming underwater *in theory*, but I'd be far happier if someone else's child was the actual guinea pig.

'Dot,' I reply, adding quickly: 'But it's her first time in a swimming pool, so . . .'

'Well, she seems to have taken to it brilliantly!' Meredith either hasn't noticed or is choosing to ignore my concern. 'Right, so what I'm going to do is count to three and then hold Dot under and she'll pop straight up to you, got it? Lots of smiles and encouragement now, Mum!'

'Um, hang on, how do you get them to hold their breath?'

'Well, obviously we can't ask them, can we?' laughs Meredith. 'Come on, Dot, let's show Mum what a clever little girl you are . . .'

But rather than reassuring me, her breezy manner is fanning my nerves and I wonder if I should refuse to let Dot have a go – although surely Meredith knows what she's doing? She's got the right accent and shoulders, after all. The other mums are closely watching this unfold, clutching their babies to them as if to say *thank God it's not me going first*.

'So they just . . . hold their breath automatically?' I persist, still gripping Dot.

'Well, it's not really a question of them actually holding their breath to start with. But babies have a very strong gag reflex up to six months. They lived in water for nine months remember? They're basically little fish.'

She says this as 'feeesh'; it sounds quite sinister. I feel the first flutters of panic.

'Yeah, but that was quite a few months ago now. She's out of practice.'

Meredith laughs as if I'm joking, but I most definitely am *not*.

'Just trust your baby, okay? She'll be absolutely fine.

And she can sense Mum's fear, so let's try to stay nice and calm, shall we?'

But that just makes me stress even more, and although I plaster on a wobbly smile, I'm sure that as I hand Dot to Meredith I'm radiating the same sort of vibes my cavemen ancestors gave off in the presence of sabre-toothed tigers. But everyone's watching, so I can't very well wimp out, can I? While I open and close my mouth in helpless horror, Meredith turns Dot round to face her, counts enthusiastically to three and then holds her under. A moment later Dot pops up to the surface, her face a picture of wide-eyed alarm – which is, after all, exactly the correct response to being drowned. A jet of water shoots out of her mouth like she's a cherub on an ornamental fountain, then she splutters, chokes and starts to wail.

Meredith, however, acts as if Dot's just won gold in the 200m freestyle.

'That was terrific, well done! See, she's a natural!'

'At what – drowning?' I snap, jiggling Dot to calm her cries while trying not to cry myself.

Meredith laughs again and I feel murderous. 'Don't worry, it usually takes a couple of times for Baby to learn to shut her mouth when she goes under,' she says cheerily. 'Now, shall we try again?'

'No!' I shriek, snatching Dot away. 'I mean, can't somebody else have a go first?'

Out of the corner of my eye, I notice Bikini Woman slip quietly out of the pool with her baby.

Dot is still sobbing by the time the class finishes and as I get out of the pool she is clinging onto me like a baby chimpanzee; when I finally manage to prise her from my arm, her fingers leave little red marks. My previous buoyant mood has been destroyed by guilt: for about ten minutes back there swimming was the absolute best thing in Dot's world, but now she's probably got full-blown aquaphobia. I'm not even sure I'll be able to get her in the bath tonight. Meredith assures me she'll be fine by next week, but as far as I'm concerned, that bitch has ruined my daughter's Olympic career.

Thanks to all the trauma, Dot falls asleep the moment I put her in the buggy, so I duck into a café for a coffee. Once I'm sitting down, I automatically reach for my phone to message Luke about the class. Despite everything that's happened, I'm ashamed to admit he is still the first person I want to tell about my day. I can't work out if that makes me a pathetic doormat or if it's a sign that we're meant to be together.

Luke and I have spoken a few times since that argument we had last week about Sigrid, but neither of us has mentioned it again. Although I haven't told him this yet, I've decided to give him the benefit of the doubt and believe his version of events, partly because – as Tabitha wisely pointed out – he does seem genuinely keen to make things right, but also because I dipped my toe in the shark-infested waters of singledom and would rather chew my arm off than go in there again. I shudder as the American's appalled expression flashes into my mind once more ...

Then right on cue, my phone beeps with a message and, as has been my habit this past week, I think, *This is it, the American has reported me, I am going to be fired. Or arrested. Guilty as charged.*

But then rational Annie pipes up and says: *Don't be daft, if he was going to make a complaint he'd have done so by now. You've got away with it.*

Sure enough, the message is nothing to do with any of that mess. What it actually says is this:

How about that lunch, Barb? Like, right now? I've got a job near yours this p.m. Riva xoxo

I break into a relieved smile. This is typical Riva – I mean, talk about leaving it to the last minute to arrange a date – but then I suppose it used to be typically me, too. (There's a party tonight, you say? It's in Edinburgh? And you have to come dressed as your favourite Mr Man? Fab, see you there!) But spontaneity is a thing, like lie-ins and attractive nipples, that is wholly incompatible with raising babies. Riva sends me the address of a restaurant and suggests meeting there in an hour. Dot will undoubtedly be awake and need feeding by then, but in the spirit of being more impulsive, I agree and push aside my worries about sticking to Dot's routine and the fact that in my Gap logo sweatshirt and maternity jeans, I'm not exactly fashion-ready for a date with the woman who dresses Zoe Kravitz for brunch.

20

The place Riva suggests we meet turns out to be a greasy spoon under a railway bridge, its façade grimy with age and pigeon poo. It's certainly not the fashion hangout I was expecting – the only hats you'll see in here are of the hard and yellow variety – but perhaps it's so uncool that it's gone full-circle and is actually cutting-edge? Anyway, I fancy a fry-up and there's plenty of room for Dot's buggy, so it suits me.

Ten minutes later Riva sweeps in, instantly filling the room like she's famous, despite barely scraping five foot. She is clad head to toe in motorbike leathers, right down to the matching gloves and boots, while her hair is as gorgeously untamed as ever.

'Hello, darling.' She kisses me enthusiastically on the lips and scrapes back the neighbouring plastic chair. 'Don't you love this place? It's so authentic.'

'You come here by bike?'

She looks at me blankly. 'Uber, doll.'

I glance pointedly at her outfit.

'Oh, you mean the leathers? Silly! This is Margiela pre-Fall. Stunning, right? Totally worth the clammy crotch ...' Then her eyes fall on the buggy. 'Oh my God, is that yours?'

I smile at her look of wide-eyed shock. 'Didn't I mention I'd had a baby?'

'No, you didn't!' She holds out her arms. 'Gimme gimme, I need a cuddle.'

I glance into the buggy; luckily Dot has just woken up. 'This is Dorothea, known as Dot,' I say, dropping a kiss on her head and then passing her over. 'Dot, say hello to your Auntie Riva.'

'Well well well, my little polka-Dot, aren't *you* just the cutest?' Riva holds her so they're face-to-face, then leans in and whispers conspiratorially: 'We'll forgive Mummy her Gap hoodie for having made such a delicious baby.'

I pull a face at her. 'We came straight from swimming.'

'Babe, the only place that top would be acceptable is if you actually worked in Gap and were being paid to wear it.' She considers me for a moment then adds, hopefully: 'Unless you're wearing it, like, ironically?'

'No, I'm afraid not.'

At least, I don't *think* I am ... Christ, I forgot how complicated fashion can be.

Riva sits Dot on her knee and she grabs delightedly at the glittering jumble of necklaces around her neck. 'Anyway, what's important is that you're here and I'm here and we can have a proper catch-up,' she says. 'I need a full and complete download, starting with how this little one happened . . .'

I forgot what great company Riva is. She has the iron-clad confidence and twinkly charisma of a Hollywood star, plus a bottomless supply of hilarious/astonishing anecdotes which always seem to end along the lines of: 'and then Kendall told Kim she had a fat arse and Kanye pulled out a bottle of George Clooney's tequila and we all got off our fucking heads!' She's so fun and sparky that it's hard not to feel inferior, and I have to remind myself that we actually used to be peers; in fact, crazy as it now seems, I'm pretty sure Riva used to be the one who asked *me* for style advice. But while I've now faded to beige mediocrity, she's still grabbing attention wherever she goes – and it's not just the flamboyant way in which she dresses; she gives off this impression that she *owns* life, that she deserves the very best of everything. Did I really use to be this fabulous too?

Riva barely bats a fake-lashed eyelid when I explain about the situation with Luke. In her world, conventional-ity is the enemy: a husband, two children and a cosy home in the suburbs would be her idea of hell. So things don't work out with the father of your child? Move on, honey! Life is too short for worries or regrets – plus there are plenty more fish in the sea (if you look like Riva, at least). She doesn't see any problem at all with the fact that

I'm potentially a single woman with a small baby; after all, she was once one too, and she's clearly aced it.

Throughout our chat Dot has been perfectly happy sitting on Riva's lap – it helps that all her beads and dangly pendants act like a ready-made baby gym – but now she's started up the low-level fussing that indicates she's getting hungry. Taking care not to flash the rest of the café, I manoeuvre Dot into place and latch her on for a feed.

'Wow, so you're doing the whole ... earth-mother thing, are you?' asks Riva, watching as I struggle to stay decent. 'That's cool. Jethro was on a bottle from day one. I don't think I even tried him on the tit.'

This seems like the perfect moment to ask the question that's been niggling at me since we bumped into each other at the dentist the other week.

'Riva, when Jethro was little, how did you manage to juggle work and motherhood? You made it all look so easy.'

Riva furrows her brow. 'What d'you mean, babe?'

'Well, as far as I remember, having a baby didn't seem to have any impact on your life at all. You carried on working and partying just like before he came along.' Worried this might sound a tad critical, I add: 'I'm only asking because now that I'm a mum, I can barely find time to brush my hair in the morning, let alone hold down a full-time job *and* social life.'

Riva pushes her food around the plate – scrambled

eggs and tomatoes, no toast – and thinks for a while. I'm transfixed by her fingernails, which are super-long and pointy, like claws, and tipped with a sprinkle of tiny black beads. I'm sorry to admit my first thought is: *how on earth does she fit washing-up gloves over those?*

'Well, I suppose Jethro sort of just … slotted into my life,' Riva replies eventually. 'I guess I was lucky; he was a very easy-going baby. And it was always just me – no dad on the scene, right? – so I had no choice but to make the best of it.'

'So you didn't have any help with Jethro at all?'

'Nah, not really,' she says, then gestures to the woman at the counter for two more teas, seemingly considering the subject closed.

I, however, have a million more questions.

'But what did you do with Jethro while you were working?'

Riva tips her head to one side, thinking hard; this is obviously ancient history to her. 'Well, when he was tiny, Jeth was happy sitting in his car seat while I got on with my shit, then as he got bigger I suppose he'd … crawl around the set when I was working. He's always been a gypsy child – he's got a curious spirit, y'know? Never happier than when we're off on some mad adventure. God, I remember this one shoot for *Grazia* …'

She launches into a story of how baby Jethro ended up charming the g-string off a famous model who then insisted on having him in the magazine photos with her, then segues into an anecdote about being in the Four Seasons in LA styling an Oscar-nominated actress and finding the then-toddler Jethro curled up asleep in a pile of couture Versace – 'I mean, isn't that the *cutest*?' – and my heart gradually sinks, because her account of motherhood with its effortless fun and bohemian glamour has so little in common with my own experience of what it's like looking after a baby on a day-to-day basis. If I didn't have a child, I'd probably be listening to Riva and thinking, *yes, that sounds both feasible and fun!* – but I *do* have a child, and personally I've never found Dot able to occupy herself for more than a couple of minutes while I 'get on with my shit', let alone for a whole day. As if to validate my point, at that very moment Dot suddenly pulls off my boob to have a look around, exposing my nipple to a table of builders. Now *that's* the reality of motherhood for me, right there! As for the whole 'gypsy child' thing, in my experience, children are so conservative and such sticklers for routine that they make Jacob Rees-Mogg look like Noughties-era Kate Moss. Or perhaps I just have a particularly uptight baby.

'But didn't you find the lack of sleep difficult?' I plough on, wrestling Dot back into place. 'Where did you get your energy from?'

'God, I honestly don't remember. Maybe I was just high the whole time!'

She laughs, but my face must betray the fact that I'm wondering whether this might have actually been the case, because she shrieks: 'Babe, I'm joking!'

At that moment the waitress brings over our teas and Riva beams at her – 'thank you, sweetheart, so kind' – then pushes her barely touched lunch to one side and folds her arms on the table, in a gesture that blatantly declares CHANGE OF SUBJECT.

'So tell me,' she says, 'what's happening with the photography?'

I hesitate for a moment, unsure how much I should tell her. My new job isn't exactly glamorous, after all. Perhaps I'll just say I'm taking a career break while Dot is little . . .

'You better not tell me that you've quit,' warns Riva. 'Out of all of us, you were the one with the real talent.'

'That's lovely of you to say.'

'Well it's true.' Then she smiles at me with real affection, and despite the fact we've not spoken in so long, it's like we're right back where we were all those years ago, hard-partying partners in crime. 'Please tell me you're still taking photos?'

And so I tell her about the Curtis Kinderbey job, and she seems genuinely interested and asks lots of questions and I begin to think that actually, yeah, it *is* a pretty fun job, and if Riva thinks it's cool then I really shouldn't be embarrassed about it.

'So what's your Insta name?' asks Riva, pulling out her phone. 'I'm going to find you now . . .'

'Um, I'm not actually on Instagram.'

She stares at me, wide-eyed and slack-mouthed, as if I'd just admitted a liking for M&S elasticated-waist slacks. 'What the fuck, Barb? You're one of the few people who actually *should* be on it!'

'I just don't have a particularly Instagrammable life these days.'

'Girl, everyone's life is Instagrammable, you just need to edit it. Give me your phone.'

'Honestly, it's fine, I . . .'

Riva shoots me a stern look and holds out her hand. '*Babe.*'

I hand it over and peer across nervously as Riva swiftly swipes through my photo feed, which is mainly filled with pictures of Dot. At least there's zero chance she'll find any dick pics . . .

'Oh my God, I love that image,' she says, eyes lighting up. 'And look at this one!' She holds up my phone with the picture of the roses and vintage Chanel bag on the marble worktop that I took in that client's house a few weeks ago.

'You've got the best eye, seriously,' Riva goes on. 'You don't even need a filter on that.'

'Yeah, I was lucky, the lighting was perfect . . .'

'Not luck, Barb – *talent*. Don't sell yourself short, babe. And that vintage Chanel 2.55 – I die! Is it yours?'

'Oh no, it . . . belongs to a friend.' I really don't want to go into the details of my sordid sideline sneaking photos of clients' possessions.

'And check out this one!' It's the photo of the Chinese vase that I took in the penthouse of doom last week. 'Seriously, you need to get this shit online. Promise me you'll set yourself up on Insta?'

I make a non-committal sort of noise, which I hope will be enough to satisfy Riva.

'You better,' she says warningly – and then all of a sudden her face lights up with the wide-eyed triumph of a Eureka moment. 'Right, I've made a decision: you're going to be my new project.'

Uh-oh, not sure I like the sound of this. 'What do you mean?'

'I'm gonna make it my mission to help you get your groove back.' She beams. 'Operation Save Barb! I mean, this estate agency job is cool for now, yeah, but we need to get you back to what you were doing before, right? And my first task – after making sure you're on Instagram and getting all the right people to follow you – will be to sort out a reunion with all the old gang.'

'That's so sweet of you to offer, Riva, really, but you don't need to go to all that trouble on my behalf, honestly . . .'

'Barb!' She glares at me. 'I'm doing it, and you're coming. It'll be fun! You can network! Is Friday or Saturday night better for you? Oh, and don't you dare turn up wearing Gap . . .'

This is getting out of hand. It's been lovely meeting Riva for lunch, but the idea of going to some pretentious private members' club with a bunch of stylists makes me sweaty-palmed with panic. Old, forgotten feelings, dating back to when the other pupils shrieked 'Big Nose' at me in the corridor, stir unpleasantly inside me. An image flashes into my mind: me, standing in a bar, surrounded by fashion people all pointing and laughing at my boot-cut jeans and Mumsnet hairdo. No bloody thanks. I need to nip this in the bud ASAP.

'Riva, I'm so glad we're in touch again, but I'm not sure a reunion is a good idea. I'm just not part of that world anymore. I won't have anything in common with any of the old crew.'

'They won't care! They'll just be psyched to see you, like I was.' She grabs her phone and starts scrolling. 'Right, I'll call Delphine, Farrah, Mimi of course, Nick . . . I suppose I should ask Tara, and Tyler – ooh, and Tomo . . .'

She mentions his name casually – I'm not sure she even knows that he and I had an on–off thing together – but the prospect of coming face-to-face with the most beautiful man I have ever seen, let alone had between my legs, sends my already agitated insides into a tailspin. Back then my quirkiness and swagger – combined with my super-cool job – made up for the fact that I'm no supermodel, but now I've got nothing to hide behind. To put it bluntly, without the Barbra Streisand make-up and kaftans, my big nose is simply that: a fucking big nose. As Riva rattles away, excitedly making plans, the idea of what Tomo will think when he sees who I am now makes my stomach plunge like I've got vertigo. There's no way I'm putting myself through that ordeal. I'll just cancel nearer the time.

21

Wednesday morning is the weekly office meeting at Curtis Kinderbey, attendance of which is non-negotiable by order of Kaiser Karl. In theory, this is a chance for the whole CK team to come together to share updates and generate ideas; in reality it's an opportunity for the pushiest sales guys to boast about their commissions and for the rest of us to watch as the huge timer projected on a screen at the end of the room ticks down the minutes to zero, like something out of *The Hunger Games*.

'What the hell is that?' I muttered to Fi when I first came to one of these meetings, nodding at the ominous black numbers on the screen.

'Grim, isn't it?' she replied. 'Karl read that Google have a timer in team meetings to make sure everyone stays focused, so now we do as well.'

We also have to stand for the whole meeting because this is what they do at Facebook, although Karl gets to sit down because he strained his groin dead lifting. I'm

pretty sure Mark Zuckerberg keeps his meetings brief –
that surely being the whole rationale behind the
standing – but Karl is not interested in such technicali-
ties, which means that everyone is sore and grumpy by
the end of the hour-long session. The only good thing
about these weekly meetings is the unlimited croissants,
muffins and cappuccinos, laid on because this is what
they do at Apple – or at least this is what Fi *told* Karl they
do at Apple. Thankfully he hasn't checked whether or not
this is actually the case. Fi and I are now thinking about
telling Karl that Microsoft sends staffers on annual all-
expenses-paid holidays to encourage blue-sky thinking.

'. . . and so I said to the vendor, "Coxtons may have
their own fleet of branded Mini Coopers, but are their
sales advisors at the end of the phone 24/7 to help secure
the best offer for your home? No! Are they prepared to
do *whatever it takes* to keep their clients happy? I don't
think so!"'

There is a smattering of applause – led by Karl – as
senior sales associate Erin Maxwell concludes her Power-
point presentation, 'Hustle and Tenacity: the Secrets of
Success'.

I lean towards Fi, who is slumped against the wall next
to me, her high heels abandoned on the floor nearby, and
whisper: 'Are you *meant* to be on call 24/7?'

'Are we fuck,' mutters Fi. 'She's just sucking up to Karl
because they're shagging.'

'Thank you, Erin,' says Karl, reclining in his comfy chair at the head of the table. 'Moving forward, I think we can all pick up Erin's ideas and run with them, yeah? Now, let's hear from Stuart on the uptick in the short-term lettings market ...'

I zone out again and look around the room at the other attendees, whose expressions run the full gamut of bored, boreder and boredest. Rudy, who is standing opposite me on the other side of the room, has his arms folded and eyes closed; when I glance back at him a few minutes later, he hasn't moved. Could he actually be asleep? My eyes wander around aimlessly in search of something to occupy the remaining 14:28 minutes, until they land on Karl's 'Brown-nose Board' (not its official name), which is where our leader sticks up selfies of himself with his heroes, mostly motivational speakers and bodybuilders, with the idea being to remind us that 'anything is pos-sible'. The rest of us are encouraged to bring in photos too, although the only non-Karl pictures currently on the board are a blurry snap of deputy receptionist Irene with her arms thrown around a startled Richard Madeley, and Kev the IT bloke doing a thumbs up next to Grumpy Cat.

I put my hand into my pocket and wrap my fingers around my phone, itching to pull it out, but in addition to lower-back pain, another consequence of Karl's standing policy is that it's impossible to sneak a look at your phone during the meeting. I posted a new picture to Instagram this morning – it's a shot of this exquisite antique rocking horse I found in the bedroom of an apartment in a church conversion yesterday – and I'm desperate to check how it's doing. Yes, just one week on Instagram and I'm already a diehard 'like' junkie.

I'd thought about what Riva had said on the bus back to Streatham after our lunch. She did have a point: why *wasn't* I on Instagram? Barb definitely would have been, but then she had plenty of material. I suppose I could fill my feed with pictures of Dot – she is, after all, the most beautiful, brilliant and fascinating child in the world, and I love taking photos of her – but I'm not sure how I feel about sharing my daughter with strangers. Out of interest, I look up Riva's profile; it is filled with pictures of her celebrity mates, white-sand beaches, copious #OOTDs (including the motorbike leathers she wore to meet me) and the occasional motivational quote. Her Insta posing was impressively on point: there was the knee pop, the casual glance over the shoulder, the adjusting the hair while standing pigeon-toed and looking at the ground laughing (experts only for that one) and the long-distance stare with hands in pockets. None of her son, Jethro, but I suppose that's fair enough. Distilled into those seductive little squares, Riva's life looked even more enviable than the glittering reality, and a quick browse through the profiles of some of her followers yielded yet more of the same: chic restaurants, vegan smoothies and thigh gaps. And how many palm-fringed infinity pools *are* there in the world? Or does everyone just take photos in the same one? *This is not my world*, I thought to myself with a shudder, and went back to nice, safe Facebook with its 80s movie quizzes, photos of World Book Day costumes and kitten gifs.

Then a couple of days later, I went to photograph a townhouse in Stockwell, and while measuring for the floor plan, I came across a gorgeous Le Corbusier chaise in the master bedroom. I get this tingling feeling in my stomach whenever I see the makings of a great photo, but I knew that this needed an extra something, so I had a rummage in the wardrobe and found a classic Burberry trench, which I draped artfully over the chaise. I spent a little while tweaking the coat and adjusting the curtains to get the lighting just right, and the resulting shot was seriously impressive. I gazed at it for a while, enjoying the way the coat's checked lining contrasted with the cow-skin upholstery and the flash of sunlight on the chrome frame. I knew it deserved a wider audience.

At first I thought: well, there's absolutely no way I can put this on Instagram. What if somebody recognised their stuff? I'd be in deep shit. Nah, not worth the risk, no matter how good the photo. But on the way to my next job, I looked at it again, and then scrolled back through all the other covert photos I'd taken over the past few weeks, and I could just see how great they'd look displayed together on Instagram. A collection of beautiful things photographed in a beautiful way; it would certainly make a nice change from all the bums-in-bikini-bottoms shots.

After putting Dot to bed that night, I Googled how many people there are on Instagram and it turns out it's something like 800 million! The chances of somebody finding my photo of their particular Le Corbusier chaise or Chanel bag would be infinitesimal, surely? And if they did somehow stumble onto my profile, they wouldn't necessarily recognise the things as their own, would they? Plus, it's not like I'd be silly enough to put a photo of myself up there.

It took me a while to come up with an Instagram handle. I couldn't use my own name, obviously, but I liked the idea of creating a whole new identity for myself. My photos look like they belong to someone who lives in Chelsea, flies private jet and has a passion for fine art, so I decided to call myself 'ArbiterofCool'. I know – ridiculous, right? There I was, in my attic bedsit in Streatham, breast-milk stains on my old Primark t-shirt and my hair tied up with a pair of knickers, making out I was Victoria Beckham's richer and more glamorous BFF.

Nevertheless, thanks to Riva following me – and getting her friends to do the same – 'ArbiterofCool' already has over 300 followers. One commenter, 'Lifestyle_Curator', actually wrote: 'wish I had your life!!!' followed by a wink, applause, and three heart-eye emojis. I very nearly replied, 'I'm sitting here eating beans out of a can LOL!!!' but instead just graciously liked their comment; no point bursting their bubble, after all. Anyway, I'm finding it a real buzz to have an audience for my photography again, and with each new 'like' or thumbs-up emoji, I feel a tiny shred of my self-confidence returning. I'm just so glad that Riva talked me into it.

When the team meeting is over – there's a mass exodus the second the timer ticks to 00:00 – I join Fi at her desk, blissfully sinking into the hard office chair like it's made out of clouds and kittens. It's still only mid-morning, but it already feels like we've done a full day's hard graft. While Fi checks her email, I get out my phone to check Instagram: sixty-two likes for the rocking horse photo already! I knew it was a good'un . . .

'Hello? Annie?'

I look up from the screen to find Fi glaring as if she's just said something vitally important and I missed it because I was fiddling with my phone. Which I obviously had.

'Sorry, what was that?'

'I was telling you that Finn's booked us a weekend in Amsterdam in April, and that I think he's going to propose.'

'Really? Wow, that's amazing!' I'm careful to sound as thrilled as possible, but alarm bells have started to ring.

'Yup. It's going to happen this time, I'm absolutely positive.' She holds out a packet. 'Munchie?'

'Thanks.' I take two and chew very slowly, trying to decide whether I should tell Fi what's on my mind, and by the time I've swallowed I've decided that yes, as her friend, I really should.

'Um, Fi, why do you think Finn is going to propose?'

She looks at me like it's obvious. 'Why else would he be booking a mini-break in April?'

'Maybe . . . to have a little holiday?'

She shakes her head, irritated. 'No, I'm telling you, he's going to ask me to marry him. The timing is spot on. It's nearly fifteen and a half years since our first kiss.'

'I just don't want you to get your hopes up . . .'

'Annie.' Fi gives me a stern look. 'He's going to do it this time. I *know* he is.'

As you can probably tell, this is not the first time Fi has been convinced Finn is about to propose. I hate to be pessimistic, but in the ten years that we've been friends, I've lost count of the number of restaurant dates, holidays, Christmases, birthdays and Valentine's Days that were absolutely definitely going to end with him getting down on one knee. Fiona is the ballsiest person I know – she once hitch-hiked across the Australian outback *on her own* – yet her attitude to marriage is straight out of a Jane Austen novel.

The last time this issue came up was on their skiing

holiday shortly before Christmas. Every day while they were away, Fi would text me:

Dinner at a mountaintop restaurant tonight – here we go!!!

Bobsledding this morning – think this is the day! Wish me luck!!!

Do u think he might propose on a chair lift?!! Hope I don't drop the feckin' ring!

When she returned home ring-free, there was the standard forty-eight hours of ranting about how she was much too good for that feckin' loser, and how he'd only have himself to blame if she dumped his sorry arse, then it blew over and they went back to being the happiest, most rock solid couple I know – until the next time a potential opportunity for a proposal arose, then we're back to planning her engagement party and debating the merits of diamonds versus sapphires. I once told Fi she should take matters into her own hands and propose to *him*, but you'd think I'd just suggested she join the priesthood.

At that moment Rudy slopes past Fi's desk, engrossed in some property particulars.

'Hey,' he says with a slight nod in my direction as he goes by.

'Hang on a sec, were you asleep during the team meeting just now?'

He pauses, looks back and nods.

'Impressive,' I say.

'I don't sleep much at night.' He turns to leave, then stops and looks back again. 'Will you still be in the office at lunchtime?'

'Yup, I've got to wait around to collect some keys.'

'Do you want to grab a sandwich?'

'Together?'

He shrugs, as if not remotely bothered either way. 'If you like.'

'Sure,' I say, a little surprised, 'that would be great.'

'Okay. Well – whatever.' Then he gives another shrug and heads off.

Fi watches him stride back to his desk and turns to me, suspicion in her eyes.

'What's going on with you and yer man over there?'

'What do you mean?' I don't think I've ever chatted to Fi about Rudy; we've always got so much else to talk about.

Fi darts a look over to his desk and back to me again. 'Well, he's barely ever said a word to me – or anyone else in the office – and now he's asking you on a date?'

I give a bark of laughter. 'I don't think you can call getting a sandwich a date.'

'I'd watch him if I were you. Not sleeping at night – I ask you! He creeps me right out.'

'Come on, Fi, you just need to get to know him. He's a really nice guy.'

'Weird, more like,' she mutters. 'Well, I hope the two of

you and your little vampire babies will be very happy together. Now, I need your help deciding what I'm going to wear when Finn pops the question . . .'

While we're clicking through 'Occasion Dresses' on ASOS, I glance over to where Rudy is sitting, typing feverishly at his keyboard, one leg frantically tapping away as if possessed. What a daft thing to suggest, that he was asking me on a date! Aside from the fact that we don't fancy each other, I'm old enough to be his mother – well, near enough.

'Annie?' I look round to see Karl's head sticking out of his office door; he spots me and beckons. 'Need you in here, Annie, pronto.'

'Be right there,' I reply as he disappears back inside.

'What's that about?' asks Fi.

'Dunno.' I shrug. 'I'll be back in a sec. Check if they've got that red skater dress in your size . . .'

In his office Karl is sitting behind his desk, an unsettling look on his face, his fingers steepled in front of him like he's a Bond villain. Put it this way: a fluffy white cat wouldn't look out of place in this scenario.

'Close the door behind you, Annie.'

I do as he says. 'What's up?'

Karl gestures impatiently to the seat on the opposite side of his desk. 'I've just taken a call from Brad Michaelson.'

Sitting down, I try to place the name. *Brad Michaelson* . . . Nah, doesn't ring any bells. 'Do I know him?'

'He's the American guy who owns that £3.2 mill pent-house on the river you did the pictures for a couple of weeks ago.'

My mouth drops open; I immediately shut it again. I try to swallow, but my mouth is so dry I just make a weird choking noise. I nod and plaster on a smile on my face, hoping it will distract from the fact that the rest of me is *freaking the fuck out*.

'It looks like we've got a problem,' says Karl, reclining in his chair with an exaggerated sigh. 'Or rather, *you've* got a problem.'

22

Now that the moment I was dreading has arrived, I feel a sort of calm acceptance. I'm in trouble, I'm not going to be able to talk my way out of it, so I'm just going to have to go with the flow, right up shit creek. It's simply the latest episode in the sorry soap opera my life has become – although if this was a plot line on *EastEnders* you'd think it a bit far-fetched.

It *is* mortifying though, sitting here opposite Karl knowing that he thinks I'm a sexual predator. I feel myself shrinking into the chair and my hands fold themselves together primly on my lap; my subconscious is clearly trying to make me appear as chaste and non-sexpest-like as possible.

Karl is still leaning back in his chair with his eyes focused beadily on me; I assume he's expecting me to grovel a bit before he fires me, which is fair enough.

'I am so sorry, Karl,' I begin, earnestly emphasising each word. 'I have absolutely no excuse for what happened; it was completely unprofessional and I can only apologise unreservedly.'

Karl stares at me blankly. 'Apologise for what?'

Well, that throws me. It's almost as if he doesn't have a clue what I'm talking about . . . Jesus, could this actually be about something else? Which would be excellent, except now I've just admitted to being totally unprofessional.

'Well, what I actually meant was . . .' I can't for the life of me think of an alternative reason as to why I might be grovelling. 'You see . . . the thing is . . .'

To my relief, Karl interrupts with an impatient wave of his hand.

'Listen, this Brad character – typical Yank – saw the pictures you took of his place and he wasn't happy. Not happy at all.'

This is so not what I was expecting to hear that I can only manage a sort of 'mmm' sound.

'Long story short,' Karl continues, 'he's decided to completely redecorate the apartment before putting the place back on the market. Apparently the current decor was too much of a "bachelor cliché".' He rolls his eyes. 'Personally, I thought it looked pretty sharp, but that's Americans for you . . . Anyway, it means you're going to have to go back once the paint's dried and take a whole new set of photos.'

'Right, I see. And – that's it?'

'Yeah. That's it.'

'This guy didn't mention any other . . . issues?'

'No. In fact, he actually made a point of telling me how pleased he was with the pictures, and was quite apologetic about causing hassle.' Karl reaches for his protein shake. 'To be honest, I think it's his fiancée that's to blame for his change of heart over the decor. He's always mentioning her – 'oh, Serena wants five bathrooms' and 'Serena must have underfloor heating'. It's crystal clear who wears the trousers in that relationship.' He gives a snort of laughter. 'Or rather, who wears the pants!'

Ah, so the American – Brad Michaelson, as I should start thinking of him – is engaged. But why should that be a surprise? He's hot, funny and kind (as proven by him not reporting my appalling behaviour): that's the holy trinity, right there. If you were playing man-bingo, Brad Michaelson would be a full house. So of course he would have been snapped up yonks ago – and by the undoubtedly stunning Serena. But while I'm shaky with relief that I'm in the clear, at the same time I feel a cold ache of disappointment. Despite our disastrous encounter at the penthouse, deep down a tiny part of me – a misguided ovary, perhaps, or a deluded pancreas – must have been quite taken with the guy.

Karl, who has been noisily slurping the dregs of his shake, clearly takes my confused expression to mean that I didn't get his joke.

'It's what Americans call trousers, Annie. *Pants*.' He

gives a tetchy sigh and gestures to the door. 'I'll let you know when you need to head over to the property to take another set of pictures. Oh, and Annie?'

I pause, already halfway out of the office. 'Yes?'

'Whatever it was you were apologising for earlier . . .' He pauses, scrutinising me through narrowed eyes. 'Just make sure it doesn't happen again, alright?'

And then he nods, as if to dismiss me, and I plaster on another smile and say a silent, heartfelt *thank you* to Karl for not interrogating me any further, because I have absolutely no idea what excuse I would have come up with. Yet although the imminent threat of being exposed as a pervert has disappeared, a brand new worry is now looming ominously in its place: I'm going to have to return to the penthouse to take a new set of photos, which means potentially coming face to face with Brad Michaelson again.

I stay well out of Karl's way for the rest of the morning, keeping my head down at the spare desk in the corner where I kill time editing photos, and the second I notice Rudy putting on his coat I make a dash for the door. I catch Fi's eye on the way out and she gives me a look that plainly says: 'You'd better watch yourself, missus, I don't trust that fella. Oh, and please bring me back a chicken salad on granary, no mayo, cheers, darlin'.'

You might think this is an awful lot to infer from just a look, but we've known each other for a long time – and Fi does have unusually expressive eyebrows.

Rudy sets off at quite a pace, striding out like he's hiking across a moor, and I have to trot to keep up: a stumpy-legged dachshund to his loping lurcher. I'm not particularly short, but Rudy makes me feel tiny – height-wise, at least. His waist measurement is probably half of mine.

'Italian place round the corner alright with you?' he asks.

'Absolutely,' I reply, a little out of breath.

And that's the full extent of our conversation on our way to lunch – but then, we're not going at a pace that invites casual chat. Besides, I've got used to Rudy's silences now, and don't find them nearly as uncomfortable as I used to.

We hit the café at peak lunch hour, but while Rudy orders at the counter I manage to grab a table. It's squashed between a large communal table and a display of boxes of amaretto biscuits, which wobbles ominously as I edge my way into my seat. There's barely enough room for one person to sit here, let alone two, and when Rudy returns with our sandwiches he stops in front of our midget table with a look that says: *and where am I supposed to go?*

'Sorry, it's a bit cosy,' I say. 'Perhaps you should sit on my lap?'

I mean obviously, I'm joking – look at my face! See my wry smile! – but Rudy frowns.

'It's okay, I'll take the chair,' he says, sliding carefully into place.

Honestly, at times I do still wonder if he might not be entirely human; he gets this 'does not compute' expression which is pretty much one hundred per cent cyborg.

Still, at least my parma ham and mozzarella sandwich looks good.

'Thanks for this,' I say, struggling to eat without shoving an elbow in Rudy's face or destroying the leaning tower of biscuits. 'How much do I owe you?'

'Don't worry, I can expense it. Karl's asked me to have a chat with you – apparently I'm meant to be your Curtis Kinderbey mentor. He wants me to check you're being adequately indoctrinated.'

He says all this with a slight grimace that suggests it's all a massive inconvenience. So getting lunch together wasn't Rudy's idea, after all? I feel a pang of disappointment. Silly as it sounds, I quite liked the fact that out of everyone in the office, Rudy seemed to have singled me out for friendship.

'Ah, right,' I mumble. 'I see.'

Rudy continues to stare at me. 'So – are you?'

'Am I what?'

'Being adequately indoctrinated?'

I scrutinise his expression; as ever, it's impossible to tell whether he's being serious.

'Do you, for instance,' he goes on, 'have any idea what Curtis Kinderbey's turnover was last year?'

'Um . . .'

'Do you know who Curtis – or indeed Kinderbey – is or was?'

I just gawp at him. Am I really meant to be able to answer that?

'Can you name Karl's favourite flavour protein shake?'

'Cookies and Cream!' I reply at once.

'Well done, passed with flying colours. I'll report back to Karl.' And then he breaks into a grin that makes his mismatched eyes shine, and I finally feel I'm back on firmer ground.

We eat for a little while in silence, the noise and bustle of the café padding the gap in our conversation, and I'm over halfway through my sandwich when Rudy abruptly announces: 'So I have news. I've got an audition.'

'Oh my God, that's fantastic, congratulations! What's it for?'

'A musical.'

I get a mental image of Rudy flailing about in tap shoes doing jazz hands.

'I'm actually not a bad singer,' he adds a little defensively, as if reading my mind.

'No, I'm sure you're brilliant,' I say quickly. 'So what's the musical? This is *so* exciting . . .'

'It's called *A Star is Born*.'

'No way! As in the Streisand film?'

He nods. 'That's the one. I'm a huge Barbra fan.'

'Me too! In fact, at one time I was *obsessed*. I used to

dress the same as her – my work friends even called me Barb.'

'Yeah, now you mention it, I can definitely see the similarity,' says Rudy, nodding, and my hand flies to my face in embarrassment.

'It's the nose, isn't it? Except Barbra makes a great big conk look a million times better than I ever could.'

As I say this, it occurs to me that my nose has been particularly bothering me lately. I once read that your nose and ears are the only parts of you that never stop growing, which is why you see those old men who look like the BFG; perhaps mine is actually getting bigger? I've found myself comparing it with other people's noses when I'm on the bus or tube, and it's rare I'll see one as enormous as mine, certainly on a girl. I used to be proud of my nose, but that was when I worked in fashion where uniqueness is prized above all else (which is why you get some truly bonkers-looking models). The real world, however, is far happier if you blend in – and that's tricky when you have the nasal equivalent of a flashing neon sign in the middle of your face.

Rudy, who has been openly scrutinising my features, asks: 'Don't you like your big nose?'

I can't help but laugh. Other people would be all, *ooh, it's not that big*, but Rudy is honest to the point of bluntness – and it's actually refreshing. I start to mutter something about how my nose and I have had a chequered history, but then, inspired by Rudy's direct manner, I start again.

'No, I don't like it. I used to, because I appreciated that it was different, but now it makes me feel . . . not pretty.' I shrug. 'I'd really prefer if it was less noticeable.'

Rudy smiles. 'You should be lucky to have such a large nose,' he declares, his voice rich and sonorous, as if he's reciting a Shakespeare sonnet. 'It acts as a rudder, and will steer you through the life's troubled waters.'

Wow, where did that come from? It's like he switched to actor mode; I get a glimpse of how incredible he'd be on stage.

Rudy is clearly pleased at the effect his speech has had. 'It's a quote from one of my favourite novels,' he explains. '*Jitterbug Perfume*. You should read it.'

'Why, good PR for the gigantic-nosed, is it?'

Rudy considers me for a while longer, and I feel myself shrinking from his penetrating gaze. Embarrassed, I turn my attention to what's left of my sandwich. After a moment he says: 'Why are you so down on yourself, Annie?'

'That's ridiculous, I am not!'

His voice is gentle. 'I'm not criticising you. I just think it's a shame that you're not kinder to yourself. You have so much to be proud of.'

I feel my insides tensing. To my horror, I feel like I'm going to cry. 'You barely know me.'

'You're right, but from what you have told me, you've had a lot to deal with in your life – things that any of us would struggle with. Having a smaller nose won't change that, though.'

I stare fiercely at my hands, at a loss how to reply. This is all too close to the bone. I admit that I have occasionally wondered whether Luke would have cheated on me if I had a cute little button nose like Sigrid. The truth is I probably *am* in desperate need of a rudder to steer me through the troubled waters of life: most of the time I feel completely out of control, careering from one crisis to the next, while everyone else seems to glide serenely along. The only time I feel remotely good about myself these days is when somebody likes one of my Instagram photos: that's how flimsy my self-esteem is right now. I swallow down the lump that's suddenly appeared in my throat; this really isn't a conversation I want to be having with Rudy.

'Thank you for the pep talk,' I manage, plastering on a shaky smile. 'You're very wise, Rudy. What's that expression . . . ? Old beyond your years.'

He considers this for a moment. 'I guess I've just always preferred hanging out with older people. My other half jokes I should be called Grandad. At least, I think it's a joke . . .'

For such an innocent, throwaway comment, this hits me like a truck; I think my jaw might literally drop. It hadn't even occurred to me that Rudy might be *dating* someone – probably because it's such a normal, human thing to do, which is totally at odds with his whole 'vampire robot from Mars' vibe. I'm desperate to ask more about this mysterious 'other half', but Rudy's already putting on his coat.

'We better get back to the office,' he says. 'I've got a viewing in half an hour.'

I nod and start to gather up my things, but as I get up to follow him out, he pauses and turns to look at me again.

'For what it's worth, Annie, I like your nose,' he says. 'It holds your face together.'

Then he sets off towards the door, and as I follow him out of the café, weaving through the closely packed tables, I find myself wondering why, whenever I speak to Rudy, I always end up baring my soul to him. He has this uncanny knack for cutting through all the social niceties and getting right to the heart of who I am and how I feel, while giving away next to nothing about himself. It's really quite unnerving.

23

As I walk into the kitchen, Jess gives an ear-piercing wolf-whistle of the type you hear from particularly non-woke scaffolders. It's so loud that Dot, who's in my arms drinking her breakfast bottle, jumps and immediately starts to howl.

'Wow, Mama looks *hot* this morning,' marvels Jess, ignoring the wailing. 'What's the occasion?'

'I'm just going to work.'

'Are those new jeans? They make your bum look awesome.'

'Yeah, well, as you kept telling me, it was about time I replaced my maternity ones.'

'And . . . are you wearing eyeliner?' She peers at me more closely. 'Yes, you've got your Barb flicks back on. Very nice.'

'I just thought I'd try something a bit different.' It actually took me five attempts to get the lines to match, which came as a shock because not so long ago I could apply perfect eyeliner in a dark club while pissed.

Jess eyes me with suspicion. 'It seems to me you're making an awful lot of effort for 8 a.m., Miss Taylor.'

'I could say the same about you,' I reply, taking in her marabou-trimmed robe, artfully messy bun and three different shades of eyeshadow.

'Me? I got out of bed like this,' she says with a Mona Lisa smile. 'Have you got time for a coffee before you leave?'

I settle Dot in her bouncy chair, where she resumes her bottle while fixing Jess with a baby death-stare, and perch on a stool at the island. A fruit bowl sits in the middle of the counter, except rather than apples and bananas, it holds Jess' five-a-day of colourful foil-wrapped condoms.

'So come on, hon, what's with all the pre-breakfast sexiness?' Jess pauses in the middle of spooning coffee into the cafetière. 'Ooh, have you got an appointment with your fuckable dentist?'

'No! I told you, I'm going to work.'

And I *am* going to work. That is the absolute truth. I'd just rather not tell Jess *where* I'm going to work – and luckily I don't have to, because at that moment a penis walks into the kitchen.

'Hey, gorgeous,' it says to Jess. 'Where's that coffee you promised . . . oh fuck, you've got a *baby*!'

The penis – or rather, the heavily muscled man attached to it – recoils, girlishly horrified, at the sight of Dot in her bouncer. I rush to cover my daughter's eyes so she's not scarred for life and Jess howls with glee.

'She's not mine, silly! This is my adorable housemate, Dottie, and her marginally less adorable mum, Annie.'

'Oh right. Phew.' The penis' owner gives a grunt of a chuckle. 'Hi, I'm Joe,' he says, sticking out his hand to me, which I shake with just the tips of my fingers because I *really* don't want to know where it's been. Nobody (apart from me) seems remotely fazed by the fact that he's starkers.

'I'll bring the coffee up in a sec,' says Jess. 'You go up and keep the bed warm, okay, babe?'

Joe grunts a farewell, turns and leaves. You can tell he's flexing his arse as he saunters out: he clenches with every step. It's hypnotic.

'That was Joe.' Jess grins, once he's safely contained upstairs. 'Quite something, isn't he? We met in the gym.'

'Yes, he's obviously very, um, body confident,' I offer, struggling to come up with something polite to say about him that doesn't involve his nether regions.

'And with good reason, wouldn't you say?' Jess smirks. (Honestly, it's like she's reading from a particularly clichéd sitcom script.) 'Anyway, I think I'm going to be working from home today. And I'll probably be working *quite hard* – just to give you a heads-up if you and Dot plan on getting back early.'

'Thank you very much for the warning.'

Jess pours me a coffee, and I can tell she's checking out my make-up again. 'Come on, spill the beans, Annie.

Since having Dot you've been so low-maintenance you've almost gone full cavewoman. Don't get me wrong, I'm thrilled you've decided to rejoin civilised womanhood, and I'll happily get Mara back again to give you a once-over, but all this' – she waves her hands in front of me – 'has got to be for something – or someone . . .' She suddenly gawps. 'Oh God, you're not meeting up with Luke, are you? Shit, please tell me you're not planning on moving back in with that arsehole?'

'God, no! I haven't even thought about that.'

And it's true, things have gone very quiet on that front – which is entirely down to me. I know I'm putting off making a decision about our future, but I'm terrified by the enormity of what is at stake: basically my daughter's entire well-being and happiness, not to mention my own. What if I make the wrong decision? It's almost like I'm waiting for a sign, for something that will definitely prove that I can trust Luke again – or, more likely, that I can't.

I take a sip of coffee, trying to decide whether I should tell Jess what I'm really up to today. I'm embarrassed to tell her the reason that I'm looking marginally less shabby this morning, but at the same time I could really do with her advice. After all, she's the one with the penis in her kitchen: she's clearly good at this shit.

'Okay,' I say, putting down my mug. 'So, this morning I've got to go back to the penthouse to take more photos.' I pause. 'You know, the penthouse *with the American.*'

I watch Jess' face as the penny drops. 'Ah, I see. The *engaged* American, would that be?'

'I haven't forgotten, don't worry. And I'm not for one moment planning on trying to tempt him away from his fiancée, if that's what you're thinking. *Christ*, no.' I shake my head for emphasis. 'Ideally I wouldn't go back there at all, but I can't get out of it – and believe me, I've tried. I even had a go at persuading Karl that the agency shouldn't take on his property because this guy's fiancée was proving so difficult, but it's a really gorgeous apartment and Karl's in line for a whopping great commission when he sells it, so . . .' I tail off, shrugging. 'Anyway, I decided that if I had to face the American again, it would be better not to turn up looking completely rough. It's going to be excruciating enough as it is without him being repulsed by my saggy jeans and dull hair. I thought that if I made a bit of an effort, he might think: "Well, she's not *that* minging, so I should probably be flattered that she tried to force herself on me".' I sigh; my logic suddenly seems, well, illogical. 'Is this making any sense at all?'

Jess weighs this up. 'I think so. You want him to see what he's missing?'

'No, no, it's not that, I just . . . Look, I'm dreading seeing him again, it's going to be mortifying, but if I have to do so, then surely I should be looking my best?'

'Absolutely. Looking hot is always your best defence.

Besides, you never know, he might take one look at your cute ass and decide to shelve the fiancée after all.'

I grimace, although I must admit that I did fleetingly entertain that exact thought while I was doing my hair this morning. 'Although,' I go on, 'chances are he'll be back in New York by now and I won't have to see him at all. That would be the best outcome by far.'

After dropping Dot with the childminder, I get a bus towards the Thames-side apartment complex, my nerves increasing at every stop. In my head I run through the speech I've prepared in case he's there, which goes something like this: 'I'm so sorry about how I behaved last time I was here. It was completely inexcusable, but I was on heavy-duty medication for my allergies' – I thought that might be the sort of thing an American would get – 'which must have impaired my judgement. I really appreciate you not taking the matter any further and can only apologise for any distress I might have caused. Now let's have a shag and forget all about it.'

That last bit's a joke, obviously. Just trying to lighten my mood.

When I arrive at the apartment complex, the foyer feels even more intimidatingly luxurious than it did before – although that could be because I could barely see straight last time I was here. I notice little details that I missed on my first visit: the curled wire at the doorman's ear, reinforcing the 'secret service' vibe of his dark glasses and overcoat, the enormous modernist chandelier made out of thousands of tiny crystals that looks like a magical floating waterfall, and the letters 'WR' inlaid across the marble floor, which I'm guessing stands for 'Westminster Reach', the name of the apartment complex, but equally could be 'Wondrously Rich'.

This time, rather than jumping straight into the penthouse lift, I buzz the intercom like a polite, sober person. After a few moments, a man's voice answers. It sounds worryingly American; I have to fight the urge to turn and run.

'Um, hello, is that Mr Michaelson?'

'No, I'm afraid he's not here right now.'

Relief rushes through me. *Thank God.* 'It's Annie Taylor from Curtis Kinderbey. I'm here to take some marketing photos of the property.'

There's a slight pause. 'Come on up.'

The lift doors glide open and I step in, enjoying the smell of wood polish and wealth, and check my reflection in the mirror. I'm pleasantly surprised by what I see, but then the lighting in here is bloody amazing: my skin looks so flawless it's like I've been heavily filtered. Perhaps when you're rich, your face is always this kind of a beautiful blur; maybe you never find out the harsh reality of what you *really* look like, because you only frequent places with super-flattering lighting. You probably float through life under the illusion you're Gigi Hadid.

I spend a nano-second wondering who the guy was who answered the intercom: the interior designer, perhaps? But it doesn't matter anyway, because I intend to be in and out of this place as quickly as possible.

The doors slide open and I step into the interior design equivalent of a black forest gateau. The previous inoffensive beige decor has been replaced by deep red velvet drapes, purple-black wallpaper and weird rococo flourishes like swirls of whipped cream. It's a migraine waiting to happen. I'm no expert, but if they're trying to sell this flat, I'd say the original neutral colour scheme would be a much safer bet than this. I can't imagine many people would actively go for this 'Dracula visits a bordello' vibe.

I glance around for the man who answered the intercom, but there's no sign of anyone.

'Um – hello?' I call. 'I'll just get started, shall I?'

A voice comes from the direction of the bedroom. 'Sure, be with you in a sec.'

I set up my camera with a heavy heart. This job is going to take far longer than I thought, as the thick curtains and autopsy colour scheme have killed off any natural light. I eventually find a control panel with at least a dozen buttons and gradually work through them, turning them on and off, trying to find the best combination of up-lighting, down-lighting and gothic-chandelier-lighting. I can't imagine what Karl is going to say when he sees what Serena has done to this place. So much for a quick and easy sale ...

'Hello again.'

I spin round at the sound of the voice behind me and the breath whooshes out of me like I've been punched in the guts. Standing there, smiling as if this isn't at all massively, bowel-clenchingly awkward, is Brad Michaelson.

Except, obviously, it's *not* Brad Michaelson.

I open my mouth to speak, then shut it because nothing comes out, then open it again and manage a strangulated 'Hi'.

'It's nice to see you,' he says.

'Yeah, you too.' I plaster on a smile, desperately trying to remember my speech, but my mind has gone blank. Fuck, what was it I was going to say? Something about allergies ...? I take a deep breath and then suddenly, as if my engine has just been jump-started, the words begin to pour out.

'I am so, so sorry about what happened the last time I was here. To be quite honest with you, I was drunk.' *What? No! Tell him about the allergies!* 'The thing is, I'd just had an argument with my boyfriend earlier that morning – well, ex-boyfriend, actually, it's all horribly complicated – and it was chucking down with rain that day and I ended up making some really bad choices because I was upset and then ... well, you know what happened next. I totally misread the signs because – like I said – I was drunk.'

Jesus. It's like I'm standing outside myself, watching as I jabber away, and although I'm mortified by what's coming out of my mouth I'm powerless to stop it.

'Anyway, I'm not the sort of person who usually drinks during the day, honestly. My judgement was obviously significantly impaired by the alcohol and I did some stuff that was out of character – very much so – which I wholeheartedly regret and apologise for.' I stare at my feet. 'This is all quite embarrassing for me,' I mumble at my shoes.

'Honestly, there's no need to be embarrassed,' says the man, his voice kind. 'As far as I remember, there were two people involved in that kiss.'

I look up, surprised. 'But I threw myself at you.'

'You were quite assertive, yeah, but I don't remember doing anything to stop you. And then you ran off like Cinderella.' He looks a bit bashful. 'That's how I've been referring to you – as Cinderella.'

'Cinderella wasn't a pisshead,' I say – although inside I'm thinking: *He's been talking about me? Is that a good thing?*

'No, that's true.' He laughs. 'Or perhaps she was a pisshead, which would explain why she ran off without her shoe. I don't want to be sexist, but I don't know many girls who'd leave expensive footwear behind.'

I smile, and begin to relax a little. Meanwhile, the more primitive part of my brain registers that he's wearing jeans and a t-shirt and is looking *fine.*

'Hey, I don't think I ever introduced myself.' For the

second time this morning, a man offers me his hand to shake – although this time I take it far more enthusiastically. 'Sam Whittaker. I'm a friend of Brad's. I'm working in London for a while and he was kind enough to let me stay in this ridiculous place of his. He pops over every now and then, just to check up and keep me on my toes.'

'Annie Taylor. As you know. But fully in control of myself this time, I promise.'

'Shame,' he says with a grin. My heart does a little leap, but I tell myself firmly that he's one of those people who are just naturally flirty. 'So what do you think of the new decor?'

'Oh, I'm no expert on interiors.'

'Hideous, isn't it? Serena's choice, I think. That's Brad's girlfriend – well, fiancée now.'

'It certainly makes quite a statement,' I say, gesturing at a metal sculpture that looks like an enormous pair of buttocks. 'But then if I've learnt anything in this job, it's that rich people really like statements.'

As soon as I say this, I regret it. For all his easy, down-to-earth charm, this guy might well be loaded too; he certainly has that air. Thankfully, though, he nods. 'Yeah, just because you can afford to make your apartment look like the Playboy mansion, doesn't really mean that you should.'

We smile at each other and I'm reminded of the easy rapport we had together the last time.

'Well, I should let you get on,' he says. 'I'll be in the kitchen if you need anything. Can I get you a drink? Vodka?'

Touché. 'No, thanks, I'm fine. I'll just zip round and then be out of your way.'

Well, that was remarkably painless. I can't believe he was so nice about it! As much as he claims there were two of us involved in the kiss, from what I remember he wasn't exactly putting his heart and soul into it. There was definite tentativeness on his part. So, all in all, extremely gentlemanly of him.

It takes me nearly an hour to finish the photos this time because: a) I'm trying to look as professional and hard-working as possible to make up for my previous misdemeanours, b) I have to keep moving stuff around and tampering with the lighting to minimise the worst design excesses, and c) – especially c), to be honest – Sam keeps dropping in and out to chat as I work, and I'm really enjoying hanging out with him. We just seem to have a natural affinity. I learn that he works in finance, has a dog called Seymour (he shows me the photo of him that he has as his screensaver) and that he lives in Brooklyn but originally comes from Toronto. He even spends quite a long time demonstrating the difference between American and Canadian accents, which is both informative and a turn-on, because it gives me a valid excuse to stare at his mouth.

After I've spun out the job as long as I feasibly can, I reluctantly start to pack away my camera.

'So that's me done,' I say, shouldering my bag. 'The agency will email Brad the photos for his approval in the next few days.'

'Great,' says Sam, digging his hands in his pockets.

'Well, I'll get out of your way then.' I smile at him, but a fug of awkwardness has descended over us again, clouding the easy connection we had a moment ago.

'Sure.' Sam bites his lip. 'Annie, I, uh, don't know that many people in London, apart from work colleagues. Would you like to get together for lunch sometime?'

I just stare at him, too surprised to respond.

'Obviously if it's complicated with your current personal situation . . .'

'No!' I virtually screech. 'No, I'd really like to. Thank you. That would be nice.'

'Great. So . . . should I give you my number? Or take yours?'

As we exchange details, I feel that thrill you get when you meet someone really fantastic and they seem to like you, too; the intoxicating buzz of what might happen. But at the same time, like the ticker on a really negative news channel, there's a commentary running through my mind: *He's only asking you out because he thinks you're easy. You're just a convenient booty call. A holiday romance* without *the romance.* Well, if that's the case I'm afraid he's going to be extremely disappointed when he finds out about my wind-sock vagina and the fact that my ginormous boobs are misshapen and lumpy with milk.

As I put his number into my phone, I realise that I'm angling it away from him so he can't see my screensaver, which is my favourite photo of Dot. I feel a nauseous lurch of guilt. What kind of mother am I, hiding the existence of my daughter to appear more – well, more what? Sexy? Available? Whatever the reason, I feel like a total shit for doing it.

'I'll be in touch,' says Sam, pressing the button for the lift, and then he leans forward and kisses my cheek, and the swirl of anticipation and lust his touch stirs up inside me makes me think that perhaps it isn't such a big deal if I don't mention Dot to him after all.

24

'Thank you so much for coming with me to my scan today,' says Tabitha, as we leave the hospital arm in arm. 'Jon would have cancelled his business trip like a shot, but I told him I'd be absolutely fine going with you.'

We step out into brilliant sunlight, as dazzling as a torch shone straight in the eyes. After months of gloom and drizzle, the warm spring weather acts like Red Bull for the soul – strangers smile at each other and people shrug off their coats – nevertheless, it's going to take more than sunshine to lift the clouds that are currently hanging over Tabby. I glance at my sister, who has her hands cradled around her bump as we make our way towards the tube station.

'Are you kidding?' I say to her. 'I'm just so glad you asked me to come with you. I want to do whatever I can to help, plus I loved getting a sneak peek at my nephew.' I smile at the memory of the squirmy little black and white tadpole on the screen. 'He definitely has your nose, Tabs. He's going to be so handsome.'

Tabby smiles that same tight, sad smile again, and my heart aches for her. I can well imagine what's going on inside her head – the worry that the doctor's words must be causing her – and I just wish I could think of the right thing to say that would make her feel a bit better. I've got to at least try.

'Hey, just stop for a second.' I guide her over to the side of the pavement out of the flow of pedestrians. 'Tabby, you've got to remember that these scans aren't an exact science. I know the doctor said the baby is measuring small, and that he wants to keep a close eye on your pregnancy from now on, but odds are the baby will be right on track when you have the next scan in a couple of weeks, and if he isn't, well ... maybe he's just a small baby. At one point they were concerned about Dot's growth too, and look at her – she turned out to be a right heifer!'

Finally, I get a genuine smile in reply. 'I just want everything to be completely fine, you know?' she says.

'Of course you do. Being pregnant is a uniquely worrying time, and if it wasn't this, you'd be stressing about something else. And don't forget that you're basically ninety per cent hormones right now, which is bound to make you more anxious. But you heard what the doctor said: all the signs are good, they just need to keep a close eye on the baby's measurements for the next few weeks. Come here.' I wrap her in a hug and we stay like that for a moment. 'It's going to be okay, I promise you,' I murmur into her hair.

I shouldn't have said that. If the last few years have taught Tabby and me anything, it's that sometimes things aren't okay; sometimes, the worst does happen. What I should have said was: 'It probably will be okay, but if it's not, I promise I'll be here to support and love you and we'll get through it together.' But I'm guessing that isn't what Tabby needs to hear right now.

'Thank you, my love,' she says, as we start to walk again. 'Anyway, what's going on with you? You seem . . . different.' She glances at me. 'Happier.'

'Do I?'

'Yes, there's a sort of lightness to you, which is really lovely to see. I've been so worried about you since Luke . . . well, you know. Things going well, are they?'

I'm dying to tell her about meeting Sam at the penthouse the other day and him asking me out, but I've decided that right now it's probably sensible if I don't mention our possible date to anyone. As much as I'd love to see Sam again, I lay awake last night agonising over whether it would actually be a terrible idea. Sure, Luke betrayed me in the most horrible way, but if there's still even a small chance of mending our relationship, then I probably shouldn't be going on a date with somebody else, no matter how much I fancy them. And anyway, is some casual, meaningless sex *really* going to make me feel better about myself? At least for now I've firmly got the moral high ground. If I go ahead with this date, I'll be heading into very murky waters, what with me not telling Sam that I have a child, or that I'm still with the child's father (or am I? God, that's even murkier) and I'm not sure I want Tabby or anyone else telling me I'm making a mistake until I've actually had fun making it. Besides, it's been nearly a week and I've heard nothing from Sam, so it may well be that he's changed his mind anyway ...

So I say to Tabby: 'I guess things *are* going well. I'm enjoying the new job and Dot's settled into our new routine – and she's sleeping okay at the moment, which makes a big difference to how I'm feeling.'

'I can imagine.'

'You've got all this to look forward to in a few months.' I smile.

'I know, I'm going to be constantly calling you up, asking questions. It'll be like 2 a.m. and I'll be on the phone: "But how do I get him to sleep?" '

'And I'll be like: "Sorry, Tabs, but I've no fucking idea".'

We laugh and I feel a huge surge of love for her, and I'm reminded just how lucky I am to have her as my sister.

We're now approaching the station where Tabby can

catch the bus home to Fulham, and I'll get the tube and then train back to Jess' place in Streatham.

'Have you got time for a cup of tea?' Tabby nods at a café across the road with a display of cakes in the window. 'We haven't seen each other properly in ages, and it would be great to hear more about Dottie and the job.'

I glance at my phone: it's already five o'clock. As much as I'd love to spend more time with her, I'm conscious of the fact that time's ticking on.

'Don't worry if it's difficult,' adds Tabby quickly. 'We can catch up another time.'

'It's just that I don't want to be late collecting Dot . . .'

'Of course, I totally understand. And I so appreciate you coming with me today.'

We hug again and I kiss her cheek and tell her that she must call me straight away if I can do anything at all, and then she sets off towards the bus stop and I duck into the station. With every guilty step, it feels like I'm getting closer to hell. This is the second time today that I've lied to my sister, and whereas the first time – 'it's going to be okay' – was arguably a constructive lie, this one is inexcusable. The truth is that Claris is collecting Dot from the childminder and having her for a sleepover tonight, and the real reason that I'm keen to get home is to give me extra time to get dressed and ready for my night out with Riva. And yes, I'm sure Tabby would have understood if I'd explained that I'm really nervous about meeting up with Riva and the old fashion gang tonight, and that the longer I can spend on my hair and make-up, the more confident I'll feel, but after the worry caused by the scan it doesn't reflect well on me to put my vanity before my sister's sanity.

As I get on the tube, I make a vow to myself to be a better sister. I've been so caught up with my own troubles recently that I've neglected her, but from now on I'm going to make sure I check in with her more often. I know she's got Jon, who couldn't be a more doting husband, and Jon's lovely parents have adopted her as one of their own, but since our own parents died, we've only had each other and now, more than ever, she needs my support.

25

Three and a half hours later I'm standing outside the unremarkable-looking black door of a Georgian town-house in Soho, behind which lies an exclusive private members' club. The last time I was here, about six years ago, was with a then red-hot Irish actor (renowned for his boozing and blue eyes) whom I'd just been working with on a shoot, and although my memory is hazy, I think we ended up kissing in the ladies' loo. Just another average Friday night for me back then.

Tonight, however, feels like A Very Big Event. My outfit for the night is Jess' red trouser suit with a plunging lacy black camisole; my cleavage levels are hovering somewhere between *TOWIE* and *Made in Chelsea*, but I think I just about get away with it because the rest of the outfit is fairly modest. My lipstick (chosen by Jess) exactly matches the colour of the suit, and I am wearing false lashes that took me half an hour to apply but were totally worth it. When I look in the mirror a stranger stares nervously back, but I'm confident that I'm looking good – which is the only way I'd be able to go through with this, as my nerves are ridiculous. My finger is actually shaking when I lift it to press the entrance buzzer.

After a moment the door clicks open and I head up to the reception desk, where a girl with a bleached wavy bob, who was probably still in school when I was last here snogging in the toilets, looks me up and down and asks who I'm here to meet, having clearly decided I'm not enough of a somebody to waste a smile on. When I mention Riva's name, however, she thaws dramatically.

'Oh, you're with Riva!' she gushes, like I'm now her BFF. 'Her party's just arrived. Head straight up, babe, she's on the roof terrace.'

The terrace is packed, but I spot Riva's curls immediately. She's sitting at a large table with at least a dozen other people crammed around it, all chatting and laughing, their expansive body language and loud voices suggesting they rule the place. So much for the 'quiet little get-together' Riva promised in her text to me earlier. Riva's crew are all so fabulous-looking that even a total stranger would know that out of all the groups here, this is the 'It' table, the one at the centre of the action. Was I once this intimidatingly cool, too? With a jolt I spot a few familiar faces among the crowd, people I haven't given a second thought to in years – although once upon a time would have known every minutiae of their lives. Tomo, however, isn't among them. Before I can decide if this is a good thing or not, Riva catches sight of me.

'Barb!' She jumps up and rushes over to give me a hug. 'You look amazing,' she says, grinning. '*Adore* the suit. Very Cate Blanchett.'

Lacing her arm through mine, she marches me over to her friends.

'Hey, people!' she booms, waving her arms for attention. 'Look who's here!'

Everyone at the table (and quite a few at the other tables as well) turns to look at me. Staring back at the mass of faces – some curious, some surprised, some bored, most beautiful – I feel my cheeks turning the same colour as my suit. I give a nervous, half-hearted wave.

'Right then,' says Riva. 'Who do you already know? There's Delphine, obviously . . .'

A waifish redhead waves across the table. 'Barb, darling, it's been too long! You look gorgeous.'

'And there's Mimi' – Riva gestures to a curvy blonde, who blows me a kiss – 'ooh, and over there, next to Farrah, is of course Nick.'

'Hey Barb, great to see you,' calls Nick, a model who, when we were last in touch, fancied himself as a budding photographer. 'You still in touch with Jay?' he adds, mentioning my old boss; he used to be obsessed with getting me to introduce them.

'Afraid not,' I reply, and with a shrug Nick turns his attention back to the model on his right.

Then Riva points out a slender middle-aged man in a trilby and three-piece-suit and says: 'And of course you know ...' But before she can finish, the man stands up, flings out his arms and shrieks: 'OH. MY. GAAAAD! Barbra fucking Streisand, is that really you?'

I look at him blankly; I have absolutely no idea who he is – and I'm usually quite good at remembering faces.

'Oh bitch, *please*,' he pouts theatrically. 'I know I'm off-duty tonight, but surely it hasn't been *that* long?'

Then he strikes a pose and I gasp.

'Madame Kiki Beaverhousen? Oh my God, it's so good to see you!' I rush over to give him a hug. 'I'm so sorry, I didn't recognise you without the wig and sequins.'

'Well, I could say the same about you.' He pulls back and looks me up and down. 'You off-duty tonight as well?'

I laugh. 'No, I'm afraid this is me *on* duty these days. Barb's retired.'

'What?' He gasps in horror. 'But why? Barb is your spirit animal, just as Madame Kiki is mine. You can't just ... put her back in the wardrobe. That's tantamount to abuse!'

'I'm afraid I have. These days I'm just Annie.'

'Well, it's a delight to see you again, just Annie.' He moves a chair between him and Riva. 'Come and sit next to me, darling. What are you drinking?'

'Whatever you're having.' I smile, relieved to be out of the spotlight.

'Excellent choice.' He waves at a passing waitress. 'Bianca, darling? Two Singapore slings for us London queens.'

Riva introduces me to the others at the table, but I forget their names as soon as she's told me, and then, with the babble of gossip resuming comfortingly around me, a cocktail appears; I take a huge gulp so the alcohol can work its magic.

'You should have seen Barb a few years back,' Riva is saying to a Kim Kardashian lookalike sitting opposite. 'She was a total fucking legend. I mean, seriously, *everyone* knew her. She used to be Jay Patterson's right-hand woman.'

This is all hilariously over the top, but the Kim clone looks genuinely impressed. It appears that Jay's name still holds currency even after he was exposed as a sexual harasser and drug addict last year.

'And do you still work in fashion, Barb?' asks the Kim-alike through over-filled lips.

'Oh no, not anymore,' I say. 'I . . .'

Before I can finish, Riva leans across and says: 'Barb works in property and design.'

My immediate reaction is to hoot with laughter, but Riva's face is deadly serious and certainly my new friend looks a lot more interested than she would if I'd told her I worked for an estate agent, which is what I was about to say.

'You should check out her Instagram,' Riva goes on. 'She has a killer eye.'

Two drinks (swiftly) down, I begin to relax and feel less of a sore thumb. I've stopped imagining that everyone is looking at me and wondering: *What's that mum doing here?* It helps that despite the five years that have passed since I was part of this crowd, they're still having the exact same conversation as when I left. All anyone is talking about is the industry: who's landed which contract, who's fallen out of favour, who's working (and sleeping) with whom. Some of the names and references mentioned are unfamiliar, and there's more talk about bloggers and influencers, but generally I'm astonished how little has changed – which means I can easily blag my way through most conversations. And if there is an awkward lull, I can simply dig out one of my endless, outrageous anecdotes from working with Jay. I'll say something like: 'Oh my God, Riva, do you remember that crazy shoot we did with Salma Hayek in Marrakech? And Jay tried to smoke oregano and nearly got arrested?' And the old gang will break into screams of nostalgic laughter while the newcomers hang on my every word with starry-eyed admiration. My ego hasn't had such a boost in years.

In fact, I find myself slipping back into this world so easily that I have moments of feeling weirdly off-balance, sort of like vertigo, when I remember how different my life is now. Nobody apart from me seems to have kids – or if they do, they're not talking about them – and everyone is drinking in that carefree, chaotic way that suggests they don't have to worry about combining childcare with a hangover tomorrow morning. Early in the evening I make the mistake of asking Riva where Jethro is tonight and for a split second she looks like she doesn't even know who I'm talking about.

'Oh, with his nan,' she says, with a vague wave of a hand that suggests it doesn't warrant further discussion. 'Now, have you spoken to Cheska yet? She's just got a job working as assistant to . . .'

The drinks keep coming and I'm enjoying myself more than I have in ages. I really hope Tomo turns up soon; I'm looking hot, right? And I'm clearly holding my own with this crowd. It would be fun to see him again and catch up with his news . . .

'Come on, everyone, selfie time!'

The Kim Kardashian clone, whose name, hilariously, is actually Kim, bunches us all together and gets the waitress to take one picture of the whole group – well, I say one, but really it's a full-blown photo shoot. As she's tapping away, editing and filtering, she looks up and asks: 'Barb, what's your Instagram so I can tag you?'

'Oh no, I'd rather you didn't . . .'

Riva laughs at my discomfort. 'Barb's got a strict no selfie policy on Instagram. She likes to fly under the radar.'

Kim turns to me, horrified. 'Really? Wow. Sure. That's, uh, weird.'

'It's just a work thing,' I explain. 'Not to mention the iPhone camera doesn't do my face any favours. It's my nose – it tends to dominate.'

'You just need to learn to contour,' says Kiki Beaver-housen, whose real name, I discover, is Edgar. 'A little shading and some highlighter and you could completely remodel it.'

I give a hollow laugh. 'I think the last thing my nose needs is highlighting.'

Riva puts her head on one side and scrutinises me. 'Babe, if it bothers you so much, why don't you get it fixed?'

'Fixed?'

'Yeah. Made smaller.'

'What, like a nose job?'

Delphine chips in from across the table: 'Ooh, you should go and see Mr Jindal. He does all the top girls.'

'Oh God, yeah, he's uh-maaazing,' drawls Kim. 'You know that blonde model in the latest Dior campaign? Caro-lina? Well, you should have seen the state of her nose before Mr Jindal got his hands on it.'

Farrah nods enthusiastically. 'Yah, that bitch owes her entire career to him.'

'I don't know,' I say. 'It just feels a bit, well, drastic. Going under the knife.'

Riva's forehead furrows in confusion. 'Why? I had my

boobs done after Jethro. It's *so* not a big deal nowadays, doll. You'd be in and out of hospital super quickly and then it would be like a week in bandages and you're done!'

'These days surgery is basically just like a sort of *intensive* facial,' agrees Delphine.

'Yeah, you should totally do it,' Mimi chips in. 'You've got the most fabulous cheekbones, it would really make them pop if your nose wasn't so' – she gestures with her hands, searching for a tactful word – 'bold.'

I have no idea what she's talking about – can cheekbones pop? – but I must admit it's very tempting to imagine I could fix my detested nose so easily. I've got a bit of money left over from my parents that I've kept back for emergencies, I'm sure that would be more than enough ...

'Here, I've got Mr Jindal's office number on my phone,' says Delphine. 'I go to him for lasering,' she adds, slightly defensively. 'Why don't you book a consultation?'

I guess there's no harm in meeting this guy for a chat. With a thrill of anticipation, I take down his number and save it in my phone.

It's past eleven when somebody mentions that Travis is having a party in Shoreditch and suggests we get over there right away; there is an immediate and enthusiastic mass exit.

Riva turns to me, her eyes shining. 'Oh my God, Barb, Travis is gonna fucking *die* when he sees you!' She grabs my arm and leads me towards the exit. 'How long is it since you last saw him? Shit, do you remember that time when we were in Cannes together? And Travis streaked down the Croisette?' She cackles with laughter. 'Man, fun times . . .'

As we make our way downstairs I laugh along with her, and although I'm pretty sure that I've never met anyone called Travis, or even been to Cannes, these seem like minor details. The important point is, I think that I *could* have been there.

We're standing outside waiting for our Uber to arrive when I check my messages. I have one from Claris telling me that Dot went to sleep like a dream, and a voicemail from Tabby. With a rush of something uncomfortably close to guilt, I hit play.

'Oh hey, Annie, don't worry about phoning back, nothing at all important, I just . . . well, I was just feeling a bit worried about – well, you know – the scan and everything, and you're always so good at making me feel better that I thought I'd give you a call. But as I said, I'm absolutely fine, just being a bit silly, that's all. Anyway, Jon's back tomorrow. Thanks again for today. Love you.'

I check the time of the message: she left it three hours ago. Still, I should definitely try to speak to her . . .

'Hurry up, Barb, we'll be late!' I look up from my phone to see Riva hanging out the back of a packed silver Toyota, beckoning impatiently.

'I just need to make a very quick call,' I say, waving my phone by way of explanation.

'No time, babe,' says Riva. 'Do it in the car.'

I hesitate for a moment. I really don't want to speak to Tabby when I'm surrounded by these people; I need privacy for this. But she's bound to be asleep by now – and she did say in her message that I shouldn't worry about calling back. I'll just send her a text instead, then she can read it in the morning.

Nick sticks his head out the front window. 'Barb, you coming or what?'

With an apologetic grin I slip my phone back in my bag, then squeeze in next to Riva and slam the door.

26

The way I see it, a hangover is basically a fun tax. The bigger the fun, the more you'll be liable to pay – with a special higher tariff for parents of young children to act as a 'fun deterrent'. Viewed in purely fiscal terms, it seems almost – *almost* – fair that I'm feeling so dire this morning, as I had such a brilliant time last night.

Honestly, I really don't know why I was so worried about seeing the old gang again. I guess it was because I thought I'd feel out of place, but all anyone wanted to talk to me about was the old days, back when I was working for Jay. I haven't felt so fascinating in a long time. None of them seemed at all bothered about what I'm up to now – which is lucky, because I can't imagine Mimi or Farrah being that interested in Curtis Kinderbey, or my thoughts on baby-led weaning. Is it terrible to admit that it was actually really nice to spend an evening being something other than someone's mum? To be appreciated for my achievements, rather than simply my body's ability to push out a baby? For the first time in ages, I felt like a valued person in my own right, instead of just carer-in-chief and head bum-wiper to a tiny, demanding dictator. The only time I got even close to mentioning Dot was when Edgar poked my cleavage and shrieked: 'Good Lord, are those new boobies?' And when I explained that they were only bigger because I was breastfeeding, his horrified reaction was priceless. In fact, the night's only downer was that Tomo was a no-show. According to Travis – who, it turned out, I *did* know: we worked together on a men's fragrance campaign once – he's living part-time in Ibiza. Travis promised that he'll make sure Tomo comes along next time we all meet up – by which time hopefully I'll have just about recovered from this God-awful hangover.

Rolling over in bed, my tummy churning like I'm on a cross-channel ferry in a gale, I reach for my phone: shit, it's already past eight o'clock. I really do have to get up. Why on earth didn't I call it a night after the drinks in Soho like a sensible person? It's all very well going to bed at 3 a.m. if you're a blogger, but I'm due at the office in less than an hour to pick up some keys. Bloggers probably don't even *have* an office, they just snap a quick bed selfie, stick it on Instagram (#bestsleepever #lovemybed #socosy), get paid thousands of pounds by a duvet company and then take the rest of the week off. And yes, I am jealous, but most of these so-called influencers couldn't frame a decent photo if they tried.

Trying to delay the moment where I have to attempt to stand, I scroll through my phone, smiling to see the contacts I added last night: Nick, Delphine, Edgar/Kiki – um, who's 'Nose Guy' . . . ? I try to make sense of it, but thinking makes my brain hurt. Suddenly a memory looms out of the fog: Riva asking why I don't get my nose fixed. Everything falls into place. Of course, this is the plastic surgeon they were raving about! I stare at the number, which now possesses an almost mystical allure. Before the rational side of my brain can kick in, I hit dial and – with a thrill of anticipation – I leave a message asking someone to call me back at their earliest convenience about booking a consultation.

At just after 10 a.m., held together by industrial amounts of coffee and under-eye concealer, I arrive outside a set of imposing black gates on a quiet street in Battersea. From where I'm standing it's impossible to see what lies behind them, but going by the CCTV cameras and general fuck-off air conveyed by the seven-foot gates and spike-topped fencing, you'd think it was a top-secret government laboratory rather than the apparently charming seven-bed period property that I've been sent to photograph.

I press the intercom, the gates slowly open and I find myself in a particularly lovely part of rural Somerset. Ahead of me, surrounded by trees, I can just about make out an enchanting three-storey house, its weathered, silver-grey brickwork swathed in greenery. As I make my way up the gravel driveway, the usual London sounds of traffic and swearing disappear, to be replaced by birdsong and the gentle hum of a mower. A couple of vintage cars and an old-fashioned bicycle complete with basket are parked near the house, arranged in such an aesthetically pleasing tableau that it must have been deliberate. Even the air smells sweeter in here. I've photographed some truly amazing properties over the past few weeks, but never have I had such intense home envy as I do right now.

I ring the doorbell and settle in for a wait: the first thing I've learnt from photographing houses like this is that it can take a long time to get from one wing to the other. It's not like your average London flat, where you can basically just turn around and open the front door from wherever you're standing in the property.

A man in tennis whites opens the front door, racket in hand. He's in his mid-fifties and looks important and cross.

'Curtis Kinderbey?' he barks. 'You're late.'

Oh come on, mate, I feel like saying. *You live in this stunning house, you're playing tennis on a weekday, you're clearly loaded – surely you can manage not to be an arsehole?*

Before I can get a word out, however, he turns and shouts: 'Natasha? Estate agent's here, darling. Could you come and deal with it? Giles is waiting for me at the club.'

And with that he walks past me without another word and heads out to one of the gorgeous cars, jumps in and zooms off in a shower of dust and gravel.

A minute or so later Natasha – for this must be she – drifts elegantly down the curved staircase, spooning something out of a bowl that probably involves chia seeds. She is obviously fresh out of the shower: her long, brown hair is wet, her feet bare and her unfairly beautiful face make-up free. Most normal people would immediately think: *teenage daughter.* But the second thing I've learnt from this job is that when it comes to rich people, wives and daughters are interchangeable. She's not wearing a wedding ring, but that could be locked in the safe (lesson number three: there's *always* a safe).

'Oh hey,' she drawls, admittedly in a very teenager-home-from-boarding-school fashion. 'So you'll just ... get on with it, right? Or do you need me to ... do something?'

'No, it's absolutely fine; if you're happy for me to go around by myself, I can just crack on.'

'Great, so, just ...' – she waves her spoon in the air – '... crack on then, yah?'

And with that she wafts back upstairs again, leaving me none the wiser as to whether Natasha is in fact Mrs Arsehole or Miss Arsehole junior.

While from the outside the house looks like a bucolic Grade II listed vicarage, inside we're firmly in Kardashian territory. It's obvious that an interior designer has been heavily involved throughout: whereas normal people gradually accumulate furniture according to their needs – a sofa here, a coffee table there – and then simply stick these things in the most suitable spot in their home, mega-rich people will engage a designer to create an entire room from scratch, often shelling out on a completely new set of furniture and decor to suit each individual space. As is the case here, this can give each room a 'themed' feel: so we have the 'ancient Roman villa' dining room, with its mosaic floor and marble urns; the cosy 'retired professor of history' study, its walls lined with leather-bound books; and the 'French chateau owned by the Beckhams' kitchen, in which a massive Sub-Zero fridge is concealed behind an elaborately carved, faux-distressed armoire.

This place is a gold mine of Instagrammable stuff – everywhere I look there's a hashtag waiting to happen – but as I have no idea how many people there are in the house, I have to rein in my urge to get out my iPhone and start snapping. I do manage to sneak a shot of a gold chandelier shaped like a gigantic hot-air balloon, though, and a dinner service decorated with ivy leaves, all laid out on the dining table as if at any moment twenty guests could turn up demanding a banquet.

Once I get upstairs, the Natasha mystery is solved: she *is* the daughter, thank God. (I'd have felt a bit queasy if she'd been the wife.) Her bedroom is your bog-standard millionaire teenager hang-out, but it's the room that leads off her bedroom that's the real eye-opener. I guess it'll be described in the property particulars as a 'dressing room', but this is a world away from the cramped space that implies. It's like stepping into a high-end spa: there's a couple of mani/pedi chairs complete with a full selection of gel polishes, salon-style backwash basins, a massage table and a row of hair and make-up stations, each with its own lavishly spot-lit mirror. Sitting alongside these is an enormous custom-made Louis Vuitton trunk branded with Natasha's initials. I pull open the lid a fraction and take a peek inside: bloody hell, she's basically got Selfridges' entire beauty hall in here! Row upon row of designer make-up, meticulously arranged: an entire drawer of eyeshadows, another of lipsticks and glosses, dozens of pencils, every imaginable shade of foundation (which is odd, because Natasha's skin is only one colour), brushes of all shapes and sizes ... basically it's an Aladdin's cave, if Aladdin was big in YouTube beauty tutorials.

After checking to see if the coast is clear, I open the trunk more widely and fire off some photos, but it's difficult to get the exterior of the trunk in shot as well – which is really the best bit. Perhaps I should take out some of the make-up and put it alongside? Working quickly, I grab handfuls of products and arrange them on top of the trunk. Perfect. And the light in here is amazing thanks to all those spotlights. Right, I'll just set up one more shot – where was that Nars palette I spotted a moment ago . . .?

'Uh, what are you doing?'

Natasha is standing in the doorway, her forehead wrinkled quizzically. As I watch in horror, her eyes take in the open trunk, the make-up scattered all over the counter and the palette that I'm still guiltily clutching. But when she looks back at me, instead of fury at my snooping, her eyes are wide with apology.

'Oh my God, I'm so sorry, I had no idea it was such a mess in here!' Natasha pads over to where I'm standing. 'Can I help you clear up?'

Wait – *what*? This is so different from the reaction that I was expecting I can only manage a nod.

She goes on: 'I don't think the maid's been in yet this morning and I'm, like, *massively* disorganised. Mummy would call it lazy, but I just don't like putting stuff away! Haha! Here, let me give you a hand . . .'

Natasha obviously hasn't had much experience of tidying – she'll idly pick up a lipstick, look at it as if she's never seen it before, test it on her hand and then drop it back where she found it – but I'm just thrilled not to have been caught.

'You have the most amazing make-up collection,' I say, once I've recovered my composure.

'Yah, I know.' Natasha has now abandoned all pretence

of helping and is examining her pores in a magnifying mirror. 'Total shame I can't wear it at school, raaarly.'

I pack the last few brushes away in the trunk. 'Well, I'll be getting on. Thank you for the help.'

'No, thank *you*,' says Natasha, flashing a brilliant smile. Clearly, she hasn't inherited her manners from her father.

An hour later I'm on the bus back to the office to drop off the keys, and my photo of the Louis Vuitton make-up trunk is already winning Instagram. Delphine, who's a make-up artist, has commented: 'omg babe – WANT!!' with six hearts and a kissy emoji, while someone called PrincessFairyGirl34 has written: 'Is this yours? Sooooo jel!' And the lingering guilt I was feeling about raking through Natasha's stuff fades away as I bask in the warm glow of rapidly accumulating likes.

When I arrive at the office I'm immediately flagged down by Fiona, who is sitting at her desk talking on the phone. When she spots me she gestures frantically towards the door and mouths: 'I need to speak to you!'

I tap my wrist, hold up five fingers and point to the café over the road; she replies with a thumbs up.

By the time I've bought two coffees for me and Fi (and a bacon and egg sandwich for my hangover) and have found a sunny spot on a bench outside the café, Fi bursts out of the office and bustles across the road.

'Hello, darlin',' she says, giving me a quick peck and

sitting down next to me. 'Jesus, you look rough. Dottie been keeping you up, has she?'

'Actually, I had a night out yesterday. With the old fashion gang.'

She turns to look at me in surprise. 'Did you now? I had no idea you were in touch with that lot again.' She doesn't even try to keep the hostility out of her voice. Fi never had much time for my fashion mates; she used to say they were boring and self-obsessed. I guess they can seem a bit cliquey, but I just think she never got to know them properly. Fi goes on: 'So how did that cosy little get-together happen then?'

'I bumped into Riva the other day and she invited me out.'

'Riva . . .? Was she that stylist with the big hair? Totally in love with herself, right?'

'Come on, she's really not that bad . . .'

Fi looks sceptical. 'Well, I'm guessing it must have been weird, seeing them all again after so long.'

'You'd have thought so, wouldn't you? But it wasn't at all. It was like I was still part of the gang. I actually had a really fun night.'

'Well, don't you go neglecting your *real* friends now you're back in touch with those freeloaders,' says Fi tartly. 'Anyway, listen, I've got something to tell you. Guess where I've been this morning?'

'Mass?'

'No, eejit, I had a viewing at the Westminster Reach penthouse. Crime scene of the Annie Taylor snog-and-run. And' – she pauses for dramatic effect – 'yer man was there!'

'You mean . . .'

'Yes! I met him. Your victim!'

'And? What did you think of him?'

'Well, he didn't seem too badly traumatised by what happened, but I think the intensive therapy has probably been helping . . .'

I give her a light slap. 'Seriously, Fi, did you speak to him?'

'Yeah, although he was leaving when I arrived so it was literally just "hi" and "bye". But I can totally see the appeal.' She nods enthusiastically. 'Great shoulders, gorgeous smile, a bit clean-cut for me but still very cute . . . Shame he's engaged, really, you two would have made a lovely couple . . .'

Fi looks at me with such sympathy that I decide to give her the full picture.

'Listen, I was going to tell you this eventually, but I actually saw him again, about a week ago.'

She frowns. 'Where?'

'In the apartment. He was there when I went back to take the new set of marketing photos.'

'What? Why didn't you mention it at the time?'

'I know, I'm sorry,' I say. 'But the thing is, Fi, *he's* not the owner – that man isn't Brad Michaelson. His name is Sam Whittaker, he's a friend of Brad's who's staying in the apartment while he's in London on business and honestly, he's *so* lovely. We had a really nice chat, he was totally cool about the whole drunk snogging disaster, in fact' – I can't keep the excitement out of my voice – 'he asked me out.'

Her mouth drops open. 'You are *joking*.'

'No! I couldn't believe it. He told me he didn't know anyone in London and asked if I'd like to have lunch with him.'

'This is amazing! You are *totally* in there.'

'Yeah, well, but I haven't heard anything from him since. And he probably only asked me out because he thinks I'm gagging for it . . .'

'Nonsense! Annie Taylor, you are a total catch and you really need to start remembering that. Besides,' she adds, shooting me a sly look, 'I thought you *were* gagging for it.'

Before I can answer, my phone starts to ring and Fi looks at me triumphantly and says: 'There you go, that's probably him now!'

But it's not Sam. It's Nose Guy – or rather, Nose Guy's office – calling me back, I presume, to book my appointment for my plastic surgery consultation. There's no way I can speak about my potential nose job with Fi here; I get the feeling she would strongly disapprove.

'Is it him?' she asks.

'Nope.' I slip my phone back in my bag. 'Nothing important, I'll deal with it later.'

'So you'll go? On the date?'

'It's not a date. It's just lunch.'

Fi gives an exaggerated huff of frustration.

'Fine, yes, I'd really like to,' I say. 'We had such a great chat – it was just easy, you know? We had this natural rapport – I literally could have talked to him for hours and I just know there wouldn't have been any awkward pauses. Also, of course, I do really fancy him. There was a spark between us, I'm sure.'

'So what's the feckin' problem?'

'It's just everything's so complicated in my life at the moment. Haven't I got enough to deal with without adding this to the mix?'

'Oh come on, he's not asking for your hand in marriage! It's perfect – he's only in London for a while. Go on, have some no-strings fun – it'll do you the world of good.'

'Maybe . . . but – what about Luke?'

Fi shoots me a savage look and virtually growls: 'What about him?'

'. . . and Dottie?'

'Well, I wouldn't take her with you when you go on the date, but beyond that – honest to God, woman, you're looking for problems where there aren't any! I don't think having a baby disqualifies you from having fun. You owe it to yourself to get out there, have a laugh and get laid, plus it might even help you make a decision about Luke. So will you do it?'

'Alright,' I say after a moment's thought. 'I'll do it.'

What I haven't admitted to her is that there is no way I'll turn Sam down if he gets back in touch. I just wanted her to tell me that I'm doing the right thing in meeting up with him – so thank God she's given me the green light.

27

> Hey Cinderella, how's it going? If you'd still like to get together for lunch, how does this Wednesday work for you? There's a place on the river near St Paul's I've been wanting to try. Let me know if you can make it, it would be good to get together. Sam.

I read the text again to make sure I didn't miss any subtleties – although having said that, I could probably spend all day trying to analyse the hidden subtext of the phrase: 'it would be good to get together'. Does that particular choice of words suggest he wants to have meaningless dirty sex with me? Or embark on a committed, loving relationship? Men can be so obtuse . . .

As over two weeks have passed since we saw each other at the apartment, I'd all but convinced myself Sam wasn't going to get in touch, but now that he actually has, the initial surge of excitement is giving way to guilt, confusion and, above all, worry. I get the feeling I'm doing something morally wrong by even thinking about meeting him. It doesn't help that Luke is currently standing just a few feet away, smiling at me like I'm the most wonderful woman on earth.

We've met up at the local playground so I can hand over Dot, as Luke is going to look after her today, and it's such a lovely morning that when he suggested I stick around for a bit, I surprised myself by agreeing. Dot's usually at home with me on Mondays, but I have an appointment this morning and Helen the childminder doesn't have space, so Luke volunteered to take the day off work and spend it with her. I can see how hard he's trying to be a good dad, and I have to admit that my frozen heart does thaw a little watching them together. Luke is pushing Dot on the baby swing, standing in front of her and tickling her feet every time she swings back towards him, making her giggle like a maniac. I return Luke's smile without even thinking about it; at moments like this, it's far harder to remember to stay mad at him.

He's the only man in the playground right now – 9 a.m. on a Monday is prime mum-time – and I might be imagining it, but I'm sure I notice some of the other women checking him out. Objectively speaking, I have to admit that he *is* a good-looking guy. He's wearing jeans and an old navy sweatshirt and looks as if he's just returned from two weeks in the tropics – although he's one of those annoying people who only has to look at the sun on TV to get a tan.

I glance down at my phone and re-read Sam's message again. As much as I like the guy (and I know I do, because if I was fully and unconditionally single I would be giddy with anticipation about seeing him again) I'm still worried it could be a massive faff – as well as morally questionable – to venture down this particular road. Plus, I'm already worrying about the number of lies that meeting up with Sam would entail: both to him and of course to Luke. I'm a terrible liar: I get this uncontrollable tic where I start tugging at my right ear. I'm just not cut out for duplicity.

I slip my phone back in my pocket and decide to reply later; it's taken nearly two weeks for Sam to contact me, it won't hurt him to wait a few hours.

Luke has now taken Dot out of the swing, much to her displeasure, and comes over to where I'm standing with her squirming and complaining in his arms.

'Do you think we can try her on the slide?' he asks.

'Sure, but you'll need to hold her.'

'Obviously,' he says, grinning at me. 'I'm not a complete novice at this, you know.'

We stroll across the playground, dodging kamikaze toddlers, and Luke puts Dot at the top of the baby slide and gently whizzes her down – 'wheeeee!' – and even though it's not exactly The Smiler at Alton Towers, her eyes go wide and she pounds her fists in that adorable way she has when she's massively excited about something.

'Aren't you a daredevil!' I laugh, as Dot sits at the bottom of the slide rocking back and forth in her enthusiasm to do it again.

'I told you she's going to be sporty,' says Luke with a proud smile, carrying her back to the top.

We watch our daughter enjoying the slide, both of us absorbed in our own thoughts, and then after a minute Luke asks: 'So what's this appointment you've got today?'

'Oh, just a routine doctor's thing.' My hand shoots up to my right ear.

'Is everything alright?' asks Luke with a look of concern.

'Yeah, it's really nothing important. Just ... women's stuff.' My fingers continue to tug at my ear; I literally have no power to control this pesky tic.

'Well, I hope it goes okay,' he says – and then he catches sight of something behind me. When I turn to find out what he's looking at, my heart plummets into my shoes. *You are fucking kidding me.*

'Mum!' shouts Luke, waving. 'Over here!'

Plastering on a smile, I watch as Lucia Turner bustles through the playground, a fearsome little cannonball of tweed, beige stockings and lipstick, her black hair arranged into a terrifying nuclear cloud that must have taken an entire can of hairspray to create.

'I didn't know your mum was coming,' I mutter to Luke as she rapidly closes in on us.

'Yeah, she loves seeing Dottie,' he replies, a note of

defensiveness already creeping into his voice. 'And I know she was keen to see you.'

I bet she was, I think, *so she can bloody well give me the third degree.*

I haven't seen Lucia since finding out about Luke's affair with Sigrid, but let's just say I will be extremely surprised if she hasn't worked out a way to blame me for everything that's happened.

'*Cara mio!*' Lucia reaches up for her beloved son's face and kisses him vigorously on both cheeks. 'Oh, and Dottie – *vita mia!*' She grabs Dot from Luke's arms and holds her up like Simba at the start of *The Lion King*. '*Amore!* What a very, very beautiful *bambina* you are. *So* like your papa at your age ...' And then, clutching Dot to her bosom, she turns to face me, and although she's still smiling broadly, her eyes slant ever so slightly into a look that says, *I've got a bone to pick with you, missy.* 'And Annie, it's wonderful to see you.' She comes in for a kiss, wafting Elnett and Rive Gauche. 'How I've missed you!'

'You too, Lucia,' I say, and it would be easy to miss the tiny sceptical arch of Lucia's eyebrow as she beams in reply.

'So, first things first.' She thrusts Dot at me. She's brought with her two bulging Sainsbury's Bags for Life, which she now holds up; I don't need to look inside to know they'll be full of home-cooked meals. 'Luca, these are for you. I can't imagine how you're finding time to cook with your busy job and looking after Dottie and all the other *so* many important things you have to do!'

'Mum, you really didn't need to . . .'

'Well, how else you gonna eat?' She very deliberately catches my eye. 'And it's all your favourites: *parmigiana, lasagne, polpette, braciole* . . .'

Luke kisses her. 'Thank you, you're an angel.'

'Oh shh now, it's nothing,' says Lucia, puffing up with pleasure like a roosting pigeon. 'Now, why don't you take Dottie to get some gelato so I can have a little chat with Annie?'

'I think she's a bit young for ice cream, Mum.' Luke laughs, but he's already taking Dot from my arms. I'm beginning to realise that this is a carefully planned ambush. *Traitor*, I think bitterly as I watch him head off across the playground. Yet before I have a chance to plan my escape, Lucia laces her arm firmly through mine and marches us in the direction of a nearby bench.

'Let's sit down, Annie,' she says cosily, as if we're the best of friends. 'We have lots to catch up on, *si*?'

When I first started going out with Luke, I got quite upset about the fact that Lucia clearly didn't think I was good enough for her son. She was always polite and welcoming enough, but there'd be subtle digs about my clothes or hairstyle, and she'd keep up a running commentary on how I should be looking after her son, pointing out where I was falling short (most frequently in the fields of cooking and housework). When I finally got up the courage to speak to Luke about it, he flatly denied that there was any sort of problem and insisted his mum adored me. At first I assumed he was lying to spare my feelings, but by the time we'd celebrated our first anniversary, I'd come to the conclusion that Luke genuinely didn't realise there was anything unusual in the way his mother worshipped him. I made peace with the fact that Lucia wouldn't be happy with *whoever* Luke was going out with, because nobody would ever be good enough for her darling boy. (Apart from maybe Kate Middleton; Lucia thinks she's the epitome of femininity and wifely good practice.) When I got pregnant, Lucia's delight at the prospect of her first grandchild was tempered by her strong disapproval that we weren't yet married, a situation that I, of course, got the blame for as well.

'I really don't understand you girls these days, not wanting to settle down,' she would say with a tinkling little laugh, and I would grit my teeth and laugh along with her, too polite to tell her that the only reason we weren't tying the knot was because her son didn't want to. Luke and I had talked about it, sure, and although he insisted that he wanted to marry me in the long term, he felt it would be 'unromantic' to propose just because I was pregnant; he would far rather wait until I'd had the baby, so we could make the wedding 'just about us'. And look how well that plan turned out.

We've now reached the bench and Lucia lowers down onto the seat with a little 'oof' noise that I've also caught myself doing lately. Oh, hey there, middle age!

'So, Luca tells me you have a job.'

'Yes, I'm working for an estate agent taking their marketing photos. It's just part-time for now.'

'You're enjoying it?'

'I am. I don't know if you remember, but I used to work in photography before I met Luke, and it's really nice to be taking pictures again.'

Lucia's lips tighten in disapproval. 'And you think it is worth it?'

'Worth it in what way?'

'Well, leaving Dot with a stranger so you can just' – she flutters her hands dismissively – 'take pictures.'

Anger surges up inside me, but I know from experience that it's pointless trying to argue with her, so instead I say, mildly: 'I am getting paid, you know, Lucia.'

'Well, if it's a question of money, then I'm sure Luca would happily give you the money that he's having to pay this childminder person.'

Damn Luke, why does he have to tell his mother everything?

'Annie, you know I love you like a daughter.' This is so blatantly untrue I very nearly laugh. Lucia adores her four daughters only marginally less than Luke; I probably rate somewhere below her chiropodist. 'But this current situation is not good for anyone. Not good *at all*. A child needs both parents. You have to move back home so Dot can be with her father. As for this job – why can't you wait until Dot is bigger? I don't know, you girls these days, so fixated on your career . . .'

I'm this close to jumping up and storming off, but I take a deep breath, determined to stay calm. 'Lucia, you do know what happened between Luke and this other woman, don't you? He cheated on me weeks after I'd given birth.'

Lucia bristles at my tone. 'Yes, Luca told me all about it, and it *is* unfortunate, but you have to remember that when a woman has a baby it is a very tricky time for the father. I should know, I had four by the time I was your age! A man can easily feel neglected and then . . .' She gives a shrug, which I assume translates as: 'and then may be compelled to put his penis into another woman'.

'Lucia, are you suggesting that Luke cheating on me is my own fault?'

'No!' She gasps, her hand flying to her chest, indignant that I'd even *suggest* such a thing. 'No, no, no!' she adds, for emphasis. There's a slight pause. 'But . . . maybe a little, yes.'

I close my eyes, suddenly feeling very tired.

'Annie, there is an old Calabrian saying – it's hard to

translate – but it goes something like: "the role of a good wife is to feed her husband's mouth, his heart and his loins".' She leans closer and lowers her voice. 'And I would say the first and the last of those are the most important.'

Right, so as far as Lucia is concerned, I'm a terrible cook and must be equally useless in bed. That can *obviously* be the only reason Luke strayed.

'Did Luke ask you to speak with me?' Out of the corner of my eye, I notice he's now heading back across the playground towards us; Lucia obviously clocks this too.

'And what if he did?' She suddenly throws up her hands theatrically. 'Annie, he is *desperate* to be a family again! I just wanted to do what I could to help, as any loving mother would for her son.' She reaches inside her black patent handbag, an exact replica of the Queen's, pulls out a lacy hanky and dabs showily at her eyes. 'You see,' she mutters sadly, 'this is what happens when you have a baby before getting married . . .'

Seeing his mother's distress, Luke rushes the last few steps towards us and drops to his knees in front of her. 'Mum, is everything okay?' he asks, his face a picture of concern. And then he turns to me with a look verging on accusatory – 'Annie? What's happened?' – and I have to dig my fingernails into my hand to stop myself exploding, because I know from experience that criticising his mama will only end in tears (mine).

'Shh, it's fine,' coos Lucia, patting her son's hand.

'Annie and I were having a lovely chat and I got a little emotional, that's all. I'm just so worried about the two of you . . .'

Luke gives her a kiss. 'Don't worry, Mum, we'll sort it out.' He glances over at me. 'Won't we, Annie . . . ?'

I set my face in a smile. 'Well, I'm afraid I have to get going, I don't want to be late for my appointment. I'll be round to collect Dottie mid-afternoon, okay?' I give my daughter a kiss, then bend to peck Lucia's powdery cheek. 'Goodbye, Lucia. See you soon.'

'Goodbye, *carissima*,' she says, as if our excruciatingly awkward conversation hasn't happened. 'You think about what I said now, yes . . . ?'

Luke is beaming at the pair of us; he clearly thinks his devious little plan has worked. I, however, am *fuming*. I'll have a think about how to handle Luke later, but at least this has helped me come to a decision about whether I should meet Sam for lunch. Even before I've left the playground, I've got out my phone and replied:

Thanks, Sam, sounds great and I can do this Wednesday. Looking forward to it. Annie.

28

The offices of Mr Rajat Jindal MB, FRCS are situated on Harley Street, the central London mecca for those wanting to get nipped, tucked, lifted or sucked. As I press the buzzer next to the discreet brass plate engraved with his name, the door opens and a woman comes out wearing dark glasses and bandages over her nose, neither of which fully cover the bruises. I get an unsettling flutter of nerves; I know what Delphine said about surgery not being a big deal, but this woman looks like she's had a fist fight, not a facial.

I'm directed to the waiting room by a receptionist who resembles one of those 'best celebrity facial features' photofits you see in gossip mags. Her face is so freakishly perfect that this must surely be Mr Jindal's handiwork – after all, what better way to showcase your skills? – and after the shock of seeing his earlier victim, it gives me a much-needed boost of confidence, although I feel more self-conscious than ever about my own ungainly features.

After filling out reams of forms and having photos of

my face taken from all angles, a nurse appears (again, with flawless facial symmetry) and ushers me in to Mr Jindal's office. Judging by her tones of hushed reverence, you'd think I was about to have an audience with the Pope.

'Annie!' Mr Jindal stands up behind his enormous desk as I enter, his arms spread wide in welcome. 'It's so wonderful to finally meet you.' (Which is charming but a little over the top, given I've only had one very brief phone call with his office.) 'Please, take a seat,' he goes on, with a blindingly white smile.

Mr Jindal is small and has the look of a man who's been drinking his own Kool-Aid, so to speak. His features are curiously feminine, and I fleetingly wonder if he actually operates on himself before realising how stupid that is.

'Have you been offered a drink?' he enquires. His voice is as neat and precise as his facial hair, which looks like it's been trimmed with the aid of a protractor and set square. 'We have the most wonderful silver-tip tea from Fujian province – would you like to try a cup? No? Well, do let me know if you change your mind . . .' He beams at me again, his hands folded neatly on his desk. 'So, you're here to talk about your nose, correct?'

'Yes. It's, well, it's been bothering me for years, really.'

He nods, staring intently at my face. 'Right, so what I'd like to do first is to find out exactly what you like and dislike about your nose.' He gets up, walks around the desk and hands me a mirror. 'Could you please take a look and point to what's bothering you the most?'

I hold up the mirror in front of me; my nose glares furiously back. 'Well, basically, it's too big.'

'So, the size is an issue, okay. Anything else? Could you be a little more specific?'

I turn my head from side to side. 'Um, well, there's a bit of a bump, here. And the tip is a bit . . . er . . .'

'Bulbous?'

'Oh. Right, yes. Bulbous.' It's not *exactly* the word I'd have used, but then I suppose it's Mr Jindal's job to call a spade a spade.

'Could you smile now, please.' I do as he asks. 'Ah yes, do you see how the tip of your nose plunges when you smile and covers the upper lip?'

I hadn't noticed that before, but he's absolutely right. Blimey. This is worse than I thought.

'Now tell me, Annie, what do you *like* about your nose?'

I exhale slowly. Right now, I'm struggling to come up with any positives.

'I suppose I used to like the fact that it looks a bit like Barbra Streisand's.'

Mr Jindal puts his head to one side and narrows his eyes. 'Yes, I do see some resemblance, but her nose is rather more symmetrical than yours.'

Well, that's told me. My final illusion, brutally shattered.

'So, you're quite correct, Annie, there is a bump here.'

Mr Jindal has now got out what looks like a pair of over-sized cotton buds and he deftly moves them around my nose as he speaks. 'The bump is half bone, which is attached to your skull, and half cartilage at the lower point. The delineation of the bony bump and cartilaginous bump goes right through the centre – here. Then, as we move down your nose, you can see that it's veering off towards the left, and as we've already discussed, the tip is rather bulbous. Could you tip your head back a little, please?' He bends down to look up my nose. 'Hmmm, yes, as I thought. You have a deviated septum. Do you have any breathing issues?'

I shake my head.

'Really?' He looks puzzled. 'Well, it may not be an issue now, but even a mild deviation can become a problem in the future.'

Wow. My nose really is a disaster area. I'd always thought it was just a little on the large side, but it turns out that it's the nasal equivalent of global warming.

Mr Jindal sits back on the edge of his desk. 'So, bearing in mind all these issues, my first job would be to file the bony bump away from the inside of the nostrils and then straighten the cartilage in line with the bump, so there's a neat, straight line between the root of the nose and the tip of the nose. My next job would be centralising the nose because, as we have noted, it's crooked. The third job would be refining the bulbousness of the tip and finally preventing the nose from drooping on smiling.'

'That sounds like an awful lot of jobs.'

Mr Jindal laughs politely. 'The rhinoplasty would probably take me about two hours. I'm a meticulous surgeon and pay very precise attention to detail.'

'And afterwards? How quickly would I be back to normal?'

'A heat-sensitive plastic splint would be attached to your nose to aid recovery. In five to six days that would come off, and within a week you'll be back out with a beautiful new nose.'

'Really, that quickly?' The image of sunglasses woman flashes into my mind. 'Won't I look a bit . . . battered?'

'There'll be some light bruising, but not much.' Mr Jindal stands and gestures towards a computer at the side of the room. 'Let's give you an idea of what I think is achievable with the surgery.'

We sit down side by side in front of the computer, where one of my photos from earlier is already displayed in merciless close-up on screen. I'm not used to seeing my 'resting' face; I had no idea quite how haggard and dour I look.

'That's not my best side,' I wince.

Mr Jindal laughs politely. 'Well, it's my job to make sure that *every* side is your best side. You deserve a nose that reflects your natural beauty.'

He starts manipulating the image on screen and I watch, transfixed, as he makes tiny, subtle adjustments to gradually create my new nose. After a few minutes, he finally seems happy and turns to me with an expectant smile.

'So what do you think?'

What I think, Mr Jindal, is that I am never going to be happy when I look in the mirror again. Now that I've seen what I have the potential to look like, the flaws on my actual face have been magnified to hideous proportions. I stare at the miraculous stranger on the screen: she's still haggard and dour, but, bloody hell, her nose is *perfect*. Mr Jindal is now rattling on about payment plans and whatever, but I'm not really listening because all my attention is focused on the image in front of me and one single, seductive thought: *Where do I sign?*

29

My lunch date with Sam has not got off to a good start. In fact, I'm beginning to wonder if it's actually going to start at all.

I was already flustered when I got to the restaurant, as I was running ten minutes late thanks to delays on the Central line, but when I finally arrived, Sam wasn't here either. And now it's another ten minutes later, I've still not heard from him and I'm sitting in the middle of a virtually empty, extremely swanky restaurant – the sort of place where if you leave your seat for even a split second, they'll have refolded your napkin – and I feel like the staff are all wondering whether I've been stood up.

I wouldn't blame them if they were, because that's exactly what I'm thinking too.

I check my phone for the umpteenth time. There's been a flurry of activity in my WhatsApp group with the girls – mostly Jess being obscene, but also a sweet message from Claris: *Just relax and enjoy yourself and try not to worry about the bigger picture right now.* I reply with kisses and almost instantly there's a message from Fi: *Is he there yet??* And then another from Jess: *Hope you've got condoms!*

'Would you care to see the wine list?'

I look up to see the waitress, who has already brought me a bottle of water and the food menu, holding out a leather-bound folder with a ravishing smile. And that's another thing: there must be a dozen waiting staff in here, but I've got stuck with the one who looks like an actress who's only here to research playing the role of a waitress in a Hollywood movie. Pretty would be okay, beautiful I could just about cope with, devastatingly stunning is another matter entirely. I thought I was looking quite good this morning – I blow-dried my hair and I've borrowed a silky blouse from Jess – but you really don't want that sort of competition on a first date. Which brings me to yet another area of concern, namely: is this actually a date at all? It's been so long since Sam and I last saw each other (nearly three weeks, in fact) that doubts and worries have gradually been crowding in and are now taking the edge off the knicker-pinging sense of excitement I'd usually be feeling before a first date with a guy I really like. Worries such as: did Sam and I really have fantastic chemistry or did I just imagine it? Is this a sex thing, a friend thing or just a lunch thing? What – if anything – should I tell him about Dot? And is that a piece of leftover breakfast granola I can feel between my teeth?

I get out my phone, flip the camera to selfie mode and am subtly checking out my reflection – baring my teeth at the screen like an angry, FaceTiming dog – and, of course, this is the exact moment that Sam chooses to arrive at the table.

'Hey, I'm so sorry I'm late, I got held up at work.' He bends down to kiss me on the cheek, but I'm in such a fluster at being caught grimacing into my phone that I stand up, leading to a clumsy clash of heads. Sam sits down, but immediately stands up again because I'm still on my feet. It's so ridiculously awkward that we both start to laugh.

'I guess we should probably do this sitting down, right?' asks Sam, the clunkiness of our greeting breaking the ice, his lateness forgiven. And then he smiles at me across the table and my tummy turns somersaults and I think: YES.

His facial hair is shorter, more stubble than beard now, giving a clear view of that kissable mouth, and he's as well-dressed as ever in a grey suit. But something more than his undeniable hotness is giving me butterflies. When I look into his eyes, I get that same feeling again, the one that made me act so appallingly on our first meeting, the notion that we are somehow *destined* to be together. Perhaps not even in a romantic way – I'm not talking about soulmates or any of that Hallmark crap – but that we're meant to be in each other's lives. There's something familiar about him, even though we're from different sides of the planet and have known each other for a grand total of about twelve minutes.

Of course, I keep all of this to myself, because I don't want to terrify the poor guy, and instead I stick to small-talk convention and ask about Sam's job.

'I'm a banker,' he says with an apologetic grimace, mentioning the name of a big American investment bank that even I've heard of. 'I work in a department called Private Wealth.'

'That sounds exclusive,' I say. 'Like how Donald Trump would refer to his piggy bank: "Yeah, this is where I keep my Private Wealth".'

Sam grins at my terrible Trump impression. 'Well, he's not one of our clients, thank God, but we do only deal with ultra high net worth individuals.'

'So how much money would I need in my account to do business with you?'

'Ten million dollars minimum.' He looks me square in the eye and smiles. 'But I could definitely make exceptions.'

I can feel the chemistry between us and I'm getting more confident that this is actually a *date* date – because surely you don't smile at someone like that if you just want to be friends? – and I get a lovely little shiver of anticipation at what might be on the cards, but then: *disaster*. The waitress-slash-starlet sashays up to our table, and I suddenly know how a sparrow must feel when a peacock rocks up and whips out its tail feathers. Like, I might as well just flap off, because honestly, who's going to throw me any crumbs now?

'Are you ready for me to take your order?' she asks, all flicky blonde hair and fluttery blue eyes.

I watch as Sam turns and gets his first look at her, my heart already sinking; his eyes widen ever so slightly – although he's far too well mannered to gawp – and he says, I kid you not: 'How you doing?' Not exactly in that Joey Tribbiani from *Friends* way ('How *you* doin'?') but there's definitely a hint of interest in his tone. Meanwhile, she transforms from the politely professional server of earlier into a brazen vixen sexpot on the prowl for Canadian man-flesh.

'I'm doing really well, thank you,' she says. 'You?'

'I'm good, thanks,' says Sam, returning her smile.

Why did she have to be our waitress? Why why why? We're virtually the only customers in the place. There's a table of four businessmen across the room from us and they've got a male waiter looking after them. Surely they should have assigned Miss World to the blokes? The tips alone would have made that a more sensible decision.

She takes our order and, to be fair, Sam does instantly turn his attention entirely back to me when she finally leaves, and he doesn't glance at her disappearing back view in that maddeningly unsubtle way blokes can have, but still, I'm definitely rattled.

'So, tell me, Annie,' says Sam, leaning forward as if fascinated in what I have to say. 'How long have you been working in real estate?'

'Not long. Just a few weeks, really.'

'It must be so interesting, being able to look around other people's homes.'

'Yeah, it is,' I say, my Instagram feed full of clients' stuff flashing guiltily into my mind. 'But it's more the photography side of the job that interests me. I used to work as an assistant to quite a well-known fashion photographer when I was younger.'

'Who was that? Would I have heard of them?'

'Maybe – he's certainly got quite a reputation. Jay Patterson?'

Sam raises his eyebrows and nods, and I'm gratified to see he's impressed. (God, I miss that look; you just don't get the same reaction when you say you work for Curtis Kinderbey.) 'Sure, I know him – the guy who was busted for drugs recently? That must have been fascinating. How did you end up working for him?'

So I tell him about my days as a full-time top photographer's assistant and part-time party girl and Streisand super-fan. I'm on far more solid ground with this subject, and as I reel out my well-rehearsed anecdotes, breezily name-dropping A-list celebrities and locations, it hits home once again just how much more of a catch Barb was: better looking, more interesting, basically a lot more fun; certainly a more fitting prospect for a Manhattan-dwelling banker type like Sam.

Sure enough, he seems fascinated by the old me.

'Well, you're officially the most glamorous person I know,' he says, after I tell him my story of Kate Moss complaining about the coffee I made for her (embellishing my role a little, naturally). 'So why did you stop working in fashion?'

I hesitate, taking a sip of wine while trying to decide how I should respond. I never like telling new acquaintances about my parents' accident, partly because it makes them feel awkward, but also because I don't want them to cast me as a victim. I get the impression, however, that Sam would probably take it in his stride.

So I say: 'My mum and dad died in a car crash five years ago and I really struggled to deal with it, so I had to quit my job with Jay.'

'God, I'm so sorry. I can't imagine how tough that must have been. No wonder you needed to take a break.' There's a flash of pity in his eyes, but it's quickly replaced by something closer to admiration. 'How the hell do you cope with something like that?'

'I didn't, really, not at first. I got loads of support – I'm really close to my sister, Tabitha. But when I was ready to go back to work, the fashion world had moved on without me.' I shrug. 'It's fine, it's a young person's game, really.'

'What are you talking about? You're still young!'

'You're very kind, but I wouldn't have the stamina any-more. Certainly not for the partying that went along with the job.'

Sam nods. 'Yeah, I know what you mean. These days I'm happier at home in my apartment than hanging out in a club where you can't even get a seat. Friends will ask me to some cool party and I'll be like, "Sorry, but I need to get home and watch *Frasier* reruns with my dog".' He shakes his head, chuckling to himself, and I smile too because he's basically signalling that he's not a player, which is excellent news. 'Seymour is like my surrogate child – I plan my life around that mutt . . .'

Okay, now would be the perfect moment to mention Dot. This is the ideal opening. I'll tell him I have a baby and that I'm no longer with the father, but it's all very chilled and civilised. His face will light up with delighted surprise and he'll ask if he can see a photo of her. He'll coo over how cute she is, then our eyes will meet, I'll feel his hand reaching for mine and he will softly admit that he's always wanted to be a father, and when can he meet her?

. . . Yeah, but that's not really the most likely reaction, though, is it?

Let's try that again: I'll tell him I have a baby and that I'm no longer with the father, but it's all very chilled and civilised. His eyes will bulge with horror and he'll stam-mer something about how that's really great, but inside he's now thinking of me as a feckless single mother look-ing for some schmuck to help raise her kid and is frantically wondering how he can get the hell out of here without being rude.

Because it *is* a bit of a passion killer, isn't it? Not just that I've got a baby, so wouldn't have as much time for lots of sexy, irresponsible fun with him, but – to put it bluntly – the fact that I am no longer box-fresh. Sam could have his pick of women; why would he go for the one whose vagina has had to stretch to accommodate a human head? After all, it is a truth universally acknow-ledged that a single man in possession of a dog is cute and a bit sexy, while a single woman with a baby is desperate and a bit sad.

Sam's a decent guy though, and he seems to like me. He'll get it, right? And if not – well, better to find out now, surely. I take a deep breath and adopt my most upbeat, breezy tone. 'So, here's a funny thing . . .'

'Right, so we've got the sea bass . . .' Oh bloody hell, Jen-nifer Lawrence is back with our main courses. Fantastic timing. And am I imagining it, or has she undone a couple of buttons at the top of her shirt? '. . . And the pumpkin gnocchi,' she says, setting down the plates in front of us, totally unaware that she's just ruined my big moment.

'Thank you, it all looks delicious,' says Sam.

Off you trot now, I think, shooting the waitress 'piss off' vibes, but she lingers by the table, smiling at Sam, and then says: 'Whereabouts in Canada are you from?'

WTF? How did she know he's Canadian?

'Toronto. But I live in New York these days.'

'My dad grew up in Montreal.'

'Do you still visit?' he asks.

'Yeah, every Christmas. My grandparents live there. I love it.'

Sam nods. 'It's a beautiful part of the world.'

I'm trying to think of something to say so I can elbow my way into their little chat, but all I know about Canada is that they have elks and a fairly hot prime minister, neither of which are going to be much help here.

'So do you get back to Toronto much?' the waitress asks, head tipped to the side in the most adorable way.

'Sure, often as I can. My parents and sister live just outside the city.'

Well, this is news to me. Now this woman is literally stealing information that is rightfully mine. I suppose Sam can't *not* reply to a direct question, but does he really have to offer her additional details? Why couldn't he have just said 'yes' and then ignored her, like English people would?

As I watch Sam and the waitress talking, a terrible thought suddenly occurs to me. What if the special rapport I thought I had with Sam isn't actually that special after all? Perhaps he's just a friendly guy who's good at chatting, and I've been mistaking his natural charisma for incredible sexual chemistry. Because, although it pains me to admit it, the way he's being with our waitress – charming, smiley, a bit flirty – is almost exactly the same way he's been with me.

In an instant, the vision of the two of us snuggled up together in his apartment watching *Frasier* reruns, Dottie on the sofa between us and Seymour at our feet, fizzles out with a sad farting noise, like a deflating balloon.

While the waitress bangs on about something called 'beavertails', which seem to be a sort of Canadian snack, I test out this new information to see how it makes me feel. *Sam just wants to be friends.* That's okay, isn't it? You can never have too many friends, and I don't have any Canadian ones at present. When he goes back Stateside we can be pen pals! Plus, if Sam *had* wanted to get involved romantically, it would all have been horribly complicated and stressful bearing in mind my current personal situation. Yes, this really is for the best, all things considered.

I stare down at my plate, but what had looked mouthwatering just a few moments ago now seems stomachturning. I poke morosely at the gnocchi, my appetite gone the same way as my good mood.

'Is your food alright?'

I look up to find Sam watching me with a quizzical smile, and now that sex is off the table it hits me just how desperately I actually want him – so much so that I can feel it as a physical ache, like period cramps. I get a vivid flashback to the moment we kissed: the softness of his lips, his warm breath, the smell of his skin. It's just so rare that you meet someone that gives you goosebumps, and for a heady half-hour back there I really thought Sam might feel the same way – and after the gut-punch of Luke's betrayal, it was exactly what I needed. But now it looks like I've misread the whole situation.

If only you'd met him after you had your nose job, whispers a little voice inside me, *then he might have fancied you*.

'Annie?' Sam is now looking at me with genuine concern. 'What's the matter?'

I open my mouth to reply, but I've been sucked so far into this vortex of self-pity that I can't find the words, so I fake a coughing fit, holding up my hand in an 'I'm-okay-just-give-me-a-moment' way, and in the time it takes me to drink some water, I give myself a stern talking-to. I can either stumble through the rest of this lunch feeling sorry for myself, which would be no fun for anyone, or I can follow Claris' advice – *relax and enjoy yourself and try not to worry about the bigger picture* – and make the most of being taken out for a swanky lunch by a lovely man without agonising over what the future might hold. Clearly, the latter is the only sane choice.

'Sorry, something went down the wrong way,' I say. 'How's the sea bass?'

We talk for a while about New York – a place I know

well from my fashion days – and then about travelling in general, and we discover that we share an ambition to walk the Inca trail to Machu Picchu, which makes my inner romantic scream, 'See, this is fate after all! You're meant to walk it together on your honeymoon!', until I firmly tell it to shut the eff up. And I discover that when I'm just being entirely myself, rather than 'mum' Annie, or 'Barb' Annie, or even 'sexy potential shag' Annie, I start to relax with Sam in the same way I would do with Fi or Jess. We manage to avoid the subject of past relationships, as I guess you tend to do when romance is off the table, which means I don't have to tell any lies about Luke. And, best of all, our supermodel waitress doesn't reappear again; it's an average-looking male waiter who delivers our pudding, then our coffee and who then hovers awkwardly with the bill because our lunch has run on far longer than it should have done and they need to clear the tables ready for dinner.

We could easily carry on the conversation, but Sam says with what sounds like genuine regret that he needs to get back to work. He insists on picking up the bill and as we walk out I feel his hand gently resting in the small of my back.

'Thank you so much for lunch, I had a really lovely time,' I say, as we stand on the busy pavement outside the restaurant.

'Me too.' His eyes are fixed on mine, and despite all my

good intentions about living in the moment, I'm hoping with every fibre of my being that he suggests meeting up again. Instead he says: 'Can I get you a taxi?'

'No, it's fine, I'll hop on the tube.'

'Okay, Cinderella.' I get the impression he's prolonging our goodbye, although I'm sure that's wishful thinking. 'Well, I better get back to the office.'

'Yeah, all that money won't count itself.' I grin.

He smiles at me. 'Well then, take care.'

Then he lightly kisses my cheek and disappears off into the crowd without a backward glance.

30

Tabby is lounging on my bed in Jess' attic room, working her way through a bowl of sweet 'n' salty popcorn, while I run straighteners through my hair. The radio is playing some half-remembered house anthem from the early Noughties. It would be a scene straight out of our teenage years – except for Dot's cot in the corner, Tabby's pregnant belly and the fact that we're drinking tea rather than contraband Baileys.

'So this woman marched up to me at the fish counter in Waitrose,' Tabby is saying, 'and she put her hands on my stomach and said, "You're obviously having a girl, you're carrying exactly the same way I was with my daughter". And I was just like' – Tabby does a pantomime gawp – 'and I told her, very politely, that actually I've had a scan and it's a boy, and she said – and honest to God, Annie, she was really cross – she said, "Don't be ridiculous, it's definitely a girl, they get those scans wrong all the time". And then she walked off, tutting to herself!'

'Oh my God, you were bump-shamed! Why do people treat you as public property when you're pregnant? It's like you're suddenly just this *vessel*.'

'I know! And she was so bloody sure of herself . . .'

Tabby reaches for the popcorn, giggling. She had another scan this week, and the baby's measurements were far more reassuring; it lightens my heart to see her looking happy and relaxed.

'God, what if she *was* right?' she adds, her handful of popcorn frozen en route to her mouth. 'We've gone for a truck theme for the nursery!'

'Well then, your daughter will be a lovely lady trucker when she grows up.'

'Not sure Jonathan's parents would be too pleased about that . . .' She nods over at the dressing table. 'Chuck me your make-up bag, will you, hon, I should at least put on some mascara before we go out.'

I do as she asks, then head for the bathroom. 'I'm going to pop to the loo and then we should probably get going.'

It's our monthly girls' catch-up tonight, and Tabby and I are meeting Fiona and Claris at a tapas bar in nearby Brixton (Jess is in Paris at a beauty conference – it's one of life's mysteries how she manages to hold on to such a glamorous, perk-heavy job when she barely seems to work). Luke is looking after Dot, and although I'm really looking forward to seeing the girls, especially as I need to give them a blow-by-blow account of my lunch with Sam, once again it's the prospect of an uninterrupted night's sleep that's making me really excited – more so than ever, in fact. I made the mistake of mentioning to one of the Little Splashy Quackers mums last week that Dot was now sleeping through the night, and since then the universe has been kicking my butt big time, with Dot waking several times every night and screaming until I stick her on the boob. Last night she woke at 1 a.m., 3 a.m. and 5.30 a.m., and although she dropped straight off again after being fed, I had no such luck, and spent much of the night lying awake, stressing about the Luke situation and wondering if I'll ever hear from Sam again. After bad nights like this I become *obsessed* with how much sleep I've had, piecing together the snatched fragments to reassure myself I won't go crazy from sleep deprivation: 'It's fine, I've had a total of ... let's see ... four and a half hours' sleep – that's plenty! Dwayne "The Rock" Johnson made seven *Fast and Furious* movies on only three hours' sleep a night! And Donald Trump only gets four hours – and he's sort of holding things together, right? *Right* ... ?'

There's a stack of baby-care books next to the loo in my bathroom, and I resist the urge to search for solutions to the sleep issue that I know won't be in there because I've checked a dozen times already. I'm thinking of starting Dot on solids next month, as she's obviously hungry, so hopefully that will improve things.

I take a final look in the bathroom mirror, squirt on

some perfume and then head back into my bedroom. 'So have you had any more thoughts about baby names?'

But Tabby doesn't answer. She's sitting on the edge of the bed staring at a piece of paper in her hands, and when she looks up at me she seems shaken.

'Tabby? What's the matter?'

'What's this?' she asks – and holds up the picture of my new nose from Mr Jindal's office. Bugger, I must have left it on the bedside table.

'Oh sorry, I was planning to talk to you about that.' I'm not sure why I'm apologising, but the look in Tabby's eyes is making me feel oddly ashamed.

'But what's it for? And who's Mr Jindal?'

I cross over and sit on the bed next to her. 'He's a plastic surgeon. I went to see him last week to talk about my nose.'

'But why?'

'Well, to get it fixed, obviously. Made smaller.'

She stares at me, horrified. 'You're not thinking of getting a nose job?'

'Well, yes, I am. You know I've never been happy with it.'

'I know you occasionally mutter some nonsense about it being too big, but I had no idea it was bothering you *this* much.' For some reason, she seems angry – and that makes me angry.

'Do you have a problem with this?'

'Of course I do! Why on earth would you want to do something like this to yourself? It's crazy!'

'I'm sorry, Tabby, but you're overreacting . . .'

'*I'm* overreacting? I'm not the one who's thinking about butchering herself!' Tabby gets up off the bed and crosses to the side of the room, as if she's so furious she needs to get away from me. 'Look, your confidence has taken a knock because of Luke cheating, I understand that, but this' – she brandishes the paper accusingly – 'is not the answer.'

I stare at my feet, like a kid being scolded by her mum. 'I have no idea why you're making such a huge deal over this,' I mutter.

'Because it *is* a huge deal! You used to love your nose, Annie, what's happened?'

'I used to love my nose because it was part of my Barbra Streisand thing, but that's not me anymore.'

'No, and thank God for that,' she says tartly. 'You were an absolute nightmare.'

I gape at her like she's just punched me in the guts. '*What?*'

'I'm sorry, Annie, but it needs saying. I know you think Barb was this amazingly fascinating person who everyone adored, and now you're just some frumpy, pale imitation of who you used to be, but honestly, you couldn't be more wrong.' Tabby is pacing around the room, getting increasingly het up. 'Today's Annie is sweet and kind and funny, and *so* much more amazing than that self-obsessed girl who thought she was God's gift just because she worked for that idiot Jay Patterson and once made coffee for Kate Moss!'

For a moment I'm too stunned to speak, partly because this outburst is so unlike Tabby, but also because I truly believed that Barb had been my absolute best self – exciting, glamorous, successful – and it hadn't even occurred to me for one moment that my sister might feel otherwise.

'Tabby, I'm going to forgive you for saying all this because you're pregnant and hormonal, and God only knows I remember how batshit crazy that can make you, but I think you're being more than a little unfair.'

'No, I'm being honest. You turned yourself into a cartoon character. You might have looked incredible, but it wasn't the real you – and I know for a fact that being Barb didn't make you happy. I was living with you at the time, remember? You were always stressing about whether Jay was about to get rid of you, how you looked, whether you were at the right clubs with the right people . . .' She gives a huff of frustration, running her hands through her hair. 'It's like you've completely rewritten history and forgotten how things really were back then.'

'That's not true,' I say, shaking my head.

'Having plastic surgery is not going to make you happy, Annie. It won't solve your problems with Luke, or bring

Mum and Dad back. I'm sorry to say this, but it's not your nose that needs fixing, it's your *head*.'

I stare at her open-mouthed, staggered by her insensitivity, and anger rushes up inside me. 'Tabby, that is bang out of order. It's fine for you with your perfect little nose and perfect little life – Jonathan would never do the dirty on *you*. *You've* never been bullied for the way you look. You have it so fucking easy, Tabby, you have absolutely no idea . . .'

I turn my back on her, struggling to keep a lid on the emotions that are threatening to burst out. I really don't want to start screaming at my pregnant sister, but this feels like a personal attack – and Tabby's the one person I thought I could always rely on. Neither one of us speaks for a minute, maybe longer, but then I feel her hand on my shoulder and when I turn around and see the tears glistening in her eyes, my anger is swept aside in a rush of love.

She pulls me into a hug, and we cling together. 'Oh God, I'm so sorry, Annie, I've handled this terribly,' she murmurs into my shoulder. 'I was just shocked by the fact that you would want to do something like this to yourself. You're so beautiful, I just wish you could see that . . .' She pulls away and looks me straight in the eyes. 'Look, if this is something you really want to do, then of course I'll support you a hundred per cent. But please, can you at least wait until your life is a bit more settled before making such a huge decision? Because you can't change your mind once you've done it. You'll be stuck looking like . . . well, like someone who's had a nose job.'

I reach for the paper that Tabby is still clutching. 'But it's quite subtle,' I say, smoothing out the creases and holding it for both of us to look at. 'Don't you think it makes me look better?'

'No, I think it makes you look like someone from *Geordie Shore*.' But she's smiling as she says it.

We have another hug and the horrible scrunched-up feeling inside me starts to ease. Tabby and I hardly ever argue; it feels like the universe is thrown out of kilter when we do.

'Come on, then, we better get a move on,' I say, heading for the door.

But Tabby doesn't follow. 'Annie, would you mind terribly if I don't come tonight?'

'Not because we just had a bit of a disagreement, surely?'

'No, I'm just not feeling too great. I'm knackered and I've been getting these crampy pains . . .' She rubs her bump; she does look quite tired. 'I should probably get an early night. You understand, don't you?'

'Sure, but why don't I stay here with you? We could get a takeaway, watch a movie . . .'

'No, you go. Have fun for both of us.'

I linger by the door, trying to work out whether she really means it.

'I'll be fine, honest,' she insists. 'Send my love to Fi and Claris.'

We hug goodbye, and I'm already halfway out the door when she calls: 'Annie, we are okay, aren't we? You're not mad about what I said?'

'Of course not,' I say, blowing her a kiss.

Nevertheless, I can't help stewing over Tabby's outburst on the bus ride to Brixton. What was it she called me? *Self-obsessed . . . a cartoon character . . .* Barb wasn't that awful, surely? And she's certainly got it wrong about how happy I was back then – as far as I can remember, I was too busy having fun to be worried about anything . . . By the time I get to the tapas bar, I've pretty much dismissed Tabby's comments as well-meaning, but hormonally misguided.

Fiona and Claris are sitting at a candlelit table in the corner, hams hanging from the rafters above them, picking at plates of croquetas, chorizo and tortilla.

'At last! You're lucky we left you anything.' Fi grins, getting up to kiss me.

'How are you, my love?' says Claris. 'Where's Tabby?'

'She's not coming. She wasn't feeling that great and . . . well, we had an argument.'

'That's not like you two.' Claris wrinkles her brow. 'What happened?'

'Well, I mentioned that I was possibly thinking about having a nose job and she flew off the handle.'

There's a stunned silence; Fi and Claris look at me as if

I've just announced I'm having a sex change. Christ, not them as well?

'Oh come on, surely it can't come as *that* much of a shock?'

'Of course it's a shock!' roars Fi. 'Jesus, woman, have you gone insane?'

'We just had no idea that you were considering something that, um, drastic,' says Claris, diplomatic as ever. 'Why would you want to change your beautiful face?'

'Because I hate my nose, alright?' I slop wine into my glass, fuming. I can't believe how old-fashioned they're being about this! I guess it's not their fault they're not as forward-thinking as Riva, but really, they could try to be a *little* more open-minded.

'Well, of course, it's your decision,' soothes Claris. 'And we'll be there for you whatever you decide to do.' She shoots Fi a significant look. 'Won't we, Fiona?'

'You don't need a feckin' nose job,' she mutters darkly, stuffing an olive in her mouth. 'But yes, of course, if it's what you *really* want . . .'

'Thank you,' I snap, far more tetchily than I intended. It doesn't help that last night's sleep deprivation is fast catching up with me.

Claris smiles nervously at me and Fi, clearly keen to smooth over any tension.

'So Tabby's okay, is she, Annie? Just a little tired?'

'Yeah, I'm sure she'll be fine after an early night.' I intend to leave it at that, but Tabby's comments from earlier are still niggling at me. 'She was in a really funny mood though. She told me I was a nightmare when I worked for Jay, called me self-centred. Can you believe it?'

I see Fi and Claris glance at each other, as if trying to work out how to respond, and immediately regret bringing this up.

'Well, I wouldn't necessarily have used the word *nightmare* ...' Claris begins carefully. 'You were very cool and loads of fun, and obviously you looked so glamorous, but you were a little ... unreliable.'

'Yeah, always cancelling at the last minute,' agrees Fi. 'And you did kind of think you were fucking *it*, what with your fancy job and kaftans and that dickhead male model who was always messing you about ...'

I look at them both, open-mouthed; for the second time tonight it feels like the rug's been pulled out from under me. 'What is this, "Bash Annie Day"? If I was so bloody awful back then, why didn't any of you tell me at the time?'

Fi takes a sip of wine. 'Well, it wasn't so much *you* that was the problem, but the people you were hanging out with.'

'Jesus, here we go again!' I virtually shriek, on the verge of losing it completely. 'Fi, why do you have such a fucking problem with Riva? Are you just jealous because I'm back in touch with that lot again?'

'No, Annie, it's not because I'm jealous, it's because I

care for you, unlike those eejits. Have you forgotten how they all dropped you when your parents died? Not one of them made an effort to get in touch. It was like the moment you weren't fun, fabulous Barb anymore, you no longer existed. God forbid they should have actually got their faces out of the coke long enough to check up on you! And then when you were ready to go back to work again, they didn't lift a finger to help you get a job.' She shakes her head bitterly. 'As far as I'm concerned, that was when they showed their true colours.'

'It wasn't their fault! You remember what I was like during that time – I went to pieces, I completely shut myself away.'

'Yeah, I remember because I was *there*. And so was Claris, and Jess.' Fi glares at me accusingly. 'Where the feck was this Riva?'

I'm shaking with anger, and it would be very easy for me to lash out and shout and rant at Fi over this, but I'm not yet so out of control that I don't realise she's only saying it because she cares about me. Besides, she's got a terrible temper; I don't want to unleash that on our fellow diners. Still, I want her to see that she's being unfair.

'Maybe Riva wasn't there for me after Mum and Dad died like you guys were, but she was just a work colleague, not one of my closest friends, and besides, she actually apologised about that the other day.' I take a deep breath, trying to stay calm. 'I'm sorry you don't like that crowd,

Fi, but I had a really fun time with them the other night, and I'm going to be seeing them again next week.' I should leave it there, but in my current point-scoring mood, something else occurs to me. 'And if we're on the subject of being supportive, Riva and that lot are being far more understanding about my nose job than you are.'

I realise what a stupid thing this is to say before it even leaves my mouth.

'Yeah, that figures,' mutters Fi sarcastically. 'In fact, they're probably the ones who suggested it . . .'

Maybe it's because this is all far too close to the bone, but something inside of me suddenly snaps.

'Right, I'm going home,' I say, grabbing my bag and jumping up.

'Annie . . .' Claris reaches her hand towards me.

'Oh come on, you eejit, don't leave like this,' says Fi.

'No, I'm sorry, I'm just really tired.' I feel like I've just done twelve rounds in a boxing ring and I need my bed. I scrabble in my purse for money and put some notes on the table. 'I'll call you tomorrow. Sorry.'

I give them both a quick kiss and head for the door. I'll smooth things over with them tomorrow; I'm too knackered to deal with this now.

31

Having been working in the world of premium property for a couple of months now, I thought I'd seen all the ludicrously ostentatious things you could do to a house – until today, and this koi carp pond.

Nothing unusual about that, you say? Ah, but this particular koi carp pond is *indoors*, located downstairs in this mansion's enormous basement extension. There's a little bridge over the pond, decorated with lanterns and a gold Buddha, and it leads to a swimming pool complex, complete with a wave machine, artificial beach and a hand-painted re-creation of Michelangelo's Sistine Chapel ceiling, so you can watch God creating Adam while practising backstroke. You get the impression the interior designer couldn't decide on a theme for the basement – Japanese Zen, Baywatch or perhaps the Vatican – and so boldly went for a mash-up of all three.

'What do you think?' I ask Rudy. We are standing by the side of the pool, the sound of lapping waves and piped Tibetan gong music echoing around the cavernous space.

'Appalling,' he mutters, face pained. 'This place is the definitive answer to the question: "How do you know if you have too much money?"'

I'm not here to take photos today; the owner, heir to a Greek shipping fortune, is such an important client that Karl wanted Rudy to accompany me on a preliminary recce so we could discuss marketing strategy – although I can't think there'll be that many potential buyers for a multi-million-pound mansion with an integral papal-themed leisure complex.

Just then Mr Eliopoulos, the aforementioned shipping magnate, strolls over the bridge. He'd gone upstairs to speak to the housekeeper; he wanted to show us how the swimming pool transforms into a dance floor but couldn't remember which button to press.

'Sorry, it's the pool chap's day off,' he says cheerily, 'but I'll make sure it's working the next time you come.'

As gazillionaires go, Mr Eliopoulos is one of the more pleasant I've met – and also one of the more flamboyant. In his statement glasses and Versace print shirt, he resembles a younger, Greeker Elton John.

'So Rudy, how do you like my frescoes?' he asks, gesturing to the ceiling. 'The painting of David is actually modelled on an old boyfriend of mine.'

'The craftsmanship is exquisite,' enthuses Rudy, his

RADA training to the fore. 'My partner is actually work-ing on a doctorate in Renaissance art, so I've visited the Sistine Chapel many times; I could almost believe this had been painted by Michelangelo himself.'

I barely manage to stifle a giggle at this blatant bullshit, but Mr Eliopoulos literally twinkles with delight. 'Really? Well, you must bring your partner to visit sometime, I'd love to get his expert opinion on some of my other works . . .'

It takes my mind a moment to process this breaking news: Rudy is *gay*? I can't believe I'm only discovering this now! I guess I shouldn't be entirely surprised – the fond-ness for musicals and Barbra Streisand should perhaps have signposted me in that direction – but I really hadn't got that impression. Not that he gives much away: in fact, getting to know the real Rudy involves as much detective work as a whole series of *Line of Duty* . . .

Mr Eliopoulos puts his hand around Rudy's shoulders and steers him towards the bridge – 'Let's head outside: I think you're going to love the treehouse guest suite and Bikram studio . . .' – leaving me to trot along behind as the third wheel.

As flabbergastingly over the top as Mr Eliopoulos' house is, as we continue the tour, my mind's not really on the job. Not only am I trying to digest this new informa-tion about Rudy, I had a bit of an awkward encounter with Fiona in the office this morning and it's still niggling at me. Fi and I did make up the day after our tapas bar argument – she obviously felt as awful about it as I did – but when I saw her earlier, I got the impression she was still a bit off with me, even though she was her usual chatty self. This in turn made me bristly with her – because surely if anyone has the right to be angry, it's me? I keep running over the negative things the girls said the other night about Barb, and I can only conclude that the real issue is that they just collectively got the hump back then because I was off having fun without them. And yes, I do understand that it must have been annoying to hear me banging on about my adventures, but that doesn't mean that I was full of myself – it was just the kind of life I was living back then. What was I meant to do: *not* tell my best friends what I was up to? Well, they'll just have to get used to the fact that Riva's back in my life; I'm not going to cancel my plans to see the old gang again this Friday just because Fiona has a problem with them.

Tour of the garden complete, Mr Eliopoulos leads Rudy and me back to the main kitchen (there are also two other smaller kitchens, in case ... well, I'm not entirely sure why, really).

'If you're happy to wait in here for a moment, I just need to make a couple of calls, and then I can answer any other questions you have,' he says.

'Of course, thank you, Mr Eliopoulos,' says Rudy, taking a seat at the kitchen island, which would look exactly like a giant marble tomb if it wasn't surrounded by jaunty bar stools.

'You have an absolutely magnificent home,' I add.

Mr Eliopoulos smiles. 'Well, I look forward to you achieving a sale price to reflect that,' he says, heading for the door. 'If you'd like coffee while you wait, just ring the bell, Minerva will fix it for you.'

I wait until he's gone, then turn to Rudy and say: 'Nice guy – and he's clearly taken quite a shine to you.'

But he barely nods, engrossed in something on his phone, so I hop off the stool and have a poke around the kitchen. I've got so used to indulging my nosiness at work that it doesn't even occur to me to curtail my snooping in front of Rudy.

Mr Eliopoulos' main kitchen has everything that I've come to expect in such a property: Sub-Zero freezer drawers, a commercial-grade six-burner range with integral rotisserie, a Dacor WineStation (like a coffee vending machine, but for vintage Viognier) and a pantry that would make Nigella drool. There are several doors leading off the kitchen to other parts of the house, but one of them intrigues me in particular: it's made of frosted glass and has what looks like a large bolt on the front. I can't see in, so I tentatively try the handle and the door swings open, letting out a gust of chilled air.

'Check this out, Rudy – it's a walk-in fridge!'

He doesn't even look up, so I go inside.

Judging by its contents, Mr Eliopoulos is imminently expecting either a legion of house guests or Armageddon. The shelves along one side of the fridge are completely taken up with soft drinks – rows of bottles of San Pellegrino, cans of Diet Coke, exotic cordials and juices – and then the rest of the room is filled with what you'd usually expect to see in a fridge (caviar and foie gras aside) except on an industrial scale. The cheese section alone boasts the same variety and volume as a Tesco Metro. But the best bit is the entire shelf of glass Kilner jars, each filled with different chopped-up fruit or vegetables, waiting, I presume, to be blended into smoothies. Lined up together they create a rainbow effect that is literally peak Instagram. Without a second thought, I whip out my iPhone; the lighting is terrible in here, but I can fiddle with the filters later. Now, if I just rearrange the jars, maybe into the actual colour sequence of the rainbow, that would look even better: first we've got strawberries and raspberries, then orange segments, then yellow peppers and what's this? – I open the lid and take a sniff – ah, mango ...

'What are you doing?' I spin round to discover Rudy watching me from the doorway.

'Oh.' I immediately straighten up. 'Just taking a few photos.'

'What for?' He glances behind him, as if to check whether someone's coming. 'I think you should get out of there, Annie.'

'I was just having a look,' I say, and I can hear the guilt in my voice. 'Professional curiosity, you know?'

'But why were you moving things round?'

I come out of the fridge and shut the door behind me. 'Oh come on, Rudy, I wasn't nicking the butter if that's what you're worrying about . . .'

But he's still looking at me in that serious, almost disapproving way he has, and I decide I should probably explain what I was up to, so he understands I wasn't doing anything wrong. I have to admit I'm also quite excited about the idea of showing him my Instagram account: I'm proud of the photos, and I'd like to be able to share them with someone whose opinion I value. As for the slightly dubious nature of the content – well, I'm sure Rudy will understand. He's a creative, like me.

'Here, I want to show you something,' I say, opening up the app and handing him my phone. 'It's a little project I've been working on.'

I peer over his shoulder as he scrolls through the photos and I can't help smiling; they look so good displayed together like a mini art gallery. It's bizarre how happy these photos make me: not just because of the 'likes' – although it's nice to know that people appreciate them – but because they put me back in touch with the real Annie Taylor, the one who used to spend her days creating beautiful images – not changing nappies and stressing about Luke.

'Annie, these photos are really good,' says Rudy. 'You have an excellent eye.'

'Thank you.' I feel a glow of satisfaction at his approval; I knew he'd appreciate them.

'Hey, is that . . . ?' He peers more closely at the screen. 'Is that the stuffed stag from the house in Clapham Old Town – Mr and Mrs Anderson's place?'

'That's the one.'

'And this.' He points to my photo of the antique rocking horse. 'It was in the nursery of that church conversion, right?'

'Yup.'

Rudy turns to look at me. 'So do *all* the things in these photos belong to Curtis Kinderbey clients?'

There's an accusatory note to his voice that makes me hesitate.

'Well – yeah. Pretty much.'

'Let me get this straight,' says Rudy, now openly disapproving. 'While you're working, you take photos of clients' possessions and then pass them off as your own on Instagram?'

'No! That's not what this is about at all. I just like taking pictures of beautiful things.'

Rudy holds out the phone to me, as if it's contaminated. 'Annie, this is wrong. You should take these down, you could get in serious trouble. You must know that, surely?'

I do know that, of course, but Rudy's sanctimonious tone has got my back up.

'It's not like I'm stealing anything. It's just photos.'

'Yes – of clients' private property.'

'God, you Millennials are so judgemental!' I give an exaggerated eye-roll, trying to lighten the mood. 'All I'm doing is sharing these gorgeous things – things that these people are *very* fortunate to own, and probably don't fully appreciate – with the wider public. I mean, you could argue that I'm actually doing something noble here: I'm like the Robin Hood of Instagram, taking photos from the rich to share with the poor!' He doesn't even crack a smile. 'For God's sake, Rudy, nobody's going to find out.'

'But if they do, you'll lose your job.'

I can't believe he has a problem with this – I really thought he'd appreciate my renegade approach, but he looks so disappointed in me.

Then something else occurs to me. 'You're not going to tell Karl, are you?'

'Of course not. I just don't want you to get in trouble.' His face softens. 'Annie, you're clearly very talented. Why don't you just find something else to photograph?'

'Like what?'

'Well for starters, something that's not borderline illegal.'

I'm trying to come up with a smart reply (I refuse to

admit to Rudy that I'm in the wrong – guilt is making me pig-headed) when my phone rings.

I jab at the answer button and bark: 'Annie Taylor speaking.'

'Oh, hey, Annie, it's Sam. Is this a bad time?'

In an instant, the sulky, bitter feeling pinching my insides vanishes. I had all but convinced myself that Sam wasn't going to call me, and at the sound of his voice I light up.

'Sam! Great to hear from you.' I very deliberately turn my back on Rudy. 'How are you?'

We do the usual small talk, catching up on each other's news, but just the fact he's phoned is enough for me to start wondering if perhaps he's interested in me after all.

It doesn't take him long to get round to the reason for his call. 'So, I was wondering,' he begins, and my body tenses in anticipation, 'if you wanted to meet for a coffee?'

Yes! 'That would be great. When were you thinking?'

'Well, this afternoon, if you're free. I scheduled the day off work as I had some personal errands to take care of, but I've finished up quicker than I'd anticipated.' There's a slight pause. 'Of course you may well be working, but I thought I'd check on the off-chance you're available.'

'I'm working right now, but could meet you at . . . two o'clock?'

'Excellent,' he says, and the smile in his voice gives me another thrill.

We arrange where to meet and I just about manage to pay attention, although the troop of cheerleaders turning cartwheels inside my head is making it tricky to focus on the finer details.

My head is so full of Sam that it isn't until I've ended the call that I realise Rudy is no longer in the kitchen; decent bloke that he is, he must have gone out to give me some privacy. I think about how I behaved to him just now and my cheeks burn: he was only looking out for me, there was no need for me to be so brattish. Right, before I do anything else I should find him and apologise – but as I head for the hallway I hear voices approaching, and then Rudy walks back into the room with Mr Eliopoulos.

'You really know your Surrealist artists,' Mr Eliopoulos is saying, his hand clamped chummily on Rudy's shoulder. 'Right, let's get this paperwork out of the way . . .'

All I can do is mouth 'sorry' to Rudy as he passes and he acknowledges my feeble apology with the briefest of nods. I was expecting a smile at least, but he still looks so disappointed in me – even a little hurt – that I get another prickle of irritation.

Yet it'll take more than Rudy's holier-than-thou attitude to put a dent in my good mood. With a virtual shrug, I dismiss his concerns as an overreaction and eagerly turn my thoughts to this afternoon's date.

32

Sam and I have arranged to meet outside the café next to the boating lake in Battersea Park. It's a beautiful afternoon, and the blue of the sky and intense apple-green of the grass and trees give me a kick that only someone who spends most of the year living under grey can truly appreciate. The sunshine has brought out all of south-west London's park tribes and the paths, playgrounds and meadows are busy with cyclists, scooting toddlers with harried adults, runners, strolling Chelsea pensioners in full uniform and dogs of every conceivable shape and size.

There's not an inch of spare space on the terrace outside the café and I'm nervously scanning the crowd trying to find Sam – while sauntering along, outwardly playing it super-cool – when I walk straight into a tiny elderly lady and stumble over the pram she's pushing, inside of which are two equally doddery Pekinese. By the time I've apologised and been introduced to Sir Snuffles and Lady Wuffles, Sam has obviously already clocked me, and when I finally spot him he's grinning at me in a way that suggests he witnessed me nearly taking out a pensioner. *Yeah, really cool, Annie.* He's sitting at a table right near the pond, sunglasses and shorts on, tanned legs stretched out in front of him, and my embarrassment quickly fades as I get a jolt of disbelieving excitement: *this gorgeous man is waiting for me!* I manage to stop myself running over, straddling his lap and snogging him, but for a moment it's touch-and-go.

'I don't know if you've watched much American football,' he says, standing to greet me with a kiss, 'but I reckon you'd be a natural.'

'Actually, that was a *rugby* tackle,' I say airily. 'We don't bother with all the namby-pamby protective padding on this side of the pond.'

'Well, I'm impressed. Although next time maybe pick on somebody your own size.'

We grin at each other, and though we're surrounded by noise and people, in that moment it's just him and me. Surely I'm not the only one who can sense the electricity fizzing between us?

Sam is the first to break the spell. 'So, gridiron Annie, I thought we might get ice cream, then take a walk – if that's okay with you?'

'That sounds like an excellent plan.'

He goes for a strawberry Cornetto (which surprises me – I'd have pegged him as an almond Magnum type) while I have a 99 Flake, and then we set off, ignoring the signposts and picking a path at random. It's so rare these days that I'm not on some sort of schedule, especially since having Dot, and I revel in the feeling of wandering without any destination in mind.

While I'm still in the dark about Sam's intentions, one thing's for sure: we are certainly compatible, chat-wise. I can't remember the last time I enjoyed talking to someone as much as him. It was probably when I was fifteen and spent three hours every night on the phone to my then-boyfriend, Matthew Liggett. I was so infatuated with him I wrote a song called 'You Will Always Be Just Mine' and sang it to him to the tune of 'Hit Me Baby One More Time', accompanying myself on my Casio keyboard (setting: bossa nova). He dumped me a week later.

As we talk, I start to piece together a picture of Sam – his values and views, what makes him tick – and the more I discover, the more convinced I am that we are meant to be in each other's lives. It's one of those amazing conversations you have at the start of a relationship, when even the tiniest thing feels significant, like proof of fate: 'Your favourite coffee is a double flat white, no sugar? Incredible, mine too!'

Yet niggling away with increasing insistency at the back of my mind is the knowledge that Sam and I can't really get to know each other at all, whether as friends or (fingers firmly crossed) as something more, until I come clean about Dot. I've tried to pretend to myself that it doesn't matter that much, but even when I'm not with her, the fact that I'm a mother informs pretty much everything I do – and it's obvious that if I'm even remotely serious about trying to get closer to Sam, I shouldn't keep it from him any longer. The problem is, it's not an easy thing to simply drop into a conversation: 'Oh, by the way, I forgot to mention – I've got a baby. Surprise!'

Thankfully, however, Sam provides me with the perfect opening while he's telling me about his family in Canada.

'My sister Ellen has just had a baby,' he says, his face softening into a besotted expression. 'Her name's Penelope and she's completely adorable. I miss her desperately – and she doesn't even do anything yet! I can't imagine how I'll feel when she actually starts talking. I'll probably have to move back to Canada just so I can hang out with her.' He digs in his pocket for his phone and brings up a photo of a baby with a mop of black hair and huge dark eyes.

'Oh, she's gorgeous,' I say.

Sam is still gazing at the phone in an endearingly soppy way. 'Yeah, she's already got me wrapped around her little finger . . .'

Before I can think too hard about the consequences, I dig out my phone. 'Now it's my turn,' I say, showing Sam my screensaver. 'This is Dot.'

'Well, she is *extremely* cute. Your niece, too?'

'Actually,' I say, keeping my voice light, 'she's my daughter.'

Sam's eyes go wide – whether with horror or surprise, it's difficult to tell – but he doesn't immediately freak out, which is at least encouraging, and he's not showing any signs of active repulsion. I would describe his expression as 'astonished with a million questions', which is about as good as I could hope for in the circumstances.

I start talking again before he can get a word in.

'She's nearly six months old. Her dad and I are separated, but he's great with her.' I don't go into the gory details – I still feel it reflects badly on me that Luke cheated. 'We're co-parenting, and I think it works as well as it can in the circumstances.'

Sam looks at the phone again and then back to me. 'She looks just like you.'

'You think so?'

'I do. She's beautiful.' He breaks into a smile, filling my worried heart with hope. 'I bet it's hard work, though.'

'More than you can imagine.' I laugh. 'But so worth it. I think I've become a better person since having her.'

As I say this, I'm surprised to realise that it's true – it hadn't even occurred to me before – and I really like how it makes me feel. Yes, the sleep deprivation is a bugger, and I could do without the back fat, but I can honestly say Dot has changed my life for the better. Meanwhile, I'm thrilled to see that Sam is still not showing any signs of imminently bolting.

'So, Annie Taylor. You work, you have a baby and you

still have time to meet up with strange men in Battersea Park. I'm impressed.'

'I'll be honest with you, Sam,' I say, as we begin to walk again. 'The job and baby don't really take up much of my time; it's meeting up with strange men that *really* eats into my schedule.'

As he laughs, it strikes me that the way he's being with me now is exactly the same as before I dropped the baby bombshell. *Perhaps he's going to be cool with this, after all?* And with that, all the tension I must have been holding inside me, in preparation for the inevitable rejection, simply melts away, and I'm left feeling as giddily light-headed as if I was perfectly tipsy on expensive champagne. I was so convinced that this would be a problem, I hadn't even considered the possibility that it wouldn't change a thing. This thought makes me so euphoric I have an urge to grab his hands and whirl around like I'm Julie Andrews on top of the Alps in *The Sound of Music*.

We're now approaching a fork in the pathway: the main trail continues on to the bandstand and there's a smaller path that at first glance seems to lead to a dead-end – a tall and impenetrable hedge – but on closer inspection carries on through a narrow opening in the leaves. Without even hesitating, this is the route we choose.

As we pass through the gap in the hedge, it feels like we're stepping into a different world. After the brightness outside, it takes my eyes a moment to adjust to the darkness: the narrow path is hemmed in on either side and above our heads by greenery, giving the impression that we're in a secret tunnel leading to the heart of the park. It's much cooler in here and the specks of sunlight that have managed to penetrate the leafy roof dapple the path in front of us. We walk on in silence, which further emphasises the fact that we're now completely alone, the only sound the crunching of our feet on gravel. With the change of scene has come a noticeable change of atmosphere between us too: anticipation hangs heavy in the air, as palpable as the buzzing of tropical insects, and growing with each step. It's like the eerie stillness before a thunderstorm: you can tell something significant is about to happen.

I glance at Sam – he's focused on the path ahead – and suddenly, out of nowhere, I'm hit by a wave of doubt. *What about Luke?* Regardless of what he's done, we are still in a relationship, and in that case me being here with Sam (and, more to the point, desperately fancying him) is wrong – or at least a very grey area. *But Luke was the one who made it grey in the first place*, I remind myself firmly. *I'd been perfectly happy with black and white.* And with that I chase any reservations from my mind.

The end of the tunnel is getting nearer now and Sam and I both slow down, as if neither of us want to leave the privacy of the passage just yet. I look at him again, but while he does seem deep in thought, he could well just be wondering what to have for his tea.

'So how long are you going to be in London for?' I ask, struggling to keep the longing out of my voice.

'Officially about three more months, but I'm thinking about seeing if I can stay on for a while.' He gives me a quick, uncertain smile. 'I like it here.'

My heart gives a little jump. Does he mean he likes *me*?

Then Sam comes to a standstill, and as I turn to face him I'm tingling with anticipation, like immensely pleasurable pins and needles.

'Annie, I'm really glad we met up today. I've been thinking about you a lot, you know. Since that first day we met.'

'When I jumped on you?'

'That's right.' He's smiling, but his eyes are gripping mine with a new intensity. I feel my breathing quicken and grow shallow as he reaches for my hand.

'Come here, Cinderella,' he says softly. 'I think we have some unfinished business.'

His fingers clasp around mine, electricity shooting through my skin where we touch, and he draws me towards him until I'm close enough to make out the golden flecks in his blue-grey eyes and the sprinkling of freckles on his nose. We stay like that for a moment, just drinking each other in, so still it's as if we're part of the surrounding foliage, then he brings up his hand and softly pushes a strand of hair away from my face: it's such an unexpected, intimate gesture that I can't help but gasp. I'm high on lust – I can't ever remember wanting someone so badly.

Then Sam leans his face towards mine; as our lips touch, I close my eyes. And in that instant, it's as if my body dissolves to liquid and I'm floating on a sea of pleasure, the waves ebbing and flowing as we kiss, unaware of anything but the warmth and smell and feel of him.

God, I'd forgotten how bloody amazing kisses can be. In long-term relationships they can become something almost utilitarian, as greetings or the prelude to something else, but this – this is better than the best-ever sex. And it goes on and on, getting increasingly intense, a release, yet at the same time a build-up, of excitement and tension that is becoming deliciously unbearable.

We pull apart for a moment, looking into each other's eyes.

'You are an incredible kisser,' says Sam, his arms tightly wrapped around me.

'I believe it's a team effort.'

He smiles. 'I'd really like to do this a lot,' he goes on, brushing his lips against mine. 'Like, as often as possible.' He kisses me again, more insistently this time. 'With you, I mean.'

'I'm so glad you clarified that,' I murmur, my eyes already closed as we lean into each other again, and then the words dissipate and float up into the leafy canopy in a haze of desire.

33

'You been at the gym, Annie?'

Dot's childminder, Helen, is standing at her front door, head cocked to one side and eyes narrowed as she takes in my dishevelled appearance.

'I'm not that keen on gyms myself.' She folds her arms. 'It's the sweating I take issue with. Although having said that, I did have a go at Zumba once and the instructor told me I had an extremely powerful pelvis.'

'Gosh, that must be . . . useful,' I say, nodding. 'And yes, I *was* at the gym, and I'm afraid my spinning class over-ran, which is why I'm a bit late. I'm so sorry.'

Helen gives my arm a kindly pat. 'Not to worry, love, you're one of my more punctual mummies, so I'll forgive you.' She stands to one side to let me past. 'Dottie's on the play mat outside, go on through . . .'

I'm still tugging guiltily at my ear as I make my way through to the garden, but really, what else could I have said? 'Actually, Helen, my flushed cheeks and bird's-nest hair are not the after-effects of a vigorous workout, but of an intensely passionate twenty-minute kiss with a devastatingly sexy Canadian – oh, and a mad ten-minute dash from the bus stop to get here, because I was so out of my tree with lust that I forgot I had to collect my daughter.'

No, in this instance a small lie was probably prudent.

Dottie is propped up against a cushion under the shade of an apple tree, toys scattered in front of her. When she spots me she breaks into a smile, showing off the two tiny white pearls of front teeth she has recently sprouted, and holds out her arms with a delighted squeal. I sweep her up and hold her to me, her head nuzzled into my neck.

'I love you so, so much,' I murmur into the silky fuzz of her hair. 'Whatever happens, you are and always will be the most important thing in my life.'

I'm trying to fight it, but now I'm here with Dot I'm suddenly feeling awful about what happened with Sam. My old friend Mummy Guilt is back and literally screaming inside my head: *What a terrible mother you are! Gadding around, selfishly indulging your baser instincts, when you have this beautiful, innocent child to look after. It's neglectful and wicked, and you should be ashamed of yourself.*

I can feel myself spinning out of control and squeeze my eyes shut, determined to keep things in perspective. *I may be a mother, but I still have every right to have a bit of fun. Now bugger off and let me enjoy the rest of the afternoon with my daughter. Oh, and by the way – I intend to do plenty more gadding, so you better get used to it, okay?*

Dot spends our bus journey home giggling at a very sweet elderly gentleman who obligingly plays 'Peepo' all the way back to Streatham, and by the time we arrive at Jess' front door, I have managed to rationalise the guilt – because after all, what could be better for Dot than to have a happy mum? – and am back on my post-Sam high.

I let myself in, calling cheerily: 'Hey honey, I'm home!'

'In here, Annie,' comes Jess' voice from the kitchen.

I dump my coat and changing bag in the hallway and make my way down the corridor with Dot on my hip. 'Jessica, you will not *believe* what happened to me today . . .'

But as soon as I get through the kitchen door I freeze, because there – sitting on a stool at the island, right next to Jess' fruit bowl of condoms – is pretty much the last person I want to see right now.

'Look who just arrived!' Jess gives me a look that plainly says: *I don't know what the hell he's doing here either.*

'Luke,' I say stupidly, staring at him, dazed. It's as if he's been conjured here by Mummy Guilt, like the Ghost of Fuck-mas Past.

'Surprise!' He gets to his feet with a broad smile, holding his arms out for Dot. 'How are my girls?'

He drops a kiss on my cheek, exactly where Sam did just a few hours ago, and it burns like a brand. 'We're absolutely fine, thank you!' I say, trying to cover my discomfort with cheeriness. Then I notice his half-empty coffee cup: he's obviously been here some time. 'Did we . . . arrange to meet up?'

'I needed to talk to you about something,' he says, cuddling Dot. 'And I was in the area, so . . .'

I don't believe that for a second. Luke has always been extremely sniffy about Streatham, even though it's barely a mile from his flat; he's also still wearing his work suit. Whatever this surprise visit is about, it's clearly important enough for him to leave the office early *and* make a significant detour.

'Well, I'm going to leave you kids to it.' Jess grabs her keys and phone and starts heading for the door.

'Don't go Jess, we can talk upstairs . . .'

'Don't worry, I've got a hair appointment.' She squeezes my arm as she passes, adding under her breath: 'Call if you need me, okay?'

After a few moments I hear the sound of the front door shutting, leaving me and Luke alone. I get a sudden, vivid flashback – Sam's lips on mine, our bodies pressing against each other – and heat floods my face.

'So, would you like more coffee?' I ask Luke, excessively jolly. 'I'm just going to make myself a cup. Gosh, it's been such a busy day, you wouldn't believe!'

'I'm fine, thanks, Annie.' He's holding Dot so she's standing on his lap, their faces just millimetres apart. She grins at him for a moment, then launches at him open-mouthed, going for his nose. 'Ouch, that hurts.' He laughs, as she collapses into giggles.

I can't help but smile. 'I forgot to tell you – her bottom front teeth are coming through.'

Luke pulls back to look. 'Hey, so they are! My little girl is growing up so fast . . .'

As always, seeing Dot and Luke together melts my heart; it reminds me of those blissful early days after we brought her home from hospital, when the three of us lived together in this crazy, sleepless, love-filled bubble . . . My mind wanders back to that happy time – but then the click of the kettle coming to boil jolts me back to the present.

'So what was it you needed to talk to me about?'

'Ah – right. Okay. The thing is, I've been doing a lot of thinking – well, more like soul-searching, really – and I've come up with a couple of ideas that might resolve our current situation.'

'Okay . . .'

'Because I can't go on the way we are now, Annie. It's *killing* me, us living apart. I know I screwed things up, but you have to let me at least try to fix it, because at the moment you're not even giving me that chance.'

I immediately feel my hackles rising. 'Well, I'm not sure it's . . .'

Luke cuts me off. 'Please, just let me say my piece, okay?'

I take in his earnest expression and the tremor in his voice, and nod mutely.

'Okay.' He exhales heavily. 'So as I understand it, our main problem is that you don't feel able to trust me because of what happened. I can *tell* you that you can trust me until I'm blue in the face, but I get that's not going to help. So what I was thinking . . . is that perhaps we should consider going to, well, counselling.'

I gawp at him, wide-eyed. Has Luke, a man for whom a stiff upper lip is a badge of honour, really just suggested we go to *therapy*? To put this in context, when one of his mates started grief counselling after the death of his beloved dad, Luke told him he was being 'weak'. To say my gob is smacked is an understatement.

'I know, it's true I've never been a fan of . . . that sort of thing,' he says, correctly reading my expression. 'But if it will help win you back, so that we can be a family again, then I'm prepared to do it.'

'Luke, I . . .'

'Hold on, I'm not finished. That's just part one of the plan.' He fiddles with his tie, as if it's too tight. 'Here, can you just hold Dottie for a sec . . .'

He rubs his palms against his trousers, as if they're clammy with nerves.

'Right. Okay.' He makes a weird clicking noise in his throat. 'So, my other suggestion – well, I suppose it's more of a *question*, really – will also hopefully prove that you can trust me, and that I am serious about being with you.' He loosens his tie again. 'Alright. Here goes.' And then, in a swift, sudden movement, he drops to his knee. 'Annie Taylor, I want nothing more than to be a family with you and our daughter, so would you do me the greatest honour and agree to marry me?'

My mind instantly goes blank, as if it's been shocked out of rational thought. My hand flies to my chest, and I think I must stop breathing, as after a few seconds I take a sudden, juddering gasp of air.

'Annie?' He bites his lip. 'You can say something now.'

'Luke ... I ... don't know what to say.' At least there's no ring; this would be a hell of a lot more awkward if he was holding out a massive rock.

He tries to smile, but it's more of a grimace. 'I think "yes" is considered appropriate in these situations.'

I stare at him kneeling on Jess' kitchen floor, and it strikes me how differently I would have felt if this had happened a few months ago. Back then, I would have assumed I'd reached the pinnacle of my entire life's happiness. Now, however, I'm afraid my first thought is: *I can't believe you've knelt on the floor in your Richard James suit. I can still remember the fuss you made that time I spilt the tiniest bit of red wine on it.*

'Annie?' Luke looks like he's seriously regretting this whole idea.

'Luke, I'm so sorry, but would you mind getting up?'

He jumps to his feet at once, brushing down his trousers, and takes Dot back. 'But I thought this is what you wanted?'

'It is – well, it was – but . . .' Surely I shouldn't need to explain to him that his timing's not ideal? 'Look, if we get married, I want it to be for the right reasons, not as a way of trying to fix our relationship. I want it to be a celebration, not a sticking plaster. So I'm not saying no, but I'm not saying yes right now either – although that doesn't mean I won't in future. Does that make sense?'

Luke nods. 'I just want to move on from what happened, and I thought this would be a good way to make a fresh start.'

'And it's a really lovely idea, but just . . .' I squeeze his hand. 'Let's take it slowly, okay?'

'Okay.' He lets out a breath and then smiles; he actually looks quite relieved. 'But you'll come to counselling, right?'

Of course we should go – it's a no-brainer. If I asked an agony aunt what we should do about our situation they would reply: *couples' counselling, duh.* I just didn't think in a million years that Luke would ever consider it, and now – well, right now all I can think about is Sam, and how deliriously happy I was this afternoon. I'm desperate to see him again, to spend as much time with him as I possibly can, to keep scratching that unbearably pleasurable itch . . .

And yet whatever happened between Sam and me – and chances are it would only be a brief fling – these feelings of elation wouldn't last forever. Relationships, even the very best of them, require hard work. Yes, right now I feel convinced that Sam and I have a really special connection, but Luke and I have history – we have a *child*, for God's sake. And okay, he's behaved appallingly, but he's now clearly trying his hardest to make it right: surely I owe him that chance? I certainly owe it to Dot.

'I'm not just going through the motions, honestly, Annie,' says Luke, picking up on my uncertainty. 'I promise I'll come to all the sessions, I'll take it seriously and stick with it. Just *please*, let's give it a go. I feel like you're slipping away from me, and I really don't want that to happen. I care so much for you, Annie; I'm willing to fight for our family. You're Dot's mum – we need to be together.'

Luke's eyes are imploring, his voice thick with emotion. Would I feel more sure about giving our relationship another go if I hadn't met Sam? Perhaps – although I'm actually far from convinced. I haven't been sure about Luke since the moment I found out about his extracurricular activities with Sigrid. Even before that kiss-of-a-lifetime this afternoon, I had been rebuilding my life without Luke in it: I had already moved on, even if I hadn't admitted it to myself.

Dot, who has been chomping at her fingers, has started to fuss and fidget in Luke's arms.

'Hey, are you hungry, little one?' he asks, stroking her face.

There's such tenderness in his gesture: it's obvious

how much he adores her. And in that moment I come to a decision – the only decision I can really make in the circumstances.

'Fine,' I say. 'Let's find a counsellor.'

'Fantastic!' He draws me into a hug, Dot pressed between us. 'I'm so pleased.'

'One day at a time though, okay?'

'One day at a time.' He draws back and beams at me. 'Thank you so much for giving us a chance, patatina, I promise you won't regret it.'

I force myself to swallow down my automatic response – *we'll have to see about that* – and instead ask: 'Would you like to stay and help bath Dottie?'

'Yes, please, I'd love that.' He looks so happy that I feel reassured; at least I'm doing the right thing for our daughter.

'You head on up and start the bath running, I'll be straight there with her milk.'

Once Luke and Dot have gone upstairs, I move around the kitchen preparing her bottle as if on autopilot; the emotional maelstrom of the afternoon has left me totally drained. I feel like I should be happy about how things have turned out, but right now I'm just desolate at the thought of never seeing Sam again. Wrong as that may be, I can't help it.

Before I head upstairs to join Luke and Dot, I check my phone; there's a message from Sam:

Hey Cinderella. Did you enjoy this afternoon as much as I did?
Hoping we can do it again soon x

I clutch my phone to my chest, closing my eyes, letting myself bask in how good he made me feel, how excited about the future. I'm not sure how long I stay like that, but I'm only jolted out of my reverie when I hear Dot crying upstairs, clearly wondering where the hell I've got to with her milk.

'Coming,' I call – and then, with the last dregs of my willpower, I delete Sam's message.

34

I've been waiting in this nightclub queue for twenty-five minutes now and it's not moved a millimetre. I know this for a fact because I'm still standing adjacent to a metre-high, poorly graffitied cock and balls, which marks the spot where I started queuing. It's not that people haven't been allowed into the club – in fact, there's been a steady flow of glamazons having a quiet word with the doorman and ducking under the rope – but not one of us plebs whose names aren't cool enough to appear on the promoter's clipboard has yet been admitted. So we're stuck here, meek as sheep in a pen, seething ineffectually whenever someone hotter or better connected than us skips the queue. To make matters worse, I'd just assumed that Riva would have put my name on the guest list, so when I arrived I strutted up to the door, feeling pretty sassy in a black jumpsuit of Jess', only to be sent straight to the back of the queue amid smirks and whispers from the other sheep. Not that I blame them, I'd have reacted exactly the same: Schadenfreude is the only power we possess right now.

I check my phone: 10.40 p.m. *Bugger*. When Riva called me yesterday and said we'd be meeting in The Club (apparently it's too cool to have a proper name) at 10 p.m. and I told her that was my usual bedtime, she had laughed hysterically – 'You crack me up, Barb!' – but actually, I wasn't joking. I'm sure it'll be worth it if/when I get inside, as, according to Riva, this place is so hot Hailey Baldwin had her birthday party here last week, but right now I would pay a day's wages to be cosied up in bed with a romcom on my Kindle. I suppose I could try messaging Riva again to see if she can come and get me, but it looks like she still hasn't read the last one I sent. I think I'll give it until 11 p.m. and then call it a night. I wouldn't be quite so unwilling to wait if the surroundings were a bit less 'murdery', but here, in this badly lit alley, just off the grotty bit of Lower Clapton Road, I get the impression that it's only a matter of time before we start to get picked off by muggers, like a herd of wildebeest being preyed on by hyenas. And as it's always the old and infirm who are first to go, I'll definitely be the first victim; everyone else here is at least ten years younger than me.

To pass the time, I take a few arty photos of the cock and balls, experimenting with different filters. Would this be something 'ArbiterofCool' would put up on their feed? In an *ironic* way, perhaps ... With this in mind, I click onto Instagram to see how my latest photos are doing. I was at the Eliopoulos mansion again this morning, and while taking the official marketing shots I also snapped a load of unofficial photos as well: the Buddha by the koi carp pond, a marble sculpture in the master bedroom, a pair of metallic Aquazurra heels that I found in the floor-to-ceiling shoe closet in the guest suite and arranged on a fur rug (#Aquazurra #fakefur #luxe #designerlife #decorinspo). I have a loyal and enthusiastic band of followers now and, as ever, get a massive kick when I see the likes and comments mounting up.

And then, as if at some hidden signal, the queue starts to edge forwards, and ten minutes later I have made it inside The Club. I'd like to say it was worth the wait, but with its strip lighting, plastic chairs and scuffed lino, the vibe in here is definitely more 'church hall disco' than super-hip hangout. There's even an old-fashioned tea hatch, of the sort WI ladies might hand out fish-paste sandwiches from to the vicar, although here it opens onto the bar. I can't see anyone I know and I'm feeling massively overdressed; everyone else seems to be wearing Nineties Grunge. I join the queue for the tea-hatch when, to my relief, I hear Riva hollering my name.

'Babe! Over here!'

Towards the back of the room there is an assortment of old leather sofas and armchairs, which have been pushed together to create a sort of VIP seating area, and it is here that I spot Riva, kneeling up, leaning on the back of the sofa and waving frantically.

'And where the fuck have YOU been, Barb?' she booms as I approach. You're late!'

'Sorry, I was stuck outside in the queue for ages.'

'Whaaaaat? You should have said you were with our party. Guest list all the way, baby!' Riva bounces up and down on the sofa, whooping, while Delphine and Farrah – who are sitting nearby – join in, although they clearly don't know what it's in aid of. I get the impression they've all been hard at it for some time.

'Well, I told the guy on the door I was with you, but he didn't have my name down.'

'What the fuck . . . ? Talia, did you put Barb's name on the list?'

A crop-haired brunette lounging on an armchair nearby looks round. 'Who?'

'*Barb*.' Riva points at me. 'Her.'

Talia looks me up and down, barely hiding a sneer at my jumpsuit, then shrugs and turns back to her conversation.

'God, I'm so sorry, babe,' says Riva, eyes saucer-wide. 'I must have forgotten. Will you forgive me?' She pouts, tugging at my hand like a little child. 'Pwetty pweeeese?'

Hmmm. I get the feeling Riva's buoyant mood tonight might not just be down to cocktails and excitement.

'It's fine, honestly,' I say, sitting next to her on the sofa.

'Awwwww, love you, babe!' Riva throws her arms around me with such force that we fall back against the cushions; she's still giggling manically some time after we struggle back up again.

If I felt like the highly esteemed guest of honour the last time I went out with Riva, this time I'm the spare part. Apart from Riva, Delphine and Farrah, I don't know anybody else who's here, and, like Talia, it clearly only takes a glance for the other guests to decide that I'm not worth talking to.

Riva is busy chatting to a beautiful guy who looks vaguely familiar – I think he might be a famous musician? – and Farrah is hanging around the DJ booth, so I try to chat to Delphine. But once we get the pleasantries out of the way, and she asks whether I've booked my nose job yet, the conversation putters to a standstill; I exhausted all my fashion anecdotes last time, so I can't even rely on those to help things along. Our lives are so different now, it's painfully obvious that we have nothing in common.

There's a sudden squeal of laughter from Riva, who is now sitting on the musician's lap with her arms around his neck. Amidst the low-key looks of most other people here, Riva sticks out like a Crufts-winning poodle amongst street mutts: she's wearing a turquoise, one-shouldered mini-dress and a headpiece in the shape of a giant pink cherry. I feel a pang of envy at her confidence and fabulousness.

'I just don't know how Riva does it,' I say, turning back to Delphine. 'Juggling her career and all this while raising Jethro. She makes me feel completely inadequate.'

Delphine wrinkles her perfect little nose. 'Jethro?'

'You know, her son.'

'Oh right, yeah. But, you know, it's not as if she has to look after him.'

'What do you mean?'

'Like, Riva doesn't do any of the actual *mum* stuff, does she? With her career – are you kidding me? She palmed him off onto her own mum when he was like, I dunno, a couple of weeks old. He was certainly *super* tiny. Riva was just so busy with work, and her mum's still pretty young, I think, so it made sense for Joshua to go and live with her.'

'Jethro,' I say, as my mind frantically tries to process what it's just heard.

'Yeah. Jethro.' Delphine nods, smoothing her hair over her shoulder. 'I mean, can you imagine *Riva* looking after a baby!' She gives a snort of laughter. 'She'd have left him at a shoot, or on a plane or something . . . So yeah, he lives with Riva's mum in, like, Croydon or somewhere, and Riva just visits when she can.' Delphine reaches for her drink, but then stops. 'Oh my God, she told me this hilarious story about going to see the kid this one time and she *literally* had to explain that she was his mum, because he thought she was his sister!'

'Um, yeah, that's hilarious.'

'I know, right? Seriously, she cracks me up . . . Oh hey, Donovan – hi!'

Having spotted someone more interesting, Delphine jumps up and disappears off into the crowd, leaving me to process the bombshell she's just casually dropped.

In a way I'm relieved, as this has now answered all my questions about how Riva managed to make parenting look such a breeze: it's because she's never done any actual parenting. If her account of motherhood sounded like a fairy tale, it's because that's exactly what it was: pure fiction. The more I think about it, though, the angrier I become. It's not that I'd ever judge her for getting her mum to raise her child – whatever works for them, it's nothing to do with me – but what pisses me off is that Riva made me feel like a failure by leading me to think she was effortlessly juggling all these balls, when in reality she wasn't even bothering to pick up the balls in the first place.

I suppose, giving her the benefit of the doubt, she might not have wanted to tell me about her mum raising Jethro because she was worried I might disapprove. I glance over at Riva, who's now licking the musician's face, and my insides scrunch up with irritation. No, she's never given a shit about what other people think. She must have known I was hoping for reassurance when I asked her about Jethro – for some practical advice, mum to mum – so why would she deliberately lie to a friend to make them feel worse about themselves?

Because she's not really your friend, says a voice inside my head, which may or may not be Tabby, Fiona, Claris, Jess or a combination of all four. And as I watch Riva's cherry hat bobbing away at the musician's face there's an ache in the pit of my stomach that feels a lot like betrayal.

'I need a drink,' I announce to no one in particular. I stand up, smooth down my jumpsuit and hold my head high as I make my way towards the bar. There is a huge crowd gathered around the hatch and I elbow my way towards the front, desperate to numb my feelings with alcohol. I'm so consumed by my inner ranting over Riva that it takes me a little while to register that standing a few feet away, his head nodding in time to the beat, is my former friend, work colleague and one-time fuck buddy Tomo.

35

I stare at him, frozen in shock. It's definitely Tomo, there's no doubt about that, but at the same time it's ... *not* Tomo. He looks, well, nothing like he used to. The only thing he'd be able to model these days would be hair-loss shampoo. His famously chiselled face is now swollen and puffy – either from fillers or boozing, it's hard to tell – and his legendary body, which once inspired a range of men's pants for Debenhams, looks soft and bloated under his too-tight Stüssy t-shirt. None of us are getting any younger, but I'm staggered how much Tomo has changed in five years.

I yell his name, but he doesn't hear me, so I jostle my way towards him and try again. This time he turns round, and – after locating me as the source of the noise – looks at me with unfocused eyes, swaying slightly.

'It's me,' I say with an expectant smile. 'Barb.'

But his face crumples in almost comic confusion. Oh come on, surely he must remember me?

'We used to work together and ... stuff. *Barb?*' I can't believe I'm having to explain to him who I am; at one stage we were almost inseparable. 'Jay Patterson's assistant?'

As ever, my ex-boss' name works its usual dark magic.

'Fuck, yeah! Barb!' Tomo reaches over and hugs me; I get a whiff of sweat and cigarettes. 'Great to see you again, babe! Fuck, it's been, like ... a really long time!'

'I know, about five years.' I smile. 'So how have you been?'

'I'm really good, yeah.' He sniffs, wiping his nose on the back of his hand. 'I quit the modelling, you probably heard. Had enough, man – it was all so fucking shallow ... Nowadays I'm a DJ. Spend a lot of the year in Ibiza – fucking amazing place, I love it ...' More sniffing. 'What about you? Still, uh, taking photos?'

'Yep, although I'm working in property rather than fashion,' I say. 'And I'm a mum now, too.'

Tomo reacts as if he's never met a mother before. 'You've got a *kid*? Wow. That's ... intense.' He narrows his eyes. 'It's not mine, is it?'

I'm not sure what my face does, but it clearly does a good job of conveying my incredulity.

'I'm *kidding*! But ... we did fuck, right?'

Jesus, what a charmer. 'Yes, we did.'

'Phew.' He grins. 'Although I'm usually pretty safe to assume that the answer's gonna be yes. Ha!'

Tomo is now in front of the hatch, and greets the

barman with a complicated handshake. 'Hey Kendo, can I grab a double JD with Red Bull? Cheers, bro.' He turns back to me and says: 'So are you still in touch with Jay? Fucking unfair what happened to him, all that drugs shit in the press. I mean, he was just the poor dude who got caught, right?' He gives a bark of laughter.

'I haven't seen Jay in years,' I say, 'but I'm here with Riva.'

'Yeah? Me too! Just like old times, eh?'

And with that Tomo takes his drink from the barman, gives him a fist bump of thanks, then turns and pushes his way back through the crowd, leaving me still waiting to be served. It seems that it's not only his looks that have faded since we last met: his charisma has gone AWOL too.

When I finally make it back to the sofas, Tomo is deep in conversation with Riva and Delphine and the possibly-famous musician has disappeared. There's no room for me to sit with them and so, after hovering awkwardly for a moment, I perch on the arm of the sofa. They're chatting about a mate of theirs called Lupo, who has apparently got into a Twitter spat with Kanye West about something, and as I listen to their competitive name-dropping ('Yeah, but you know what Jay and Bey can be like . . .') it strikes me that I'll never be part of this world again – and for the first time I realise this is actually a good thing. Just a few hours ago I'd have been desperate to join in, to prove that I was still cool, but after the events of this evening I really can't be arsed. *I'm too old for this shit*, I think, as I gulp down my drink – and it's a terrifically liberating feeling. I get a sudden longing to be hanging out with my *real* friends, and with it comes an uncomfortable prickle of guilt: they were absolutely spot on about Riva; I was just too stubborn to admit it. I'd really like to phone them right away, to smooth things over, but Tabby and Claris are bound to be asleep and Fi is on her minibreak in Amsterdam. It then occurs to me that I haven't heard a peep from her while she's been away – usually I'd have had a dozen texts by now giving me a blow-by-blow account of Finn's failure to propose. Oh God, have I totally screwed up our friendship?

'Hey babe, didn't see you there.' Tomo shuffles along the sofa, patting the space. 'You can squeeze up next to me.'

'You still here, mama?' Riva shrieks. 'Thought you'd be tucked up in bed in your Gap jim-jams by now!' She cackles wildly, clearly completely wasted, and I have a sudden urge to knock the stupid cherry off her head.

Then Tomo leans closer to me, his face slick with sweat, and fixes me with a look that once would have been irresistibly seductive, but is now somewhere between menacing and constipated. 'So Barb, I'll be coming back to your place later, right . . . ?'

'Actually, it's not Barb – it's Annie. And no, I'm afraid you won't be.'

He snakes his arm around my back and down towards

my bum, which he gives a rough squeeze. 'Oh, I think I will . . .'

'No,' I say, taking his hand – probably more firmly than I intended – and shoving it back in his lap. 'You most certainly will not.'

Tomo glares at me, holding his hand as if gravely injured. 'Jesus, chill the fuck out. I was just having a bit of fun.'

Riva gives a withering snigger. 'Come on, babe, don't kill the vibe. No need to overreact, yeah?'

I look at the pair of them, taking in their glassy-eyed expressions, twitchy movements and ugly grimaces, and suddenly the charmed life that I always thought Riva and her friends were living doesn't look anywhere near as shiny and enviable.

'Well, I think I should be getting home,' I say, jumping to my feet. 'It is *way* past my bedtime, after all! Delightful to see you all, look forward to catching up again some other time.'

And with that I turn and stride towards the exit before any of them can say a word.

I burst through the door and then stop outside, buzzing with adrenaline, closing my eyes and taking a deep, calming breath. Relief floods through me; I feel like I've had a lucky escape.

'Annie? Is that you?'

I turn towards the sound of the voice and there,

leaning against the wall, a cigarette clasped elegantly between two long fingers, is Edgar – alter ego of Madame Kiki Beaverhousen – and I'm relieved to see he's smiling at me with genuine warmth. I needed to see a friendly face right now.

I greet him with a kiss. 'Giving Kiki another night off, are you?'

'Madame Kiki would *never* deign to be seen in a shithole like this,' he says with theatrical outrage.

'So why is Edgar here?'

He shrugs. 'Nowhere else to go, darling ... Are you leaving?'

I tell him about my night, about Riva's lies and the shock of Tomo's transformation, and he just nods, unsurprised.

'They're like the Lost Boys – you know, from *Peter Pan*? I don't think they'll ever grow up. They'll always be frozen in time, back when they were twenty-five and at peak fabulous. Riva may have another few years left in her, but Tomo – well, it's all over for him, he just can't see it. That lot have had their moment in the sun and younger, cooler kids are rushing in to take their place, but they'll never admit it to themselves. It happened to me too, of course, but at least I have the self-awareness to realise I'm now a relic.' He smiles at me. 'You're very lucky that you got out when you did, darling. You'll always have the memories of that time, but you've moved on – and quite rightly so.

You're building a life with meaning . . .' He takes a final drag of his cigarette and stamps out the stub.

'Are you going back into the club? I can come with you, if you like.' I feel like I should offer; he suddenly seems so miserable.

But Edgar shakes his head. 'Please, darling, go home to your family. Because that's where I would be if I had one.'

When Edgar has disappeared back inside, I take out my phone to order an Uber. When it comes to entering the destination, I'm about to put in Jess' address when I pause – what was it Edgar had said? *Go home to your family.* Without a second thought, I type in Luke's address.

I call his mobile from the car, but there's no answer – which I guess is unsurprising, seeing as it's nearly 1 a.m. I know that he'll be home, though, as he has Dot with him tonight. When we're about halfway to Clapham I get a moment's doubt, and nearly tell the driver to take me to Streatham instead, but after tonight's events I have an intense, almost primal urge to see my daughter – and besides, if Luke and I *are* going to give our relationship another go then I'm sure he won't mind me turning up unannounced. He might even be pleased.

As we pull up outside his flat, I'm relieved to see that the light in his bedroom is still on. I press the buzzer and a few moments later he answers the intercom. 'Hello?'

'Oh hi, Luke, sorry, it's me.'

'Annie?' He sounds shocked – but I guess it *is* late. 'What are you doing here?'

'Long story . . . Can I, um, come up?'

There's a pause; a pause that goes on for longer than I'd expect in the circumstance. 'I was just getting into bed.'

'I know, I'm really sorry, but I'd love to pop up and see Dottie.'

'She's asleep.'

'Of course, but I won't wake her up. I just want to see her.' Stuck out here on the doorstep, I'm beginning to feel a bit stupid; so much for thinking Luke might be pleased to see me – he sounds anything but. Clearly, I should have listened to my gut and waited until morning. 'I'm sorry, Luke, but I'll be really quick.'

'It's not a great time right now, Annie,' he persists.

'What do you mean?'

'I'm just tired, okay?' There's an edge to his voice.

'Please, just five minutes?'

A heavy sigh, then a pause. 'Fine, but make it quick.'

There's a buzz and click as the lock finally opens.

36

Luke takes a little while to come to the door; when he finally does, he's wearing an old t-shirt and a pair of boxers, and to my relief doesn't look nearly as cross as he sounded on the intercom.

He drops a kiss on my cheek. 'Sorry about that, I was half-asleep and you took me by surprise.'

'I know, and I am so sorry for turning up like this, but you won't believe the night I've had . . .'

Luke rubs his hand across his face, looking uncomfortable. 'Listen, it really is lovely to see you, but I meant what I said – I *am* tired. It's been a hellish week at work.'

'Of course, I'll just go up and see Dottie then go back to Streatham and leave you in peace.'

He smiles. 'Well, hopefully *this* will be your home again soon, so you won't have to go anywhere.'

I return his smile, but his words leave me oddly unsettled. Until now, I hadn't really given any thought to moving back to Luke's flat – Dot and I have become perfectly content in Jess' attic – and the prospect knocks me off-kilter. Shouldn't I be feeling happy about it? Well, I guess the idea of Luke and I getting back together is still fairly new; we'll just take it one step at a time . . .

Dot is lying on her back in her cot, her hands thrown above her head like she's at a rave, and my heart twinges with happiness as I gaze at her in the soft glow of the night light, drinking in every tiny detail. I lean down to kiss her, revelling in her smell and the buttery-softness of her skin.

'I am so lucky to be your mum,' I whisper, stroking her cheek. 'I promise I am going to make your life as wonderful as it can possibly be.'

Luke comes to stand next to me, sliding his arm around my waist.

'We made a good baby,' he says softly.

Our eyes meet and in that moment, standing there over our sleeping daughter, I think, *it's going to be alright after all*; then together we creep out of the room and back downstairs.

'I'm really sorry to throw you out,' says Luke as we return to the living room. 'If I wasn't so knackered I'd definitely be asking you to stay.'

His eyes skim suggestively over my jumpsuit, lingering on the deep V of the neckline.

'Don't worry, I get it.' I smile, reaching for my phone. 'Right, I'll just see if I can get an Uber . . . Looks like it'll be here in seven minutes.'

Luke nods. 'Can I get you a glass of water while you're waiting?'

'That would be great, thank you.'

While he heads into the kitchen, I gaze around the living room; the pile of bills that was sitting above the fireplace has now been moved, but other than that nothing has changed. It still looks exactly like my home – and I'm sure, in time, it will feel that way too.

Most of the furniture in here belongs to Luke, but there are a few items that came from my parents' home, my favourite being the Turkish rug that is now in front of the fireplace. This rug features prominently in many of my childhood memories: playing Twister on it with friends, lying across it to watch cartoons, listening to my dad tell the story of how he and Mum found it in an antiques shop while on honeymoon and had to haggle down the price. In a surge of nostalgia, I go and sit on it now, enjoying the comforting roughness of the wool against my palms, and get a flashback to a game Tabby and I would play where we'd pretend the rug was a magic flying carpet. At the thought of my little sister, I feel another rush of guilt and a lump forms in my throat; first thing tomorrow I need to call her and apologise for that stupid row over my nose job. Tabby was absolutely right: it's not my nose that's been the problem.

Then from my position here on the floor, I notice something sticking out from under the nearby armchair.

Intrigued, I lean over and pull it out, and when I see what it is I get a sudden dropping feeling in my belly and a hissing in my ears. It's a boot – a cool, slouchy, studded boot – that I know won't fit me, because I clearly remember trying it on before and joking with its owner about the tininess of her feet compared to my own size sevens.

'You're so lucky, the Buddha has big feet,' Sigrid had said, and her tinkling laugh sounded like wind chimes in a summer breeze.

Numbness spreading through me as if I'm being deep-frozen, I reach under the chair and retrieve the other boot, and then a handbag. I look inside: it contains a half-eaten bag of Brazil nuts, a wallet, lip gloss and some vegan condoms. Of all the emotions that are rushing in and jostling to fill the void inside me, the strongest of these is vindication: *I bloody knew I was right not to trust Luke.* Quickly followed by confusion: *can vegan condoms only be used by vegans? And what if one of the partners eats bacon . . . ?*

'I am so sorry, Annie.'

With a start I look up: Luke is standing in the doorway, my glass of water in hand, just staring at me. His shoulders are slumped, his face etched with regret; he clearly isn't even going to try and talk his way out of this, which is at least something.

'Where is she?' I ask, surprising myself with my calmness.

'Upstairs. In the bedroom.'

I let out a rush of breath. 'I want to speak to her.'

He just nods and then turns and heads upstairs. Like me, all the fight has evidently gone out of him. For my part, I'm suddenly dizzy with exhaustion and have to fight the urge to lie down and go to sleep. I check the Uber app: only four minutes until I can get out of this mess.

I listen as Luke's feet cross the bedroom floor above me; there's a muttered conversation – a female voice, slightly raised – and then after a moment the sound of two pairs of feet descending the stairs. Sigrid material-ises in the doorway, as ethereally beautiful as ever, her silver-blonde hair hanging down in two plaits like a char-acter out of *The Lord of the Rings*. She is fully dressed, which is a relief, but her lacy blouse is on inside out.

'Here we are again,' I say pleasantly.

'Annie, please don't jump to conclusions. Luke and I have just been talking things over. He reached out to me for help, and I . . .'

'Oh, give it a rest, Sigrid,' Luke mutters. 'Annie's not stupid.'

Sigrid's perfectly symmetrical features crumple in irri-tation, but at least that shuts her up.

I turn to Luke. 'So what was all that crap you said to me about wanting to be a family again?'

Before he can answer, Sigrid says: 'It was actually *me* that suggested the counselling, Annie. Luke was so des-perate for Dot to grow up with two parents, in a happy family like he enjoyed in his own childhood, and obviously I wanted to do whatever I could to help him achieve that goal.'

'What, by fucking him? Yes, I can see exactly how that would help . . .' I give a heavy sigh, but I'm more pissed off than devastated. 'And the marriage proposal? That your brilliant idea as well, was it, Sigrid?'

'No, that was . . .' Sigrid stops herself, then glances at Luke, as if wondering if she's said too much; judging by his expression, she clearly has.

All at once, the pieces fall into place. 'Oh my God,' I gape. 'It was your mum, wasn't it, Luke? Lucia put you up to it!'

He just looks down at his feet, shuffling awkwardly, his silence speaking volumes.

I think back to the conversation Luke and I had in Jess' kitchen. It hadn't occurred to me at the time, but I don't actually remember him telling me he loved me, not even once. It was all about how much he wanted the two of us to get back together so we could be a *family* again for Dot – exactly as Sigrid has just confirmed. Luke doesn't want me, he wants a devoted mother to raise his daughter and iron his shirts while he carries on with a mistress, just like his own father probably did before him. And perhaps that arrangement would work for some couples – but definitely not for me.

My phone rings; it's the Uber driver, asking where I am.

. could easily stay here and ask Luke a million more questions, but I've already got the only answer I really need.

'I'll move the rest of my stuff out of here next week,' I
say wearily. 'And we'll have to meet up to discuss how
we're going to work out the co-parenting arrangement.'

'Of course. I truly am sorry, Annie, I never meant to
hurt you.'

'So you keep saying.'

We look at each other, and for the first time in ages it
feels like there's something close to honesty between us.
It turns out my subconscious was holding me back from
reconciling with Luke for good reason: deep down, I must
have known I was right not to trust him. I start heading
for the door, feeling curiously upbeat.

'Annie, please, wait.' Luke reaches out to me, as if to
stop me leaving, but then seems to think better of it. His
arm drops by his side; he looks utterly defeated. 'God, I'm
such an idiot . . .'

Despite everything that's happened, I actually feel a bit
sorry for him. 'Don't worry, Luke. It'll be okay.'

And do you know what? I actually think it will be.
When we first got together, in the wake of my parents'
accident, I was broken – I needed him to care for me
while I pieced myself back together – but now I know I
can cope on my own; I'm stronger than I ever thought
possible. And if the last few months have taught me anything, it's that Luke and I work well as co-parents. He

might be an appalling boyfriend, but I've got to admi
he's a fantastic father: together, we'll make sure that Do
has the wonderful life she deserves.

As I open the front door, I hear Sigrid pipe up behind
me: 'Annie, I feel it's important I share my feelings about
where we find ourselves now . . .'

I turn to look at her, taking in the pout and pleading,
puppy-dog eyes.

'And I'm sure Luke would *love* to hear all about that.' I
smile, and close the door in her face.

37

'He only went and put a FECKIN' RING ON IT!'

Fiona is holding her hand right up to my face, fingers spread – although it would be impossible to miss the large diamond glinting in the morning sunshine.

I scream, making the woman sitting at the next table spin around.

'Ohmigodcongratulations!' I reach across the table and give Fi a huge hug, nearly toppling our coffees in the process. 'This is AMAZING! What happened? Right, I need every single tiny detail . . .'

It's first thing on Monday morning and Fi and I are meeting at our favourite café near Curtis Kinderbey for a pre-work coffee and catch-up.

'I'm so sorry I didn't let you know what was going on over the weekend,' says Fi, her eyes shining as brightly as her new ring, 'but when we got to Amsterdam on Friday night, Finn confiscated my phone. He said he wasn't going to have another holiday ruined by me live-texting the entire weekend to my best mate.'

I'm hit by a wave of love for her. 'I am still your best mate then?'

'Whaaaaat?' she roars. 'Of course y'are!' She grabs my hand and crushes it in hers; Lord knows how someone who takes a Topshop size six (petite) can have a grip like Thor. 'I feckin' hate it when we argue.'

'Me too. And for what it's worth, you were absolutely right about Riva and that lot.'

'What happened?'

'Another time – we've got far more important things to discuss now. Starting with exactly how Finn popped the question.'

She breaks into a grin. 'I tell you, darl, it was so feckin' romantic I nearly puked . . .'

Half an hour later I have been given a full rundown of every moment of their weekend in Amsterdam, plus a comprehensive preview of Fi's wedding plans, including her thoughts on the dress, cake, her mum's hat and the music for the first dance. Fi is in her element: I'd always assumed 'glowing with happiness' was just a figure of speech, but she's lit up like the London Eye on New Year's Eve.

She's just taking me through a suggested itinerary for her hen weekend, which I, as chief bridesmaid, will be tasked with arranging (I'm already worrying about where to get 26 'sexy leprechaun' costumes), when the alarm on her phone starts beeping.

'Feck it, I've got to run,' she says, glancing at the screen. 'I'm due at a viewing in ten minutes. Can we finish this later? Lunch?'

'Absolutely.'

Moments later I stroll into our office, still beaming at Fi's news. I'm almost as elated as if it was me who was tying the knot; actually, no, I'm infinitely *more* excited about Finn proposing to Fi than I was when Luke popped the question. God, was that really only a week ago? With everything that's happened since then, it feels like months ago. I should probably tell Fi about it at lunch, but I don't want to put a downer on today. Not that it's actually such a downer: in a weird way, I'm beginning to think that discovering Luke and Sigrid together was actually a good thing, and even before hearing Fi's lovely news I woke this morning feeling rather chipper. I think I must have done all my mourning for our relationship the first time Luke betrayed me, and now I'm just more relieved than anything that we can move on with our lives without any more bullshit. And, of course, there's another upside to Luke's treachery: now that our relationship is beyond repair, I'm free to see Sam again for lots of lovely guilt-free kissing and more. He messaged me last night and asked if I wanted to meet him for dinner on Friday: a proper date! I'm leaving it twenty-four hours to reply, just

so I don't seem overly keen, but I've already booked Jess'
beautician friend Mara for an intensive once-over.

I haven't even made it to my desk when Karl's office
door flies open with such force it slams against the wall,
making everyone in the office look up. He sticks his head
out, his hair glinting under the strip lights as if var-
nished, and jabs a finger in my direction.

'You – my office – *now*.'

He sounds mightily pissed off, but I'm so buoyed up by
Fi's engagement that I can certainly cope with a bit of
grief from Karl.

'Shut the door and sit down,' he barks as I come in. He's
tapping at his keyboard and doesn't look up, so I do as he
says and wait for him to finish. He's obviously been busy
with the fake tan over the weekend; his skin is a shade I'd
describe as 'intense fishfinger'.

Karl finishes whatever he's doing on the computer and
then faces me, folding his teak-tinted hands on the desk.

'Here's the thing, Annie,' he says. 'You're fired.'

As my jaw drops, so does my stomach. '*What?*'

'You're fired. Gross misconduct.'

Before I can say another word, Karl turns to his computer, hits a few buttons and spins the monitor around so
I can see it. On the screen there's a video still of a bedroom: with a plunging feeling in my guts, I recognise it as
the guest suite in the Eliopoulos mansion.

'Security camera footage,' snaps Karl, although he really doesn't need to explain.

He presses another button and the video begins to play. After a moment I appear at the bottom right of the picture carrying my camera. I walk around taking photos of the room from various angles, looking impressively professional, and I'm desperate for Karl to fast forward to the money shot because of course I know what's going to happen. I sit watching in silence, my cheeks pinking with humiliation.

Five minutes into the footage, the onscreen Annie walks back to the doorway, sticks her head into the corridor to check she's alone, then comes back and begins rummaging through the drawers and wardrobes. Christ, I look so guilty! Watching this for the first time, I could well believe this was footage of a thief caught in the act. I find the Aquazurra heels in the wardrobe – oh God, did I really have to try them on? – then take the fur throw off the bed, arrange the shoes on top of it and take a painfully long time, far longer than I actually remember, to get the perfect photo. After another few minutes of this torture, Karl finally stops the video.

'You're lucky Mr Eliopoulos doesn't want to press charges. He's an extremely important man, and this' – he points at the image of me frozen on screen – 'is a disgusting invasion of his privacy.'

I drop my head in shame. 'I'm so, so sorry, Karl. I know I've let you and the company down.'

'You're damn right you have.' It's clearly taking him a huge effort to keep his temper. 'We've now lost his business because of your stupidity. What the eff were you playing at?'

I give a hopeless shrug – because really, what can I say? 'I just like taking photos of beautiful things,' I manage eventually, the only excuse I've ever had for my dodgy sideline – which is clearly no excuse at all. Even I can tell how pathetic it sounds, but there's no way I can tell Karl about the Instagram account; he'd probably have me arrested.

'You could have had a great future here, Annie, but you've destroyed any trust I had in you, damaged Curtis Kinderbey's reputation and, in the process, lost me one hell of a potential pay cheque. I have no choice but to dismiss you without notice, as of right this second.'

'I understand,' I say in a small voice. 'And I really am extremely sorry.'

Karl shakes his head, his lips drawn into an angry line, then flicks his hand in the direction of the door. 'And don't bother running off to Coxtons asking for a job,' he calls after me. 'I've already warned Darren Wilson about you.'

When I get outside Karl's office, my face burning with shame, I return to my desk and quickly gather up the few personal items I'd left there, shoving them into my bag before anyone can ask what happened.

Stupid, stupid Annie. What the hell am I going to do now? Sure, this job might not have been the most artistically fulfilling, but the pay was pretty good, the hours flexible and I was actually enjoying it. Thanks to my ludicrous need for approval from a bunch of strangers, I'm now the unemployed single mother that I feared I'd end up when this whole mess started. Ridiculously, I'm almost as upset about the fact that I'm now going to have to kill off ArbiterofCool's Instagram account: I must have known I'd get caught in the end, but those photos really made me feel good about myself. It would be tragic if it wasn't so bloody pathetic.

Desperate to get out of the office, I make a dash for the door – but just as I reach for the handle, it opens from the other side and Rudy nearly slams into me.

He stares at me, taking in my crumpled expression and general wobbliness, but doesn't say a word, just waits for me to explain. We've barely spoken since that disagreement over my Instagram account, but he's looking at me with genuine concern.

'You were right about the photos,' I mumble, eyes on the ground. 'And now Karl's fired me.'

A pause. 'Do you want to go for a coffee?'

I nod miserably, chewing my lip.

He holds back the door: 'Come on then.'

Rudy orders our drinks in takeaway cups (I'm grateful he senses this isn't a conversation I want to have in a busy café) and then we walk the few streets to the common – me, as ever, jogging to keep up with his stride – where we find a quiet bench.

As soon as we sit down, I say: 'Please don't tell me I told you so.'

'I'm sorry this has happened, Annie.'

'I'm an idiot,' I mutter. 'An insecure, attention-seeking idiot.'

'Perhaps, but you're also a very talented idiot. You may have misjudged the subject matter, but those photos were fantastic.'

'You don't have to be nice to me, Rudy. I know I've screwed up. I just got such a kick out of that stupid Instagram account. It made me feel . . . I don't know – *worthwhile*. Like more than just a mum . . .'

We drink our coffee in silence for a little while; even though this is my second double shot of caffeine this morning, my earlier burst of positivity has fizzled out completely. The enormity of what's happened is sinking in, leaving me deflated.

I sense Rudy looking at me and turn to find his mismatched eyes studying me in that intense way he has. I used to find his stare unsettling, but now I find it oddly comforting – like he's cutting through all the crap and bluster and seeing the real me.

'This was never your dream job, was it?' he asks. 'Like me, you've just been marking time, waiting for your next move. But there was always a risk you'd get too comfortable in this job and end up being stuck in it forever – well, now that's not going to happen.'

'Yeah, because I'm going to be an unemployed single mother.'

'Well, that would be the glass-half-empty approach. Alternatively, you could see this as a chance to turn your talent for photography into a career you really love.' He sips his coffee. 'You're wasted taking pictures of property, Annie. I've seen your photos of Dot – you've got a gift for capturing people in a really fresh, unique way.'

'But the Curtis Kinderbey job was safe. There's so much change and confusion in my life right now, I really needed that stability.'

'I get that.' He nods, staring out at the common, thinking for a moment. 'Did I tell you I got that audition? The part in *A Star is Born*?'

'No!' I break into a grin. 'That's fantastic, congratulations!'

'Thank you.' He gives a coy, very un-Rudy-like smile. 'I handed in my notice to Karl last Friday – we start rehearsals in a few weeks. The reason I'm telling you this now, though, is that I very nearly *didn't* hand my notice in. I've wanted to be an actor for as long as I can remember, yet it took me a week to decide to accept the role because I kept thinking: "I'm doing really well as an estate agent, perhaps I should just stick at it. What if I never get another role after this one . . . ?" What I'm trying to say, I suppose, is that the unknown can be scary, but sometimes you need to take a risk and see what happens, otherwise you might end up regretting it forever.'

'So you're saying that this is my moment to take a risk and see what happens?'

'Perhaps.' He gives a shrug of his narrow shoulders. 'At the very least, it's a better way of looking at your current situation, rather than sitting there moping about being a failure.'

We lapse into silence again. A woman passes pushing twin babies in a double buggy with a preschooler on a bike behind her and a dog trotting at her heels, and I spend a few moments marvelling at how she's even managed to leave the house.

Then out of the blue, Rudy says: 'I hope you don't mind me saying this, Annie, but you really need to start believing in yourself.'

I look down at my hands, my cheeks flushing, because I can't deny he's got a point.

'I get the impression you never think you're good enough,' he goes on. 'Not a caring enough mum, not a successful enough photographer, not an interesting enough person. But that really is bullshit, because you're enough just as you are. You are the fabulous Annie Taylor:

talented photographer, doting mother, fantastic friend and disgraced estate agent.'

I give a snort of laughter, elbowing him in the ribs.

'The point I'm trying to make, Annie, is that you're unique, so you need to stop concerning yourself with what anyone else is doing and worrying what they might think of you, and get on with living your own life the way that you choose to.' Then he sits up straight and gives a theatrical toss of his hair. 'Because you don't have to wear Barbra's kaftans to have her attitude.'

I smile at him. 'Rudy, that is probably the campest thing I've ever heard.'

'Darling, I'm an *actor*.' He pauses. 'That sounds so much better than estate agent . . .'

Despite my own woes, it's wonderful to see the change in Rudy this morning: he seems noticeably lighter and happier – younger, almost. It's like he's finally getting the chance to live his true self and the effect it's having on him is inspiring. And I can't deny he seems to be remarkably perceptive when it comes to me and my various dilemmas. I think back to the kind things he said about my photography, and how I should be using my talent to develop a more exciting career. Perhaps, I think, hope finally flickering to life inside me, this could be my chance, too?

Rudy drains the last of his coffee. 'Well, I better get back to the office,' he says, lobbing his cup into a nearby bin.

'Of course,' I say. 'You're very wise for a child, aren't you?'

'I lied about my age – I'm actually forty-eight.'

'Makes sense.' I smile. And then, on a sudden impulse, I blurt out: 'Rudy, what's your boyfriend's name?'

He turns to look at me, narrowing his eyes. 'What's this about?'

It's a fair question – and I'm not actually sure of the answer – but I plough on regardless: 'Well, you know pretty much everything about me and my life, but I know next to nothing about yours. I don't even know where you live.'

'That's because you've never asked,' he says, clearly amused. 'I live in Chelsea.'

'What? But that's really . . . posh. Are you loaded?'

'Yes,' he replies, in that unerringly blunt way he has. 'Well, my family are.'

I sit in stunned silence for a few moments, struggling to get to grips with this new version of Rudy. At least this explains why he knows so much about rich people's antiques and art: it's because he's one of them.

'And in answer to your earlier question,' he goes on, 'I don't have a boyfriend. I do, however, have a dwarf lop-eared rabbit called Methuselah, and a wife called Annabelle.'

A *wife*? I just gawp at him: this is a shock on so many levels that I don't even know where to begin. 'But,' I stammer, 'but when we were at Mr Eliopoulos' place, you told him you had a male partner.'

'No, I just said I had a partner. Mr Eliopoulos assumed it was male, and he seemed happy to have come to that conclusion, so I didn't see any point in correcting him.'

'But why not just say "wife" in the first place? "Partner" doesn't seem quite, well, *significant* enough for someone you're married to.'

Rudy dismisses this with a wave of his hand. 'People get far too hung up on labels – they tend to bring baggage with them. I find them unhelpful.'

'But she *is* your wife, so why wouldn't you describe her that way?'

He considers this for a moment. 'I guess it's like the word "mum". Yes, you have a child, but aren't you so much more than just someone's mother? I think "partner" gives a less restrictive view of Annabelle, who's a wonderful and interesting individual in her own right, and far more than just my wife.'

I can't deny he's got a point; after all, haven't I been struggling with this very thing – my identity – since Dot was born? Rudy is looking amused at my obvious confusion, but I'm feeling terribly guilty that I'm only learning these fundamental details about him now – and for pigeonholing him so flagrantly (because *of course* straight men can be Streisand fans). I'm about to tell him how

sorry I am for being a self-centred prick when, as percep
tive as ever, he gets in first.

'Don't worry, Annie, I know you've had a lot on your
plate lately. I can give you a full rundown on my love life
another time.'

Then he gives me a Rudy-hug goodbye – all spiky
elbows and awkward back-pats – and sets off in the direction of the office.

'Oh, and Rudy?' I call after him.

He pauses. 'Yes?'

'Thank you. You're a true friend.'

His face lights up in his lopsided grin, then he turns
and strides away, his long, black coat flapping about his
legs like Sherlock in hot pursuit of Moriarty.

After Rudy has gone, I sit back on the bench again; Dot
is at Helen's and I have nowhere I need to be until lunch
with Fiona. Propping my elbows on my knees and my
chin in my hands, I gaze out at the view in front of me:
across the green is the duck pond, surrounded by gaggles
of crust-wielding toddlers, and beyond that I can just
make out the brightly coloured dots of children darting
about the climbing frame in the playground. Meanwhile,
the path in front of me is a blur of mini scooters and their
kamikaze drivers. If an alien had just landed on earth, it
would assume our planet was peopled by tiny, hysterical,
dinosaur-loving pygmies. No wonder this part of London
is known as Nappy Valley.

There's a giggle nearby and I turn to see a baby wad-
dling towards me, chasing after a ball, his arms
outstretched and face apple-cheeked with delight. As so
often happens, I automatically frame the photo in my
head: I can see it would make such a gorgeous picture
that I almost reach for my phone – but no, I've learnt my
lesson. Instead, I watch as the little boy's mum takes a few
snaps, although I can tell from here that the angle won't
be that great.

Then all at once the seed of an idea plants itself in my
mind, quickly finding fertile ground and putting out
roots, and by the time I eventually leave the common
over two hours later, I'm feeling pretty sure that Rudy
was right: being fired from Curtis Kinderbey might actually be the best thing that could have happened to me
after all.

38

'Right then, do you want a Brazilian, a Hollywood or a Brentwood?'

Mara is looming over me on her portable treatment table, spatula in one hand, waxing strip in the other.

'Brentwood?'

'It's my own creation, named after my hometown – like a Brazilian, but with a glittery landing strip.' She looks very pleased with herself. 'I can do silver, gold, pink or rainbow.'

'Just whip the whole lot off, Mara,' yells Jess from the doorway, as she passes by with Dot in her arms. 'Mummy's getting laid tonight.'

'It's just dinner!' I shout back. 'Oh, and Jess, would you mind heating up that sweet potato mush in the fridge for Dot?'

I hear Jess murmur her assent from the kitchen.

Mara tips her head on one side, still contemplating my bush.

'I could wax the hair into the shape of his first initial? That's very popular with my ladies with hot dates.'

'Um, no, I think I'll just have a tidy-up, thank you, Mara.'

'If you like.' She shrugs, unimpressed at my lack of pubic panache.

As Mara heats up the wax, my thoughts turn again to tonight's plans. I am jumpy with excitement about seeing Sam again and the prospect of continuing that kiss where we left off. Even a 5 a.m. wake-up call from Dot hasn't dampened my spirits. We are going to meet at the penthouse for a pre-dinner drink, then Sam's booked a table at a new Scandinavian restaurant that Jess tells me is the hottest place in town right now, although I've never even heard of it. Once upon a time I had my finger firmly on the pulse of the London social scene; nowadays we're barely on nodding terms.

'So who's the lucky bloke then?' asks Mara, as she starts to slap on the wax.

'His name's Sam. He's Canadian.'

'Ooh, I love Canada. I had a holiday in Vancouver a couple of years back and it was amazin'.' She pauses, her spatula hovering just above me. 'Tell you what, how about we wax the hair into the shape of a little maple leaf? Like on the Canadian flag? Bet he'd love that.'

'That's a really great idea, but maybe another time,' I say quickly.

Two hours of intensive prep later, I check out my

finished look in Jess' hallway mirror and can't help breaking into a delighted grin. My freshly highlighted hair is now shorter, cut into a far cooler, more shaggy style than before. I've dug out a brightly patterned vintage minidress that in my fashion days I'd style with platforms, a feathered cloak and shitloads of beaded necklaces, but today have toned down with flats and hoop earrings. And Mara's magical lash extensions have worked like an instant facelift, emphasising my eyes and cheekbones, while distracting attention from my – well, you know.

As always when in front of a mirror, I turn my face from side to side, examining The Nose from every angle. While it'll always be the first thing I see, I think my hatred of it is softening slightly. Yes, it's massive, but when you put it together with all my other facial features, it does sort of make sense. I'm still keeping Mr Jindal's number, just in case, but I'm feeling cautiously optimistic that my nose and I can learn to love each other again. I guess the tumultuous events of the last few days have knocked some sense into me.

'You look beautiful.' Jess appears behind me in the mirror and kisses my cheek. 'Now off you trot and have a wonderful time.'

I turn to look at her with a melodramatic gasp. 'Is that all you've got to say? No last-minute condoms to press into my hands? No lecture on the merits of reverse cowgirl versus the Viennese oyster . . . ?'

'Not tonight, Annie.' She smiles. 'I don't want you to worry about anything, just have a fantastic evening. You bloody well deserve it.'

I give her a hug. 'I love you,' I say, as I open the front door.

'Love you too.' And she waves as I set off down the path.

I'm just saying hello to the sweet old man next door, who's outside pruning his hedge, when Jess hollers: 'And the Viennese oyster is *way* better than the reverse cowgirl when it comes to penetration, although obviously it does depend on the actual cock . . .'

I consider taking a taxi to the penthouse so I arrive in as flawless a condition as I have left the house, but for old time's sake I hop on the bus. The first time I made this journey, I was blind drunk, the second I was terrified, but now, as I sit here on the top deck again, there's just an overwhelming feeling of happiness and excitement. It's been one hell of a week, but I have my darling daughter, brilliantly supportive friends and a night with a gorgeous man ahead of me: life could be a lot worse.

I've just got off the bus and am walking the short distance to Westminster Reach, enjoying the sight of boats chugging along the Thames in the evening sunshine, when my phone starts to vibrate. I check the caller ID: Tabby.

'Hey, sis!'

'Annie! How are you?'

'I'm good, just on my way to meet Sam.'

'Of course, that's tonight, isn't it? Well, I won't keep you. Have a fantastic time.'

'Don't go, I can talk a bit longer. How've you been?'

She takes a breath. 'Oh, fine, you know. A bit up and down, but I guess I should expect a few wobbles!'

Something in her voice gives me pause. 'Wobbles?'

'Yes, you know – butterflies. But then it's a major thing, isn't it? Having a baby. Becoming a mum. Being responsible for another person for the rest of your life.' Tabby literally gulps, like a cartoon character. 'I'm sure everyone feels a bit . . . *panicky*. And then of course there's the birth itself and, you know, all the pain and stuff. I'm sure the way I'm feeling is totally normal. Don't you think?'

Her voice is high and unsteady, as if she's battling tears; I know my sister well enough to know when she's putting on a brave face.

'Is Jon there with you?' I'm now standing outside the entrance to Westminster Reach; I can see the doors to the penthouse elevator through the glass wall.

'He's in Hong Kong on business. But I'm fine, Annie, *really*, and the last thing I want to do is worry you, tonight of all nights. Let's speak tomorrow.'

I imagine Tabby curled up on her sofa at home, all alone, overwhelmed by the enormity of what's about to happen to her. I hate the thought of her struggling with this on her own.

'Tabby, the way you're feeling *is* normal, although that

doesn't mean it's not bloody scary.' I come to a snap decision. 'I know what you're going to say, but I want to come
over.'

'You can't, you've got your date! Honestly, Annie, I'm
just being feeble, I wouldn't dream of ruining your night.'

Just then I catch a glimpse of my reflection in the
building's expanse of glass: the usual flurry of anxieties
over my hair, clothes and general blah-ness fails to materi-
alise, and instead of the familiar inner turmoil, there's
a calmness and confidence that I haven't felt for years.

Hello, Annie, I think with a smile. *It's nice to see you again*.

'Tabs, I've made up my mind,' I say firmly. 'Sam will
understand. It's far more important that I spend this
evening with you.' I head back towards the road, my hand
already out to hail a taxi. 'I'll be there in half an hour.'

On the drive to Fulham I send a text:

I'm so sorry, Sam, I've got a family emergency so I'm not going
to be able to make it tonight. I really hope we can reschedule xxx

A moment later I get a reply:

Of course – I'm disappointed but I completely understand. I hope
that everything is okay x

Reading his text, I get a gut-churning flutter of panic:
why didn't he mention anything about rescheduling our

date? Why only one kiss to my three? Perhaps, after I cancelled at such short notice, he won't be bothered to
rearrange. I think about our amazing kiss, and what
tonight might have held, and wonder if I've just made an
enormous mistake . . .

No, that's nonsense: Sam is a nice guy – of course he'll
understand. If the situation was reversed, I have no doubt
he'd do the same for his sister. Besides, the most important thing right at this moment is Tabby, and that I'm
there for her, just as she always has been for me.

39

Dot and I are just arriving at the playground on Saturday afternoon when the clouds that have been gathering all morning dramatically darken and burst. Rain is bouncing furiously off the swings and there's a mini torrent pouring down the slide: it looks like we'll have to go to the soft-play 'fun zone' at the leisure centre instead – aka, the seventh circle of hell.

I'm just struggling to fit the impressively un-user-friendly waterproof cover over Dot's buggy when my phone starts to ring.

'Hey Fi,' I say, wedging the phone under my chin inside the hood of my mac, while I try to work out which bit of Velcro sticks to what.

'Annie, where are you?'

'In the park with Dot – well, actually leaving the park en route to the soft-play centre, as it's just started chucking it down. What's up?'

A long pause. 'Did you see Sam for dinner last night?'

'No, I couldn't make it after all. Tabby was in a state about the baby, so I went to see her instead. The poor love was in floods of tears when I arrived, but we ordered a Chinese takeaway and by the time we'd had half a crispy duck and watched *Bridesmaids*, she was feeling loads better . . .' I finally manage to fix the waterproof cover in place and struggle to my feet, soaked but triumphant. 'I was gutted to have to cancel, but I'm sure Sam'll be in touch to reschedule soon . . . or maybe I should phone him? I was the one who blew him out, after all. What do you think?'

But there's no reply.

'Fi? Are you still there . . . ?'

'Yeah, I'm here,' she mutters. 'Ah, feck it. I need to tell you something, Annie.'

'Well, go on, then,' I say, wheeling the buggy around the spreading puddles. Dot smiles up at me from under the cover, perfectly snug and dry; meanwhile, my jeans are clinging wetly to my skin and I can feel water sloshing inside my trainers.

'Right y'are, then,' says Fi. 'Okay.' Another long pause. 'So, we had a viewing at the penthouse this morning at 10 a.m. – you know, Sam's penthouse – and I went over a bit earlier to make sure I was there when the clients arrived. There was no answer when I pressed the buzzer – *nobody's home*, I think to meself – so I head on up. Anyway, it was dark in the apartment, the curtains were still drawn, so I

ACKNOWLEDGEMENTS

I do hope you've enjoyed this book, as without you, dear reader, I wouldn't have the joy and privilege of being able to call myself a writer. Out of all the millions of books out there, thank you so much for choosing to read mine.

Thanks as ever to my amazing agent, Rowan, and to Eugenie and Liane for looking after me while Rowan was busy working on her own masterpiece.

I feel extremely lucky to be published by the wonderful team at Quercus, with particular thanks to Emily Yau for her encouragement and wisdom.

Thank you also to Kathryn Taussig, for taking a chance on me several times over.

A huge thank you to the real-life Fiona, Claris, Tabitha, Tomo and my gorgeous goddaughter Dot, for allowing me to borrow their names.

Writing this book coincided with losing my gorgeous mum to cancer, and without the support of certain people the story would still be half-finished and I'd be a blubbering wreck. Particular heartfelt thanks to Lisa Potts, Freya Williams, Carrie Lazarus and Sue Terrill for their love and support.

And finally, grazie mille to my wingman Oliver: the top one percent of all husbands. The elite. The best of the best.

ALSO BY CATE WOODS:

Percy James has everything a girl could want:
a comfy flat, a steady relationship and a
truly lovely group of friends.

Then she is approached by Eros Tech. Eros is 'the
future of love' – an agency that brings together
soulmates using phone data. Percy has been identified
as a match for one of Eros's super wealthy clients.
The only problem is she already has a boyfriend . . .

But what if this is *destiny*? Would you – could
you – pass up a chance to meet your one true love?